CAIN'S BLOOD

GEOFFREY GIRARD

A TOUCHSTONE BOOK
PUBLISHED BY SIMON & SCHUSTER

NEW YORK   LONDON   TORONTO   SYDNEY   NEW DELHI

Touchstone
A Division of Simon & Schuster, Inc.
1230 Avenue of the Americas
New York, NY 10020

First Touchstone hardcover edition September 2013

TOUCHSTONE and colophon are registered trademarks of Simon & Schuster, Inc.

For information about special discounts for bulk purchases, please contact Simon & Schuster Special Sales at 1-866-506-1949 or business@simonandschuster.com.

The Simon & Schuster Speakers Bureau can bring authors to your live event. For more information or to book an event contact the Simon & Schuster Speakers Bureau at 1-866-248-3049 or visit our website at www.simonspeakers.com.

Designed by Ruth Lee-Mui

Manufactured in the United States of America

1   3   5   7   9   10   8   6   4   2

ISBN 978-1-4767-0404-3
ISBN 978-1-4767-0406-7 (ebook)

dedicated to

Barbara O'Breza and Joe Truitt

for the nurture

What are little boys made of?
Snips and snails, and puppy-dogs' tails,
That's what little boys are made of.

A Brief History of Cloning

I t started with peas.

An Austrian monk named Mendel tried some biology experiments in the small garden of the monastery where he lived and worked and prayed to God. It was the 1850s. Charles Darwin was still drafting *On the Origin of Species* and the first Neanderthal remains had just been found in a cave near Düsseldorf. Mendel's religious order, the Augustinians, believed the pursuit of truth through scholarship was essential toward spiritual enlightenment, and Mendel's particular scholarly interest had turned to the study of heredity: How life-forms pass traits on to their offspring.

To explore this, he grew peas. Thirty thousand pea plant "children" carefully bred from specific pea "parents." He meticulously pollinated and wrapped each pod, then examined and recorded their most minute detail: blossom color, pod hue and shape, and pod position. Thirty thousand times. It took seven years, and he became partially blind from squinting at all those peas.

He authored a single treatise on his conclusions and presented it at two meetings of the Natural History Society of Brünn, who subsequently published "Experiments in Plant Hybridization" in the club's official journal. In the document, Mendel proved how specific genetic alleles (which he called *factors*) in the parent peas controlled the traits of the children peas. Some factors were strong/dominant, and others were weaker/recessive, and the strong prevailed when the two met in an offspring. He started mapping these factors and eventually could predict exactly what the offspring plant would look like.

He'd invented modern genetics.

Very few people read his paper, however. He wasn't a "real" scientist, the real scientists decided. He was just a monk with a small pea garden, and his work had more to do with ordinary hybridization than the emerging field of Inheritance. And so he was almost completely ignored, and his findings were to be cited only three times over the next fifty years.

Mendel next tried bees. He kept five hundred hives with bees collected from all over the world: African, Spanish, Egyptian. He built special chambers for the various queens to mate with foreign suitors and promptly bred a new species of hybrid bee that produced more honey than any other bee on earth. Alas, Mendel's bees also proved more aggressive than any other bee on earth. They stung the other bees, his fellow monks, and then struck Brno, a nearby village. He had to destroy every hive, and killed ten thousand bees.

He returned to plants, which didn't sting, but tried something other than peas—a kin of the sunflower family called "hawkweed"—and it didn't work out. He was unable to corroborate his original conclusions. Mendel grew depressed and stopped doing experiments of any kind. When he died, the abbot who ran the monastery burned Mendel's notes and unpublished essays on Inheritance. It was another fifty years before the scientific community rediscovered his original paper.

The professionals now liked, and understood, what they saw. Using Mendel's principles and evidence on the biological machineries of Inheritance, they summarily progressed from charting peas to charting frogs. From frogs to mammals. They figured out how to craft detailed maps of DNA and isolated where each factor resided. Once isolated, analyzed each factor to understand how it *really* worked. Once understood, explored how to *modify*.

They eventually cloned a sheep from a single strand of DNA. A small animal-sciences research institute in Scotland took one cell from a parent donor, wedged it into an unfertilized egg cell that'd had its nucleus removed, zapped it once with good old-fashioned electricity, and made another animal. Identical. Two of—ignoring, technically, the mitochondrial DNA within the donor egg—the exact same sheep.

They named the 98 percent copy Dolly, and Dolly became famous. It was 1996.

Now, it was game on. The next several years yielded an explosion of "clones."

Japan constructed Noto the Cow. Thousands of Notos. The Italians cooked up Prometea the Horse. Iran made Hannah the Goat while South Korea made Snuppy the Dog and Snuwolf the Wolf. The Scots made pigs; the French, rabbits. Both China and India grew duplicate water buffalo. Spain and Turkey, bulls. Dubai crafted the exact same camel a hundred and four times.

The United States, ultimately, did it better—and more quickly—than everyone else combined. More labs, more commercial interest, bundles more money. Cloning and biogenetic research were added to every pharmaceutical company in the nation. Even university students were making clones, and California alone has more colleges than all of Germany, France, and Great Britain combined. Within a decade, Americans had created Cumulina the Mouse. Ralph the Rat. Mira the Goat. Noah the Ox. Gem the Mule. Dewey the Deer. Libby the Ferret. CC the Cat. And, at last, Tetra the Monkey. Mice to livestock to primates. Ten years.

Cloning humans, by the way, is still completely legal in the United States. Everyone just assumes it's not. A few states have banned it. Most haven't. And Washington keeps out of the way. Presidents may publically denounce it and advocate for moratoriums, but no such halts have ever actually been enforced. The Human Cloning Prohibition Acts of 2003 and 2007 were both voted down by Congress, and the 2009 version has been waylaid in various subcommittees for years. American scientists can pretty much do whatever they want as long as they don't overtly use federal dollars. Human cloning remains legal in twenty other developed countries.

When Sir Ian Wilmut, the scientist who led the team that cloned Dolly the Sheep, was asked about the possibility of cloning humans, he replied simply, "It would be naive to think it possible to prevent."

And he was right.

CAIN'S
BLOOD

Prologue: A Field Test

One of thousands performed during the longest war in U.S. history. An irresistible opportunity for assessing the potential effectiveness of newborn policy and products in model test environments, thus fulfilling the primary tenet of all military research and development: *What hasn't been tested doesn't work.* Everything, from new camouflage and body armor to computer-driven bullets and laser cannons directly out of *Star Wars*. Recon systems, satellites, advanced combat rifles, pesticides, cold-storage warehouses, radio sets, and lamps all had their turn. This field test, from a purely scientific standpoint, was no different.

The two helicopters were stealth-modified Black Hawks on loan from the 160th Special Operations Aviation Regiment (SOAR), an airborne Army unit known as the Night Stalkers. They swept over the village, silent and veiled as buoyant shadows caught in the valley's cold predawn winds. The target had been rated mostly empty. Mostly enemy. And, suitably remote.

As the helicopters passed overhead, one of the passengers, a man the Night Stalker crew had never seen before and would never see again, dropped a canister no bigger than a Pepsi can into the village square. Hell, it *was* a Pepsi can, and it bounced and skittered in a dozen different directions before settling against a mud-lined furrow running along the village's lone dirt road. The Black Hawks were halfway into the next valley before the handful of village watchmen even thought to shoot after them.

The gunfire awoke Tahir al-Umari, who rose slowly and grumbled at his stirring children to remain quiet as he pulled on sandals. Outside, there was random shouting and dogs barking. In the doorway, with arms crossed and tilted forward enough to see down the path some, he called across to a neighbor who'd struck a similar pose. "U.S.," the man replied simply. Tahir nodded, rubbed at his nose in thought as the soft winds off the adjacent black mountain slipped down, cool across his face. He was one of a dozen families who still lived in the outlying village, the rest having vanished over the last ten years. He and his sons now owned and worked eleven acres, and nine were planted with poppy. Allah willing, when the others departed, he would plant wheat and saffron again. *One day soon.* Now, perhaps, it didn't matter. The Americans would come back or send the Afghan narcotics police to burn the fields. He'd heard they possessed some sort of virus that could kill an entire crop in hours. He thought, *I will lose everything.* He thought, *Maybe this is a good thing.* And, *Now maybe the Taliban will move on to some other place.*

Automatic fire from the center of the village. The distinct clacking of AK-47s. Then excited voices became screams.

Tahir and his neighbor locked eyes across the distance between them, both with hands half lifted in confusion. *A raid by the Americans?* The neighbor quickly retreated into his house, while Tahir stepped fully outside.

"Daddy?" His youngest daughter's voice emerged from within, and he turned. His wife and other children had crowded in the doorway behind her. Whispering. His oldest son, thirteen, had pulled on his jacket and shoes.

"Stay inside," he told them, eyeing the boy especially. "I'll be right back."

He stepped hurriedly down the uneven dirt pathway, skirted the other mud-brick homes alongside. Another man followed him, a small crowd moving together toward the sounds of boisterous cursing and gunfire. More shots were fired and Tahir crouched low in the shadows. It sounded like an entire clip emptying. A woman beside him moaned a half-prayer, and he shooed her still with his hand. The air tasted funny, he realized. The back of his tongue was acrid, like he'd been chewing on something plastic.

He caught the eye of a friend, both men finding the courage to creep toward the end of the street together. There, the headlights of a stock-still van cast a muted glow onto the cramped main square. Bodies lay there, sprawled and twisted like a collection of his daughter's cloth dolls dropped absently to the ground. Like, except for the widening pools of blood.

"They're . . . they're shooting themselves," someone whispered from the shadows beside him, the voice both retreating and truthful. Tahir watched as one of the Taliban fighters shot another and then immediately brought the rifle beneath his *own* chin in a sudden ruby spout. A day laborer named Rafeeq scrambled to seize the dropped rifle but was shot down as two more Taliban charged into the square shouting more curses and commands. One noticed other onlookers across the square from Tahir and turned to fire. Four shadowy figures of various sizes spun and collapsed. The soldier cast off his now-empty rifle and stumbled toward the dead as if drunk, pulling free a handgun. Fired unremittingly into the first corpse. Then he turned and faced Tahir.

Tahir froze with nowhere to escape. The man pointed the gun and shot. Nothing. The clip already emptied. Still the man stood, wrist jerking half a dozen times, as if he'd actually been firing at Tahir. There was something in the man's expression. His eyes. *What is wrong with his eyes?* Tahir shuddered.

Another fighter pounced beside this one and clubbed him in the head with a rifle. The man with the strange look went down and the second straddled him, driving the rifle butt into his face. Again and again and again.

Tahir stumbled backward, withdrawing in panic with the others. His eyes were stinging. Smoke from the rifles, he thought, a new chill suddenly nagging at the base of his very skull. Screams echoed behind him, and Tahir had to turn.

A woman—Padja's wife, he thought—had been pulled down by two other men he knew well. Her face pushed to the ground, her *chadri* ripped away as both men struggled with their own pants. Tahir stopped his retreat. "No," he shouted at them. Found himself moving forward to stop them. Found himself watching the woman's body writhing beneath them, struggling to be free. Her exposed loins lifted and vulnerable for their every pleasure. For his too if he so desired. Tahir shook that sudden awful thought away. He advanced closer. "No," he said again, but the word came out too slow, like in a dream. The worst dream.

Padja's wife had rolled over, shamefully opening herself to them. But, the man on top of her was now screaming. Clutching his face, something dripping and red hanging between his fingers. His cheekbone glistened in the first rays of the rising sun. From beneath, Padja's wife smiled at Tahir. Blood running down her chin. Her eyes. *Something in her eyes.*

Tahir crumpled. Crawled, his head vibrating. Shadowed figures both scrambled and lumbered past him in every direction. The unnatural taste and smell of plastic utterly filled his throat, his nose. Screams swathed the village, echoed off the looming mountain, where dawn burned crimson. His mind crowded with incessant and infinite thoughts, awful thoughts, buzzing like a million insects. Over this unrelenting swarm, he reflected, *This is what Hell sounds like.* And also, *I must get home.*

He staggered back down the street, propping himself against other homes to keep himself upright. Inside each, more screams. Mothers and brothers and babies howling together as one. Their cries joining the churning clamor in his head.

Someone grabbed him from behind. He turned, struck out. The boy collapsed. A friend of his sons. The boy had a knife, and Tahir took it from him easily. Used it just as easily. Stabbing again and again. Again.

He stepped more confidently down the path now. The swirling, immeasurable thoughts had finally become one. Only one.

He inspected the dripping knife. Smiled.

His family waited inside their house as he'd left them.

His daughter came to the door first.

"Daddy?"

clone n.

From the Greek word *klōn* for "twig."

(1) a group of genetically identical cells descended from a single common ancestor;

(2) an organism descended asexually from a single ancestor such as a plant produces by budding;

(3) a replica of a DNA sequence produced by genetic engineering;

(4) one that copies or closely resembles another, as in appearance or function

> *O Muse, sing through me*
> *of that man full of skills,*
> *who wandered for many years*
> *after he destroyed the sacred city of Troy,*
> *and saw the cities of many men,*
> *and learned their manners.*

THE ODYSSEY

THEODORE/7

This boy was every boy.

The standard model. The kind you'd purchase at Walmart if they had a "Boy Aisle." T-shirt, long gym shorts. Straight bangs falling over a rounded face. Big blue eyes. The fixed, playful grin of a pirate. Twelve years old, legs too long, deep summer tan, fidgeting in his chair. Earbuds draped around his neck for later.

He'd raped his first victim with a metal bar wrenched from the bed frame, then carefully positioned the body and bar as lewdly as possible for her family to find. Another woman, he'd bitten off both nipples before strangling her with a pair of stockings that'd been pulled so tightly around her neck, they'd cut down to the bone.

He'd done these things. This boy.

Theodore.

Done more, actually, according to his summary file.

Or his DNA had.

Despite his best efforts, Castillo had not yet established any well-defined distinction between the two. He wasn't so sure the two scientists standing behind him had, either.

The two men looked nothing like Castillo's idea of scientists. No lab coats, or pens, or beakers. These guys wore khakis and matching light purple dress shirts with the DSTI logo, matching holsters with Tasers at their hips.

Castillo assumed he did not look exactly like what they'd expected either. He wore jeans and a faded gray T-shirt. Probably needed a haircut. He'd left his guns in the car.

They stood together in Observation Room #4 of The Massey Institute, a small residential treatment facility in Radnor, Pennsylvania. According to the institute's website, Massey was an "Adolescent treatment center where teen boys can develop healthy behaviors, improve their self-esteem and learn to positively express their emotions." Mental health, anger management, eating disorders, drug and alcohol rehab, etc. Treatments included a combination of group and individual therapy, experiential therapy, and cutting-edge medication. Fifty-student maximum with an 8 to 1 student/teacher ratio and a staff of one hundred additional health professionals caring for the students. All boys.

Massey was owned and operated by the Dynamic Solutions Technology Institute, which had its own facility on the other side of the wooded property. According to *its* website, DSTI was a private biotechnology company with two hundred employees that "specializes in the development of therapeutic, pharmaceutical, and cell-based therapies."

One of the room's walls was a one-way mirror allowing them to secretly watch the boys next door.

"Phase One, where Applications maintains the bulk of its research, is restricted therapeutic cloning," Dr. Erdman, the division head, the one with square silver glasses and short white hair, continued. "What most people might call 'stem-cell' research. Induced pluripotent stem cells, primarily. Nerve, skin, and bone cells. Just microscopic building blocks." His voice remained distant and flat, and Castillo wondered if the geneticist might still be in shock. Based on what he'd been told about last night—the murders committed by kids like these—it would have been understandable. "These subjects were part of Phase Three."

Castillo looked back to the mirror. Breathed deeply, thinking. Sitting beside the first kid was another boy the lab had tagged as Jerry.

Jerry was far beyond a "microscopic building block."

His file read that he was fifteen years old. Read that his former self enjoyed intercourse with dead girls and fastening their corpses to copper wires for electrical shock experiments, which he meticulously documented and photographed. Kept breasts as souvenir paperweights. The file also noted that his former self, the "Original," had been executed more than ten years ago.

The Original . . .

Another teenager, named Dean, watched ESPN from the couch. Twenty-seven bodies had been uncovered on "his" property way back in 1973. After authorities found the torture room.

Castillo said, "I assumed we were at least ten, maybe twenty years from . . . from this."

"Most people do." Dr. Erdman pulled off his glasses to wipe them with the bottom of his shirt. "For those in Washington who know better, the biotech lobby has become rather substantial in the last fifteen years. We're already a multitrillion-dollar industry, and this work is a natural extension of that research."

The last kid, labeled Andrei: The original form of his DNA had committed fifty-three murders in the Ukraine, according to his sheet. The Russian press had called him "The Rostov Ripper." *Hell of a name*, Castillo thought. This guy's preferred method was to first cut away his female victims' eyes and then casually eat their uteri after his victims couldn't "see him" anymore. *Fifty-three* murders. Castillo had served fifteen years, mostly in the field, and still he struggled with that number. The boy was apparently a new addition to the group. He'd recently turned ten years old.

"Where do you get the DNA?" Castillo asked.

The second doctor, Mohlenbrock, a stout man built like a Tolkien dwarf, actually chuckled. "Where don't you?" he bragged. "Archived evidence. Autopsy samples. We had John Wayne Gacy's brain here on loan for months and grabbed millions of good cells from that. We can use anything from hair on old brushes to flaked-off skin cells on clothes bought from family members. Hell, half these guys are still alive, and they just sign the stuff right over."

Castillo studied the first boy again.

THEODORE/7 the file and photo read.

A *clone*. The genetic carbon copy of another human being.

Eyes. Skin. Brain. Bones. Blood.

Every damn cell. Copy, paste.

And not just any human being but one developed in a lab across this very property toward the scientific aim of isolating, understanding, and harnessing violent human behavior— this boy was the genetic offspring of an infamous serial killer. A killer whose name even Castillo recognized, although he couldn't remember if it was the good-looking guy out west or the chubby one who dressed like a clown.

Ted Bundy.

This kid's DNA had history. This DNA had celebrity status. This DNA had killed.

Considering the boy's face, Castillo decided Bundy was probably the good-looking guy. Considering the file, he was definitely a monster. Castillo looked for something in the kid's eyes, anything, that revealed the kind of person who'd slowly and rhythmically beat a woman to death with a piece of plywood while masturbating with his free hand. He saw nothing but a normal twelve-year-old boy and the partial ghost of his own reflection in the tinted glass.

"How do you keep them here?" he asked.

"Massey is a regarded, and rather exclusive, residential treatment facility. Many of the students were born the customary way and enrolled genuinely at considerable costs to their parents. The cloned boys, however . . . Their adoptive parents, consociates of DSTI, naturally, have enrolled their sons here."

Castillo rescanned the file.

```
BD: June 10, 2002       SCNT: January 1, 2000
IMP: January 10, 2001   FH: N300
```

"What's SCNT, Doctor?"

"Somatic cell nuclear transfer. IMP is embryo implant. FH is the female host. Look . . ." The doctor shuffled his feet behind Castillo. "Perhaps this was a mistake. We thought it might be easier for you to understand the rest if —"

"No," Castillo stopped him. "This is helpful, thank you." He turned from the one-way mirror and re-sorted the papers in his folder. "And the six boys who escaped . . ." He reread the parent gene names, having only half recognized two of them.

```
Albert Fish. Jeffrey Dahmer. Henry Lee Lucas.
Dennis Rader. Ted Bundy. David Berkowitz.
```

He stopped, frowned. "I thought the kid in there was Ted Bundy."

The doctor looked uneasy. "Theodore *Seven*."

Castillo allowed himself an extra moment to process the implication before speaking. "Exactly how many 'Theodores' are there, Doctor?"

"With respect, we're focused on finding the six boys who've escaped." Dr. Erdman reset his glasses. "We were assured you are quite qualified for this sort of thing."

Castillo stared back, holding up the briefing they'd pulled together for him. Now, perhaps, there was something in his look that exposed his own particular skill set. Because Erdman literally took a step backward. "The six," said Castillo. "You'll want to cover their homes. They'll likely make contact."

"We have men watching each home already," Dr. Erdman replied quickly, plainly relieved Castillo had spoken first.

"Good." Castillo nodded. "I'll need the complete files for each boy who escaped. Everything you have. Grades? Known friends? Coaches? Jobs? Hobbies? Whatever you know about these kids. The trail will grow cold in a hurry."

"Absolutely." The scientist shot a quick look to Mohlenbrock. "Being gathered for you even as we speak. Psychiatric and medical reports, the—"

"And the three hostages," Castillo interrupted. "Personnel files on Dr. Jacobson and the two nurses. Santos and . . ."—he checked his notes—"Kelso. Any email and phone records you have."

Erdman frowned. "Is that really necessary? They're hostages. Or already dead. Surely every minute we wait—"

"Measure twice, cut once, Doctor."

"What's that?"

"Measure twice, cut once. Something my dad often said."

"Was he also a CIA assassin?"

Castillo looked up and smiled. *Jesus, these assholes are cocky*, he thought. *With the accountability in this massive fuckup, you'd think they'd want to keep their mouths shut and heads down until the Big Boys get everything back in FDA-approved order. CIA? The guy doesn't even understand who it is we're working for.* "No," he said. "He drove trucks for UPS. And, I'm troubled with your assumptions regarding my role."

The issue had troubled him ever since he'd first been called. He'd commanded half a dozen Joint Special Operations Command arrest/capture missions over the last seven years, but his real specialty had always been leading JSOC *kill*/capture teams. Enemy bomb makers, financiers, high-level leaders. While Colonel Stanforth had confirmed that this assignment was the former type of mission, Castillo also knew well that missions had a funny way of shifting directives midstride.

"Let's make this perfectly clear," he said evenly. "I'm here to help locate these six kids. If I can find them, I will apprehend. That's it. Only reason I was brought in. If I suspect for one minute that these kids, or anyone else for that matter, have been targeted for elimination to suppress what happened here, I will personally drag your asses to jail. Understood?"

"Fully," Erdman replied.

Castillo didn't give him a chance to extend further apologies, explanations, or, maybe, out-and-out lies. "Regardless, the point is, I can run outta here right now to track down six teenaged boys in a world that's got some fifty-seven million square miles to hide in. Or, I can do a little homework and maybe start narrowing the game's boundaries down a bit. Why are Dr. Jacobson and the two nurses not among the dead, I wonder. Maybe they were kept alive to help provide cars, money. Maybe they're still alive because they're also part of this. Were any of them disgruntled? Selling trade secrets to a competitor or another country? Had any of them maybe gotten in a romantic situation with one of these six students? Anything you give me could answer these questions and help." Castillo's thoughts had drifted again to Uzbekistan and the hills of northern Pakistan, other places he'd had to hunt down men. He shook it off. "You're a man of science," he said, pointing the folder at Erdman. "Which course of action do you think affords our highest probability for success?"

"Understood," Erdman said. "I meant no disrespect."

"And none taken. May I examine the victims now?"

Another nod, brief and perfunctory. "Follow me."

Castillo cast a final look into the other room. "Unbelievable," he murmured. "How did it ever get to this?"

Erdman smiled for the first time since they'd met. "It started with peas," he said.

THE LAND OF NOD

Most of the bodies were in the rec room.

The room's walls were painted a striking light blue color that immediately reminded Castillo of the Aral Sea, the fresh dark splatters of blood even more conspicuous than they would have normally been. He tried to pretend they were coral.

Three men in light hazard suits and masks, employees of DSTI, scuttled about the room still, gathering more evidence, snapping more pictures. By this time tomorrow, it would look as if absolutely nothing had ever happened in the room. But it wasn't tomorrow yet. It had been no more than twenty hours since the boys' escape.

Castillo followed the two scientists within and slowed to study the first body they came to. It was splayed across the room's foosball table. The sheet someone had covered it with was soaked through, and he could perfectly make out the shape and facial outlines of the person it covered. A modern Shroud of Turin, still dripping blood over the little plastic soccer players onto the field beneath.

"Who is this?" he asked.

"Dylan."

Castillo waited.

"Dylan Meinzer. Produced from the DNA of Dylan Klebold, Columbine."

"Right." Castillo forced himself to simply accept this information as nothing more than standard intel. Now was not the time to really think about what it was they'd been telling him. The cloning strangeness. He focused instead on facts, his mind pulling up what it could. He remembered that Klebold and his buddy—couldn't recall the name— shot up their school a good twenty years ago, murdering a dozen fellow students, and then offed themselves in the school library. This, if he believed what they'd been telling him, was that same boy's clone. One of them, at least. "And you've confirmed that's the other kid?"

The other body had been bound and positioned with telephone line and network cables to the railing that led to the second floor. Castillo eyed the dark shape half hidden beneath the sheet, embossed in blood and standing with its arms still held outstretched like some Halloween prankster. "One of the Erics." Dr. Erdman flipped through a few pages of his clipboard. "Eric Palmer, Eric *Six*. Blood and PCR tests match up."

"Have they found the skin yet?" Castillo asked. Another black-and-white question. Black-and-white questions were safe. Manageable. *Just stick with those, and get out of this place as fast as you can.* It had been more than a year since he'd seen even a drop of blood. Here, there were several pools.

"No," Dr. Erdman replied. He sounded embarrassed.

Castillo looked down again at "Dylan" and furled back the sheet. The body beneath had been flayed, completely and immaculately. The skin cut away at every turn so that the boy, except for a few grisly pot-holed gouges out of his arm and between his toes, looked like something out of a Michelangelo sketchbook. The debrief he'd been given upon first arrival had suggested the other one looked exactly the same. "Why did they hate these two so much?" he asked.

Sudden, bright interest flared in Erdman's eyes. "Is it that obvious?"

"Sure. This kid was alive when they skinned him." Castillo looked into the corpse's lidless dark eyes. "I . . . I've seen this before."

More interest, less scientific this time. "Where was that?"

Castillo ignored the question and replaced the sheet. "You can tell by the hands." He approached the second body. "The arms out like this. Instantaneous rigor mortis. Like a drowning victim's last spasm. These two drowned choking on their own blood."

"The others never . . ." The geneticist followed Castillo deeper into the room. "Frankly, the others never took to these boys. It was a mistake to have those two here." His voice grew more vague, perceptibly clinical in its detachment. This was merely summarizing data, preparing an imminent report. "Naturally, 'spree killers' were never the same as the others."

"Naturally." Castillo hid the accompanying damning grin. "So, how do you know it's not Eric Three or Four?" He made sure to make it sound more like a genuine question than a challenge. The anticipated pissing contest seemed worse than usual with this lot. A bunch of khakied Betas with delusions of Alphaness, the kind of men he'd struggled with most of his life. As one ex-lover—a Ph.D. candidate in some-or-other bullshitty subject whom he'd met while taking courses at the University of Maryland—had put it wryly during her breakup speech: "The hardguy schtick was fun until I realized it wasn't just a schtick." While he'd been off fighting in two wars, competence had somehow become an offense back home. He could try and talk as softly and "nice" as he wanted, but it didn't matter. People too often still saw their own weaknesses in the skills and confidence he'd fostered in the military, and that was always a dangerous thing. It'd never been an issue in the field. "Doctor?" he prompted.

Erdman, to his credit, hadn't taken offense. "There are ways. If there's one thing we know around here, it's DNA. Besides, the other Erics all terminated during gestation. You've heard of Dolly the Sheep, I imagine. Near three hundred copies of that animal died during pregnancy before the one we all know was actually born. Most all clones still terminate prior to birth."

Castillo looked at the doctor. *Terminate*, he mused. *These pricks speak just like we did in the Army.* But this wasn't a damn sheep Erdman was talking about. It was a room *overflowing* with dead kids. *Black and white. Stay with the black and white.* It was too much to take in the rest of the room at once, all the bodies. Instead, he focused only on what was directly in front of him: bloody metallic pellets the size of a small flat pill. "The transmitters," he blurted. "Tell me about those."

A dozen had been left on the pool table in the obvious shape of a smiley face, the gaps between the pellets drawn in with blood. The half-stripped body of the school's psychotherapist remained sprawled facedown beside. She, too, now covered with a bloody sheet.

"Each subject is implanted at birth for their own safety."

Castillo leaned closer for a better look. "Of course. To keep track of them."

"It appears they each cut them out. We assume they carved up Eric and Dylan looking for them. To discover where they were implanted."

"Maybe," Castillo said. "These guys seem to have found and cut out their own transmitters easily enough. I think, perhaps, this knife work on these two was mostly for, what, *fun*? Either way, question for you: How'd these kids even know to look for them? Did they know they'd been implanted?"

Erdman shrugged. "No," he said. "I wouldn't think so."

Castillo took in more of the room in more small, controlled segments, deliberately cataloguing the other evidence of recent history sprinkled throughout. The security guard brained against the steps. The torn and bloody nurses' uniforms. Crimson scrawling of curse words and giant cartoon dicks on the walls. Half a dozen small bodies swaddled in sheets; those students not invited, for whatever reason, to come along on the group field trip.

According to Erdman, the institute had started summer session the week before, most of the students having returned home for two months. Castillo tried not to think about what might have happened had all fifty boys still been in residence.

The glossy arterial spray splattered in streaks across the huge flat-screen and Xbox. He swallowed. *More coral.* Dissecting what had happened here, the who and the how and the when, would take time. The digital images from the security cameras had been deleted during the night. Nothing remained to provide his logical next step. *What in God's name happened here?* His vision narrowed to a pinpoint. He felt it go, felt the scramble to regain control. *Blackandwhite Blackandwhite.* He turned to Erdman. "Where's Jacobson's office?"

"Right through here."

He followed Erdman toward the far left corner, kept his eyes locked on the doctor's back. They'd stopped at a door, where Erdman waved his hand across a security sensor on the wall. The sensor flushed blue, showing a spectral replication of the hand and the blood vessels within. "Vascular recognition." Erdman turned as the door bolts clicked open. "Matches the unique vein pattern and heart rate in your palm to stored scans. As unique as fingerprinting, but more difficult to fake because it requires flowing blood."

Castillo nodded, allowing himself the distraction of the technology. "No more fear of Play-Doh or cadaver fingers fooling the system. Would it have picked up and refused an accelerated heart rate?"

"Yes." Erdman seemed curious.

Control flowed back for Castillo, like it had never been lost. A relief to be talking about simple security, gearhead stuff. "So, then, who opened it last night? Who had access?"

"The security log shows Dr. Jacobson opened this door at 10:13 p.m."

Castillo and Erdman left the obvious unspoken for now. *Why Jacobson? And, if a hostage, why hadn't his heart rate been up?* "Only one security guard?" Castillo asked instead. "I would think that when working for the Department of Defense—"

"Massey has only the one. The labs, the DSTI building, are far more secure."

"Why's that?"

"Here you are . . ." Erdman pretended not to hear the question and motioned toward an already-open doorway. "Dr. Jacobson's office."

The room proved spacious and expensive. It had also been totally destroyed. The chairs and dark sequoia coffee tables splintered into pieces. The cabinets emptied. Built-in shelves split and bare, the books in lopsided piles on the floor. Someone had clearly tried to start a fire with some of the paperwork. Mirrors and framed pictures had been demolished into shards of glass, and several computers and monitors were smashed, so that the whole room glittered beneath the harsh, unnatural lighting recessed above. The large desk was covered in blood that pooled along the edges of the missing doctor's laptop.

"This the teacher's blood?" Castillo asked. "The one from the stair-well."

"Mrs. Gallagher," Erdman confirmed. "Right. She would have been sixty next month."

Castillo looked around, pointed to the swaddled cloth in the sink of the understated wet bar tucked into the corner of the office. "And that's the . . ."

"Yes."

Castillo nodded, made to examine the room casually, while his mind absorbed the information. Mrs. Gallagher's entrails and uterus not ten feet away. *This is worse than Towraghondi,* he thought suddenly. *God, I didn't think that was even possible.* To clear his mind, he tried focusing on the only two things in the room not completely destroyed. The fish tank, which, though tinged slightly pink with blood, was still intact with a dozen saltwater beauties still swimming about.

And the framed needlepoint behind the desk. Old English lettering:

And our LORD set a mark upon Cain,

And he dwelt in the land of Nod,

on the east of Eden.

"He nicknamed it the 'Cain gene' early," Erdman said behind him. "Cain XP11. For Cain and Abel."

"Got that part. First killer ever. Cute. What's the 'XP11'?"

"A coding gene which influences the protein transcription and en-zymatic activity of DARPP-32, dopamine, and cAMP-regulated phos-phoprotein."

"Don't be a dick," Castillo said. *So much for playing quiet and nice.*

The doctor held up his hand in apology. "Dopamine influences anger. In short, MAOA, or monoamine oxidase A, helps govern dopa-mine levels and is a keystone for high biological plausibility in antiso-cial spectrum disorders and psychopathy. Each chromosome of human DNA carries a million different strands with specific instructions on what that person's genetic makeup will be. One particular location, a strand labeled XP11, controls the MAOA gene. When there's an anomaly on that strand, it characteristically indicates abnormal dopamine levels, potentially influencing a genetic predisposition to abnormal violence. Does that help?"

"Better, thank you. And these clones are created so that your team can better study and . . . develop this specific gene." Castillo met Erdman eye-to-eye. "To ultimately, I assume, harness violence."

The geneticist weighed his options, clearly deciding how much more Castillo was allowed to know. "Yes," he said. "And to cure it, too. We're not here only to construct weapons, Mr. Castillo. In the last ten years, this pioneering research has tendered more than fifty patents to medicate depression, bipolar disorder, Parkinson's disease, and PTSD."

Castillo glanced at Erdman to see if the PTSD reference was deliberate. *A slam? How much do they know about me?* The geneticist's expression revealed no intended insult.

"Parkinson's?" He followed that path instead.

"Remedial manipulation of dopamine levels will eventually cure the disease. We're in clinical trials now on several innovative products toward that selfsame purpose."

"And you test on these kids?"

"No, no," Erdman shook his head. "Not at all. You're not . . . If we want to test a new protein or antibody, or whatever, we have mice and monkeys and human volunteers for that. The boys are where we *harvest* the new proteins and antibodies. Perhaps it's easier to think of these boys as living drug factories, flesh-and-blood bioreactors. A single pint of their blood contains thirty grams of genetically enhanced human protein and is worth millions."

Castillo's face must have revealed his revulsion at the idea.

Erdman sighed. "A traditional protein-development factory would cost four hundred million and take five years to build. Subjects in the Cain project cost one hundred million each and take a single year. Each boy is projected to produce six hundred million in profit in his lifetime merely by donating a little blood a few times each year. I know what you're thinking. It was not the boys' choice. The ethical implications are, admittedly, complicated."

"Complicated. Or inhumane."

"A question we should debate later, perhaps. Today, there are lives at risk, yes?"

"Fair enough." Castillo willed his voice to stay even. "Why'd you even tell me? The clones, I mean. You guys might have just told me six violent kids were missing."

"Colonel Stanforth said you'd figure it out eventually anyway."

Castillo nodded. It was a nice compliment from a trusted mentor, but: *Could I ever have really imagined this?* "Why killers? Shouldn't we be cloning little Einsteins? Kobes? I don't know, Eddie Van Halens?"

"Who'd pay?" Erdman replied. "Fifty years from now, the consumer market might sustain such programs. But, at this stage, start-up costs are in the hundreds of billions. Not many industries can undertake that. Oil. Telecommunications, maybe. But, who'd we clone for *them*? The military's driven human technology for ten thousand years. And, if some good comes from that, the medicines for instance, all the better."

"OK. Then, so why *well-known* serial killers? Wouldn't it have been far easier, safer, to grab your run-of-the-mill psychopath? The prisons must be filled with them."

"Tens of thousands. A million, maybe. But Jacobson, who directs the program, always wanted the *most* violent. Not just gangbangers or family annihilators. He wanted consummate psychopaths. Serial killers. And most of those men, the ones society eventually catches, become famous."

"And no girls here. Safe to assume males are more prone to violence."

"Safe?" Erdman's smile was genuine, a scientist discussing his favorite subject. "Genetically and statistically undeniable. It's not even close. The chromosomal allele for this mutation travels only on the X chromosome. Think of this allele as the genetic antidote, a code in the DNA that can 'fix' the violent abnormality. Remember enough high school biology? Females are born from XX chromosomes. So they've got a likely chance to have a cure for any aggressive mutation in the womb."

"And men are XY."

"Very good, you remember. So, men have only a fifty-fifty shot of carrying the natural cure to an overly aggressive XP11 strand. We're hereditarily predisposed to retaining the affliction."

"Half the world is hereditarily predisposed to violence?"

"We make up ninety-five percent of the prison system. Ninety-nine percent of rapes. And ninety-nine percent of death row." The smile turned wry. "Guess you can say it's in our blood."

"Guess you can." Castillo nodded. "What was in the fish tank?"

Erdman blinked. "Sorry?"

"Speaking of blood, you can tell there's some floating in the fish tank. Someone may have only dipped their hands in, but looks like the rocks were disturbed also. A child could tell something was tossed in there. So, what was it?"

Erdman pretended to check his notes, clearly already knowing what'd been found. "It was a key," he said. "We don't know to what yet. Nothing here or his other office across the compound at DSTI. We're still looking into it."

Castillo thought about requesting the key to see what Erdman would do but figured it wasn't worth adding to the evident animosity; locks had stopped being an issue more than a decade ago. He asked, "Was Jacobson's lab office also destroyed?"

"No. Nor is there any record that he even went there last night."

Castillo didn't respond. He leaned on the edge of an upturned desk and reached down to retrieve one of the splintered picture frames. The photo inside showed two men shaking hands. The first man was a former vice president. The other, a tall, lean, gray-haired man who looked like someone you might bump into on a private golf course. *Except smarter*, Castillo decided. *Much smarter.* Someone who truly understood the world's secret levers and cogs. "This Jacobson?"

Erdman nodded.

Castillo scanned the room. "The boys and he were in some kind of group meeting, yes?"

"First and third Thursday of every month for this group. Our psychiatric head, Angela Corwin, and Dr. Jacobson always run the session together. Ran." Down the hall, Dr. Corwin had been found nude and murdered in her own office. "Though I didn't think he'd make this one."

"Who?" Castillo had lost track of the present. "Who wouldn't make it, Doctor?"

"Jacobson. Been out for weeks," Erdman said. "Pneumonia or . . . Just said he wasn't feeling well. Was working from home. Came in only yesterday. Last night."

"Why would a geneticist take any part in such talks?"

"Dr. Jacobson's core discipline is behavioral neuroscience. His achievements in genetics evolved from that."

"And who assigns particular students to specific group meetings?"

"Varies. Case counselors. Occasionally, Jacobson himself."

"Right." Castillo squinted at Erdman, finally voiced the obvious. "So Jacobson let them out. This was all intentional, premeditated even. You guys good with that? Explains the trouble-free escape, the transmitters, the missing security recordings. Why *these* six kids. The key. His own disappearance." Castillo could tell from the scientist's expression that DSTI had already considered this possibility, and maybe right from the very start. They just hadn't wanted to concede it out loud yet.

"But why?" Erdman asked. "Why would a man do something like that?"

"Was he disgruntled?"

"How could he be? DSTI was practically his company. He could do just about anything he wanted."

"'Just about.' What *couldn't* he do? Was he working with a competitor? Influencing the stock market? Did he have money issues? Or maybe he did it for the same reason you guys do a lot of things around here." He waved his hand, encompassing the acres of laboratories and observation rooms surrounding them. "To see what would happen."

The geneticist looked directly at him, brought the clipboard to his chest. Cleared his throat. Castillo got the distinct impression that something of what he'd said had struck a little too close to home. *Interesting.*

"So," Erdman said. "What now?"

What now?

Castillo thought again of just leaving all this blood and moving on. Going home. Rather, *making* a home somewhere. A new life. *That had been the damn plan, hadn't it?*

But the words came to him then, an ancient mantra he'd commandeered and employed for more than a year now: *"I will endure it, having in my breast a heart that endures affliction. For ere this I have suffered much and toiled much amid the waves and in war; let this also be added unto that."*

Can I reappropriate the line for this task also?

He'd been in the Army for fifteen years and served with Delta Force most of those. He'd learned the art of finding people there. *Hunting* them.

"Now I'll do my job," Castillo said.

The scientists at DSTI had told him that only six boys had escaped.

They were not being entirely truthful.

HOUSE CALL

Albert could not sleep again.

His head filled with too many thoughts. Each idea, memory, and image leading to another as he stared up at the shadow-lined ceiling.

Final exam in Spanish. No clue, gonna fail. Gym first bell. Why bother getting dressed? Never understand a word the asshole teacher says anyway 'cause the fucking guy's from Honduras or somewhere. Don't ever go nowhere. Never even been on a plane. So fucking lame. Retarded. Bullshit class anyway. Wetbacks should just go home. Learn English like everybody else. Adrienne Haller and her fantastico tits. Two rows back. About always see her big giant nipples. Love to watch her. Her mouth. Love to watch her mouth. "¿De dónde venéis?" the mouth says. "¿De dónde venéis?" Wanna see that new movie, the one with that one guy. Sometimes, she runs the pen along her lip. You know what she's really thinking about. Probably has stinky breath. Ashtray-breath like my bitch mother. Haller's a big freezer, probably. Cock tease. Heard Mike Gaffney was looking for me after school. Wants to kick my ass or some shit. Another total cockwad. Need a fucking car. Go somewhere. New York. Or Vegas. Or Honduras. Anywhere. Take Mrs. Nolan somewhere and check out her nips awhile.

He'd already jacked off three times. Trying to relax. To get tired. He just wanted to sleep. No more thoughts. He had to keep busy or they came back again. Every night. Sick of YouPorn and RedTube and the shitty pictures in his shoplifted *Hustler* magazines. The one girl had dark hair on her arms. *Like an animal.* Ripped those pages out and flushed 'em down the toilet with his jizz all over them. *Sick. Freak. Me.*

Mrs. Nolan. Right across the street. No more than a hundred feet away. He turned onto his side and looked out the window toward her. Her bedroom. *She probably jacks off sometimes too. She's, like, forty but even old people do that stuff. MILFs do, for sure. Lies in bed and jams away with a giant purple thingee. Probably her own fingers too. Probably sick of that gay husband. Chris. Faggot. Bet she'd love—*

Noise from the living room. Something breaking. His drunk mother stumbling over the end table again. No doubt pouring herself a last round of Jack and Diet Coke before bed. If he was lucky, she'd go straight to sleep. Some nights she'd come in and start laying into him. Retarded shit about his grades or friends or keeping his music too loud or other stupid shit. Like she was starting shit to start shit. *Drunk bitch.*

He would talk to Jacobson. He always had pills or something to make the worst thoughts go away. For a while.

Mrs. Nolan walks around in her black thong underwear. Seen it. Just last week. When she bent over to pick up the newspaper. Sure like to get my hands on dat ass. Stupid virgin. I should have done that fat bitch with Kevin when she was all fucked up, passed out. Whatnot. I could kill Mike Gaffney. Just shoot him in the fucking head with the gun in Mom's closet. Or Mr. Faggot Nolan. Whatever. Or me. BAM! No masa Española. She thinks I'm a loser anyway. Freak. Who'd fucking care anyway? She would. Mrs. Nolan. He reached into his shorts. Fourth time would ache a little, but it was worth it. Imagined her beneath him with her arms over her head, tied to something maybe. A bedpost, he guessed. Those rail things. Something. *Keeps saying NO but that's because she doesn't want to take the blame when they get caught. Squirming beneath him. Can't make out her face. Adrienne. Mrs. Nolan. Mommy.*

Shit!

Someone standing outside his room. Heard the creak. If his mom caught him again . . . He remembered that ordeal well enough. She'd vanished for a while and then come back to tease him about it for hours. Would not drop it. Like it was her fucking job or something. He quickly pulled his hand away. "What?" he snapped at the dark. Tried to sound tough with his heart thumping halfway out his chest. Wiped off the spit from his hand on the sheet.

The door opened a crack, and a shadow stepped into the den television's ghostly light. He thought it might be Russ, his mom's latest boyfriend. *No.* This guy was too tall. Some new guy who'd come by to fuck the bitch. Another asshole who'd probably end up laying into him someday for looking at 'im wrong.

"What?" he asked, sitting up. "What the fuck—"

The shadow man now stepped fully into his room.

But it didn't make sense. Not at all. *Why is he here?*

"Dr. Jacobson?"

"Hello, Albert. I'm sorry if I alarmed you."

Just like that. As if Albert had somehow willed the man into the bedroom with his earlier thoughts. Like some kinda genie lamp. The boy stood from his bed. "I don't—"

"Nothing to fear, son," the man said, his face still half lost in the room's shadows. "Not anymore. Sit. Everything's going to be fine now."

Several darker shapes in the living room behind the doctor, but Albert couldn't make them out. "Where's . . . where's my mom?"

"First we need to talk," the doctor said.

"Why? Why are you here?" Albert found he'd sat back down as told, but he'd pulled the blanket close to his chest as some childish protection. "We're not supposed to, ummm, meet again for, like, two weeks." He squinted as the doctor loomed. "What's that?"

"This, Albert, is a folder with all the information we have about who you are." Dr. Jacobson had taken a seat at the end of Albert's bed. Casually crossed one leg. "Who you *really* are."

"What do . . . you mean, like, those tests and stuff?"

"We're done with all that. This concerns where you come from." He'd placed the thick folder on the bed. "Your 'family tree,' you might say. Go ahead. Have a look."

"This about my dad?"

"It's about you," the doctor corrected. "Only you."

The boy reached out carefully and took the folder.

ALBERT/5.

And inside: ALBERT HENRY DESALVO. (11/3/1931–11/25/1973), and a picture.

"Is this . . . ? Who is this?"

The black-and-white photo so very familiar. As if he'd seen it before, when he knew that he had not.

Dr. Jacobson smiled beside him, and then spoke briefly to Albert about things like cloning and DNA and "Self." Before Albert could even imagine a response or question, Jacobson nodded back to the folder as if it alone now held all remaining truths. So Albert examined it again.

There were photocopied newspaper headlines. "Boston Strangler Escapes from State Mental Ward" and "Boston Strangler Murdered at Walpole Prison." There were labeled pictures of old ladies: Anna Slesers (55), Mary Mullen (85), Nina Nichols (68), Helen Blake (65), Ida Irga (75). And also faded shots of their dead bodies. Then, the younger ones. Sophie Clark (20), Patricia Bissette (23), Beverly Samans, (23), Joann Graff (23), Mary Sullivan (19). Albert thought, *The Sullivan girl has gay hair but is still kind of hot. Blond. Pretty eyes. Looks a little like Mrs. Nolan.*

He kept reading. About his adoption. And DeSalvo. Didn't understand it all. The DNA stuff. But yet it still somehow explained everything. His "mother." His thoughts. His whole damn stupid life. How much time passed he did not know. An hour? Ten minutes? He ignored the strange noises from the other room, ignored Dr. Jacobson, who sat quietly watching him throughout. Finally, he looked back up.

"Albert DeSalvo." He tried the name on his lips. Not McCarty, his adoptive name. The loser name all those assholes at school knew. But DeSalvo. His real name. "The 'Boston Strangler,'" he whispered into the darkness. *My real name.* The words like magic. He'd never felt . . . *better?*

"You . . . You made me?" Albert said.

"No," Jacobson replied from the shadows. "Like one of the first gods, you made yourself."

Albert looked at the doctor and noticed for the first time that there was blood on the man's pants. It did not change his single overwhelming emotion: *PEACE.*

"Thanks," Albert said.

Dr. Jacobson patted the boy's knee and stood. "Every person should know who they truly are," he said. He proceeded to the bedroom door, and Albert trailed slowly after.

Albert had no idea where his mother was, his fake mother, but there were several figures shuffling into the hall and out the front door. Boys. He wondered if there were others.

Others like me?

The doctor retreated behind them.

"What should I do now?" Albert called after them.

Dr. Jacobson did not pause or answer. He didn't need to.

As the two cars backed away, Albert understood that his front door had been left wide open. Into the night. Where Mrs. Nolan was probably still wide awake, too.

And waiting for him.

SECRET ROOM

JUNE 03, FRIDAY—HADDONFIELD, NJ

Jacobson's house sat alone atop a short wooded hill in a pricier section of Haddonfield, New Jersey. Old ivy, new construction. The country club no more than a mile away. Earlier, in the dark and from a distance, Castillo had carefully walked its perimeter. Even from afar, he could plainly tell someone else had already broken into the house before he'd arrived. A splintered back window, the board used to pry it open still laying beneath. Castillo picked the lock of the back door.

The inside of the small estate remained dark, and Castillo took his time inspecting it. A typical house. Sparse. Couple of empty guest rooms. He'd been told the geneticist was not married. He found emptied file cabinets, not a laptop in sight. Didn't seem like it was the six missing kids or Jacobson who'd done it. The place wasn't trashed, only picked over. DSTI, or someone else working for the Department of Defense, or maybe—still not out of the question yet—a foreign player, trying to sweep this mess under the carpet.

Probably DSTI, Castillo decided. He'd spotted a car at the end of the street. One guy, maybe two, watched the house. If they'd been professionals, like he was, he'd never have spotted them. And the break-in was amateur. He assumed they'd gone with the busted window to feign a routine burglary, and it would have been easy enough to grab a couple TVs, or Jacobson's gold cuff links to bolster that charade. But they hadn't. He smiled at the half-assed attempt at a plausible cover-up, not surprised that they'd visited the house. Always trickier, however, to get the job done right while being misled by the very people you'd been brought in to help. An occupational hazard he was all too familiar with.

Walking the house's dark, silent halls, he found himself truly alone for the first time since Colonel Stanforth had called, since he'd genuinely understood what the mission was about. It was not a good feeling. Being alone meant too much time to think about what he'd seen, to question the ethical and legal implications of what was being done to those boys in the name of defense and profits. He wasn't naïve, by any means. He understood the way the world worked—had certainly been involved in covert activities that had been ethically and legally debatable. But this . . .

He trailed his hand along the wood-paneled wall, studied the corner into the next room. Found what he was looking for. *Got you!* He traced his finger down the left frame of the concealed door and found the small keyhole. *And just behind that door?*

Castillo again felt the overriding urge to just get out, drive straight to the airport and back to New Mexico. *Fuck it.* He'd found other ways to make money, after all. Other ways to get through another day without the Army. But then Stanforth had called. And despite all he'd worked on, the sessions and meditations, the "life-after-war" he'd prepared for, it'd felt damn good to get that call. *OK, so I should have said no.* The moment Stanforth had mentioned the kids, he should have hung up. Smashed the phone into a hundred pieces. But he hadn't. One call and he'd instantly felt part of things again, the real deal, not just running routine security for some regional insurance company, *pretending* to be a soldier. Not the guy forced into retirement at thirty-five with an honorable "medical" discharge. Not the guy everyone was talking about behind his back.

Damaged goods. Fucking NUT JOB.

But *THIS,* he thought, leaving the mysterious hidden door and whatever-lay-behind-it as he stepped into the next room, *THIS is who I am. What I do.*

He'd enlisted at eighteen. And from the half million soldiers in the U.S. Army, he'd become one of only two thousand selected to join the elite Rangers. They'd taught him counterterrorism, counterintelligence, desert warfare operations, and demolitions. From those two thousand Rangers, forty had been selected to join Delta Force. There, he'd captured men named al-Jazari, Binalshibh, and Sheikh Mohammed in places like Yemen, Somalia, Iran, and Pakistan. He had twenty-three confirmed kills. He'd earned a degree in international economic history. Awarded three Purple Hearts, four Bronze Stars for valor, two Silver, and a Distinguished Service Cross.

Goddamn it. Was this a guy who should be sweeping corporate office buildings for competitors' bugs or riding shotgun in oil fat cat limousines as needless security? In answer, his mind kicked up an image of the dog-eared paperback stowed in his gear, and one of a hundred underlined quotes: *Look you now, how ready mortals are to blame the gods. It is from us, they say, that evils come, but they even of themselves, through their own blind folly, have sorrows beyond that which is ordained.*

Then, naturally, he thought of her. And, not for the first time today, he thought of calling.

In the dark house, alone, Castillo called his boss instead.

Anything waited behind that damn door. Best to check in before he discovered any more than he was supposed to.

Colonel Stanforth had also officially gone civilian. He was a "Mr." Stanforth now, just like Castillo, but he still worked for the DOD and its Special Activities Division as a "consultant." Nothing, of course, anyone could ever really confirm for the newspapers, or Congress, or in a court of law.

"Our new friends aren't playing nice, sir," Castillo told him. The "sir" had come out as easily as a breath. To not say it would have been as absurd as if his own mother was no longer to be called "Mom."

"*Old* friends," Stanforth corrected on the other end, a clear reminder to Castillo that the Defense Department's relationship with DSTI was protracted and still valued. "How's it lookin', kiddo?"

"Fine, sir. On-site at Jacobson's home. A lot has already been removed, however." Castillo peered out the window toward the surveillance crew. "Our friends, old or new, didn't advise they were coming out here."

"They're panicked. Not surprising, though. This isn't exactly routine for them. For any of us."

"Yes, sir."

"I'll get you a complete inventory of everything they took," Stanforth said. "And I'll make sure it doesn't happen twice." The first sign of irritation skiffed his words. Despite his "not-surprising" patter, Stanforth plainly felt screwed with. That wasn't good for the eggheads at DSTI.

"Copy. Request more men on this. Need a full team."

"No can do. We've already got men checking out the various home locations," Stanforth said. "That'll save you some footwork. If they find anything, I'll pass it on. The rest, the tough part, needs to be fast and quiet, kiddo. That's you. Fox News goes apeshit when some drunk teenager gets lost in Aruba. What do you think they'd do with this?"

And if something goes wrong . . . tough shit, "kiddo." You're gone and this never happened. Castillo considered the inherent threat in every special-ops mission: Even in formal missions, if he'd gotten caught or failed in a way that would have brought unwanted attention back home, Command could and would have denied all knowledge of his actions. And this wasn't even special ops anymore. Uncle Sam'd run him out more than a year ago. This was freelance. Moonlighting. Gun-for-hire. In the end, they could erase Castillo as likely—and easily—as they'd write him the check for his "consulting fees."

But, Castillo reigned in his paranoia some: *Is it really fair to doubt Stanforth?*

It was Colonel Stanforth, and Stanforth alone, who'd come back for him in Iran. Gotten him out of that "jam" when most others would have scrubbed the whole thing with a tidy M.I.A. and simply left him to suffer more torture and to eventually, if blessed, die. It was Stanforth who'd called him back twenty-four hours ago. And it was Stanforth trusting him now. Castillo knew he owed the man a hell of a lot more faith than what he was giving him. Only problem was that Stanforth also knew it.

"There was a key," Castillo said. "Jacobson left it at DSTI as some kind of clue. Guy *wants* to get caught. Wants us to find something."

"They know what it goes to yet?"

"A hidden storeroom," Castillo said. "I'm standing outside it now."

Stanforth laughed. "That's why I called you."

"What will they do with these kids once I find them? With Jacobson?"

"Just find them," Stanforth replied. "DSTI has the kind of specialists and facilities to treat such minds. They'll be provided for."

"Not eliminated."

"You have my word."

Castillo knew he should let it drop. *Just follow your orders* . . . yet he found himself speaking again: "Then what?" he pressed. "They vanish forever? Spend the rest of their lives locked and medicated in some institution?" *What in God's name are you doing?*

There was silence on the other end for too long. Enough to let Castillo know he'd overstepped. He was forced to wait while Stanforth decided whether or not to discharge him again on the spot. "What would the courts do with them?" the colonel finally said. "They've murdered a dozen people. Look, Castillo, are you up to this job or not?"

Am I?

"Yes, sir. Sorry."

"Unnecessary. I knew this would be a tough first assignment back. Especially with the kids. But you're the best I got for this, and that's a goddamned fact. I wouldn't have called you otherwise."

Castillo quickly processed his options, wrestling with each of Stanforth's words. "First assignment back" meant there'd be others. *Best we got.* If he could only shut his fucking mouth and do his job like he'd done for nearly twenty years, it really was a path back. Stanforth had all the necessary connections and clout to get him into one of the big private military companies. Like a lot of the other guys who'd come home, Castillo could become a private contractor. Mercenary. There were a hundred PMCs to choose from. Put all his talents to use again.

But then there was the "especially with the kids" comment. Proof that Stanforth knew about the dreams, about Towraghondi. About the boy. Of course, they'd have reports, records.

How much did she tell them?

Let it go . . .

"Permission to access the room?" Castillo asked.

"Granted. And, Captain . . ." Not "kiddo" or his squad nickname, Castillo noticed, but something much more official. And, since the rank was no longer accurate, something much more personal. "I'm augmenting your clearance on this one. Whole new ballpark."

"Understood."

"I hope so. 'Cause it gets ugly in a hurry."

"How ugly?"

"Hell's still uglier."

"Yes, sir."

"But there ain't no going back. Not ever."

That I know, Castillo thought. "Copy."

"Keep me informed, Castillo. Keep smart."

"Will do." Castillo ended the call. Put the phone away and withdrew the snapgun again to pick open the hidden door. It didn't take long.

Then he put the electric pick away and, for the first time in months, drew his pistol.

The small room proved empty of life, and Castillo promptly put his pistol away. The space, as he'd imagined, was the size of a walk-in closet. Perhaps a panic room originally. It held two file cabinets overstuffed with printouts and CDs and flash drives and vials of blood. Dozens of notebooks, in various shapes and sizes, filled with handwritten notes. Jacobson's notes.

The room also had a small plastic container with a rotted corpse inside.

The container was plugged into the wall and proved cold to his touch. Sleeping Beauty was wrapped in plastic and only half the size of the box, in two halves laid side by side. It was also very old. Decomposing but still somewhat preserved, like something dragged out of a pyramid, so it was of no pressing concern to Castillo.

Instead, he spent the next nine hours skimming through the files and Jacobson's private diaries, watching the lopsided stacks of videos and CDs. Making copies. Taking digital images of everything with his smartphone.

By morning he had more questions than answers.

But he knew this: If Hell was uglier, it probably wasn't by much.

In one of the recordings, a young boy is being beaten. The digital camera is on the ceiling of the bedroom, probably in a light fixture. The video shows this process going on for months. The man, or "father," even looks directly at the camera occasionally. Castillo shudders each time. The guy knows it's there.

In the next footage, a young boy is only screamed at by his father, but never touched once. The boy is called a "retard" and an "asshole" and a "faggot." And the boy is crying. The video shows this going on for months. By appearance, the two boys in the two recordings are the exact same boy. The rooms are different, however, as are the fathers. Adoptive fathers, Castillo assumes. "Consociates" of DSTI, using Dr. Erdman's word. The boys, in a data stamp on the bottom of the video frames, are named Dennis/6 and Dennis/10. They are clones. Castillo's job is to hunt down Dennis/6, the boy being physically abused. *Dennis Ten is not my concern*, he says to himself a dozen times.

In the next recording, another boy, John/3, is encouraged to help kill a cat with a hammer. John/5 is encouraged to play with Legos. According to the attached notes, both of these boys were crafted from the DNA of John Wayne Gacy. Suddenly one dead cat doesn't seem so bad. Castillo found an accompanying folder on "John," who killed and raped thirty boys and young men in just six years back in the 1970s. Police found twenty of the bodies in his crawl space. There were a dozen pictures for Castillo to look at. The original mug shots and pics of Gacy as "Pogo," the infamous clown character he often dressed as for community parties and events. Color printouts of the paintings Gacy did while in prison: mostly birds and clowns and skulls. Jacobson's notes reported Pogo/Gacy was executed by the state of Illinois via lethal injection in 1994. But wait! Castillo's eyes slid back to the flickering videos. Here were two more. Clones built by DSTI. POGO LIVES! And now clone Pogo is only ten years old. And *this* one clone Pogo kills a cat on film. But this *other* Pogo clone builds elaborate castles out of Legos.

Nature/Nurture.

At least two years' worth of behavioral studies connected to carefully designed environments, according to the videos' time stamps, have been recorded and evaluated as part of ongoing research. Hours and hours of tiny Pogos. Half being tortured in the name of science . . . or national defense.

Hours and hours of weeks and years.

Castillo watched as much as he could.

He clicked on another flash drive's .wmv file.

A coffin is lifted awkwardly from the ground by three men. In the digital video, it is night—the best time for grave robbing. It is raining. The men are dirty and soaked from digging all night, fresh mounds of dirt completely surrounding the grave. One of the men Castillo knows as Dr. Gregory Jacobson. Filmed in night vision, the rainwater runs dark as blood from the mounds into the gaping black hole beneath. When they lift the coffin, its rotted bottom splits open from the weight of the lead lining inside, and the casket's contents spill free. Jacobson waves the other men off and the coffin is laid back down. Tilted strangely, half in the grave and half out. They open it from the top and the camera zooms in as the casket is pried open. Rain falls on the man inside for the first time in what could be hundreds of years, the figure wrapped in a decaying burial shroud. The video shows Jacobson's fingers pulling the cloth open, tearing it free. The shroud splits easily. Beneath, the corpse's chest. Ribs. Neck bones. Jacobson rips the shroud open further to reveal the skull. Teeth. Clumps of hair. Strips of wrinkled, rotted skin along the skewed jawbone. The rain falls on everything. Jacobson runs his fingers along the crown of its glistening skull. He looks up at the camera. The rain splashes down on his face. He is laughing. And, though it could be the rain, it also looks as if he is crying.

In the last video, a boy is drawing. The same blond boy, maybe ten, is playing piano. He looks twelve and is playing Guitar Hero on his PlayStation. He is surrounded by balloons and blowing out the candles on a birthday cake. The camera is not hidden now. It's handheld. A home movie.

And the boy talks to the camera. And the man holding the camera talks back. And the boy says, "Dad, give me a break."

Castillo recognizes the boy in the video some. His features.

He recognizes the house in the video completely.

Easy enough. It's *this* house.

Jacobson's house.

OUR BASEST TRAITS

JUNE 04, SATURDAY—HADDONFIELD, NJ

[From the journals of Dr. Gregory Jacobson]

12 Oct— . . . psychopathic subjects rated "H" or greater remain among the lowest asymmetry scores for monitored offenders. During interview, subject continues to illustrate classic psychopath criteria: superficially charming, unmotivated, manipulative, inadequate sense of shame, paucity of emotion. I asked the subject how he would feel if I put a gun to his face and robbed him. He said he'd find a way to escape, give me the money, or fight me to take the gun. When I pressed him on the issue of how he would "feel," not what he would think or do, subject had no response. None. MMPI scheduled for next session. C-Subject's custodian contacted to increase maternal neglect by 2.0 degrees, fm abuse by 1.0.

9 Nov—Lunch with Dr. Carla Bayliff (Tulane), who is heading a symposium next spring and asked if I would be interested in being guest of honor. Perhaps. Reviewed impact of common functional polymorphism in MAOA on brain structure and function. Low expression variants found on subject's MRIs. Erdman maintains reservations on limited test group. Recorded pronounced limbic volume reductions and hyperresponsive amygdale during emotional arousal. Marked diminished reactivity of regulatory prefrontal regions compared with the high expression allele. The clearest link between genetic variation and aggression is located on the chromosome XP11.23. This is the true mark of Cain. XP11 is the new number of the beast.

22 Nov— . . . subject's MAOA levels remain identical to DNA patron. Latest blood tests confirm sustained low serotonin, norepinephrine, and dopamine levels. Dogs bark as they are bred. Note to visit John and Albert at secondary environments. Voxel-based morphometry prescribed to canvass subject's brain for regional volume changes related to genotype.

He requested his room be painted tan. A genuine emotional preference or mimicry of conventional exchange? He asked again about his mother today. Falsehood has a perennial spring. Perhaps I should never have brought him here.

6 April—Dreams should remain banished to the night. In the sun, they become vile trespassers. The Triazolam shots abridge REM sleep, but now they have somehow found me in the day. I could not see her face again. The warmth spilling from her insides was like a mother's blanket enfolding me. I awoke at my desk, drenched in sweat, my belly warm and wet with semen. I heard from Rochester today and everything is now arranged. Mankind remains ceaselessly motivated by genetic characteristics inherited from ancestors long buried. Individual experiences of childhood can modify, inhibit, or augment these, but can never truly erase. I shall be there when he is lifted again from the earth.

04 May—Tumblety's DNA is a match, and I am filled with abundant joy. It is, as I'd always hoped it would be, comforting to find our basest traits in our forebears. It absolves us.

Castillo tossed Jacobson's journal back inside a box with the rest. Mostly technical jargon and arbitrary fortune-cookieish dictums on violence and heredity.

A stack of clinical studies on various known serial killers (Castillo hadn't heard of any of them). A partial aerial shot of Afghanistan (likely) someone had marked with a series of colored circles growing out from the small village at its center, and the word "SharDhara" scrawled across the top (familiar almost, but not enough). Papers on Supermale Syndrome, XYY children, and something called Klinefelter's syndrome. PCR printouts from a machine Jacobson kept in the same room, which mapped double helix pairings Castillo couldn't understand in the slightest, though he remembered the significance of "MAOA levels" from Erdman. Some graphs comparing oxytocin and vasopressin levels for several subjects made even less sense. But there were also color photos of mutilated victims. Sliced and broken. These Castillo understood perfectly. Crimes, from the clothing and photo qualities, from the early 1900s through present day. There were maps of East London from the nineteenth century. Old photos of someone named Francis Tumblety, and an old pamphlet written by this same guy entitled *The Kidnapping of Dr. Tumblety*.

He'd gathered from Jacobson's journals that Francis Tumblety was the withered stiff he'd spent the bulk of the night with. A quick Google search revealed Tumblety was a Jack the Ripper suspect who'd died in 1903. Jacobson, according to the journals and film, had collected this guy's DNA six months ago.

```
"Tumblety's DNA is a match, and I am filled with
abundant joy."
```

But a match with what? Castillo wondered. The journals were vague. *With Jacobson? With some other clone?* Castillo didn't think on it too long, because the dead guy wasn't the most puzzling, most twisted part.

That was reserved entirely for the *other* CDs.

The footage of Test Group #2.

Children being beaten and worse. Jacobson's journals and reports confirming that the various forms of abuse had been methodically ordered, *prescribed*, in the name of science.

Castillo leaned into his hands and rested against the desk. It had been a long day. He'd grown too numb to think. The whole thing was fucking insane. He thought of prayer, but his only thoughts for God right now were angry thoughts. The colonel had been right. There was no going back.

"*If any god has marked me out again for shipwreck, my tough heart can undergo it.*" Another favorite Homeric passage came to mind. "*What hardship have I not long since endured at sea, in battle! Let the trial come.*"

He checked his cellphone. 0614 hours. He called the number they'd given.

Who am I trying to convince?

"It's Castillo," he said and could hear the anger in his own voice. Knew already it had been stupid to call.

"Yes?" Dr. Erdman replied at the other end. His voice sounded strained. It'd been a long day and night for everyone. Castillo wondered how the cleanup was coming along. "I was informed by Stanforth you'd found something and instructed to leave you alone until you were finished. Are you?" Erdman tried to sound bored, but Castillo could tell the bioengineer was terrified about what Castillo might have discovered. *With good cause.*

"*Wer mit Ungeheuern kämpft,*" Castillo replied.

"Go on."

"Something Nietzsche pointed out. 'Who fights with monsters should—'"

"'—beware that he, himself, does not become a monster.'" Erdman finished the quote. "Profound. Cliché. How does it relate to the immediate matter at hand?"

Castillo's laughter was harsh. "What do you see when you look in the mirror, Erdman?" *I shouldn't have called.* It was confrontational, unnecessary. The kind of call he would have made a year ago. Merely spoiling for a fight. *Any* fight. Wanting to lash out at someone for the shit he'd been forced to watch all night. An emotional reaction that had no place in the operation. *Damn it. Why did I call him?*

"What most men see, I imagine." Erdman's reply brought Castillo back. "I hope you've acquired meaningful information of some kind to assist in the prompt resolution of this matter. Stanforth assured us you would."

"Meaningful information." Castillo stopped any impending threats from bursting forth. Slowed his speech. "One, Dr. Gregory Jacobson—your boss—is undeniably insane. His personal journals are filled with violent disjointed fantasies and a connection to some Victorian murderer named Francis Tumblety, an Englishman who died a hundred years ago. There's video of Jacobson and some other folk digging up this man's grave. In fact, I'm standing over, I believe, what's left of Mr. Tumblety's corpse."

"Yes?"

"Not surprised yet, I see. Two, for the sake of marketable pharmaceuticals, bioengineering prospects, and potential military applications—otherwise why would I be involved?—DSTI, a highly financed but little-known genetics lab, purposely breeds monsters. Testing clones of humans known to possess violent behavior. Sponsors the abuse of children . . . No wait, my bad, sponsors the abuse of only *half* of them for the sake of nature/nurture environmental testing."

"Those tests were discontinued years ago and, officially, never happened."

Deny. Deny. The videos *had* been time stamped years ago and so might have been discontinued. And the public disavowal of some wrongdoing was not unfamiliar to Castillo. It sometimes went with the job. However, this . . .

"Understood," Castillo pressed. "How familiar are you with the full environmental testings, 'subject insertions,' of Phase Three, Doctor?"

Erdman paused on the other end. "Jacobson had plans, but we never . . . DSTI rejected his proposal. If anything was done, he did it on his own."

Deny. Deny.

"Well." Castillo rubbed his eyes. "His notes indicate that's exactly what he did. Adopting out infant genetic psychopaths to unknowing parents to see how the 'killer gene' would play out. Paid for it himself when you wouldn't."

"DSTI rejected the proposal, as it tendered virtually zero benefit to our primary objectives."

"So you've now noted twice. Guess he had motive to become disgruntled after all, huh? His records also indicate that he, himself, was one of the adoptive parents."

"Did you find . . . ?"

"A stolen clone? Nope. Not yet, Doctor."

There was a long pause on the other end of the phone. Then Erdman spoke again. "Jacobson practically launched DSTI himself and is one of the preeminent bioengineers in the world. He was permitted many freedoms."

"Clearly. Did you know he had a son?"

"Of course."

"And that the boy is a clone from your lab?"

"Yes."

"How many more could there be then? How many families have these children been placed with? Jacobson's notes are iffy. Coded."

"We don't know for sure. A dozen, perhaps. All other embryos have been accounted for. We'll need to see his notes."

"Good, he wanted you to see them. He left the key for a reason. I've made my copies and will leave the originals for you. Pick 'em up here in an hour. You can send me e-copies of what, if anything, you found earlier when you tried to clear this place out. But it looks like I've got what I really need here already. Your six missing students was barely the beginning. Jacobson's going to find these other adopted kids, and then he's going to set *them* free, too."

"Why do you think so?"

"It's in the journals. He clearly wants the cages emptied. So, if I have this right, by week's end, there could be as many as eighteen of these kids loose in the world?"

Erdman returned absolute silence.

"Perfect," Castillo said. "You guys need to start understanding I'm on your team and I can't do my job when I'm being lied to. On that note, any idea what 'SharDhara' is? Person? Place? Something to do with Afghanistan?"

"No."

"No? He's got a map of a region *in* Afghanistan, a blast radius and what look like mortality numbers here. Estimates. Figures. Readings of some kind I can't make heads or tails of."

"Doesn't mean a thing to me. How did you find the room?"

"I'll be in touch." Castillo hung up and tapped his chin with the phone, thinking. The fight with Erdman had already become one more reason to call her. Practically as if he'd done it for that purpose.

So many reasons to call. A dozen more *not* to.

"Damn it," he cursed quietly in the empty room.

He tapped in the number from memory.

0630. Might not even be at work yet. *Would I call back if she wasn't?*

She answered on the first ring, "Kristin Romano."

Her name alone, or even the sound of her voice, would have been enough. Combined, it felt like he'd been shoved out the back of an HC-130 into a six-mile HALO-style free fall.

Kristin Romano.

When he'd returned from Iran, he'd spent another year recovering at the Walter Reed Medical Center in D.C. There, Colonel Stanforth made sure he'd gotten the very best treatment available for the physical damage he'd endured. Psychological healing had come harder. The biggest hindrance, he'd always known, had been himself. But the assembly-line treatment of Veterans Affairs hadn't helped much either. The first two psychologists he'd worked with kept piling on the pills. Had figured if they'd kept him a zombie another forty years, he'd get over the torture and the fact that the Army had decided he should be pinned with a bouquet of shiny medals and then retired at age thirty-three as swiftly and quietly as possible. It hadn't gone well. He'd even punched out one of the guys during a session.

Then came Doctor Kristin Romano. Captain Romano. *Kristin.*

She'd stopped his prescriptions immediately, her methods more connected to activities like journaling, art therapy, meditation, and even, eventually, more woo-woo exercises in things like astral projection and channeling.

To start, however, she'd simply invited him to spend the week camping with nine other vets somewhere in the Adirondacks for a bunch of touchy-feely Oprah bullshit. Sit around the campfire and talk about your feelings like a gaggle of pussies. He'd said six words the first two days, and none of the other guys had been much better. The third night, she'd set up an actual sweat lodge miles from their cabins and left the ten men completely alone for the rest of the night. He couldn't remember who'd started it, but they'd started. Talking. First one guy, then the next. Things they'd seen, done. Most of it was things they *should* have done. They took turns crying and screaming and laughing. It had been midmorning the next day before anyone realized they were cold and there was no more firewood. Ten brothers now. Ten singular experiences had become only one. Group talks continued the rest of the week. At the end, she'd given each man a copy of *The Odyssey* and said, "It took Greece's greatest soldier ten years to finally make his way home after the Trojan War. Give yourselves a fucking break."

He'd read the book religiously ever since, meditated on and memorized passages each night, Odysseus's adventures suddenly a very real allegory for *every* returning soldier. Each week, he and Dr. Romano had discussed what he'd read. They'd discussed more easily than ever before what he'd done and witnessed in the Army. His kills. His capture. The torture. Some of the boy, of Shaya. They'd eventually gotten to his childhood and future plans. Then *hers*. And then love. Or lust. Or both. But it had happened. And the fact that she'd been married and had a young daughter made the eventual ending even worse. When he'd vanished on her, it had been quick and clean. Like an execution, as if the whole affair had been nothing but ten months of fucking to pass the time. Hell, he half remembered implying that. Maybe to make her hate him, make it easier. But in the end, he'd left for one reason: He loved her.

Worse: She knew it.

"It's Castillo," he said.

Silence.

"Been a while, I know." He could feel himself scrambling, like a man desperate to deploy a parachute in the last few thousand feet. "How . . . how are things?"

"What can I do for you, Captain?"

It was the voice of a total stranger. *Fine*. That's what he needed to hear. He was safely on the ground again. *Almost*. "Not a captain anymore," he said. Doubtless, she'd already heard that. As far as he knew, her notes on him had been applied as part of the procedure. "Discharged ten months ago. I need your help."

Her voice changed. "Have you had—"

"No, no. Nothing like that. I'm fine. You cured me, remember?"

She laughed softly. It sounded forced but was still familiar enough. He thought he'd somehow already forgotten it. "You were never 'sick,'" she said, and he heard a more genuine smile. "What can I do for you?" The stranger's voice returning some.

"Nothing," he said. Waited. Thought again of hanging up. "I don't know."

"Articulate as always."

Castillo absently straightened some of the papers on Jacobson's desk. Thinking. Thinking, *Why the hell did I call her?* Saying, "I need your help, Kristin."

"'Kristin'? Wow . . . what's the—"

"I'm in something now that's . . ." Castillo breathed more deeply, memories clouting him. "OK, here's the thing: I've got a couple psychological reports to figure out for a case I'm working on. But it's all just a bunch of numbers and bullshit shrink jargon I can't decipher."

"OK . . ."

"I'm gonna need a little help figuring some of this shit out. And maybe, I guess, I also need someone I can trust." *And maybe someone who can help hold me together through this first assignment back. Just once . . .*

"You were never a 'maybe' guy." Her end of the line grew muffled. Probably shutting her office door. "Not a minute ago, you told me you were finally out. What the hell they got you working on now?"

"I can't tell you. You know that."

"Yes," she said, her turn to sigh. "I know that."

"Will you help me?"

Pause.

"Kris?"

"Yes," she said.

"I'd just need you to look at the files and maybe give me personality profiles. Who these guys are, how they think. Six subjects. You have time?"

"Do I have . . . You know, this is fucking nuts. Whatever. Send me the files. I'll get to them as soon as I can."

"Also, if you could, any generic profile data you can pull together on sociopaths would be good. It'll all arrive by courier later today."

"OK." More confusion in her voice. "Not a problem."

"Thanks. Means a lot."

"Was there anything else?"

Castillo thought. Maybe he'd try something like *I'm sorry I left the way I did. What the hell have you been up to the last ten months? How's Allie? How's that damned husband of yours doing?* Or maybe . . . "No," he said. "I better go anyway. Whenever you can get to it . . ."

"I'll look at it today."

"Thanks. I, ah . . . Talk soon."

He shut the phone and put it away. Drew his 9mm pistol in its place.

He'd replay the call in his mind many times again later. He'd think of her. Later.

Now it was time to find the clone.

PLANS SHARED

Jacobson watched the fading moon from the back porch of a small ranch house in the outskirts of Salisbury, Maryland, as a bruise-colored dawn emerged underneath. The only other light was from a single hallway fixture deep inside. Leaning back in a wooden rocker, legs outstretched, the backpack at his feet, a slender, assuaged smile rested across his face. His boys had grouped around him in a lopsided semicircle, quietly smoking cigarettes and drinking the beer they'd found in the fridge. Nurse Santos lay freshly entombed within the tomato and pepper garden not twenty feet away. The whole of creation seemed still, waiting.

"During the Middle Ages," the geneticist said, "people believed Cain lived on the moon."

"That's gay," one of the boys laughed. Dennis. Jacobson eyed the boy, analyzed him.

"Why'd they think that?" another voice asked.

Jacobson gently turned to Ted, the boy who sat closest. Beautiful Theodore. The same angelic face that had once charmed, raped, and murdered thirty women. "Do you know what happened to Cain after he killed his brother?" he asked the teen.

"He lived in the land of, ah, Nod," Ted replied. His voice was deep, about to leave childhood behind forever. "Like the poster thing in your office."

Jacobson nodded. "Good. And then what?"

The boy thought, shrugged. "Dunno."

"Anyone?" Jacobson knew the other boys were half listening at best. Distracted. Excited. "*Nod* means 'wander' in Aramaic, the language of the Bible, and most faiths believe Cain 'wandered' the earth. Cursed. Unable to die."

"Like a vampire," Jeff said. Aptly, his words sounded deep and hoary, as if spoken by something that had newly wrestled itself free from its tomb. Still, Jacobson could hear the clear echo of his own adopted son in the older voice. Three years separated them, but it might as well have been a thousand. In the end, it would bear out that only one true Jeffrey Dahmer traveled through time untouched, unfettered. In the end, his progeny, *all of them*, would spill blood as effortlessly and jubilantly as the original.

"Funny you should say that." He pointed at the boy as elusive memories of talking to his own Jeff half arose in his mind. *Where is he now? Already discarded by DSTI? Or, perhaps, even now finding his true self as these unchained souls are doing.* "Hebrew Apocrypha suggests Cain eventually met Lilith, Adam's first wife. That she taught the world's first killer to drink blood for power. That they had many children together. Demons and monsters, if you believe in such things. Other ancient texts claim Cain was the bastard son of Satan and Eve."

"That's gay, too," Dennis giggled. And several of the other boys laughed.

Jacobson smiled with them. *It's their time, too.* "In either case," he concluded, "he is said to have lived forever as a nomad, finally begging people to end his boundless suffering. No one did. Eventually, or so they believed, he fled to the moon itself." He looked up again, and some of the boys looked with him.

"Yeah." Ted stared. "It kinda makes sense. Some nights, you know, when there's that weird feel in the air. Like something bad is going to happen . . ."

"Like tonight!" Henry hooted.

"Like tonight," Ted agreed, but his voice revealed he recognized that tonight's revelries were over.

Jacobson leaned forward. "And today," he assured the boy. "And the next day, too."

Now all the boys were listening.

"Today, we will part," said Jacobson, and the boys shot each other quick looks. Many had been waiting for this, already grown tired of doing everything Jacobson told them, and he knew that. He wondered how far some would make it. "You are all free in every possible way. I ask only two more things of you."

"Fuck that," Henry laughed.

"Shut up." Ted glared at the other boy, and Henry just shrugged. Ted turned back to Jacobson. "What?"

"Two lists," answered Jacobson, reaching into his shirt pocket and handing one paper directly to Ted and the other to Dennis. On each, scribbled words. "Names and addresses of others. Others like you. Like Albert. Like John here."

John was the boy they'd found hours ago. When Jacobson had explained what he was, the boy had gone into the next room and beaten his own little brother to death with a baseball bat from the garage. All this while the other boys had been having fun with John's adoptive parents, now both nude and still and bloody in the family's dining room. After all that, there'd been no question about what to do with John. He was a keeper. And now, a new day emerging, he was inside, putting on the makeup, getting ready to drift with them in perpetuity.

"I have folders with specific information for each in the car."

"You want us to free them, too," Ted confirmed.

"Oh, yes."

"Why can't you do it?" Henry asked.

Jacobson's eyes flashed in the darkness, something in them the boys had only seen once before. When it had all started back at Massey. When the "quiet old man" had pulled Mrs. Gallagher into his office. "I have other responsibilities now." His voice too had become another voice altogether. Terrible, like some provoked god. "You'll indulge me, yes?"

"Sure, yeah. Just asking." The boy's words shook some with his reply.

"Not a prob, Dr. Jacobson," Ted said carefully. "What else?"

Jacobson reached down into the backpack and brought something out for them all to see. They each crowded for a closer look.

"What is it?" Ted stood, and Jacobson handed him the canister.

It looked just like a Pepsi can.

INTRODUCTIONS

"I won't hurt you," Castillo said into the empty room.

Not really empty. Not by a long shot. He had far too many years of coming into rooms where people were hiding to think that. But he'd passed this room far too quickly when he'd first walked the house. He was supposed to be alone. But the tan room. He remembered passing through an empty tan room.

"He requested his room be painted tan. He asked again about his mother today."

"Perhaps I should never have brought him here."

The closet. The smallest movement, and he turned with the sound.

"Come out," he urged. "You can come out now."

The slatted door folded open. Castillo aimed.

The boy seated inside beside a wicker hamper was maybe fifteen. Sandy blond hair. Glasses. Lanky. Familiar. The boy from the home videos. But also somewhat familiar from the clone photos he'd received at DSTI. Castillo just couldn't remember which boy it was. There hadn't been enough time yet to really study and memorize their faces properly. And Jacobson's notes didn't reveal which one he was either.

Not one of the original six breakouts. This kid was something differ-ent altogether.

Jacobson's adopted son.

"It's OK," Castillo told him. "I won't hurt you. You alone?"

The kid nodded. No weapons that Castillo could see.

"Where's your dad?" He lowered his pistol. One down, fifteen or so to go. *More than you can handle. Six might—maybe, hopefully—have been doable.*

The boy shrugged.

"Come on out of there." Castillo waved him forward and eyed the rest of the room. "What you doing in there, man?"

Another shrug.

"Hiding from me, I guess," Castillo said. "Out now. Easy. Every-thing's cool."

"You're with them."

"Who? Come on out."

"DSTI." He crawled free clumsily, borderline comically, but eventu-ally stood up. Kid was thin, but already as tall as Castillo. "Right?"

"Stay right there. You live here, don't you?"

"Yeah."

"I'm gonna check you for weapons, OK? Take it easy." Castillo pat-ted the boy down. "Who else lives here?"

"My dad. I don't have any—"

"You're doing fine. Sit down right here," Castillo said as he pointed to the bed. "When was the last time you saw him?"

The kid didn't reply.

"Relax, I just need you to answer a couple questions is all."

"He said they'd kill me."

"Who would? DSTI? Your dad say why?"

No answer.

"Did he say why they'd want to kill you?"

"A 'liability.' He said I'm a liability."

Castillo sighed. "Hey, listen. I'm not going to kill you. Or your dad or anyone else. I'm just here to help get everything back to normal. You understand? 'Cause your dad's in some real trouble. I'm trying to help him." Castillo set a chair opposite the boy. "You're safe."

The boy shook his head.

"I asked, 'When's the last time you saw him?'"

"Last night."

Castillo sat. "Great. OK, so then what happened?"

"Happened? Nothing. He . . . nothing. We talked."

"About?"

The kid shook his head again. "Just talked. Then . . . he left."

"Tell you where he was going?"

"No."

"You sure?"

"Yeah."

"Ever been to DSTI?"

"Me? Yeah, lots of times."

"Why? When?"

"I don't know. My . . . my dad took me."

"What for?"

"I don't know. He worked there, so . . . sometimes stuff with the other guys."

"What kind of stuff?"

"Just stuff. At Massey."

"You go to school there?"

"No. Home schooled. Tutors. And I don't think any of the guys ever really thought of it as that. As a school, I mean."

"So, what? A treatment center? What were *you* being treated for?"

"I don't know. I thought . . . I was, like, in a bad car accident years ago and, so, like, rehabilitation and stuff. Memory issues. Speech specialist. I don't know. My dad wanted me to go sometimes, so I went."

"What kind of things would you guys do there?"

"Like group talks. Or, um, I don't know. Like, mostly group games, I guess. IQ tests and—"

"Stuff, got it. Anyone else at Massey or DSTI know you live here?"

"Sure. Just about everyone. You gonna arrest my— Are you gonna arrest Dr. Jacobson?"

Castillo shrugged now. "I'm not a cop, man. But I need to find him. And soon. Him and some of the other guys."

"Something happen?"

"Why would you say that?"

"You said my dad was in trouble. And guys with guns keep coming to my house."

Castillo nodded, the kid clearly referring to DSTI's earlier visit. "Fair enough. Yeah. Something happened. Some people got killed."

"Who? Did . . ."

"Not your dad. Some students, a couple of other employees."

"Did he . . . ?"

"'Did he?' What? You think your dad might have done something?"

"Don't know."

"Me either. Some of the other students might be involved, though. And now they're missing. You know these guys? Albert? Henry? David?"

Castillo waited while the boy looked away, mouth moving slightly in silent thought. "Some. I guess."

"You guess. What about Jeff or Dennis?"

"No."

"What's that?"

"No. I never met a Jeff."

"OK, OK. Look. I'm gonna have to find these guys. And your dad. Do you have any idea where any of them might be?"

The kid shook his head.

"Know where the other guys live?"

"No."

"What about your dad?"

"He lives here."

"No, I mean does he have somewhere else to go? Parents? A brother? Girlfriend?"

The kid shook his head each time.

"He travel much? You guys ever travel together?"

"I guess."

"Where?"

"Don't know."

"Where?"

"Like, Washington. Ohio. New York. Um, the beach and stuff."

"Which beach?"

"I don't know. Hatteras. Florida Keys. Stone Harbor."

"Nice." Castillo pulled out his digital camera. "D.C., huh?"

A nod yes.

Castillo filed through the pics he'd taken. Pics of Jacobson's journal entries.

"What about, well, St. Louis or Baltimore. You two ever been there?"

"No. My . . . He went there sometimes. Conventions and stuff."

"Yeah? How often?"

"I don't know. Couple times a year, I guess. He brought me back a Ray Rice jersey."

"Cool."

"I guess. They took it. Took everything."

Castillo surveyed the kid's room. Emptied bookshelves and drawers. Lines where posters had freshly hung. Where a fish tank or something had once rested on the chest of drawers. Now no proof he'd ever existed. Wholly emptied by DSTI. Castillo would not think about what they would have done with the boy had they found him.

"He said they'd kill me."

Castillo put his phone away. "I think you could maybe help me," he said.

The kid started to get up. "I don't get how—"

"Stay right there, man." Castillo waited while the boy sat back into place. "The thing is, I think you've been telling me the truth. That makes you a very rare bird today. I'm bettin' you could maybe even help me figure some things out. These guys are quite like you. Where you've been, they'll go. People always stay in their own environments."

"Those guys have nothing to do with me."

"Sure."

"So . . . You're not gonna turn me over to DSTI?"

"DSTI?" Castillo shook his head. "Nah. They didn't even tell me you existed."

The kid looked as if he'd just been told he was dead. "Oh," he managed.

"And I think you can help me."

"You really think so?"

"Maybe."

"How'd you find the room?" the boy asked. "The hidden one, I mean. . . . The other guys didn't."

Castillo nodded. "Got an idea of the house's layout from the out-side. You kinda look at it and imagine room sizes and where walls and rooms *should* be. Something to always do before entering an unfamiliar structure. When I got inside, something didn't add up."

The boy thought about that for a moment. "I could maybe . . . help, I guess. Maybe help you look for them."

"Maybe, pal, maybe. You know what most of 'em look like. Kinds of places they talk about going? Even places your dad has been."

"I guess. And you want to help them? Not just . . ."

"I do," Castillo said. And it felt good when he said it. *It felt like the truth.* "I want to help them all get out of this OK. Your dad, too."

"Sure. That's, um, cool."

"Yeah, I guess it is. You really sure you wanna help?"

Am I really sure I want your help?

The boy looked around his emptied room. "I'm sure."

"Well, best get started then. This house is gonna get swarmed again in about thirty minutes. I'd tell you to grab some clothes but looks like they wiped you out pretty good. Probably for the best. Anything you want to take?"

"They already took everything," the boy replied. "We can go now."

Castillo stood and held out his hand. "Shawn Castillo."

The boy half stood also, frowned, and shook back.

"Hi," he said. "I'm Jeffrey Dahmer."

YOUR BEST BET

Castillo drove north up Route 70 through a long channel of dark pine and strip malls. There was no particular reason for heading this way. It was chiefly somewhere away from Jacobson's, away from DSTI. Somewhere where they could talk. Where he could maybe figure out where he really *should* be driving.

He'd not wasted five more minutes at the house, sneaking the boy out a side window away from the pitiful surveillance team and through a backyard to his own waiting car. It had already been a long day for both of them, and it wasn't going to get better for a while. Jacobson and the six clones had a twenty-hour lead, which would have been an eternity if they had been men trained to avoid capture. Castillo's salvation was that they weren't. Regardless of their origins, they were basically a bunch of runaway teens. Jacobson could be another story. He appeared insane, perhaps, but that didn't mean he hadn't prepared properly to vanish into thin air. According to his diaries, he'd been messing with the whole Tumblety-corpse-thing for a year. But a Jack-the-Ripper wannabe was the least of Castillo's concerns.

Hi, I'm Jeffrey Dahmer.

Jacobson's son, his adopted son, his clone of the world's most in-famous serial killer, shrank in the passenger seat while Castillo stared straight at the road ahead, thinking. Every so often, he could hear the kid sniff back tears.

"I need you to remember everything, anything, your dad told you," Castillo said, not looking over. "Anything could help." The boy kept silent, and Castillo tried again: "The last time you spoke, what exactly did he tell you?"

"I don't . . . I don't know."

"You don't know."

"I told you, I don't remember."

"OK, Jeff, he comes up to your room and . . . what? Were you asleep or . . . ?"

"No. I was reading. Whatever." He turned away from Castillo and instead stared out the window.

Castillo had hated using the boy's name. Even though this was Jef-frey *Jacobson*, he couldn't shake off the *Dahmer* reality any more, appar-ently, than the kid himself could. No matter how difficult the name was to say or think, he also knew it was the easiest way to keep a subject's attention.

"He said he needs to talk to me," the boy continued. "Then he says, 'I'm not your real father.' Gave me some folder with information about . . . He says, 'You're actually the clone of this famous murderer guy.'"

"He'd never told you any of this before?"

"No."

"Got it, so then what?"

"Then he said they'd kill me and then he left, and then, so yeah. . . . That's it." The boy used the back of his hand to wipe away fresh tears. "Bet you think I'm a total pussy, huh?"

"Because you're crying?" Castillo really looked at the boy for the first time in twenty minutes and tried to see him just as that: a boy. It was, he realized immediately, a distasteful thought. Because he knew exactly what Jeff really was and because of the kind of life awaiting the kid even in the best circumstances. "Anyone who'd think that just proves nothing bad's ever really happened to 'em." He had enough damned dead kids on his conscience to deal with. "What'd you do?" he asked, chasing away the thought.

"What?"

"After your dad left, what did you do?"

"Nothing."

"Must have done something."

"Walked the neighborhood, I guess."

"Anywhere special?"

"No." Jeff shook his head. "Just around. It was dark when I got back, I could tell people were in the house, so I hid."

"Your dad drives a white Avalon, yes?"

"Yeah."

"You drive yet?"

"No. Supposed to get my temps and stuff this summer."

"What about that folder your dad gave you?"

"Wasn't there when I got back. Nothing was."

"Yeah. You're doing great, kid. Just hang in there." Castillo tapped at his smartphone. "This is a list of the students who were killed during the breakout," he said as he handed the phone over. It was nine names. Nine dead kids. "You know any of these guys?"

"I don't know," the boy said. "How many Henrys are there?"

"Too many," Castillo agreed. "Last names only, then."

"Him." The boy extended his hand and finger to the name.

"Careful, touch screen."

Jeff read out four names. "They were . . . I don't know," he said. "They were nice kids."

"That seems to be the consensus." Castillo took the phone back to pull up the list of the six who'd escaped. Like the nine dead, their *adopted* names.

```
Albert Young. Jeffrey Williford. Henry Roberts.
Dennis Uliase. Ted Thompson. David Spanelli.
```

"Know these guys?" Castillo asked, giving the phone over again.

"They . . . They're, ah, clones, too?"

"Yes. Know 'em?"

"Henry and Al. And David. But David . . ."

"David what?"

"He'd never . . . I can't believe he'd do this."

"What makes you say that?"

"He was chill, that's all. Kinda funny. Friendly. I don't know."

"Maybe he *isn't* part of this," Castillo said, making a mental note on David. "Maybe he and some of the others are caught up in it as hostages, or . . ."

"I don't know."

"And Henry and Al?"

The boy visibly shuddered.

"That bad?"

Jeff nodded. "It was the way they looked at you. How they looked at *everyone*. Like you were a mouse and they were cats kinda thing. Always with this smile. Like they could do whatever they wanted to you. I don't know. Sounds retarded, I know."

"Not at all. And it helps me figure out who the leaders in this group may be. You know where these guys like to hang out?"

"I don't know. On Xbox? Movies, maybe. Um, Henry was into paintball."

"Anything else? David? Ted?"

"No."

"That's OK. It's a good start. We've already got eyes on the six homes of these guys. You and I will head back and hit some local malls, theaters, and wherever the hell folk play paintball. A lot of these guys lived near DSTI. Figure King of Prussia Mall. Wawa. Your average person tends to hide in places they already know."

"These aren't 'average' people."

"They're civilians." Castillo took the phone back, searched, and handed it over again. "And that's average enough for me. Look at this for me."

The screen showed a bunch of dates and numbers that didn't make any sense.

And this:

McCarty AlBaum

One drawing on each page surrounded by the seemingly random numbers and letters. *Dates?* Castillo wondered again.

"Are these . . ."

"Those are from your dad's journal," Castillo explained. He could tell the information startled the boy some, and he pressed ahead. Black-and-white questions worked for everyone. "Who is M. Carty?"

Jeff shrugged.

"Do you know any Cartys or McCartys or . . . ?"

"No."

"Think."

"No."

"What's this bird?"

"Dunno."

"Al is Albert, yes?"

Shrug.

"Has to be," Castillo said.

"I guess."

"Albert Fish or Albert DeSalvo?"

"Who is that?"

"Famous guys named Al."

"Famous for killing people."

It wasn't a question, and Castillo nodded. "What do you think that is?" He nodded down at the phone. "This squiggle. A music note? Did your dad play any musical instruments?"

"Not that I know. And that's not like any note I've ever seen. Is it a nose?"

"You play?"

"I guess."

"You guess?" Castillo spotted a doughnut chain ahead. Somewhere to pull over, make some calls, turn back toward Philadelphia. "What do you play?"

"Bass."

"Cool." Castillo squinted up at the rearview mirror. It was time to get hold of Pete Brody, for sure. Call Colonel Stanforth again. Ox, maybe. He needed so much more info. *Where to start?* It was a long shot at best that the malls would turn up anything. "Maybe it's some kinda DNA thing? Like a scientific notation of some kind."

Shrug again. "Maybe."

He half watched Jeff exploring the phone, looking at some of the other pics from the journals.

Hi, I'm Jeffrey Dahmer.

"How's this?" said Castillo. "Your father adopted out one of the Albert clones to a family named Baum. Al Baum . . . How's that sound?"

"Sure," the boy said absently, lost in his father's scribbles.

Castillo had earlier logged into a lower-level NSA database. "There are twenty thousand Baum families in the United States."

"Is that a lot?"

"Too many for us." He slowed to pull into the Dunkin' Donuts.

"What are you doing?"

"Relax. Gotta turn around anyway. And I've got some people to get ahold of. Folk who could help point us in the right direction. Maybe grab you some food."

"Not hungry."

"Not a problem." Castillo deliberately parked the car in the one spot where the sun's position likely blinded the store's lone outdoor security camera, if it even worked at all. He felt the need to hide Jeff— would have to disguise the kid when they had a breath.

"I need five minutes," he said. "After, we'll hit some of the spots you know about. Then probably set up camp somewhere in town to grab some sleep and start digging into the data. Sound good? Good. In the meantime, you stay right damn here. I'll be over there. But listen . . . hey, Jacobson, listen." The boy turned again at the sound of his name. An easier name for Castillo to utter. "If you try and take off, or whatever, I'll catch you easily and drive you straight back to DSTI. Got it?"

The boy nodded.

"DSTI claims that you don't even exist to just about everyone. Are you sure you got it? Any time today you go and call the cops on me, ask someone for help, make a scene or anything . . . you need to know that every path leads you straight back to DSTI. And I'm gonna keep this next fact as simple and honest as I can, OK?"

"OK," the boy said, curious.

"No one's told me to find you," Castillo said. "I'm only supposed to find six boys and your dad. That's it. No one is paying me to find *you*. In my book, you're on my team now."

"What if—"

"If," Castillo stopped the question, "they decide you're a 'liability' and want me to capture you specifically? I promise to give you some money and a week's head start. Fair?"

The boy looked away.

Castillo reached out awkwardly to tap his shoulder. "Hey," he said. "I don't really understand what's going on yet. And I know you're not too far behind me. But I know if the goal is getting you, you *and* your father, out of this safely, right now I'm your best bet."

Jeff turned and considered Castillo's face. It was amazing the way kids didn't even try to hide it. He was sizing Castillo up.

Castillo thought, *If it was me, I'd take off.* He had no clue if the boy would really be waiting in the car when he got back. "Don't move an inch. I'll be right back."

"Here . . ." Jeff handed back the phone.

"Nope. Got another for that. Sure you don't want anything?"

The boy shook his head.

"Then keep looking through those pics. Let me know if anything jumps out at you. Places. Names you might recognize. Something about where your dad might be. We need to find these guys fast." It was mostly a lie. Castillo knew the way the world really worked. "Fast" was relative. Only thing that mattered was if the operation was completed successfully. Not how long it took.

"From this? It's just pages of weird cartoons and scribbled numbers." Jeff stared in wonder. Or horror.

Christ. It was the first time Castillo had successfully visualized the boy as someone's actual son, as an actual teenager who should have been playing Call of Duty or getting laid. Probably scared out of his mind. Everything he'd ever known as truth was, as of hours ago, now completely wrong. To top it off, his father was clearly a flaming madman. Castillo suddenly wanted to convince the kid everything was gonna be all right, only he couldn't think of a thing that wasn't a complete lie. Instead, he tried the truth. "Your dad sure ain't making this easy."

The boy kept his eyes glued to the phone. "No shit," he replied quietly.

Castillo almost smiled as he closed and locked the door.

GROUND ZERO

It was early morning, and Saturday, yet the courtyard was still more than half full with people grabbing ten minutes of fresh air and buying some fancy coffee or a meal before returning to whatever work it was they did on the inside. Stanforth watched from a wood bench on the northwest side. To pass the time, he played an old favorite game: Trying to imagine what each of them was currently working on. *Which project? Whose department?* Looking for some clue within the fact that they'd picked up breakfast or dinner. Maybe something in the way they carried themselves, or a loose comment as they passed by. Not an easy game when most were civilians and some were from other countries. It was simple for all of them to get lost in the swirl. *Message of the hour, it seemed.*

He, himself, wore khakis and a white polo shirt. Sunglasses resting on the end of his sharp nose against the sun in his face, a half-eaten hot dog and a Sprite in his hands. Almost like any other graying D.C. vacationer who'd somehow wandered away from one of the tour groups. *Almost.* But there weren't any tours on Saturdays. And when the pretty dark-haired secretary in the sensible skirt had smiled back at him not five minutes ago, she'd seen right through his civilian attire in half a second. She'd seen West Point, and the medals, and the retired chairman of the American-Afghan Security Affairs Committee, and the senior military adviser. She'd recognized the power and pedigree as clearly as if he'd been holding a sign. They almost always did. The ones worth a damn.

Trapped within these five walls, it was a helluva good game. Framing the trees and warm sun and chirping birds was the most powerful building on earth. For fifty years, they'd called the park in the dead center of the Pentagon "Ground Zero" because everyone knew the Russians had twenty nukes aimed right at it. Today it was the Russians *and* the Chinese and probably the North Koreans, too. Hell, when they didn't have nukes, the fuckers dropped your own planes on you. Otherwise, it was a terrific park to buy a proper hot dog and enjoy another morning.

He spotted his appointment, Executive Deputy Burandt, across the yard, moving toward him. Even from a hundred yards away, Burandt looked worried. *Asshole.* Stanforth stared straight at the man and finished the hot dog. *The golden age of weapons development and this fucking guy is worried about something that would never even reach page three in any newspaper.*

Half of all federal research dollars went to the military—as much as research in medicine, energy, the environment, transportation, manufacturing, and agriculture *combined*. More than thirty thousand private companies supported R&D.

In short, a lot of people were paid to imagine and produce new weapons for Uncle Sam. A quick fifty billion dollars, to get imaginative, but that was merely a start. Most real R&D was done under the "black budgets" of the four military branches, adding up to another five *hundred* billion to toy with. These special budgets were so highly classified that not even the president knew how the money was being spent. Hell, it was four fucking years before anyone told Truman they'd built a hydrogen bomb. And, oh, how that unhindered money did roll. When the Cold War ended with no enemy in sight, the Department of Defense still somehow managed to double its budget. And after 9/11, forget about it. With the daily-touted threat of global terrorism and two brand-new wars, the budget kept growing with more than half of it falling safely within these mysterious parameters. *Five hundred billion dollars.* Unaudited. Unwatched. Unstoppable.

In '94, an Air Force research lab in Ohio admitted to secretly working on bombs filled with synthetic pheromones and aphrodisiacs to make enemy troops "turn gay." They'd be too busy sucking cock to actually fight back. Put the whole Don't Ask, Don't Tell into a bit more perspective. The same lab also worked on methods to create giant swarms of bees. The Navy spent twenty million dollars teaching bats to carry explosives. For fifty years, the men in this very building had supported and encouraged the scientific study of everything from invisibility and time travel to ghosts, mind control, talking dolphins, and telekinesis.

Trying to figure out how each could be used as a weapon.

There were bound to be some fuckups along the way. Like this one. Another bump in the road. And, if after five years as executive deputy to the commanding general, this mealymouthed Caltech fuck didn't get that . . .

"Good morning, sir," Stanforth said.

Executive Deputy Burandt sat beside him. "Where are we?"

Stanforth took a sip of his soda. Birds stirred and chittered in the trees behind their bench. "DSTI is locked down tight," he said. "Not a problem."

"All military assets are secure?"

The word *SharDhara* sprang immediately to mind. Castillo had asked about it, and Stanforth had lied right back. *Nope, doesn't mean a thing.* How could it? Most of the civilian players directly involved had been eliminated. How Dr. Jacobson had learned about the field test, he'd have to figure out later. Erdman maintained all toxins were secure. Now there were more pressing matters. "Doesn't seem to be about those," he lied again. "This seems to be about the boys only."

"Make damn sure. How bad is it?"

Stanforth had also decided to remain quiet about Jacobson's secretly adopted clones. Those could all be gotten rid of neatly under separate cover. Besides, there was no way his solution to that new problem would be approved, anyway. *Easier to ask forgiveness than acquire permission.* Best to stick with the original situation. "Thirteen dead," he said. "Nine kids. Maybe three hostages."

"Wonderful."

"It's messy, but it'll clean up quietly and hastily. Most of the dead officially never even existed. It helps. After our chat here, I've got other appointments to array a few resources nearby, and then I'm heading straight back to New Jersey to oversee any remaining tidying on-site."

"And the . . . the 'boys'?"

Stanforth nodded. "A couple of scared teenagers. It's probable that one of the chief geneticists, Dr. Gregory Jacobson, is helping them. Appears he's been planning this for years and may have a few resources of his own already set aside. But, he's also off his rocker. We'll find them."

"Then what?"

"You really want to know?"

"No."

Stanforth leaned back.

"What do you need?" the executive deputy asked.

"Keep the FBI off my ass. If they arrest one of our targets or a teenaged John Doe, freeze it. These kids probably shot their kill wad already. If not, help keep it off *Nancy Grace*. If anyone starts asking why DNA from a guy who's been dead for twenty years is showing up, ditto."

"Jesus H. Christ, Stanforth. Fucking clones?"

Stanforth smiled. "You really want to know?"

Burandt squinted into the sun. Shook his head. "I want this entire undertaking, this damned company, shut down. Today. Eradicated. Permanently."

"No," replied Stanforth. "You don't."

The executive deputy turned, glaring. "Look, you son of—"

"Most R&D dollars go right down the fucking drain. You know it, I know it. Ninety percent of this shit never leads to anything. We've funneled DSTI maybe fifty million over the last decade. Pocket change." He counted off with his free fingers. "In return, you've got the 5HIAA toxin, IRAX11, biodrones . . ." *Easier to ask forgiveness . . .*

"IRAX11 was terminated."

Stanforth shrugged. Jacobson, it seemed, had somehow gotten a lot of intel about SharDhara. Results. Recommendations. Chatterjee, undoubtedly, must have gotten to him before they'd safeguarded against such leaks. *Before the fine Dr. Chatterjee went bye-bye.* "Doesn't change the fact that it worked," he said. "Let's not toss out too many babies with the bathwater."

"Fine. But get this cleaned up. How long?"

Stanforth set his cup down on the ground. "Don't know."

"Unacceptable. We're giving you forty-eight hours."

"And then?" Stanforth provoked.

There was, as expected, no answer. *He* was the answer.

"Bin Laden took thirteen fuckin' years," Stanforth said. "And half this goddamned building was looking for him. This is the real world, partner. If the assholes at CNN and Fox don't understand that, I'm quite certain you do."

Burandt snorted his accord.

"I've got my best man working on it," Stanforth assured him. Those few he knew as good or better than Castillo were engaged halfway across the world or still with the DOD. Castillo was perfect. Close, self-employed, and desperate. Easy to discard, if necessary, when it was all over. "And if he doesn't get the job done, the kids will be dead in a couple months anyway."

"Why so confident?"

"How much you know about Dolly?"

"The sheep?"

"Her lab name—her real name—was 6LL3. Died at six years old. Most sheep live to twelve. But there were giant black tumors growing inside 6LL3's chest. And her legs already had arthritis. She couldn't stop coughing blood. So they put her down. In the biopsy, they found surprisingly shortened telomeres, the parts of the cell connected to age, and figured these midget telomeres were passed on from the 'parent,' who was six years old when the DNA was taken. Genetically, Dolly was already six years old the day she was born. Weird, huh?"

"So what? These boys are already in their fifties . . . or?"

"Let's just say they're closer to death than we are. Special prescriptions are given by DSTI to suppress the deterioration, the tumors."

"This . . . this Jacobson character probably covered that."

"Appears none of the medication was taken. He either forgot about it in all the excitement, which I doubt, or he wants them to die as much as we do."

"Why would he want that? And, I don't want anyone to—"

"Sure you do," Stanforth stopped him. "If you don't want to know, then don't know. But don't dare drop platitudes from the sidelines. At the very least, these damned kids deserve your honesty. You want them as dead and gone as I do. As to Jacobson, who knows. Maybe he figures it'll end soon enough anyway. A couple of months, worst case. But we'll find them before that."

"Fine." Burandt stood, patted a wrinkle from his shirt. "'Worst case.' How much damage can they do in the meantime?"

Stanforth looked up from his sunglasses. "There've been more than sixteen thousand murders in the U.S. in the past twelve months. Almost a hundred thousand rapes."

The executive deputy nodded.

Stanforth shrugged. "What's another fifty?"

AT THE PARK

When Ashley saw the clown, she knew for sure.

Before that, it had only been a suspicion, prompted by that inimitable nervous tickle in her stomach that hinted that she might now be in a threatening situation, that something bad could happen. Could. But not fear. Not yet. Not nearly enough to make you grab your two children and run screaming for the car. That'd be too embarrassing.

The two cars pulled in beside each other on the gravel parking lot. Both filled with kids, teenagers. Mostly all boys. *Why come to a playground?* A girl among them. Older. Dirty hair hung over her eyes. Moving strangely.

Ashley turned back to find her daughter still winding through the top of the park's small wooden castle. She absently handed little Michael another pretzel stick and looked back toward where two other mothers had been having a picnic lunch with their own children. Was overly relieved when she saw they were still there, chatting away.

"Pox," Michael burbled beside her. "Pox." Pox, Tik, Mop. The ever-evolving official language of young Michael Steins, fifteen months.

Made-up words she collected in a small diary to share with him some-day.

"Pox," she smiled. "Pretzels."

Michael giggled.

Two of the boys had already taken seats at the swings and were using their feet to twist themselves up in the chains. Another pair was wrestling atop the seesaw. *Fine*, Ashley thought. Only trying to recapture some half-remembered joy of childhood. First weeks of summer vacation. Very Holden Caulfield. They'll be bored in five minutes. The girl was probably just high.

Ashley fumbled for her cellphone, half remembered she'd left it in the car. She started packing their things. "Honey," she called out to Cassie. "Honey?" Wanting to get her attention without using her name. Why, she wondered, was that suddenly so important? Her daughter moving away from her deeper into the castle. Ashley stood and trailed after her. Clapped her hands. "Honey, come on now. Time to go."

Her daughter turned. "Whyyyyy?" she whined from the top para-pet, her dark pigtails hanging over a yellow dress.

"Come down, honey. Hurry up."

The four-year-old scrunched her face in displeasure.

Closer, several of them looked older than teenagers. Young men.

"Come on." Ashley waved her down. Can't get up there quick enough. "We'll get ice creams on the way home."

"Mikey, too!"

Don't say his name, baby. Don't say his damned name.

"Yes, yes. Let's go now, honey."

A horrible sound. Van doors shutting.

Ashley spun around. The other table suddenly empty. The other mothers VANISHED. The other children already somehow collected, small bags of books, toys, *Glamour*s and Pringles already packed. Their SUV somehow at this very moment backing slowly out of the long gravel parking lot. Leaving her alone.

With *them*.

She turned back to her daughter and almost collapsed to the ground as the whole park seemed to tilt. She was gone. Her daughter. Where once there'd been a little girl, there was now nothing. *What do I . . . dear God, this is really happening.*

Ashley approached the castle like a half-formed ghost.

She's gone. She's really gone. What have these monsters done to my—

"Shit!"

Her daughter appeared with a squeal at the bottom of the green tube, sliding to the end until her feet dangled above the mulched ground.

"Cassie . . . Goddamn it!"

"What, Mommy?" She climbed off the slide.

"Nothing." Ashley fought the urge to collapse again. "I'm sorry, baby. Come on, let's go." Yanking her back toward the picnic table.

She saw the clown then. Standing perfectly still by the cars. A demonic scarecrow.

Watching her. And her children. *My children.*

A red suit with white frills and buttons and a matching red hat. Huge blue triangular eyes like a jack-o'-lantern. Its mouth bloodred and covering the entire bottom half of the face. In the shape of an enormous smile.

Now, she knew.

Scooping up the rest of their things and slinging the bag over her shoulder. Dragging little Michael in one arm, pulling her daughter with the other.

"Pox," Michael said. "Pox!"

"In the car, baby. Hush now."

She looked up at the swing set, clearly saw the girl there for the first time. A woman. Her "boyfriend" slowly and mechanically pushing her swing from behind. The woman's face masked behind grimy hair, head drooped to the side. What Ashley had thought was a shirt was not. The woman was nude from the waist up. What she'd figured was a shirt's pattern was dried blood.

"What's wrong, Mommy?"

Ashley staggered forward to her car. Michael started crying.

"Mommy, what's wrong?"

"Shut up," she hissed, wrenching her daughter closer. "Please, baby, just . . ."

One of the boys laughed.

She'd reached the car.

"Pox," Michael yelped again. "Pox!"

"Pox," Ashley replied in a half laugh that shuddered through her whole body. "Pretzels. That's right, baby."

She had the door half open when they finally stopped her.

The first boy squatted down to playfully wave a finger at her daughter. The girl's eyes were wide, her grip on Ashley's hand like a vise.

Another boy reached out and touched Ashley's mouth.

"Please . . . ," she stammered over his probing fingers.

Around the back of the car, a third shape moving toward them.

A horrible thing made of white and blue and red. One she'd somehow been waiting for.

"Pox." The clown smiled at them in a bloody grin that now filled the whole world. "Pox?"

Michael giggled.

II

DNA n.

short for deoxyribonucleic acid

(1) A nucleic acid capable of self-replication and synthesis which carries genetic information in every cell;
(2) Two long chains of nucleotides twisted into a double helix and joined by hydrogen bonds between the complementary bases adenine and thymine or cytosine and guanine;
(3) Sequence which determines and transmits individual hereditary characteristics from parents to offspring: see also genetic code;
(4) DNA: see also Do Not Alter;
(5) DNA: see also Do Not Ask

While Odysseus pondered thus in mind and heart,
Poseidon, the earth-shaker, rose up a great wave,
dread and grievous, arching over from above,
and drove down it upon him.
And the wave scattered the long timbers of his raft
but Odysseus bestrode one plank.

THE ODYSSEY

AND THE MONSTERS

DSTI was founded by Dr. William Asbury and incorporated in 1977. Its chief executive officer was Dr. Thomas Rolich, M.D., Ph.D. Its director of research was Dr. Gregory Jacobson, recipient of the Zonta Science Award and The Genetics Society of America's prestigious Novitski Prize for "exhibiting an extraordinary level of creativity and intellectual ingenuity in genetic scholarship and application." Castillo lifted this from DSTI's corporate website.

The rest came from Brody. Pete Brody had worked on half a dozen missions with Castillo as the chief analyst from the DI, the CIA's Directorate of Intelligence, and was now working in the private sector, something to do with Wall Street. His choice, but he'd still seemed genuinely interested when Castillo had called earlier. "I'll see what I can find," he'd said.

Ten hours later, and Castillo had info DSTI had not quite included on its website. "They were acquired as a subsidiary by BioStar in 1990 to obtain several of DSTI's cloning patents," Pete reported. "BioStar is a subsidiary of Goodwin Bio-Med, formed by the Nerney Institute in

'87. Nerney's a sister company of Terngo Engineering, who designs and builds vehicles and industrial machinery for the U.S. Defense Department."

"Go on," Castillo said. He'd stopped taking notes.

The boy, Jeffrey, still lay asleep in a bed across the room. At least he looked asleep. Castillo wasn't sure. The kid had dozed off a few times in the car, but for no more than a couple minutes. Probably needed to sleep for a *week*. It had been a long day crisscrossing Pennsylvania to search the local malls, convenience stores, and high schools. They'd even checked out several local paintball fields. Shown pictures of the six escapees and Dr. Jacobson to fifty-plus kids. Questioned various store employees. Nothing.

He'd gotten maybe an hour of sleep himself. *Maybe*. He wasn't sure. Like that, his chronic insomnia had reverted from being a disorder worth fighting back to an occupational advantage.

He'd pulled into the motel around 1900. Dyed and cut the Jacobson kid's hair. Wasn't sure if DSTI or anyone else would be looking for him, but the kid's father had convinced him he was dead meat—a "liability," the kid had quoted—if he was caught. Maybe the boy took some comfort in the fact that Castillo hadn't killed him yet. Castillo doubted it. Since Erdman hadn't been particularly forthcoming with the knowledge of Jeff Jacobson's *existence*, Castillo felt no real compunction to share with Erdman what, or *who*, he'd found. For now, he'd get what he could out of the kid and turn him back over to DSTI when the idea wasn't so repugnant.

If he could get anything at all, that is. The malls and paintball fields had been a bust, and the kid'd looked catatonic throughout, in full-blown, understandable shock. After the haircut and dye job, Castillo had had him look at some more of his father's journals, see if anything made any sense, and that hadn't gone much better than the first time. The boy barely read them, had mostly looked like he'd wanted to throw up. *Who could blame him?* Castillo felt the same way and had never even met Gregory Jacobson. While this lunatic was this fucking kid's father and the guy—

"Terngo's prime shareholder," Pete was saying, "is Plainview Inc. I've no doubt you know them."

"Intimately." Castillo had lived within their version of reality for ten years. Everything from lodging and meals to laundry, Internet access and gym equipment. They were Halliburton's little brother, but with a forty-thousand-person staff, including foreign mercenaries, not by much.

"Annual revenue of one hundred billion dollars," Brody said, "including an additional ten billion a year from the U.S. Department of Defense."

"That's a lot of money to trickle down."

"'Tis. DSTI is also partially and directly funded by Johns Hopkins University, which receives another two billion annually for federally funded research and development. Mostly, again, from the DOD."

"Incredible."

"Remember, Castillo, it's simply a giant global shell game meant to hide one thing from all of us: the money."

"And the monsters," Castillo said. "Anything else?"

"There've been some deaths."

"Go on."

"There was a plane crash ten years ago. Three DSTI geneticists and a marketing VP. Twin-engine Beechcraft King Air over Kentucky heading to a conference in Nashville. The NTSB concluded likely cause was the flight crew's failure to maintain adequate airspeed, which led to an aerodynamic stall. None of the other typical causes of a small-plane accident—engine failure, icing, pilot error—appeared to have been involved. The company plane was not required to have a cockpit voice recorder."

"Convenient."

"And a couple of suicides."

Castillo nodded against the phone, focusing his thoughts. A "couple" didn't sound too bad, not when each year more vets killed themselves than died in actual combat. "How many?" he said.

"Three. Over the last twelve years. Above average for a company that size, statistically."

"Suspicious otherwise?"

"Aren't they always?"

"No." Castilllo had heard enough. "That it?"

"Most recent suicide was a Dr. Chatterjee, Sanjay Chatterjee. Hung himself two years ago. Family started a fuss, wouldn't believe he'd do such a thing, but then they vanished back into India. Need more?"

"Might later. Is that cool?"

"'Tis. You want the names of the other dead employees?"

"Email 'em to me. Thanks, Pete." Castillo ended the call.

He watched Jeff again. The teen looked remarkably peaceful. Castillo couldn't remember ever being that young.

He checked his phone for the time. Kristin had sent a text message midday that she would call him back directly before ten. An hour from now.

No response yet from Ox. Probably never would be. It'd been a long shot anyway.

Ox was another war pal he'd first met in the field almost fifteen years ago. If Erdman and Stanforth didn't know who or what SharDhara was, Ox was an *hombre* who just might. He was a notorious enthusiast and purveyor of government cover-ups and conspiracies and one of those individuals who always knew a guy who knew another guy who knew . . . and so on. Always good for the latest bit of military gossip, even as paranoid as some of his musing often got. The real trouble with Ox was getting hold of him. When he'd retired, he'd more or less vanished with a bunch of other survivalist whackballs into the hills of Tennessee, or West Virginia, or someplace. Castillo hadn't seen him in years, and they'd only spoken on the phone once since his own return to the States. He did still have specific directions on how to contact the man using a special nym server with an untraceable email address, PGP key pairs, and some anonymous remailer based in Norway. *Insane.* His email to Ox had probably gone straight to Santa's workshop in the North Pole. As he'd hit Send in the Dunkin' Donuts parking lot, only one thing had been for sure: If he did somehow actually get hold of the guy, only he and Ox would ever know it. Anything less, and the man would never contact him back. Part of his charm, Castillo supposed.

He checked the FBI feed again for any new crimes, made some unproductive notes, and then rummaged back through the images of Jacobson's journals for another hour before his phone rang as promised. He rushed for the door.

"Hey," Castillo said, stepping outside quietly. It was surprisingly warm, the day's heat still lurking on the night's breeze. He surveyed the mostly vacant lot. His perusal widened to the traffic on the bordering streets, no direction seeming any more promising than another beneath the reddened moon. "Thanks for getting back so—"

"I've looked at the files you sent," she said. Paused.

"Thanks, I . . ." Too many thoughts folded in on him again, and nothing he could say to her. He cast his eyes back to the ground. "What can you tell me?"

There was another pause. Enough that he knew she was still deciding if she should lecture him, hang up, or just give him the info he'd asked for and continue on with her life. "How much of the situation *can* you share?" she asked, choosing Option Three. "Any?"

"Just know I gotta find these guys."

"OK, look: All six are classic loners, with documented sociopathic tendencies ranging from just-above common all the way to full-blown psychopathic monster. Three are lacking almost every benchmark of ordinary human social development. And some of these numbers, to be honest, don't even make sense to me. How well do you understand the terms?"

"*Sociopath*? *Psycho*? Assumed they were the same thing."

"They're similar but different disorders, especially in the way they manifest. Which could help you know what to look for. Even though they're always lumped together, you should probably understand the two beyond some vague *Webster's* definition before you go much further."

"It's why I called you." He'd found the outside stairs leading to the motel's second and top floor. He took them unhurriedly, stretching his legs, relishing the feeling of warm air against his skin. Yet somehow still cramped, chilled. Nervous.

"All right. About one half of one percent of Americans could be diagnosed as sociopaths or psychopaths. So says the National Institute of Mental Health."

"Two million psycho killers?"

She laughed softly, the sound tender and familiar. "Not at all. There are degrees to everything. Ninety-eight percent of that two million are only sociopaths, and most sociopaths are little more than flaming ass-holes."

"Skip the technical jargon, please."

"Guys with no regard for the feelings and rights of others. Care only about Number One, steal for the hell of it, moody guys who screw over coworkers, start bar fights out of boredom, won't talk to their kids . . . that kind of thing. True psychopaths are much, much rarer. The difference is important, and also horrible."

"Go on."

"First, how they're the same. They both manipulate to get what they desire with no true sense of right or wrong. See people as targets, opportunities, and believe the cliché that the end always justifies the means. And so lie with almost every breath. And steal. And sometimes even rape or kill. Both are unable to empathize with their victims' pain, and even hold *contempt* for their victims' distress. Oblivious to the dev-astation they cause, lacking remorse, shame. Both usually surface by age fifteen; often cruel to animals, have an inflated sense of self, no aware-ness of personal boundaries. Feel entitled, spoiled. Shallow emotions, incapacity for love. Need stimulation and enjoy living on the edge, and believe they are all-powerful, all-knowing, and warranted in every wish. Both carry a deep rage."

"Copy. How different?"

"Sociopaths have a life history of behavioral and academic difficul-ties. They're less organized; they struggle in school and work. They'll often appear nervous and easily agitated. They act spontaneously in in-appropriate ways without thinking through the consequences. So, they typically live on the fringes of society, without solid or consistent eco-nomic support. They have problems making friends, keeping jobs, tend to move around a lot. Since they disregard most rules and social mores, their crimes are typically spontaneous because they don't give one damn *and* don't care if you know it. The prisons are filled with these guys. Most of us would not be comfortable with a sociopath in the room. You would totally know he was there."

"But not so Mr. Psychopath."

"You got it. Mr. Psychopath, as you say, is extremely organized, secretive, and manipulative. While he also has no regard for society's rules, he *understands* them. He's studied them for years like it's a job, and he can mimic the right behaviors to make himself *appear* normal, even charismatic and charming. He's often well educated, can maintain a family and steady work. He's learned The Game, and he's playing it to win using our own rules against us. You would be comfortable with a psychopath in the room because you would never know he was even there."

"Would *you*? I mean, could you spot one in a room?"

"Doubt it. I might. Here's a tip they taught us at Columbia. Watch the hands. When normal people are struggling for a word, maybe the name of an obscure actor or, like, a foreign phrase from some language they half know, we often make those little circles with our hands or fingers, right? It's natural. It helps stimulate the segment of the brain that finds and makes sense of unfamiliar words. For serial killers, however, almost *every* word and phrase is an unfamiliar bunch of lines. All of the crap normal people say to get through the day: 'Yes, I'll be at work on time tomorrow,' 'Yes, it IS a gorgeous day,' 'Yes, I love you, too' . . . they might as well be speaking Greek. As they're *always* struggling for the 'right' words, they often employ their hands to help, and a killer's wrists and fingers can get spinning like little windmills to get through the next twenty seconds' interaction normally. If you see that, think of it as the start of a witch's spell."

"And get the hell out. Interesting." He'd noticed that Jeff's shrugs and grunts were his go-to mode of communication, rather than actual sentences. He'd written it off to being fifteen and terrified, but . . . "Exactly what I was looking for. Anything else you can tell me about this language thing?"

"Sure, OK. In one test, people were given a huge list of words randomly selected from three categories. Made-up words like *frizzdirt* and *champstal* and more common words like *pencil* and *canoe*. And then words like *mother*, and *peaceful*, and *lonely*. Words that have deeper and complicated meanings. A pencil is just a pencil, but *mother* and *lonely* have six billion nuanced meanings that could keep you up talking all night if you were talking with the right person."

"Yes," he agreed, maybe a little too quickly, not caring if she read too much into it.

"OK, so in the test, they flash these words up at the testee, and when he recognizes it's a real word or not, he hits a certain button, and it records how fast he identified it. For normal people, the third category was always the fastest, by about thirty percent across the board. They'd see *grandpa*, or *country*, or *love* and know instantly: *That's* a word, *bam*, button pressed. Next. But for the tested serial killers, the psychopaths, not so much. For these guys, there was no difference between the time to recognize *pencil* and the time to recognize *mother*. None. It took the exact same amount of time. The doctors' conclusion was simple and unanimous: The two categories clearly meant about the same to the serial killers. They were nothing special, merely more words in the world. *Mother* and *love* were as meaningless to a serial killer as *pencil* or *canoe* were to normal people."

"I wonder if the doctors got it wrong."

"How do you mean?"

Castillo thought a second. "Maybe the exact opposite was true. Maybe the times were exactly the same because to a killer trivial words like *pencil* and *canoe* actually have *more* meaning than they do to the rest of us. Maybe for him, every damn word counts."

"Maybe. I see higher-than-average IQ and WAIS-IV intelligence scores here. Most of the files you sent, however, are tracking MAOA levels and testosterone. More interest in their balls than their brains, and these guys all seem to be males, *cubed*. A lot of potential violence here."

"What do you know about the 'XP11' gene?"

"Not familiar. What's that?"

"Some kind of coding gene thing that affects dopamine levels."

"OK, right. Yes, the 'anger gene.' I have read about it. Something to do with the MAOA gene. Makes perfect sense." A short, tense pause. Then words again, too casual. "What in God's name are you working on, Shawn?"

"I'll be done soon. What can you tell me about the individual boys?"

"Fine. Subject David, is it? Yes . . ."

David. The one Jeff thought was "chill." "Yes."

"Start here because I can tell you he's probably the least of your worries based on these annotations. Has some sociopath tendencies, but he's more midlevel antisocial personality than anything. Nomadic. Schizoid, avoidant features. Nothing a program of risperidone couldn't take care of."

"An antipsychotic? Didn't think you liked the drugs, Doc."

"Don't usually. But sometimes it makes sense."

"Would he travel with a pack? Work in a group?"

"Probably not by choice. These notes are fractional, but I'm still surmising an almost complete lack of interest in social relationships, a tendency toward a solitary lifestyle, secretiveness, emotional coldness. He's not into the group scene. Of course, he's also a teenager and so quite drawn, and susceptible, to peer influence."

"Anything else?"

"Just more numbers otherwise. Biochemical analysis. Drugs, I assume. Not sure what, but they're obviously testing something on several of these guys."

"Would that surprise you? Preclinical testing on kids? Psychological experiments. That kind of thing."

"Sadly, not at all. Seventy percent of foster kids are on some kind of state-sanctioned behavioral medication, with a lot of it still officially in test mode. There's some evidence we've tested AIDS meds on these foster kids also. But that's the meds. The experiments are far worse."

You have no idea. "What do you mean?" he asked.

"The University of Iowa once got hold of twenty orphans for a study on emotional reinforcement. Half stuttered, and half spoke perfectly normally. The stutterers were praised for their speaking skills and the normal-speaking kids were mocked and scolded for their 'terrible speech.' This went on for months. While the stutterers showed no significant change in facilities, the normal-speaking kids now all stuttered. Every one of them. The experiment got the nickname 'The Monster Study.'"

"Good name," Castillo said. *It isn't really. They used it too soon. Should have saved it for Jacobson and Erdman.* If making a kid stutter was monstrous, what to call the study that prescribed beatings and molestation? "What happened to the kids?"

"The study ended directly before World War II and the results were buried for fear of comparisons to the Nazis. The lead researcher went on to become one of the nation's most prominent speech pathologists. Two of the subjects later committed suicide."

Castillo shook his head. Tried to ignore the footnote and press on. "What else on these six guys? What to look for?"

"Al seeks approval more than the others. He displays an inability to take criticism, and he needs more recognition. He'll need, want, an audience and the support of the others. Ted's probably the most aggressive. A classic predator. Will probably go where the girls are. Teen nightclubs, I guess. Think a *Jersey Shore* scene . . . *Friday Night Lights*. The mall? Wherever teen boys meet girls nowadays. Start there. Let's see. The other two . . ." She struggled, looking for their names and files.

"Henry and . . ." He caught himself. Didn't want to say the name.

"Jeff," she said for him. "Wow, let's get to him in a second. Henry is more like David. Probably carries anxiety in social situations, odd behavior, unconventional beliefs. But he also shows an elaborate and exclusively internal fantasy world. I can see him lost in movie theaters, playing video games, that kind of thing. Now Jeff."

"What about him?"

"Probably the most dangerous in the group. Languid schizoid. Depressive. But there's rage hidden in these observations and numbers. Comments indicate he's likely homosexual. Maybe narrows down your hunting ground some. Physiologically, there's an imbalance in his blood tests that's . . . I don't know. Like I said, some of these MAOA numbers don't even make sense. They're off-the-spectrum high, so they can't be right. But I can tell you the guy should be locked away. Now. I could have another doctor look at these profiles, maybe—"

"No. No one else. Best to treat as highly classified."

"Loud and clear." No mockery in her tone.

"There could be at least five of 'em together," he said. "Ten maybe. Could they get along? How long? Will they follow a pattern?"

"Sounds like a bad joke. Five psycho killers and a priest walk into a bar . . ."

"Funny. How long? Could, would, these guys go on a killing frenzy together?"

"Most serial killers work alone, but not all. There are plenty of known cases of pairs. The current Smiley Face killer in the Midwest could be a group of people. Your guys, however, are textbook psychopaths, with massive egos, god-sized narcissism, and a grandiose sense of self."

"Another thing, as you pointed out, they're teenagers." Castillo thought of Jeffrey Jacobson waiting below. "How relevant?"

Kristin sighed in thought. "They'll need the pack more, probably. Most serial killers commit their first murder in their late twenties, finally acting out on one of the specific elaborate violent fantasies they concocted as a child. They're the same most all of us have as children, but where the rest of us grow out of such fantasies because we've developed socially and are afraid of how society will respond, these guys don't. Even more than most psychopaths, these teen versions especially don't give a damn what other people think. How much did you give a shit about consequences at seventeen? So their social development, organically prone to limitations from their psychopathy, will suffer even more thanks to their age. Freud said a child would destroy the whole world if he had the power."

"Noted."

"From these records, I'd say most of these patients are in an accelerated stage of sociopathic behavior for their ages. Destroying the world is probably high on their to-do list, along with withdrawing from reality and entering a fantasy world. Adult psychopaths pick one, maybe two, fantasies to develop, to plan, to perfect over the years. Making a fantasy real takes preparation, precision, and time. Even Mr. Psychopath understands such limitations when he's twenty-eight. But if you're a kid, like the guys you need to find, the very moment they think of a fantasy, boom, they think they can make it come true. They're after instant gratification for their childish, godlike appetites."

"And think they can get away with it."

"Best part of any fantasy, isn't it?"

"I don't know," Castillo said. "Thanks. Really. If I come across any more—"

"I'll be here," she said, then added, "You sound like hell."

"Thanks a lot."

"Honestly, Shawn. You don't sound good."

Castillo tensed. Was she offering to help him with the profiles as an old friend with history or as his therapist? "Just been a tough couple days," he explained, hoping to prove he had no need for the latter. "Hey, Kris, I—"

"Try and get some sleep," she said, her voice too cold, too clinical again. Another pause. "But if you need anything else . . ."

"Talk later. Thanks."

He stood for a minute on the second floor of the motel, his hands on the rusting blue banister. Memories swirling in his head of her, of the two of them, in another reality and time. His breathing grew harder, his hands clenching the railing.

Castillo swapped his thoughts back to the now. Away from her.

The Jacobson kid, the clone, hadn't panned out. Hadn't provided a solid lead yet. Couldn't decipher his father's notes. Castillo didn't blame him, but he thought maybe it was already time to cut the boy loose. Jeff Jacobson was probably slowing him down anyway.

Is that really the reason you want to get rid of him?

He'd given the kid plenty of chances to escape, almost hoping he would so the decision would be out of his hands. One phone call, and DSTI would come and collect him. Some small token of success he could offer up to Stanforth and the other science jerkoffs.

Whatever the reason, *Best get rid of him now,* Castillo thought again, moving back toward the steps.

Back toward Mr. Psychopath.

FORMS NOT FOUND
IN NATURE

JUNE 04, SATURDAY—RADNOR, PA

Dr. Patrick Mohlenbrock cupped the fetus in his left hand, holding it up to the light for a better look. Its tiny head dangled awkwardly off the end of his forefinger as fluids from the incubator dripped down the geneticist's wrist. One of its small hands had reflexively latched onto the tip of Mohlenbrock's plump gloved thumb.

Six weeks, the chart read. So much had already started, but the option of speeding up gestation to adulthood or continuing to retard development for another couple of years was no longer his to make. DSTI was cleaning house. Or, at least, temporarily sweeping certain programs under the carpet. It would be easy enough to start again after the attention was off them.

Mohlenbrock didn't mind. He'd never cared much for Project Cain anyway. That had always been Jacobson's hard-on. Mohlenbrock's lay elsewhere. Therapeutic cloning had already become the trillion-dollar industry everyone expected it to be. While Nasdaq was a slowly sinking roller coaster, the biotechnology indexes continued to garner record gains every year. It was time. IVF, transgenic foods, commercial eugenics, pharmaceuticals. Americans were already paying five hundred bucks a year to store the DNA of their pets and loved ones. The dot-com orgy would prove pennies compared to what was coming, and he was sure as hell not going to miss it.

We must never approach the temple of science with the soul of a money changer. He could still hear Jacobson's reproof. *Fuck Jacobson.* Jacobson was the fuckwad who'd gotten them into this jam anyway. His fascination with the XP11 gene, his fanatical deals for more funding with the powers that be. *And where the hell is he now?* Dead? Maybe murdered by the special children he'd bred, or, as it was rumored, running around the country on some unknown crusade to free clones DSTI hadn't even known about. *Fanfuckingtastic.*

And, in a few hours—unless Erdman could talk Stanforth out of it—even worse than that. Much worse.

Mohlenbrock almost hoped Jacobson wasn't dead yet. Because he knew well what would soon be sent to look for him. Adequate pay-backs, on balance, when DSTI and everyone associated with it would lose everything if things didn't get cleaned up quietly. A lot of people, people like him, would probably go to jail, too. They'd already chemically lobotomized half a dozen kids. A frat-house cocktail of various antipsychotics, neuroleptics, and antianxiety inhibitors that included an intentional overdose of Thorazine. While they hadn't removed any part of their brains, they hadn't really needed to. The twenty-first century's liquid lobotomies worked as well.

"This the last of it?"

The geneticist turned to the voice. "Yeah," he said. "Of these."

Dr. Erdman nodded from the doorway and surveyed the room. Forty cylindrical incubators, which ran from the floor to the ceiling, were lined in five long rows. Almost half had already been removed, and only their wide bases remained. Three more DSTI workers had begun dismantling those, too. A fourth employee hosed down one of the emptied cylinders. Its surface reflected a light blue glow across the lab's floor. There were two large steel bins on wheels lined with black plastic in the center of the room.

The rest of the pods were still occupied. The clones inside ranged from five weeks' gestation to four years', each floating serenely in the piss-colored liquid inside. In another room were six more that had been physically matured to twenty years in less than eighteen months. A different project altogether, really. Stanforth wanted to keep those, for now.

"So," Mohlenbrock asked fairly cheerfully, considering the late hour and the day they'd had. "Any word yet on the whereabouts of our little monsters? How's your boy Stanforth going to—"

"Focus on what's here," Erdman said. "They have the situation well covered on the outside. Admit it, you'll be glad when Jacobson's gone."

"Jacobson was always a threat," Mohlenbrock agreed.

"Then what's the issue?"

"You really think they, we, can control that . . . Control it?"

Erdman shook his head disapprovingly at the word choice, but Mohlenbrock didn't care. DSTI could come up with all the cutesy names they wanted to. Didn't change the truth. Pakistan and Afghanistan and all those other "stans" was one thing. This was the United States they were talking about. It was abject lunacy. Erdman, however, wasn't looking for an argument. "That's the least of my worries," he said.

"Oh?"

"Just get this cleaned up." Erdman stepped from the room. "Stanforth should be here in an hour."

Mohlenbrock watched him go, then looked back down at the experiment growing cold in his hand. *Its eyes were closed, thank God.* The fetus was just six weeks old, yet already seven inches long and almost nine ounces. Already a hundred billion neurons firing away. It had vocal cords, the genitals of a man. A thyroid gland already pumped male hormones into its premature brain: testosterone artificially laced with genetic rage and cruelty.

"Stanforth should be here in an hour." And we want him to see we've all been good little soldiers, don't we?

It gasped suddenly. Barely a tiny sucking sound, then another. New lungs fighting for their first taste of air. He felt the tiny shape shift against his wet palm.

What thoughts are even now forming in its primal brain? What terrible thoughts?

Mohlenbrock had forgotten already if it was another clone of Bundy or DeSalvo.

He reminded himself that it no longer mattered.

He reached for one of the steel bins.

An hour later, in another room down the same hall, three men argued about what to do next. The Soldier, Stanforth, was winning the argument. The Scientist held firm. The Suit, DSTI's CEO, mostly kept quiet.

"We've used them successfully before," Stanforth said.

"With consequences," reminded Dr. Erdman.

"There are consequences in everything, gentlemen. Surely things have advanced in a year."

"For better or worse?"

Stanforth shrugged. "It's *your* project. Enlighten me."

"Well," the company CEO managed, shooting a glance to Erdman. "What do you think?"

Stanforth openly snickered at the man's feebleness. He also turned to Erdman, whom he was actually starting to like. The guy wasn't another pussy brainbox or goof like Jacobson had been. He seemed to have a broader worldview, which was important at the moment.

"They're dangerous," Erdman said.

"No shit." The colonel fingered the tank's acrylic panel. "That's why we made them."

"Don't you . . . ," the CEO, Rolich, began, hesitated, then began again. "Don't you trust your man—Castillo, is it?—to do the job? You're the one who told us to be patient. To let him do his job."

Stanforth turned sharply. "His job, you dumb cunt, was to find six boys. *Not* twenty. Sure, he'll probably uncover a couple before it's over—guy knows how to do *his* fucking job—but Jacobson's notes suggest there are clones spread all over God's country. Clones you didn't warn me about. Clones, I notice, you don't deny are missing. And that bullshit is on you two. Not us. You knew Jacobson was bat-shit crazy, and you didn't make him vanish. Worse, you looked the other way when he fucking raised one himself. And if you didn't know, well, I suppose that's even fucking worse. We were prepared to wipe up your shit once or twice. Not twenty fucking times."

"Does Castillo really think he'll find the others?" Erdman asked.

"He called an hour ago. He's working on it. I trust him. More than I can say about you two fucks. So we're clear, if I find out you've ever lied to me again, we'll kill both of you."

"Can we get more men?" Erdman asked, sidestepping the warning.

"You're already using half a dozen of my best. Most are on cleanup, which is the most critical charge at the moment. And anyone better who I'd trust is deployed abroad and dug deep. Besides, any more men, and this thing could blow wide open. Small teams keep things quiet. And we know *this* soldier will keep his mouth shut."

"Can it keep its jaws shut?" Erdman asked.

"Indulge me, gentlemen." The colonel looked at Erdman. "But we may start with only the one. I'll assume it's almost ready to go." He left the room quickly, cutting off any possible protestation.

"Yes, sir," Dr. Erdman called after him.

Behind him, the body in the tank shifted.

They spent the rest of that whole night preparing for the proposed mission.

Dozens of shots. Tailored fluids and DNA, sophisticated anti-angiogenesis enzymes and chemo-preventive agents. Therapeutic exercise, joint mobilization, dry needling, cryotherapy, iontophoresis. Maps. Photos. Blood samples to taste and smell.

And, finally, clothing.

At first glance, in dark rooms, it looked entirely human.

WHAT A KILLER LOOKS LIKE

JUNE 05, SUNDAY—MARCHWOOD, PA

This is what a killer looks like, Jeff thought.

His glasses lay beside the sink. The mirror was half fogged with steam from the shower he was pretending to take as he squinted into the glass. Castillo was in the next room doing something CIA-ish with his gazillion laptops and the maps he'd taped up onto the wall.

They'd spent all day in this sketch motel, Golden Ranch Inn, somewhere north of Radnor. They weren't out hunting bad guys like yesterday. Now they were sitting around for hours and hours, and it was boring times a thousand. Jeff watched TV and pretended to sleep while Castillo researched and waited. Waited for what? Murders, it turned out. Castillo had told him there were three hundred homicides a week in the United States. *Three hundred people? Murdered?* "Every week," Castillo had replied. "Fifty a day. And while half are boyfriends and best friends and coworkers and gang morons, the other half are unsolved. Those are the ones I'm interested in."

Jeff had done the math easily enough. That was seven thousand unexplained murders every year. Strangers killing other strangers for the thrill of making someone else die. And each one was now a little red dot for the map on the wall. Castillo had tapped his laptop and, gradually, right there, right on that map, was every reported murder in the last forty-eight hours. Every rape. Every missing person. Some red dots were bigger than others, like Polaris or Sirius shining brighter than the rest in a night sky dripping red with dozens of little crimson marks. "The more brutal the murder, the better," Castillo had said. "I'll find these guys." He'd said it was only a matter of time and of marking, starting to articulate some lines along the various highways, and looking for possible paths. The lines already ran in a hundred different directions.

"Just like connect the dots," Jeff had noted quietly.

"Just like." Castillo had turned and stared at him. "But with dead people."

Castillo totally hated him. Jeff knew that for sure. Whenever the guy went out to make one of his secret phone calls or something, he'd always come back into the room all agitated. Like he was disappointed Jeff was still here. Even sent Jeff out on some fool's errand to Subway in the middle of the damn night. Gave him a hundred-dollar bill for a couple of subs. Totally hoping he—the freak—would take the hint and split. Guess all those early threats about dragging him back to DSTI were obsolete. Guess Castillo didn't want that shit on his conscience after all.

This is what a killer looks like.

But the freak hadn't taken the bait. Instead, he'd returned from Subway and handed Castillo a list of all the places he knew his father—his fake father—had ever gone to. Conferences and cities and colleges and stuff. It was a pretty long list, but Castillo didn't seem too impressed. *What an asshole.* Best to stay out of the guy's way. Jeff stayed mostly in his bed pretending to be asleep, or watching TV with the sound down while Castillo worked on his laptop and messed with his map. After ten-plus hours of that, he'd asked Castillo if he could take a walk around outside a bit. Stretch his legs, get some fresh air. Something, anything, to get the hell out of the room.

Castillo had waved him off like a fly, no doubt hoping Jeff would leave for good.

Outside proved even more horrible than in the motel room, the nightmares from sleep sneaking into the waking world as nightmares and hallucinations directly from his father's journals. *I'm going crazy*, Jeff thought. *Or always have been*. If the hallucinations weren't enough, there were the very real dangers lurking outside. Some drunk or stoned guy had gotten all up in his face as he'd wandered back to the motel room. Crude and hostile, and no less evil, probably, than the guys Castillo was looking for. *Or me . . .*

It was best, safest, to be here, hiding in the bathroom. *Invisible*. It was simple to do now. He'd become the invisible boy. On the very first day they'd left Haddonfield, Castillo'd run into an Old Navy store and returned in ten minutes with two full bags: two pairs of jeans, a bunch of T-shirts, and a hooded sweatshirt, everything either blue or dark gray, in the most generic styles the store carried. If Jeff was holding the clothing he'd bought in his hands, he still couldn't have described it. Then, in the motel bathroom, Castillo had cut and dyed Jeff's hair. It was now short and brown. Castillo told him he could only wear his glasses when they were safely in their room. *How am I supposed to spot those guys without my glasses?* Not a single person on earth would notice, let alone *recognize*, Jeff one bit if they saw him. He'd ceased to exist. Exactly like Castillo wanted. Like his own father had wanted. His *fake* father.

He'd been reading a new fantasy novel the night his fake father had come in and told him that (a) I'm not your real father and (b) you're actually the clone of a famous murderer and (c) DSTI will want to kill you and (d) I do love you but (e) I'm leaving, good luck. It had been a lot to take in at once. When his fake father drove away, Jeff had chased after the car as it vanished down the street. One more thing: He still missed his fake father.

Jeff tried to picture himself as he'd been just a day ago. Happy. Normal. Then he imagined himself at eighteen, the same age as Jeffrey/5. The other boy his fake dad had built in a lab. The one Castillo was chasing after. The one who'd probably helped kill all those people at DSTI. Eighteen years old. A couple years from now. Maybe *that* Jeff had grown some sideburns or a little soul patch. Probably a couple inches taller.

He wondered how old all the others were. The other *Jeffs*. How many were there in the world? According to the notes his father had handed him that first night, he was really Jeff/82. Another seventy copies had died, by both flaw and design, prior to his own birth. *Seventy!* So he was one of, then, maybe four, five, *ten* other Jeffrey Dahmer clones that'd survived.

He thought of a joke he'd heard: *What's worse than a barrel full of dead babies?*

He could only remember the last, maybe, five years of his life. The rest was kinda hazy. His father—his *fake* father—had told him stories about things they'd done and filled in memories as best as he'd been able. But his fake father had clearly lied a lot. *Hadn't he?* It was hard to know about anything for sure. His fake father had said there'd been some kind of car accident and that was why he couldn't remember so well. Why he had no mother. His fake father had shown him pictures of an accident once, had said that's why his head hurt sometimes, why he saw things that weren't there.

The punch line: *A live one at the bottom, trying to eat its way out.* He thought, *That's me.*

Sometimes he even saw *people* who weren't really there. Familiar faces in a crowd or imprinted in the scenery. There was the Asian guy. A couple different black guys. The big blond kid. There one second, gone the next. Like ghosts or some kinda déjà vu. All those years, he'd thought it had been people he'd known once. Maybe before "The Accident." An event as fictitious as all the rest. But now he knew better. He'd seen their pictures in his folder. The same faces he'd glimpsed so many times before. The second part of the déjà vu. Ghosts caught on film. Inherited memories of some kind.

His victims.

This is what a killer looks like.

He next tried to imagine himself at twenty-five. As Jeffrey Dahmer #1. The Original. The one in the files his fake father had given him. The one who murdered seventeen people. Jeff didn't know much about him. Had never even heard the name before three days ago. The folder his father had given him with all the details had been taken when the DSTI guys busted into his house. He knew only what he'd managed to glean that first night. That Dahmer'd been born in 1960 and lived in Ohio and that his dad was a chemist. He knew that Dahmer committed his first murder at eighteen. That he was just getting started. That he got found guilty on fifteen counts of murder and was sentenced to a separate life term for each and every one. Almost a thousand years in prison. Jeff couldn't even imagine *one*. Didn't matter. Two years into his sentence, another prisoner beat Dahmer to death with a broom handle. The guy claimed that "God told him to."

And that's the face he was looking for in the motel mirror: the face smashed apart with a broom handle because that's what God wanted.

It wasn't too hard to imagine at all. He'd seen the pictures in his file. Brown hair dye wasn't enough. It was still the same face underneath. Add a couple of pounds maybe. Not too many.

The very last face seventeen people saw right before they were murdered.

Yeah, no doubt about it. It was the same face in the mirror.

His face.

This is what a killer looks like. . . .

Jeff turned on the hot water faucet all the way. It took another minute to steam the mirror completely. He imagined the outlines of faces forming in the mirror's emerging coating of vapor. But his own had vanished completely.

Thank God, he thought.

Castillo turned to eye Jeff as he came out of the bathroom.

"What's wrong?" the boy asked.

Castillo shook his head, ignored him, peered out the door's peephole again.

"What's goin' on?"

"Nothing," Castillo said, watching. "Couple of drunk assholes."

"Those are the guys who—"

"Yeah, your friends from earlier. You should have stayed the fuck inside."

"Sorry. You said—"

"No, that's totally on me."

"Can't we just ignore them?"

"No. Eventually the police are gonna show up. Whole goddamn motel is empty. Eventually, cops'll maybe come knocking on our door asking what I heard. Don't want to have to explain my car or you, or even *me*, to them or anyone else." Decent places brought too many cameras and registrations. But the cash dives, you still stuck out like a sore thumb. Should have stuck to motels in the middle. *Damn!* "Another Sunday night in Mayberry."

Another empty beer bottle exploded off the motel parking lot.

"Get dressed," he said and opened the door.

Four doors away. One car, an old dirty Omni, and one red Dodge pickup were parked unevenly in front of an opened room door. Loud music and bright light came out of the room. Air was streaked with the whiff of pot. Two girls and three guys leaned against the door, sat on the hoods and tailgate. Late twenty-somethings. Hard to tell. Guys all had half-assed beards, short hair. Two in their wifebeaters, showing off cheap tats and emerging beer guts. Couple of locals. One of the guys was "playfully" shoving one of the girls with his drunk hand in what Castillo assumed they both took as some kind of hilljack foreplay. The girl was half laughing, half shying away.

"What up, motherfucker?!" one of them yelled as soon as Castillo stepped outside. The posse cackled.

"Yo," Castillo said. "You guys mind taking the party inside some?"

"What the fuck for?" He had the attention of all of them now. There had been a fourth man in the room, and he stepped outside. Castillo assessed each. Two were pretty stoned.

"Just getting a little rowdy is all, man," Castillo lifted a hand to the newest arrival. "Someone's eventually gonna call the cops, you know."

"Fuck the cops!" More laughter. "Fuck you, too, man."

"Shit, bro. You callin' the fuckin' Five-Oh on us? Thought you was cool."

"No, man," Castillo said as he held up a peaceful hand. "Ain't calling the cops. But this place got a manager, couple other people trying to sleep. Someone else might. Letting you know it's getting kinda loud is all."

"Bill's the manager here. He knows us. No one knows you, hard guy. So . . . How 'bout you get the fuck back inside and go beddy-bye or what the fuck ever. Faggot."

Castillo waved. "Sure thing, man."

He reentered the room and shut the door. "Pack up," he said.

Jeff had already dressed as he'd been told. "We gotta go?"

"Yeah. Not worth it." Castillo assembled his own notes, holstered his gun and phone beneath his shirt. Tossed his two laptop cases in the gym bag with his clothes.

Knocking at their door. Banging.

Castillo dropped his head. "You gotta be fucking joking . . . you good to go?" He looked at Jeff.

"Yup."

Castillo nodded. The damn kid was ready before he was. Not bad. "Stay close," he said. "Get in the damn car." He opened the door.

Two of the guys stood outside. "Hey, man, wanted to apologize is all," one said. "You know. No hard feelings, bro." Held out a hand, grinning.

"Sure, man. No problem." Castillo ignored the shake, nodded for Jeff to continue to the car.

Three voices jeering as one: "You-guys-going? That-your-kid? Bet-you-sucking-dicks-in-there."

Castillo exited the room, blocked them from Jeff. Smelled their drunkenness. Assessed.

"You fucking leaving 'cause of us, man? Shit, man, now I feel all shitty. Fuck that. Damn."

"Checking out anyway," Castillo said. "You got the place to yourself."

"Hey, hardguy," the bigger of the two said. "How about we gonna call the cops on you, hardguy. Bet you cornholing that kid hard in there, huh? Fucking faggots. You wanna suck my cock now, hardguy?"

Castillo sensed Jeff turn to him for direction. "Just get in the car," he said.

"Hey, man. You call the cops on us? You fucking did, didn't you?"

The red pickup truck had started moving.

No, no, no, Castillo was thinking. *Don't be that obvious.*

They were. The pickup came to a stop behind his car.

Castillo opened the passenger door of his car, ushered Jeff inside. "Lock it." Shifted to the trunk.

Three voices: "Where-you-guys-going-man? Ain't-going-nowhere. Wanna-beer-kid?"

Castillo put his bags in the trunk, shut it. Surveyed the four guys again. Guy One had a buck knife at his hip. Guy Three, one of the stoned ones, maybe had a gun. *Maybe.* Yeah, Castillo decided. He did. He'd gotten out of the pickup with it freshly jammed in his belt. The two girls and the final guy had gathered in a loose semicircle to watch. Better than breaking beer bottles, he supposed.

He noticed Jeff squirming in his seat for a better look.

Shit.

"You guys mind moving the truck?" Castillo said.

"What truck?" the Big One said, snorted to his pals and stepped closer. Just enough.

"Look, man, I don't—"

Castillo had hit the man's throat with the back side of his hand. Stepped back and kicked. The man's kneecap audibly exploded. Before he'd hit the ground, Castillo was already moving around him toward Guy Three. Gun Guy.

He closed the distance quickly, too quickly for someone stoned.

Grabbed the man's wrist, pulled. Something snapped. Castillo ignored the shrill scream, forced Gun Guy to the ground with a twist of the broken limb. Punched three times directly into the nose with the heel of his hand. Then took the pistol. Tossed it onto his hood.

The last two came at him together. Good. Castillo eyed the girls: not running, not scared. Merely watching. Guy One had pulled his knife as Castillo thought he would. Both already looked damn unsure. Castillo smiled.

"We gonna fuck you—"

Keep talking, asshole. He'd already covered the gap between them. The movement with the knife was clumsy, probably the first time the guy had ever tried it for real. Castillo sidestepped, grabbed his arm, pulled forward and back, as he'd been trained a thousand times. As he'd used in the field a dozen times. Another loud snapping sound and the knife, still in Guy One's hand, was now pointed at Guy One's back. Stab, stab, stab. . . . It'd be that quick to finish it. Castillo fought against the trained reflexes. Instead, he turned the wrist more than usual. With another loud snap, the knife dropped. The man howled like a nervous hound dog.

Castillo grabbed his neck with both hands, pulling the head down to the hood of his car. Felt the nose go. The man fell back, his howling stopped. There'd be too much blood in his mouth. Castillo turned to the last.

"Hey, look, man . . . I . . . look, I don't wanna . . ."

"Sorry, friend. Only way this works." Castillo came low, took out the legs first. And then followed with a palm to the lower jaw. Lights out. Kid never even made a sound.

The whole thing had taken about twenty seconds.

The other three guys were moaning around him. Not moving. Or not moving well. Probably still didn't know what had just happened. Probably'd never seen so much blood, not even on some deer they'd shot. Blood had a way of freezing normal people. One thing was for sure: None of them would ever admit one guy had done this. Which was why he had to embarrass all of them. The girls might joke about it privately later, but they would never dare make it public.

He patted Guy Three, found his keys.

"You wanna move this fucking truck, please," he shouted and tossed the keys at the girls. One of them rushed to pick them up. He took the gun off the hood and stepped around to his own seat. "Find better people to hang around," Castillo said.

The girl nodded, got in the truck. She couldn't have been more than sixteen herself. Castillo shook his head and got into the car. "Fucking animals."

He started the car. The truck retreated and he pulled away.

Jeff was still staring at him.

"What's your fucking problem?" Castillo said.

Jeff shook his head. "Didn't say a word."

"Good. Keep it that way."

And he did.

JACOBSON FREE

JUNE 05, SUNDAY—INDIANAPOLIS, IN

[From the journals of Dr. Gregory Jacobson]

June 5—. . . What is broken when one can bring himself to kill another? MALES are responsible for the blood and violence of every culture, every country, every age. And serial murder is the masculine zenith of this same gender-based lust for dominance and execution. It is the asocial equivalent of our philosophy, mathematics, music, et al. To wit: There is no female Mozart because there is no female Jack the Ripper.

June 5—. . . In violence, we forget who we are. The men and women who passed me today who looked me in the eye who know nothing of what I truly am. Veritas Lux Mea. Since the Renaissance, God's Death, we have presumed to elucidate violence through Science. Before, when I was T., they presumed anthropometry could reveal the mark. Rapists were blond, pedophiles had long left feet, murderers were homely with smaller foreheads, etc. This was scientific fact. Absurd? Any more than claims of possession by Satan or other

primitive gods? Any more absurd than our pursuit of the Cain gene?
XP11.23–11.4 Do we only need to look there? No. I am still marked.
NOW ART THOU CURSED FROM THE EARTH. In violence,
we remember who we are.

Her hair was wrong.

It had to be the hair. It was a little too short. Too clean. Everything else was perfect.

The body positioned two-thirds of the way across the bed, on its left side. The shoulders were flattened to the mattress. Head turned to the left cheek. Legs spread. The left thigh at a perfect right angle to her trunk. The other at an obtuse angle. One breast under the head, the other under her right foot. Liver between the feet. Intestines on the right side of the body. Spleen on the left. The flaps he'd removed from her abdomen and thighs were on the bedside table.

The Thing on the Bed.

Like in the pictures. Like in the dreams.

Jacobson dragged the kukri knife gently along her forehead. *Do I cut again?* He'd already hacked off her ears and nose. *Do I rip some more?* Slashed away her lips and down over the chin. Her eyebrows and lids, her cheeks. Picture-perfect. She'd lived for almost two minutes while he'd cut her. Hemorrhaging slowly, painfully, from a deep slash across her throat that went down to her spine. The carotid artery filling her rent windpipe and then flooding her lungs as he continued his work. He'd started next on her abdomen. Then her face. *Was this the moment I did wrong?* Perhaps he was supposed to start with the face. He simply did not know this detail, forensics in 1888 not being what they were today.

Jacobson closed his eyes and leaned back, letting the vulgar smells of the tiny room fill his nose. He could suddenly feel the warmth of the blood on his face as something wet trailed down his left forearm, and his mind chased after the promising sensation.

His very first memory, his first recollection of childhood, of being, began with a dream. He'd been four or five at the time. He'd woken, screamed for his parents, found he'd wet the bed like a baby. He hadn't been able to stop crying. His father had spanked him that night. The dream returned later. He didn't recall exactly when, but it had. A month later, a year. He'd screamed and wet his bed again, but he did not call out for his parents this time. He made sure his terrified sobs were as quiet as possible, and only his bedroom's darkness was there to comfort him. Boy became man, and still the dream came. Once, or twice, or ten times a year. He no longer screamed or cried anymore. He simply woke up, methodically cleaned himself.

In the dream, he is in a small, dark room. There is a fire in one corner and a bed in the other. And, there is something on the bed. Something evil. He'd always known that part, felt it. That the thing on the bed wants him closer. Wants to fuck him, consume, destroy. *Completely.* That it wants *INSIDE* him. He also knew that it was much stronger than he was. That he would ultimately surrender to its wishes. He could not—not ever—win.

As the years passed, the Thing on the Bed became more detailed. In his teens, he learned that it was a woman. Soaked in blood. Ripped open. That it was still alive. Years later, it spread its misshapen legs wider and thrust its hips lewdly at him. It burbled blood from its missing lower jaw. In time, it *spoke* to him. In his twenties, he stood over it. He held a blade.

There were other dreams. Other women. Each became more familiar over time. But none had ever returned as much as the first. These eventually became fantasies he carried into the waking world. Girls he saw at school, some of the women he worked with, a stranger in a bookstore. He could picture them on the "dream bed," ripped open and waiting for him. Sex proved unspeakable. He could not ejaculate unless he imagined pushing into the Thing on the Bed. When a much younger man, he'd dated only two women because of this. He'd asked the last if she would play out a silly fantasy with him: tie her up, pretend to cut her.

It had not gone well.

He'd avoided women thereafter and focused on what he hoped was his true passion: science. But while his career as a geneticist flourished, he closed his eyes to the darkness each and every night, knowing that he was an aberration. Monster. Until . . .

Until that day. May 22, 1990. During a conference in Baltimore, a colleague had been reading a book, and, curious, Jacobson had picked up the paperback. Straightaway, everything made sense. *Everything.* Right there, in black and white, on page 176.

The Thing on the Bed.

It was real. SHE was real. The woman in his dreams.

Mary Jane Kelly. Murdered on Friday, November 9, 1888.

He spent the next hours reading the book from cover to cover. Then again. And again.

Jack the Ripper: Memoirs of the World's First Serial Killer.

He was—needless to say—unsurprised that one of the many suspects was named Tumblety. An old family name, and old family gossip. His mother's biological and ne'er-do-well father. Long since lost and banished to time and rumor. But time and rumor meant nothing to genetics. *What else*, Jacobson had marveled, *is passed on through RNA and amino acid sequences?*

His research and efforts refocused, the geneticist studied the off-spring of killers, and then the killers themselves, eventually creating their clones.

Searching for the root of evil.

But not to cure. Simply to understand. Appreciate. Enlighten.

To find the basest traits of our forebears absolves us.

He'd waited more than twenty years to unearth Tumblety's DNA and confirm their genomic link. Twenty years to explore alternatives, cures, but ultimately assenting, verifying, to the fact that our lifeblood, our physical quintessence, is inescapable.

Now if he could only finish what was started. Reach the same release his own blood had once known. Mary Jane Kelly's singular blood-drenched murder had somehow ended the Ripper's career. Over the years, Jacobson had studied every report he could find, knew the crime scene details and images as well as he knew his own face. The very same molecular fabric of his own body, his own mind, the very blood pumping through his veins, had been there in 1888.

Then, and now. The Thing on the Bed. They were the same.

He looked back down at the bed. The fire's shadows cast unevenly over the mutilated shape there. He sighed. No. She was not the one. Not yet. But there was still time. *Please, God* . . .

He would simply have to try again. He gently traced the blade sideways across the skin on her thigh, cleared away a thin trail between pools of blood.

Placed the note card there.

RESEARCH & DEVELOPMENT

JUNE 06, MONDAY—HARRISBURG, PA

The Senators were playing some team called the Erie Seawolves.

The ballpark was mostly full, five thousand plus, and Castillo had substituted their seats to the very edge of the Monday-night crowd. Jeff sat quietly beside him, watching the field with the genuine and innocent wonder of a bygone era when people could still be amazed by a baseball game.

A couple batters in, the kid jumped up from his seat, said he needed to hit the bathroom, and Castillo was fine with that. He needed some time to think alone anyway. He'd spent the morning adding more red dots to his "Murder Map," and the lines still ran in a hundred different directions. Soon he'd have to pick one of them to follow. So he needed something. *Anything*. Even if from a man half crazy.

The call from Ox had come early morning. Castillo had said they were in Pennsylvania, and Ox had suggested the Senators game as a place to meet. Castillo still had no idea where the guy had called from. Simply said he'd be there.

Castillo watched Jeff working back through the crowd to their seats.

Hopefully, the mysterious man would materialize as promised. The guy's whole demeanor had definitely changed after Castillo had mentioned SharDhara. Maybe he'd finally get some answers.

Ox materialized at the bottom of the third inning.

He was a black man shorter than the boy, with rounded gold glasses, a slender goatee, and a shaved head beneath a new red Senators baseball cap. He wore a matching silk pants suit of burgundy, a pair of large Chinese-style goldfish embroidered in crimson across the shirt. He hugged Castillo warmly, then shook Jeff's hand. "Marvelous night for baseball," he said to him. "Marvelous."

"Covert as ever, I see," Castillo said, eyeing the outfit.

Ox sat, crossed a leg, studied the ballpark. "Covert enough." He grinned. "No one's looking at me. Who we rooting for?"

"*Everyone's* looking at you," Castillo said. "What's SharDhara?"

Ox cocked his head. "Subtle as ever, yourself, I see. Maybe I never heard about any such thing."

"Maybe." Now Castillo smiled. "And maybe you drove nine hundred miles just to tell me that. Or to see the Seawolves?"

"Maybe I drove *eleven* hundred miles to see an old friend." Ox raised his hand for the beer vendor. "What'd you contact *me* for anyway?"

"You know something about everything."

"Hell I do. You want one?"

"No." Castillo waited while Ox paid for his beer. During the exchange Ox's face had gone blank in thought. No emotion, no response as he focused on the game below.

"That bad?" Castillo asked.

"First you tell me what you into."

"Can't." Castillo shook his head. "Sorry."

Jeff had stopped watching the game to study the two men. Ox's eyes were narrowed some, a tinge of irritation. "A taste, then," the man said. "Make sure you and I are on the same page, is all. I don't want any unspecified nastiness coming upon me and my family. Understood?"

"Fair enough," Castillo replied, leaning in. "A private company is doing shitty things for our former bosses. Horrible shitty. Involves experiments. Kids. Civilian deaths. And someplace or someone named SharDhara. No clue what that means, but I can tell when people are bullshitting me, which they are on this topic. And it got your black ass down here in a hurry."

"So it did. That's a fair taste." Ox kept looking at Jeff. "You one of 'the kids,' I suppose."

The boy looked at Castillo, who nodded it was OK to reply. "I am, sir," he said.

"You don't seem too surprised by any of this," Castillo noted.

"Nothing's surprised me since I was four. I notice, conversely, *you* still are."

"Surprised?" Castillo leaned back in his chair. "I admit I am."

"Why I love you, Castillo." Ox looked across him to Jeff again. "This's a man still believes in good guys and bad guys."

"I've worked some 'morally questionable' operations in my day. I know lines have to be crossed sometimes."

"'Lines crossed'?" Ox snickered, then sipped his beer. "You know your history, boy?" He'd kept his eyes trained on Jeff, but Castillo knew he was still talking to him. "Know the Nazis?"

"Sure," Jeff replied.

"Sure, sure. Nazis famous for killing millions and conducting lethal experiments on humans, right? Famous for being evil? And these UNITED STATES OF AMERICA"—as he spoke, his voice lowered, *sotto voce*, then rose into the thunderous boom of an Alabama preacher—"got rid of the evil Nazis. Problem is, at the exact same time, the U.S.A. was *also* conducting lethal experiments on humans."

Jeff and Castillo shared a knowing look.

"Still is," Jeff said.

Ox winked. "Still is, baby. Still is." He turned and watched the next batter. "Let me tell you two a story. Dr. Cornelius P. Rhoads, American scientist, puts cancer cells into a bunch of people, who, surprise, die. His subjects are dirt-poor Puerto Ricans, so no one gives a shit, right? Sorry," he added, "just being honest. Uncle Sammy invaded Puerto Rico in 1898. It's now 1931. A Puerto Rican politician named, ahhh, Pedro Campos gets hold of some letters in which Rhoads brags about killing these people, and ol' Pedro goes to the press. Puerto Rican and American. Guess what they do. *Nada*, baby. Instead, our Pedro is promptly arrested for being a 'terrorist' and spends the next *twenty years* in a Puerto

Rican jail, where he's declared insane and *this* country now uses *him* as a subject for radiation experiments. Irony squared, yes? Want more? During this exact same time, Rhoads, the fine doctor who'd purposely killed a dozen people and then bragged about it, is promoted to run the U.S. Army Biological Warfare Department. The American Association for Cancer Research even names an award on his behalf. That's the punishment for a dozen murders. More? Dr. Rhoads *personally* arranged for the radiation experiments to be conducted on Pedro Campos. Rhoads later wrote, 'All physicians take delight in the abuse and torture of their unfortunate subjects.' Research it yourself sometime online. Some days it's almost funny. See, before you can truly appreciate SharDhara, you gotta know your history, gentlemen."

"Why I contacted you," Castillo said.

Ox sighed, shook his head. "All right, look, man. . . . The Department of Defense recently admitted, despite a dozen different treaties banning research and development of biological agents, it *still* operated biological-agent research facilities. More than *one hundred* sites across the nation. Including two dozen major universities. All them bitches making *something*. When the Manhattan Project scientists finished the world's first atom bomb, they started a second project: injecting plutonium directly into hundreds of American men, women, and children. Their mission was to study the effects of exposure to atomic weapons. Their very first test subject was a civilian who'd *simply had a car accident near the lab.* Ten years later, these same scientists were dropping lightbulbs filled with *Bacillus subtilis* in the New York subway system, to see · how effective biological weapons would work on a large population. Within four days, a million New Yorkers were infected."

"What's *Bacillus subtilis*?" Jeff asked.

Perfect, Castillo thought. *Exactly the kind of exchange that could get Ox going back in the field.* If Ox really truly knew anything that could help, it'd work its way out soon.

"Common flu bug. No biggie. Practice, brother. They love to *practice.* Ten years later, the Senate confirmed that more than two hundred populated areas in America were deliberately contaminated with biological agents between '49 and '69. San Fran, D.C., Key West, Minneapolis, St. Louis. *Everywhere*, man. The CIA had forty *different* universities and drug companies working on this. More ancient history, but you'll connect the dots easy enough. Then on to MK-ULTRA: covert drug tests secretly given to military personnel, mental patients, whores, and the general public to study if psychotic drugs were a potential weapon. LSD, heroin, morphine, mescaline, Mary Jane, whatever. Keeping brothers high 24/7 for weeks to see what would happen." He looked at Jeff. "They teach you anything about Tuskegee in school?"

"I don't go to school. I . . . but, yes, I know what Tuskegee is."

Ox tilted his head, curious. "OK, Private, what you know about it?"

"Scientists got a bunch of poor farmers, African-Americans, in the South and gave them fake treatments for some disease. They could have cured them, but let more than a hundred die to see what'd happen."

Ox nodded in approval. "Not bad. How you know that?"

"My dad's a scientist."

Ox looked at Castillo, who held up his hands in surrender.

"His dad's most definitely a scientist," Castillo confirmed. He watched Ox trying to make heads or tails of the boy's role. *Maybe should have left Jeff waiting in the car.* But maybe he secretly hoped Ox would figure it out. ALL of it. Because at present his only confidant in the world was the teenaged clone of Jeffrey Dahmer.

"Well," Ox said, "it wasn't any old scientists. It was the U.S. Public Health Service, and they infected hundreds in Guatemala also, most of them institutionalized mental patients, with gonorrhea and syphilis without their knowledge or permission. The infected were even encouraged to pass the disease onto others as part of the study. And today, white people have the balls to laugh when black folk claim the government is secretly sterilizing the brothas through fast-food chicken franchises."

Castillo shook his head. *Was it possible . . . ?*

"We could do this all day, man, but you get the point. Take your pick. Project Artichoke. Project Paperclip. Third Chance. QK-Hilltop. Project Derby Hat. Chatter. Camelot. Montauk. MK-SEARCH. MK-NAOMI. MK-OFTEN." He'd put his beer down between his feet and was marking them off on his fingers faster than Jeff could count. Castillo had heard the list before, a part of the man's go-to script, but he listened to it quite differently this time. Knowing that "Project Cain" or

"CAIN XP11" could be somewhere someday in the roll made the others real for the first time. "Project 112. Project SHAD. DTC Test 69-12. H.R. 15090. Big Tom. Fearless Johnny. The Philadelphia Experiment. Program F . . . have fun brushing your teeth tonight, son. . . . Operation Whitecoat. Ancient history, I know. Need something more current? More relevant? OK. How 'bout chemtrails. Or HAARP. Or Plum Island. Or SharDhara. . . . But we won't find out the real truth about those until years from now, when it's finally been declassified. When someone's too damn old to worry about being silenced and finally talks. When it's old news. When there's worse things to think about. Memories are short, man. Agent Orange, who gives a shit? That's Woodstock, man. Ancient history. Gulf War syndrome? Again, who gives a shit? Twenty years ago already. DX111. Fuck, brother." He turned directly to Castillo. "How 'bout all the stuff they tried on us. Pyridostigmine bromide, NAPP pills, organophosphate pesticides, depleted uranium, Khamisiyah. We had *this* talk before, you and I."

"We have," Castillo agreed. The battlefields and soldiers of his career *had* been crammed with experimental drugs and materials.

"Volunteer army, who gives a shit, right? Bury our shit another ten years and it'll sound like we're bitching about mustard gas at Meuse-Argonne. It wasn't until 1995 that we learned four hundred Americans had been injected with plutonium to see what would happen. There was an apology. Always is. The U.S. apologized for the experimentations on Pedro Campos in 1994. Apologized for the LSD tests in 1995. Apologized for Tuskegee in 1997. Apologized for Guatemala in 2010. How long before they apologize for what they done to us, man?"

"Or us?" Jeff said.

Ox looked at the boy. "You'll be dead first, little man."

"Hey, dude." Castillo's whole body tensed. "Come on. Give us a break."

Ox held up his hands in apology. "Sorry, sorry. But listen, both of you now. You remember MK-ULTRA, the LSD tests. Check it: Dr. Frank Olson was the acting chief of the Special Operations Division during the whole project. Man knows the experiments are, what'd you call it, 'morally questionable' and so he up and quits. Maybe plans to go to the *New York Times* or Mike Wallace or some shit, right? Thing is, a few days later it's reported Olson's committed suicide by jumping out a thirteenth-story window. That there'd been LSD in his system. Course, his family does not believe ANY of this and fights for the truth for the next forty years."

Castillo could only think of the late Dr. Chatterjee, DSTI's most recent suicide.

Ox continued. "When Good Guy Olson's body was finally exhumed in 1994, the medical examiner termed the death a 'homicide' and pointed to cranial injuries that indicated Olson had been knocked unconscious *before* he exited the window. Of course, the United States apologized for that too and then paid his family $750,000. You understand yet? What they're willing to do? These fucking people. You think a dozen, a hundred, kids matter to these guys?"

"I don't," Castillo agreed. "So tell me about SharDhara."

"Secondhand info, brother. All I got."

"I'll take it."

"Hollyman. SFC Hollyman. Met him through a guy I knew down at the VAMC in Miami. It was hinted Hollyman, who'd spent some time at the hospital, might be a guy I wanted to talk to. Total nutball was the official consensus, but my buddy knew my ideas on what a total nutball is can be different than other people's, so . . . I track this guy down. Company B, Second Battalion, 7th. Took a while but we eventually get talking. Or drinking. I don't know, you know how it goes. Anyhow, eventually he comes around to SharDhara. Like that's all he's been wanting to talk about the whole time anyway, you know. Dancing around it, 'classified' blah blah, all those rounds and war stories, waiting to get to SharDhara. He dropped with a small team in '08. Six guys escorting a couple spooks straight out of Langley. Real Black Ops bullshit. SharDhara was a village, typical backwoods shithole. Taliban mostly. Sub commander, maybe twenty fighters. Local IED depot. Hollyman figures it's a standard hit and go, right. Blow the IEDs, maybe pop the sub commander and then outsy. Then he's ordered to pull on the old NBC."

"Like a Hazmat suit," Castillo explained for Jeff. "*N*uclear *B*iological *C*hemical. For possible WMDs like sarin or mustard gas. But that's not what this was . . ."

Ox shook his head. "Hollyman said the village was, and I quote, 'All fucked to holy hell.'"

"How?" Castillo and Jeff exchanged looks again.

"Everyone dead," Ox replied. "*Everyone*. Whole damn village. Bodies shredded by a hundred bullets, folks hacked to bits. Missing limbs. Ripped apart. Bitten. Men and women raped. They couldn't make sense of it. Some kinda Taliban reprisal, they thought, but the Taliban were as dead as the villagers. Kids dead with knives, what looked like self-inflicted wounds. Found one survivor. An old crazy woman they found in one of the huts. He said she was eating the dead. Just sitting on the floor, eating the bodies that surrounded her."

"Zombies?" Jeff said.

Ox shook his head. "Wasn't that crazy. The dead were dead. The old woman was simply insane. Hollyman said he wanted to pull the trigger himself. Spooks wouldn't let him. They took the woman away, told Hollyman and the others to make it look like the Taliban had taken out the village. Burn it all, clear out the IEDs. They did. And all the while, he said, the Spooks were collecting samples."

"Samples?"

"Air samples. Dirt. Water. Tissue and blood from the dead. Spent half the day collecting what they needed, then burned as ordered. The bodies, fields, livestock, dogs, everything."

"What did he think it was?" Castillo was trying to shake the images now painted in his head.

"What do *you* think it was? He said they'd tested something. Something biological had been used on these people. He didn't know what it was, but he said he'd never seen nothing like it in his whole life. Said the woman, the woman's eyes . . . not even in his nightmares. Hollyman was his detachment's senior medical sergeant. He'd seen plenty to have nightmares about. But this . . . Said he'd burned *things* that day. Not people. *Things*." Ox's voice trailed off.

"Anything else?"

Ox shook his head. "That's it, man. I don't . . . you know."

"You know how I can reach him? Would he talk to me?"

"Gone, man. Two years now."

"Dead? How?"

"Benelli M1014." It was a standard-issue combat shotgun.

"Suicide?" Castillo thought again of the "suicides" and "accidental deaths" at DSTI. How easy to put scare quotes around those words now. "Or do you think they . . ."

"He wouldn't be the first." Ox brought his beer back up and finished it. "It's been open season on scientists for fifty years. We in the golden age of chemistry and biology, man. More than three hundred Iraqi scientists been clipped since we showed up. Accidents, bombings, suicides. . . . More recently, it's been the Iranians. Check and see yourself which Iranian scientist was mysteriously blown up, misplaced, or poisoned this month."

"But that's our enemy. You're talking the United States government eliminating U.S. civilians."

"'Civilians,'" Ox said with a laugh. "There you go again. Men who design weapons aren't civilians. Don't care whose team they're on. You want dead Americans, go to bioweapons. It's been a decade of those DNA guys going down. How'd that line go? *The truth is out there*."

"American scientists were killed?" Jeff gulped. "By the government?" Castillo knew the boy was thinking about his father. After everything he knew, everything the man had done to him, the kid was still worried about his *padre*. Amazing.

Ox made a gesture as if he'd been a magician revealing something hidden in his hands. "DNA expert Dr. David Schwartz stabbed to death in Virginia. DNA expert Dr. Don Wiley, Harvard man, shows up floating in the Mississippi. DNA expert Dr. David Kelly, who worked for the U.S. Navy, found dead after somehow slashing his wrists *and* throat and then dragging himself a half mile away from his home. DNA expert Dr. Franco Cerrina found dead in his lab at Boston University: Cause of death still unknown. DNA expert Dr. John Clark, guy who ran the lab that made Dolly the Sheep, and spoke out against cloning afterward, was found hanging in a remote cottage. Bioweapons expert Dr. John Wheeler found dead in a Delaware landfill. Bioweapons expert Dr. Robert Schwartz found murdered in his home in Virginia. Bioweapons expert Bruce Edwards Ivins, of the United States Army Medical Research Institute, found dead from an apparent overdose. Of *TYLENOL*! No autopsy was permitted. Look it up yourself. You think it's the, what, the French killing all our guys? Islamic sleeper cells? Like I said: LSD guy not the first. And sure as shit won't be the last. More to the point: Once is happenstance, twice is coincidence, *TEN* times is Clear-the-Fuck-Out. You all right, Castillo? You lookin' a little puzzled."

"I'm fine." Castillo looked at Jeff, then back to Ox. "For the record, I don't own a Benelli M1014."

"*Entiendo*. What else you need?"

"I don't know yet." Castillo stared out over the outfield, tried to clear his mind. "But this helps. If I need to—"

"You contact me anytime, Castillo. You know that."

"Thanks." Castillo stood to leave.

"How's my girl Kristin doing?"

"She's fine."

Ox shook his head. "You aren't together no more."

"Never were." He tapped Jeff to move. "Come on."

"Yeah, right." Ox smiled in memory. "You know, I still do that ghost routine of hers sometimes. Just to talk to familiar faces. How sad is that? Talking to ghosts."

Castillo sighed. "You ever think sometimes *we're* the ghosts? That those other guys are all back home now mowing the grass or watching TV or some shit? And we're the ones who never made it back?"

Jeff had risen slowly beside him.

Ox studied them both again. Nodded his head.

"Yeah," he said. "All the damn time."

NIGHT TERRORS

JUNE 06, MONDAY—HARRISBURG, PA

S oon, the man whispers, a promise, and steps toward his bench of tools. A rusted kerosene lantern casting fluid shadows along the cave wall behind, shadow grotesque as the man hunches unnaturally under the low ceiling. Others in the adjacent tunnels, holes, their foreign jibbering dim and whispered like prayers beneath the hum of generators and exhaust fans. It smells of piss and sweat and blood, someone laughs. Two emptied chairs beside the dark stains of torture pooled below, each of the two bodies already dragged away and only their heads remain propped on the small wood table watching. The man chooses his favorite scalpel to make more shallow incisions along the chest and genitals, peels the flesh. Cursing, damning, pleading but the words are garbled sounds, not words at all anymore. Glare angrily from the open eye, the other swollen over and crusted in dried blood. No. Don't do this. Still, the man steps closer and presses his thumb against the mouth to push back the upper lip. Writhing in the chair, the blood-soaked ropes holding tight, screaming as the blade raises. Brings the scalpel once more to the gums. Then to the body again. Then the gunfire erupts in one of the tunnels and sound echoes like thunder. Drops the wet scalpel onto the table beside the two *heads. Watching. Someone shouting somewhere, the sound of a man dying. The man with the scalpel is holding a rifle, arguing, afraid. Other shapes bursting into the room. One body lifted into the air and then, like a black ghost, rises a meter off the ground. Blood splashes across the cave's gray-brown rock. Something else now stirred in the shadows. A thin, dark shape that drifts like smoke. You scream.*

Castillo jerked up straight in his bed, gasping for air. Scanning the dim room.

The cave was gone. The black thing was gone. The man.

The man.

His own scream still echoed in his memory. Reality reemerged, quickly and in huge swaths. Awake. Real. Room. Motel. Back in the U.S. Pennsylvania. Just a dream. Nothing's there. No one's there. Nightmare.

Still, his hand remained jammed in the bag by his bed, wrapped around the pistol he kept there. His heart pumping a million beats a minute again. He touched his free hand to his chest. *Calm down. Calm down.* His mind fought for the words, the specific words to help. His own frantic breathing filled the whole room. Nothing coming to mind. *Think! Focus!*

He looked across the room to the other bed.

The boy, Jeff Jacobson, lay there. Head turned asleep.

Maybe I didn't really scream out. Maybe he imagined that also. He let go of the gun. Pressed his hands against his face. Opened his palms enough to let the unsteady breathing pass through.

"Strange man, escape this spell and bethink thee now of thy native land, if it is fated for thee to be saved . . ."

The quote finally came to mind, and he said it to himself again and again alone in the dark. His hands found his chest. Ran along the scar tissue rigid and embossed beneath his T-shirt.

He thought of getting up. Tossing on the light. Waking the boy up. Someone to talk to.

But the boy wasn't a boy.

He was a clone.

And the clone of Jeffrey Dahmer.

A monster. And it was best to let monsters sleep.

Castillo checked his watch. 2300. He'd only been asleep thirty minutes. He needed another couple hours at least. He lay back down. Focused on his breathing.

Sleep. *Shake off this trance . . .*

The nightmares almost never returned twice in the same night.

Almost never.

EMILY

Emily led Allison into the apartment slowly on purpose. She didn't want her little sister to miss a thing. It smelled musty, like sex, like a dirty gym locker room. Like too many boys. Allison had paused in the doorway, and Emily took her arm to gently lead her beyond her warning instincts. The door shut behind them.

It had been a couple months since she'd last seen Allison. Ever since Emily'd moved out of the house, or been tossed out, or whatever it was that had happened, they weren't that close anymore. But a simple phone call was all it had taken. A big sister inviting her old pal over to watch a video and grab some pizza. Allison said yes almost immediately. She was a nice person that way. Always had been. Pretty, too. Even prettier than Emily remembered. Grown her hair out long and straight, which the boys would like, for sure.

Two of them, Al and Jeffrey, were watching TV again. Al liked to bite. Jeffrey was the only one who hadn't yet done her, or her roommate, actually. He liked boys, it seemed. So he, John, and Ted had gone across the hall one night. Surprised the thirty-something chode who lived there. That had been too funny. The nurse, Ms. Stacey, sat between them on the couch, the head tilted slightly to one side. Her eyes were bare, dark slits, the whites behind still fluttering wildly. They'd opened her stained button-down shirt all the way again so that both her tits hung out freely.

None of the three seemed to have noticed when Emily entered the room. "That's Jeff and Al. Ms. Stacey," she introduced her sister to them anyway. "And John, of course."

Slumped in the room's other chair was a boy dressed as a clown. His red and blue makeup was smeared and patchy, his collar stained a dark red where his chin rested on the top of his chest. A bag of Doritos rested on his crotch. A huge, red, puffy ball dangled over one eye from his lopsided hat. He turned sluggishly as they entered the room and tracked their movement deeper into the apartment, his red lips listlessly forming into a moronic smile.

"Emily?" She felt her sister tugging her arm.

"Hey." A low voice from the kitchen behind them. "You're late. This her?"

"Allison," Emily said, smiling and leading the girl forward. "My baby sister. Ain't she the sweet sweetest li'l thing?"

"Sweet, sweet." The boy laughed. He looked older than the others by a few years. Long, wavy dark hair and incredible blue-green eyes. Like turquoise almost, and always changing depending on the room's light. "But she ain't no baby, is she?" These incredible eyes roved unhurriedly over her sister while he bit at his lower lip. "What up, Allison?" he said. "I'm Ted."

Allison had lowered her head.

The dried blood on the kitchen floor looked like any other stain.

"You being mean to my friends?" asked Emily.

"No, I . . ." Her sister's voice trembled. "I . . . nice to meet you."

"That's better." Ted stepped closer, grinning with a distinct, and totally fucking hot smile Emily had grown to recognize. *This was gonna be fun, fun, fun.* How they'd come together was simple enough. Some kid named Al had friended her on Facebook six months before. Another smartass on the web who liked sending her dickpic Snapchats and private IMs about wanting to rape soccer moms while their daycare brats ate Happy Meals and waited for him to finish. Joked about blowing up a mall, sending body parts flying in an unholy rain of Payless shoes, Abercrombie boxers, and blood. ROFL.

Then, one day, this guy sends an email and says he and a buddy are heading to Ohio. Would she be cool if they stopped by to party some? They'd bring some pot or X, he said. The kid was probably way younger than he was pretending, but she wasn't past hooking up with a high school boy. Emily wrote back: SURE. WTF?

But it wasn't just Al and a buddy who showed up at her door.

It was five guys.

And they'd taken their time with the two girls. Emily and her roommate, Kim.

Days.

"Nothing to be afraid of, right?" Ted was saying to Allison. "Your sister said you were pretty cool. She sure got the pretty part right." He touched the side of Allison's face. "Fourteen, huh? No kidding. You a party girl? You wanna party like your sister here?" He winked at Emily.

Emily liked Ted the best.

Ever since the first time he'd fucked her. Raped her. Made love. She didn't know what to call it. His hands closing so tightly around her throat as he'd forced her to the living room floor. The life and air leaving her body as one. Her roommate's frantic screams, muffled with duct tape, so very close, other shapes moving above them both.

Then Emily had looked into his eyes and seen it: Nothing. No rage, not even amusement. Nothing. Thrusting into her like a piece of machinery, the blackness of death spreading over more of her teary-eyed vision. The guy honestly didn't care if she lived or died.

She'd never cum so hard in her life.

He'd known it when she had and laughed. Then he'd squeezed harder until everything went black. She'd awoken hours later when he was doing her again. "I thought you were dead," he'd smiled.

Oh, yes. Emily liked Ted the best.

And Ted wanted more. Always wanted more. More than her or her roommate.

Emily knew who to call.

Allison. Her sister.

Pretty, perfect Allison. Ms. School Play, and Ms. Cheerleader Squad, and Ms. Honor Roll. Fourteen. Another fucking Taylor Swift clone. The good girl. Princess of the known world. At least according to their mother. *Not* the screwup. The stupid one, the druggie, the slut who'd had the abortion. College dropout. Nineteen years old and working second-shift food services at Walmart. Princess of Nothing.

Until now. Because now, now she'd finally found her King of Nothing.

She'd heard of Badge Bunnies and Buckle Bunnies, girls who got wet for cops and cowboys and such. A few, she now understood, got off on guys who hurt people. Killed. And these guys claimed to have some shit that would kill, like, *thousands* of people. She could hardly sleep, she was so fucking turned on. *I'm a Blood Bunny*, she thought. Grinned.

Oh, Mom, if you could see us now.

"What was that?" Allison asked, her eyes grown wide like one of those anime cartoon girls.

Emily giggled. They could all hear Kim in the bathroom again, thumping and mewling in the tub.

"Come on." Ted put his arm against Allison's back. "I'll show ya."

Down the hall, the sounds became more distinct. The strange gargling noise, the slow and steady THUMP of something hitting a wall.

"Emily?" said Allison.

The bathroom door was open a crack, and Ted pushed it back with one hand, positioned Allison to look within. It was dark inside, the hall light barely illuminating the smears of blood surrounding the bathtub, black against the shadowed tile floor, the wall.

THUMP. Movement in the tub. The body shifting back and forth in the darkness.

"Not sure how much she really feels," Emily said behind them as she peeked in on her roommate. "She's so far down the K-Hole."

She'd been amazed how easy it was to buy ketamine on the street. Totally like the boys told her. These guys knew about everything.

THUMP.

"The cuts are below the elbows and knees," she told her sister, "so it was easy to stop the bleeding."

"Easy?" Ted laughed. "Like hell."

"Well," said Emily. "Easy enough."

"Yeah," he agreed. "I guess it was."

One of his hands held Allison against the door frame, keeping her from collapsing.

"What . . . what did . . ." Allison fought for the right words. "Emily?"

"Shhh, sexy. Don't you worry about any of that," Ted told the girl as the thing in the tub burbled and flopped. "We were just having a little bit of fun is all. You like to have fun, don't you? No? Your sister told us you were a fun girl."

"Fun, fun, fun. When did he take her lips?" Emily asked.

"I don't know. After you left to get her, I guess." Ted shook his head. "That crazy retard'll eat anything."

Albert had already taken so much. The hands, feet. Both breasts. An eye. Emily did not understand why. She just thought it was kinda funny. She did not yet understand that Al was a clone of Albert Fish, who'd fried in an electric chair way back in 1936. That he'd earned names like The Werewolf of Wysteria, The Brooklyn Vampire, and The Boogeyman sixty years before she'd been born. That he'd raped, murdered, and eaten as many as a hundred children. Sent letters to his victims' parents describing every detail. "'How she did kick, bite, and scratch,'" one letter reported. "'It took me nine days to eat her entire body.'" Al's Facebook profile had had none of this. LET'S PARTY, Al had written. SURE, she'd written back. And then she'd given her address. Now this.

"Kinda wish they'd left her alone," Ted concluded.

"I like her like this," another voice said behind him. "Better time. This the sister?"

"Yeah." Ted turned. "Say hi to Allison."

"Proof of God, she is."

"Yeah, for sure," Ted agreed. "Allison, this is Henry. He's a good guy."

"You going first?" the new boy asked.

THUMP.

"Nah," Ted said. "Go ahead. A promise is a promise."

"Cool." Henry took hold of Allison's arm.

"Back in one piece," Ted reminded him.

Henry puckered his lips. "You got it, Captain America."

Allison turned to her sister and started to speak, but no words came out of her mouth. A rasp of breath as Henry pulled her down the hall toward the bedroom. She struggled some, but not enough that it would matter.

"I'm gonna watch," Emily said.

"Like hell. What am I supposed to do in the meantime?" Ted's face looked frustrated, angry.

"Not a prob," she said and pulled out her cellphone. "Gimme a sec."

His pupils had dilated, eyes grown almost completely black. Like something dead.

"Hey, Mom," Emily said into the phone, waving the boy away. "It's me. Yeah, hey, listen. Yes, I know it's late. But, hey, Allison's over here. Yes. I don't know. But she's pretty upset about something."

Ted grinned.

"No. You should probably come over." Emily rolled her eyes.

Muffled screams trickled from the end of the hall.

My dear little sister. Another Princess of Nothing.

"Yeah, Mom," Emily said. "We'll be waiting for you."

THE MURDER MAP

JUNE 07, TUESDAY—HARRISBURG, PA

McCarty.

It came with the afternoon list: One of seven more dead people discovered in the last twenty-four hours. But so very different from the others . . . Familiar. Castillo stepped to the desk, grabbed his phone. Scanned over a hundred images he'd taken until he found the right one.

"Got you!" The sudden sound of his voice like thunder in the small room. All morning had been silence: the boy watching the muted TV, Castillo at his laptop, distracted, the night's events—the dream—still fresh in his mind.

"I got you, you son of a bitch." Castillo pumped his fist at nothing, hurried across the room to the map. Happy to leave the brooding thoughts behind if even for a minute.

"Who?" Jeff sat up some.

"Don't worry about it," Castillo replied. "Just more dead people."

"Oh."

He felt like a dick the moment he replied, and the kid's childlike response only added to the feeling. It was unfair to think of the kid only as a "monster." Whatever the boy's origins, he really needed to think of Jeff as a scared and abandoned fifteen-year-old.

Have to. Don't I?

"A couple new names came in. I don't know. But, it's someone. And it's somehow connected to this. Three new homicides in Delaware. Police found them a couple hours ago. I've got about an hour before it hits cable TV. Two different homes. Goddamn, I got you guys." He grabbed his red pen and marked the map. "Husband and wife. A Mr. and Mrs. Nolan. Shot. Another woman killed in the house across the street. Want to guess her name?"

"No."

"McCarty. Nancy McCarty. Chicken girl."

"M. Carty."

"Looks like. Want more?"

"No."

"Seems her teenaged son is missing. *And* the prime suspect." Castillo grabbed the remote. "Yes, yes. Now we're cooking, kid. Let me see if it's on goddamned Fox News yet. Shit. Wanna guess his name? The missing kid?" He put the television on. Found the news channels.

"What is it?"

"Al. Albert McCarty. Age fifteen. Fuck, yes. Albert Fish, maybe. Or Albert DeSalvo. Both names are in your dad's notes. Good. Nothing on TV yet." He put the set back on mute. "Where was that . . ." Back on his phone, flipping through the digital pics of Dr. Jacobson's journals. "Pack up. We're leaving for Delaware five minutes ago. M. Carty. You son of a bitch. McCarty. So . . . so, then what's with this damn chicken?"

"It's not a chicken," Jeff said. "It's a hen."

"Chicken. Hen. What's the difference?"

Jeff looked away, retreated, began to pack the book bag Castillo had bought him.

"Forget that shit," Castillo said as he waved his hand. "You got something to say, kid, say it."

Jeff dropped the bag. "You said they got . . . that those three people got killed in Delaware."

"So?"

"They're the Blue Hens."

"What?"

"Blue Hens. The University of Delaware sports teams are called the Blue Hens."

"What the hell is a—"

"It's the state bird."

"You've gotta be shittin' me. How do . . ." Castillo stared at his phone. "Is that all this is? McCarty in Delaware. That's the big secret code?"

Jeff shrugged.

"Maybe. So what're these, then? These birds? This circle? The squiggle?" Castillo waved Jeff over and pulled up the next image, staring at the screen.

Jeff slid off the bed. Joined Castillo as he thumbed through the original images.

"Stop," Jeff said.

AlzBaum

"OK," Castillo urged, "so what the hell is that?"

The teen stared. Tilted his head. "Could be . . ."

"What? *Could be* what, damn it?"

Jeff glanced briefly at the Murder Map.

"What? Go ahead . . ." Castillo turned and urged Jeff toward the wall with the map.

Jeff turned his head, studied the map. Stepped toward it, crossing the room like he was sleepwalking. He ran his finger across the red dots and half-formed lines. "What's this?" He pointed to a small cluster of blue dots.

"Missing persons." Castillo was up and standing beside him. "A mother and her two children last seen at a playground in Ohio. Little park right outside McArthur. Maybe a custody thing, husband. Maybe something else. Why?"

Jeff turned and looked him in the eye for the first time in three days. "Because I think I know what the squiggle is."

"Go. Yes. What?"

"A snake."

"A snake?"

Jeff nodded.

"Why do you think this is a snake? It could be anything."

"Now we know it's places. The Blue Hens, Delaware. The pictures are places."

"Maybe."

"Then *maybe* it's a snake. It looks kinda like Serpent Mound."

"Kinda? What the hell is Serpent Mound?"

"Some old Indian burial site built in the shape of a giant snake. Something my . . . my dad took me to once."

"Where?" Castillo's eyes were wide.

Jeff dropped his finger on a spot in southern Ohio. "Right here."

Castillo put his own finger over the missing family in McArthur, Ohio. A third person could have then drawn a line between their two fingertips. A straight line and less than a two-hour drive.

"It's not Al Baum," Jeff said. "It's Albaum. Just like McCarty. And the picture is a hint to the location."

"Yup," Castillo agreed. "Goddamn."

He snatched up his laptop, typed. Some database in Washington whirled. Spit out names and ages and addresses. *Thank you, Homeland Security Act.* "There are only two hundred Albaum families in America," he reported aloud, still clicking.

"Better than twenty thousand Baums, huh?" Jeff commented.

"Hell, yeah," Castillo answered. *Kid has a quick mind. Smart.* It'd been the exact same number Castillo'd stated days ago. He further refined his search on Albaum.

"How many Albaum families in Ohio?" Jeff asked.

Castillo turned, smiled. "One," he said.

ANOTHER SON

The man who finally came into the visiting area didn't look like the guy from the pictures, the one with the dopey eyes and crazy hair. This guy was balding, with a slim gray mustache. Much older. He wore the same dark blue prison suits as the other guys. He smiled. Looked kinda nice.

David knew this same man had once murdered six people with a .44 revolver. Blinded another. Paralyzed an eighteen-year-old girl. For a year, on and off, he'd simply walked the streets of New York shooting total strangers.

David Berkowitz. The .44-Caliber Killer. The SON OF SAM.

And SAM, whoever the hell that was, had apparently been quite fertile.

Because David was *another* son. And cell for cell and genome for genome, the man he'd been made from now sat directly across from him. Just forty years older. As if it wasn't a thick acrylic window separating them, but some kinda freaky mirror.

David knew this because it was in the file Dr. Jacobson had given him. From the same DSTI files he knew he fought depression and had some anger issues, but nothing a few meds and maybe a little counseling couldn't keep in check. And when the other guys were going nuts that first night, the night Jacobson finally lost his friggin' mind and set them all loose, he'd honestly just kept out of their damn way.

Sure, he'd helped skin Dylan after the kid was dead—*thought* he was dead, he'd told himself every day after—but that was only so the others would think he was doing *something*. Maybe give him a break. He'd seen what Ted and Jeff were doing to the other DSTI kids who weren't playing the game. So, yeah, he went along with it. But, all in, he was still cool. He wanted no part in the murder stuff. Or, didn't think he did. He'd shaken those other guys as quickly as he could. Was ecstatic when Jacobson had split the two groups up. Even promised he and Dennis would find all the kids on Jacobson's list. Others like him. Kids born to kill. Would have promised anything to get away from Ted and Henry and Jeff.

Not that Dennis and Andrei were much better . . .

"I know you?" the man on the other side of the freaky mirror asked. His voice sounded funny coming through the small vent at the bottom of the glass. Like a shitty cellphone even though they were sitting a foot apart.

"Sorta," David replied.

"Sorta? You look real familiar. What's your name, kid?"

"David."

"No kidding. Two peas in a pod, how about that?"

"Yup."

"So who are you, and to what do I owe this visit? They told me you had some kinda letter to get in or something."

"Um, Dr. Jacobson thought . . ."

"Ah, I see. Good old Gregory Jacobson. Haven't heard from him in years. You his kid or something?"

"Sorta."

"Again with the sortas. And he 'sorta' set this up?"

"Yes. I . . . I needed to talk with you. He gave me that letter to get in. Said that was OK and made some phone calls, I guess."

"You guess. Well, you got about ten minutes, kid. What ya want to talk about?"

"Do you feel bad about killing those people?"

"You're one of those beat-around-the-bush kinda guys, huh?"

"Do you?"

The man crossed his hands. He smiled, but it wasn't a nice smile this time. "Every damn day," he said. "You writing a school report or something?"

"I'm just . . . trying to figure things out. I have . . ."

"You have what?"

"Strange stuff in my head, you know. Kinda confused nowadays."

"Yeah? Is that what this is about? You must be one of those kids he works with down at that school. Yeah, sure. Strange stuff in your head. I used to talk to the dog, you know. Thought he was possessed by a demon and he told me to kill people. 'Strange' like that?"

"Something like that."

"Really? Shit. Sorry, kid." The man freed a pair of glasses from his shirt and fixed them to his nose. "You talk to your parents about this?"

"Mom's dead. Dad's . . . well . . ."

"Old man's a shit, huh?"

"Sorta." David smiled when he said it.

The man chuckled behind the glass. "You got friends?"

"Not really. They . . ." He thought of Dennis and Andrei sitting out in the car in the prison parking lot, waiting for him. Andrei, whom he'd picked up just days before, per Dr. Jacobson's orders. The one he'd freed. The one who'd killed that homeless dude last night. Kept hitting him with the hammer even after . . . "They're kinda bad."

"I hear you, man. I had the same, growing up. You know. Adopted, shitty dad, immoral friends, the whole nine yards . . ."

"I know."

The man studied him for a moment before speaking again. "Yeah? You seem to know a lot. You know Jesus Christ?"

"Not really."

"No?" The older David leaned forward. "*For whosoever shall call upon the name of the Lord shall be saved.'* You read the Bible?"

"No."

"Start. You're not alone, brother. God's servants are always facing the trials of this corrupt world. Jeremiah, John the Baptist, Paul . . .

we each endure tremendous suffering and temptation at the hands of the great enemy. Satan and all the evil spirits who wander through the world seeking the ruin of souls."

"Satan."

"Got lots of names."

"Cain."

The man smiled big again. "*And God said, What hast thou done, Cain? The voice of thy brother's blood crieth unto me from the ground.*' Sure . . . but it's not just murder, kid. All, and I do mean all, have sinned and come short of the glory of God. We're born with sin, each of us. And the price for that sin is death."

"Death . . ."

"But, David, the gift of God is eternal life through Jesus Christ, our Lord. We can turn away from sin and choose His greater Light. Always wish I'd learned this sooner."

"Do you really believe that?"

"Baby, I was once an iniquitous man addicted to pornography, a devil worshipper who studied Satanism, a slayer of Life who wandered the streets at night hunting pretty girls to execute. The Son of Sam."

"And now?"

"Son of Hope. '*With people this is impossible, but with God all things are possible.*'"

"If you could go back—"

"Can't." The man shook his head. "Can't, can't, can't. . . . But I . . . no. I'd surely find another way."

"Really?"

The man studied him again. Tilted his head as if recognizing something for the first time, but unwilling to accept it. "David . . ."

"Yeah?"

"Nothing," the older man said quietly. "It was nice, ahhh, meeting you. Good luck."

"You, too," David said.

CREDENTIALS

The address led to the home of Frederic and Wendy Albaum and their eleven-year-old adopted son, a few miles outside of town, halfway between an abandoned auto-parts store and the local cemetery. The two-lane country highway was called Pickerington Run by the locals, but the signs Castillo had followed read Route 28. The last car had passed more than fifteen minutes ago. A long dirt driveway ran up to the shadowed three-story farmhouse. It was night when Castillo and Jeff finally arrived, the darkness adding to the town's overall temper of barrenness and isolation.

He liked it. It reminded him of home. The trailer back in Thorough, New Mexico, shaded and lost at the foot of the Featherhold Mountains, the nearest neighbor an acre or more away on either side. And it reminded him of northern Iraq or parts of Pakistan: tranquil, boundless. Like, he imagined, walking alone through Eden. The whole world laid out by God as boundless scenery for solely one man. Castillo had paced off the perimeter of the house twice. Television light blushed through a second-floor side window, steady blooms of silver and blue against the closed curtain. The rest of the house appeared empty.

Lifeless. There were three cars in the driveway, each with Ohio plates. Nothing out of the ordinary.

He knocked at the front door. Nada. Rapped again harder. Glanced in both directions at the outlying neighbors. Nothing there either. No sounds within. Castillo was actually fine with that. All the possible scenarios he'd run through in case someone answered the door sounded absurd. *Excuse me, Mrs. Albaum, I was hoping you could answer a couple questions about your son's genetic makeup.* Or *Hi, Eddie. Curious. Ever jack off in the graveyard down the street?* Honestly, the real openings he'd come up with didn't sound much better.

He tried the door. Locked. Bolted, too. Castillo examined the front windows, chanced a peek inside. Nothing either. Thought about calling it a day. He'd simply head right back up the road into town and the Motel 6 where he'd stowed the kid. Get some sleep. Double-check some things with Stanforth. Follow up on Albert McCarty, the missing Delaware kid. Maybe visit the Albaums the next morning when . . .

But there *was* the giant snake, the effigy site, fifteen minutes away. And the Albaums. Who, upon further searching, had two sons registered in the local school system: Austin (age 17) and Edward (age 12).

And Jacobson's enigmatic notes were filled with data on a boy called Ed.

Jacobson, or DSTI, or whoever, could have doctored up the boy's birth records and whatnot easily enough. Something that would take less than thirty seconds and no more than a thousand dollars, if that, depending on how far up the operation went.

This had to be right.

Castillo backed away from the porch and followed the side of the house, keeping to the night's shadows. Several blowflies were fluttering in the back door's window.

This door was also locked but proved a cinch to crack. Castillo opened a gap.

The smell inside was immediate, faint, and too familiar.

Death.

Castillo drew his pistol.

•   •   •

On his bed, Jeff had laid out four sheets from the dozens Castillo had printed for him to study while he went out to check on the house.

Rich Ⓧ Ardson   Size ✕ More   H Ⓥ Owell   Gil 🐦 Ronan

The last names, if they were right about Albaum, were easy enough: Richardson, Sizemore, Howell, and Gilronan. But the stupid pictures were nothing but a big bunch of maybes. Jeff scanned Castillo's "Murder Map," searching for any town that made sense. But there were thousands. Castillo had told him to focus mostly along Route 50. Still, it was hundreds of possibilities. "Hundreds is better than thousands," Castillo had said when he'd left.

Five hours ago! Jeff eyed the room's small digital clock again. Castillo'd said he'd probably be gone awhile, but five hours? Had he found the boy? The clone? Had something bad happened? He refocused on the printouts. He'd made his own lists and notes next to each name and symbol, his blocky lettering right next to his fake father's scribbles. Beside Rich Ⓧ Ardson (was it a heart or a bow and arrow?), he'd written down everything from Bowmansville, PA, to Points, West Virginia, and Athens, Ohio. Then there was Hunter. Or Sherwood Forest? Or Center Point? Or maybe even Loveland? It was maddening. The bird could easily be Birdsville, Maryland, or the Baltimore Ravens, or Birdseye, Indiana. Maybe Odon, Indiana, because he had two ravens as messengers. But then Jeff crossed it out because Odin was spelled wrong. The other two symbols: something about a moon, and a bug with a hat? No clue. None.

And besides, even if he could figure it out: Then what?

More of the clones would be found.

For the first time he stopped to think: But then what? What happens to them?

And me?

He brushed the printouts aside and eyed Castillo's other files.

Castillo had left them in a pile on the chair on Jeff's side of the room. Almost like Castillo wanted Jeff to take a look. More and more, Jeff was starting to believe that everything Castillo did was part of some kind of test or plan. That there was a reason behind all of it. Jeff stood over the desk. His fingers ran over the same folder again. JD658726h56-54, it read on top. He'd already peeked inside. Jeffrey Dahmer/5. The one Castillo was after. Jeff had already flipped the folder open twice before. Enough to see the name. To see pictures of the boy he would soon become. Or was. Whatever else was within, he didn't know.

Didn't want to. And, at the same time, wanted to.

His eyes traced Castillo's book instead. Castillo kept it in his duffel bag, and Jeff had seen him reading it late at night when Castillo thought he was sleeping. Jeff riffled through its pages, curious. *The Grace of the Witch. The Beggar at the Manor.* He knew of *The Odyssey*, the Greek guy trying to get home and Lotus people and all of that, but he hadn't ever read it. Castillo had made little notes throughout in the book's margins. Underlined and bracketed stuff, too. A lot of the pages dog-eared. Jeff read one of the underscored passages:

```
I am a man of much grief, but it is not fit that
I should sit in another's house mourning and
wailing. It is wrong to grieve forever without
ceasing.
```

Then flipped to another, one Castillo had put a star next to:

```
Since it is not possible to elude the will of Jove
or make it vain, let this man go alone over the
barren sea.
```

Jeff wasn't sure what it meant, but he inspected some of the other marked passages.

```
To me, O stranger, thou appearest now a different
man from what thou wast before, thou hast other
```

```
garments, and thy complexion is no longer the
same. Thou art certainly one of the gods who
possess the whole of heaven.
```

Jeff closed Castillo's book, swung his eyes and hand to the folder again.

```
JD658726h56-54
```

He propped it open some. The first page was numbers and a picture. The numbers made no sense. The picture was . . . The picture was what he would look like if he was cool. Cool? He cleared space on the small desk and opened up the folder.

There were a lot of numbers. The next page. More numbers. Asymmetry scores, MMPI fmab, MAOA, karyotype levels. And so on. It meant nothing to Jeff. His heart weighed a thousand pounds. His hand was shaking. What would the next page reveal? He'd expected everything spelled out. Black and white.

THIS IS WHAT WE HAVE LEARNED ABOUT JEFF.

THIS IS HOW MUCH OF A KILLER JEFF REALLY IS.

THIS IS WHAT JEFF SAID ABOUT WANTING TO MURDER AND EAT PEOPLE.

There was none of that. Only more numbers. A person reverted to nothing more than a bunch of charts and graphs. No different, really, than a high school science class lab trying to figure out the pH levels of Ivory soap or the density of tomato juice. No more than Mendel and his stupid peas. He turned the pages over one after another. Nothing.

Until the second-to-last page. There, a few notes someone had typed. *His father?* Another one of the smiling shrinks at DSTI? Maybe it was Mrs. Jamieson. She was one of the smiliest shrinks they had up there. And apparently dead now.

```
need for stimulation/prone to boredom, lack of
realistic long-term goals
```

```
propensities to risk-taking behavior—promiscuous
sexual behavior? deprecating attitude toward the
opposite sex—likely homosexual, lack of interest
in bonding,
```

```
conning/manipulative, inclinations of excessive
boasting
```

```
Ritualistic behavior/OCD? how much alcohol
introduced? killed cat with bb gun. buried?
```

That was all. Then another page of numbers. Jeff turned back to the notes and looked for anything else to compare, or contrast, Jeffrey Dahmer/5 and himself, Jeffrey Dahmer/82. It did not say if the *other* Jeff had musical talent. But he only played bass and not particularly well. Maybe it meant nothing. *Or everything.* Jeff wondered if HE had any real long-term goals. Promiscuous sexual behavior? Stupid. He hadn't even kissed a girl yet. Or any guy either, for God's sake! He wondered if tapping his knee all the time was OCD. Or making sure his books were lined up in certain ways on the shelf. Or that he would never ever use the last bit of milk left in the jug but would pour it out into the sink. *Did that count?* He'd never killed an animal. But he'd found a snake once and picked it up with a stick. *Did that count?* He and the kid in this folder were genetically, physically, the exact same person. Beyond the blue eyes and blond hair, what else linked him to the original killer?

"Asshole," he cursed his father—*their* father—in the empty room.

He closed the folder, stuffed the whole thing down to the bottom of Castillo's pile.

Jeff crossed the room and retrieved his scattered notes from the floor and end of the bed. The last clue had led them straight to Serpent Mound and, probably, a clone in Ohio. He'd seen it almost immediately once he'd really thought about it. His dad had taken him there. He could remember walking up the high steel observation deck to look down upon the ancient burial mound. Of all the little pictures to draw, why that? Had his father known his adopted son would recognize it?

And Jeff thought, *Serpent Mound was on purpose. For me to figure out.*
And Jeff thought, *Maybe they all are.*
And Jeff thought, *Why?*
Something to ask later. If he ever got a chance.

The clone was named Edward Albaum.

Like the others, he'd been manufactured at DSTI. He was eleven years old. His family had been murdered. When Castillo found him, the boy was watching television.

There was a folder of information in the kitchen. Notes left behind by the others for Edward to study when he was ready. From the files, Castillo now knew that the Albaum boy's DNA had come from the brain tissue samples of Ed Gein. The name wasn't too familiar to most people, which was kind of surprising. Maybe because the name was so simple and ordinary; hard to remember. The actual guy, however, was far from simple or ordinary. Ed Gein's acts became the true-life inspiration of such horror-movie legends as Leatherface in *The Texas Chainsaw Massacre*, Norman Bates in *Psycho*, and Buffalo Bill in *Silence of the Lambs*—three of the most famous horror movies ever made. Period. All from one guy. How was that for monster credentials?

But Castillo knew that the movies didn't even share the whole truth. That the truth was too horrible, even for horror movies. Women dangling from meat hooks and necklaces strung with body parts. Skulls in the kitchen stained with vegetable soup and pudding. Suits of skin stitched from half a dozen bodies he'd dug out of a nearby graveyard. Reupholstered furniture of human skin, hearts in a pot in the kitchen, organs in the icebox . . . all the rest.

All the rest. Castillo was already tired of looking up the historical specifics. They always netted out to the same with these men, anyway. Mutilation. Necrophilia. Rape. Torture.

Pain. Fear. Death.

The detached freedom to do whatever they wanted, while also imprisoned by some Other inside that angrily demanded they act upon those same freedoms. It was a contradiction—an enslaved freedom.

This little monster sat on the couch where Castillo found him, waiting. Waiting for what, exactly, the boy had no clue. Neither did Castillo.

He'd simply make the phone call. "Found one. He's not one of the six." And then give the kid's address. DSTI would send people. After that . . . After that, who knew? Castillo only needed to get through the next couple hours.

He studied the boy. Cropped, dirty hair. The kid looked tired, like he'd done a couple weeks fighting beside the 7th Cavalry Regiment in Fallujah. His glossy eyes staring at ESPN on the television with little or no recognition of what they were really seeing.

For Ed Gein, aka Edward Albaum, it had been four days A.C.

After Cain.

After the others had arrived in his driveway, as they had elsewhere before, as they would somewhere again. After they'd burst from their car like trolls breaking free from beneath some bridge and raced up the steps into his family's house. Smashed his father's face with a golf club as teeth bounced and pinged off the living room wall. After they'd dragged his mother and big brother upstairs.

In an hour, Castillo'd managed to piece together most of what had happened.

After Cain.

Five boys. One of them dressed like a clown. A single carload of the most infamous serial killers in history on the ultimate road trip: Bundy, Lucas, Fish, Gacy, and Dahmer. But not the Dahmer waiting for Castillo back at the hotel room. The fifteen-year-old kid with glasses and a kind voice, another kid altogether. Cloning was funny that way. And these others had let this boy in on their little joke. They'd told young Ed—as they, themselves, had recently been told—who he was. How he'd been born. Built. That the man who'd been visiting him every six months for "games and tests" as an "education specialist" was actually a geneticist named Jacobson who'd been paying his parents fifty grand a year to keep their mouths shut about their nontraditional adoption and his visits. They'd even showed him the bloody naked woman they'd had in the trunk.

The five boys had left him with that information and then, as they'd been finished with the rest of his family, had gotten back into their car and driven off. Leaving him, for the first time, it seemed, to decide his own fate.

The first thing the boy had done was to cover his family's faces with open notebooks to hide their vacant, glassy gazes, the steadily graying skin. He'd emptied the pantry for food. Found cash in his mother's purse. Gotten himself up each morning for the last week of school. Afraid, he'd told Castillo, of where the police would put him if they knew his parents were dead. Afraid he'd be blamed. Afraid they'd make him live with strangers.

Afraid.

Castillo couldn't worry about that today. He wouldn't. He'd make the call, and in a couple of hours, the good doctors from DSTI would arrive. What happened then, where those men decided to reshuffle their eleven-year-old lab rat, was not his concern. It wasn't his mission. His mission was explicitly to apprehend these boys, them and their genetic brothers. To bring them back to DSTI. Back to the test tubes and computers. The neurochemical testing and mind games. Back to the lab where they'd each been made. And how long before they authorized other options if capture proved too problematic? He remembered his empty threats to Erdman about reporting them all if he suspected any mistreatment.

My mission.

What would they really do with these kids?

Make the phone call. *I found one.*

Me and Jeff.

After Cain.

AFTER MRS. NOLAN

Albert McCarty didn't really know what to do.

He was at a rest stop somewhere halfway up the New York turnpike. After Mrs. Nolan, he'd taken his mom's car and driven to Mike Gaffney's house to shoot him and his parents. But they weren't home. He'd waited for almost an hour, but he'd gotten bored and left. He didn't know where Adrienne Haller lived. And he sure as fuck hadn't felt like waiting for school the next day.

So he got on the highway and drove. North. He figured he'd go to Boston. Home of his father, the "Boston Strangler." Except Dr. Jacobson said the Boston Strangler guy wasn't his father at all. The Boston Strangler was him. *Him* him. It didn't make any sense really. No more sense than what he'd done to Mrs. Nolan, he supposed. Or what those kids Jacobson brought over had done to his mother. To his fake mother. *Whatever.*

Getting to Boston somehow *did* make sense. The question now was HOW. He wasn't stupid. The police would be looking for his mom's car eventually. There'd be, like, announcements up on the highway signs any minute. MISSING TEEN. DELAWARE LICENSE. TRE542.

KILLED THE NOLANS. GOT FREAKY WITH THE MILF TOO!

He needed another car. A car the police wouldn't be looking for. He'd never hitched a ride before. Seemed like it'd be easy enough. But he didn't want some pervert trucker picking him up. Making him suck dick or something weird. He had fifty-five dollars for gas and food and the gun with seven bullets. *Should be enough to get anywhere*, he figured. *But who to approach?* A family was probably best. His mom told him if he ever got lost, he should go to a family. It was safest. The irony was really fucking funny. *But which one?*

Albert sat atop one of the picnic tables, his feet up on the seat. The rest stop lights fully lit the night. He had a cold Mountain Dew and a half-eaten package of peanut M&M's he'd bought from the vending machines. Everyone assumed he was with one of the other families. Everywhere he looked was another to choose from. All afternoon and into the night, they kept coming in. Every shape and size. Some with babies. Some with a couple of teens who looked no different than he did. People on early summer vacations. Driving to the shore, or Grandma's, or whatever. *Now all I have to do is pick the right one and . . .* and what? Ask for a ride? Say I'm lost? Ask for help? Take the car at gunpoint? Wait for a single mom and stick the gun in her right tit and say *Drive, bitch, or I shoot your ugly kids?* Then he could do to her what he'd done with Mrs. Nolan. It wasn't as easy as it sounded.

He gulped down the rest of his Dew and tucked the candy in his pocket for later. He needed to drop a deuce. Or take a piss. Or something. Something *not* this. Albert trudged to the bathrooms again. He'd been trying to take a dump all day, couldn't. Ended up just beating the bishop every time. He looked over the other travelers again as he crossed the picnic area. By the time he got out, there'd be a whole new batch to pick from. He'd find a good one then. *This time, for sure.* He'd figure it all out then. He passed an old guy on his way into the bathroom. Even held the door open for him to let him pass by. "Thank you, sir," the old guy said. "Sure," Albert said, and smiled. He wanted to bust out laughing so bad. Inside, there were two guys taking a piss. They were talking like they knew each other, and Albert went past them to the second stall.

He got in and turned to lock the door. Dropped his pants and sat down. He hadn't taken a shit in almost three days. Too nervous or something. Or maybe too fucking pumped. *Whatever.* He listened as the other guys cleaned up outside by the sink, started the hand dryer, and laughed about something. He heard the bathroom door open and close again. The dryer kept going. Then silence. Peace and quiet. He tried to relax. Thought about jacking off again.

Then Albert saw the feet. The toes of two black boots in the space beneath the door, standing directly in front of his stall. Just stood there, still, lifeless. They could have been empty, like someone placed them there as a joke. . . . *A pair of pale green boots with no one inside them!* Like that Seuss book one of his day-care teachers had always read. He wondered if—

The guy outside was still staring straight at Albert's stall door.

Albert unfurled a handful of toilet paper and shifted in the seat to let the guy know someone was inside. Still the boots did not move.

The stall door rattled.

"Busy," Albert cried out.

Nothing. The boots did not move. And the door was shaking again. And now the bolt on the inside was clattering against the latch.

"Busy! *Occupado!*" Albert said more loudly. "Sorry, man."

Freaky. He could hear the guy breathing. Sniffing, almost. Like he had a cold or something. Like he was trying to smell what was inside. Albert felt for the gun in his jacket pocket. "Look, sorry, man," he said. "There are like three more stalls . . ." He'd decided to shoot the guy if he shook the door one more fucking time.

Still the black boots did not move. Albert fumbled in his jacket to free the gun.

The boots were gone.

He hadn't even seen them leave. He'd looked away for a second to mess with his jacket, and by the time he'd looked back, nothing.

Albert pulled his hand away from his jacket. Leaned back in the toilet seat. His eyes scanned the floor for the boots. He didn't see them anywhere. Didn't hear the guy moving around either. Didn't hear that weird breathing. "Screw this," he mumbled. Reached down to grab his pants.

That's when he noticed the shadow against the inside of the

bathroom stall. And, only then, recognized the sensation of someone standing close to him.

Albert looked up and had half a moment to figure out Who or Why or How someone was suddenly hovering at the top of the stall *above* him.

His bowels emptied quite easily then.

BLOOD TRAIL

JUNE 07, TUESDAY—CHILLICOTHE, OH

Jeff ate steadily but quietly, the uneasy silence between them amplified by the bustling diner. "You gonna eat your bacon?" he asked, eventually breaking the quiet.

Castillo looked up, collected himself. "No, go ahead."

The boy reached over to his plate and took the two slabs of half-cooked bacon. Castillo looked away as Jeff started stuffing the greasy meat into his mouth. He couldn't help but wonder what other slippery meats had once passed over those same lips. What gristle those sharp teeth had once chewed into. The same tongue savoring the taste of dead human flesh.

It wasn't fair, Castillo knew. This kid was not THE Jeffrey Dahmer. Not technically. *Nature/nurture, right? Hell, the rest of the world knew the boy only as Jeff Jacobson. This kid had never done a damn thing.* He stopped staring, stopped trying to think about it, and looked down at the road map beside his plate. He dropped a finger onto the map. "Unity, Ohio, and Lovett, Indiana."

Missing persons in Ohio, a couple of women. In Lovett, Indiana, two teens had been found hanging by chains from a tree. Both bodies soaked with gasoline and then burned. On CNN, the Lovett sheriff said he thought it was related to drug trafficking. Castillo didn't see it that way. He saw only the fresh blood. A fresh trail looking more and more like a straight line. "They're heading west," he said. He ran his fingers in a subtle squiggle across the map. Jeff didn't look up from his plate. "Route 50," Castillo added. "From what the Albaum kid could tell me, it looks like the original group picked up someone named John a couple of weeks before they came for him. John, he said, had been dressed like a clown."

"What?" Jeff asked.

"That's what he said."

Jeff retreated to his food.

"You know," Castillo pressed, "John Wayne Gacy was infamous for dressing up like a clown sometimes. A character named Pogo."

"I don't . . . I don't know who that is."

"John Wayne Gacy?"

Jeff shook his head.

"Did you ever meet a boy named John?"

Jeff ignored the question. Seemed not to have heard it.

Castillo tried again. "Did you ever meet a John?"

"Ever in my life?" Jeff stared at his plate. "Sure. Probably. A kid on my soccer team two years ago was named John Vincent. Does that count? But if you mean a John connected to Massey or DSTI . . . the clown kid? The *clone* kind? Then no."

Castillo glanced around their booth. "Let's keep it down a bit," he said. "Got it?"

"My bad," Jeff replied, then looked up and added in a whisper, "No, I don't think I ever met a John at Massey. I already gave you all the names I could remember."

"Fair enough. The Albaum boy said the clown was definitely named John and that a guy named Ted did most of the talking. But he couldn't remember the other names. When I tossed some names at him, he thought he remembered Al and Henry but wasn't sure. He was pretty positive he never once heard a *D* name."

"David and Dennis."

"Might not be with these guys."

"David wouldn't be."

"So you've said," Castillo replied.

"And my . . . Dr. Jacobson wasn't there, was he?"

"He was not with them."

Jeff used his fork to knock a piece of pancake back and forth on his plate. "What about Jeff?" he asked. "Did this kid run into a Jeff?"

Castillo looked straight at the boy. He wished they were both quiet again.

"Or"—Jeff laid the fork aside and looked up, noting Castillo's discomfort—"are we just supposed to pretend you're not looking for a Jeffrey Dahmer clone?"

"I am," Castillo said. "The boy wasn't sure if he'd heard that name or not. He did, since you ask, remember a tall blond guy."

Jeff thought about this. "So, what happens to him now?"

"Albaum? He's halfway to Pennsylvania. Back to DSTI."

"What happens to him now?"

"I don't know."

"They're just gonna kill him."

"Fuck off. Why the hell would you even say that?"

"I told you. My dad said they'd kill me if they ever caught me. Now they have this kid."

"Well, Daddy ain't thinking too clearly these days, is he? I'm sure the kid'll be fine."

"Are you?"

Castillo sipped his coffee. It had grown cold.

"How long before you turn me over to them?" the boy asked.

"They don't even know you're with me."

"But they know I exist. You'll need to turn me in eventually."

"You're helping me do my job."

"And when I can't? Or won't?"

"Don't know. Guess I'll decide then."

Jeff nodded again. Castillo's matter-of-factness had taken the steam out of his growing anger. There was nothing left to say, really.

"Here's what I know," Castillo said to change the topic. "Based on what the Albaum kid says, I think a couple guys split off, together or alone. Guys like David, maybe. I think Jacobson . . . I think your father has also gone on alone."

"I think that, too," said Jeff.

"It's this group heading west I'm most worried about." Castillo ran his finger along Route 50. "There are murders and disappearances all over the country, but if I wanted to draw a straight line down Route 50 today, I finally could. *This*," he tapped the map, "this is the fresh game trail. You ever gone hunting?"

"Isn't that what we're doing now?"

Castillo made a noise that sounded like a laugh but wasn't. He reached for his cold coffee. "You figure out any more of your dad's notes?"

"Maybe. I think the bird might be Hitchcock, Indiana."

"*The Birds*. Like the Hitchcock movie?"

"One of his biggies. My father and I watched it together one night. He said it was a classic I should probably know. He made popcorn."

"Go on."

"I think the monkey is Salem, Illinois."

"What monkey?" Castillo pulled out his phone to thumb through the images.

"The monkey with the graduation cap."

"Is that what this thing is? And Salem? Why isn't he wearing, like, a witch's hat?"

"Salem, *New Hampshire*, is a small town where Scopes went to high school."

"Scopes."

"The Scopes Monkey Trial."

"Uh-huh. And how the hell would you know that?"

"The guy who prosecuted Scopes in court, the William-Jenner-Bryan guy, he spoke at Scopes's high school graduation. This was, like, ten years before the trial. Just coincidence. Still, Bryan claimed later he remembered Scopes in the audience and that he was all laughing and being a jerk and stuff."

Castillo leaned back. "I repeat . . ."

Jeff shrugged. "My dad was a scientist. What 'the hell' do you think we talked about?"

"Your dad's still a scientist. You think these pictures might be clues just for you?"

The boy shrugged again, and Castillo mirrored the move perfectly.

Jeff smiled. "Anyhow, Salem, Illinois, is on Route 50."

"What about the other pics?" Castillo asked.

"Nothing." The boy shook his head. "I need more time and . . . and maybe it would help if you update the, um . . ."

"The 'Murder Map'? As soon as we get back to the car. We'll follow it west. Hitchcock. Salem. Worst case, we're wrong and can cross off another town. On the way, I wanna stop at that park outside McArthur. Maybe find something. Was just told, though not released publicly yet, a pair of witnesses say they saw some teens there that day. Nice job, man."

Jeff looked up again. The question he wanted to ask next suddenly became clear to both of them.

What about my dad? What about going after my dad instead?

He didn't ask. And Castillo was glad.

"Hey," Jeff said instead. "Is it OK if I order a slice of pie or . . . ?" His face was already wet and shiny with bacon grease.

For a moment, Castillo thought it was blood.

"Sure," Castillo said, looking away.

dependent variable n.

(1) Two related variables that are dependent on each other are known as dependent variables. The variables that are free to roam are known as independent variables. The independent variable and dependent variables are plotted against each other in a two-dimensional graph when carrying out a scientific experiment. The vertical axis of the graph is used to plot the dependent variable.

(2) a variable whose value is consequent on change in the independent variable. The dependent variable is always the response or reaction to the independent variable. Also called *criterion variable*.

> *Easy is the word that I shall say*
> *and put in thy mind.*
> *Those who are dead*
> *shall draw near the blood,*
> *and there shall speak the truth.*
>
> THE ODYSSEY

GETTING CLOSER

Goebel Park. Days before, a mother and her two children had, it was believed, vanished here. The cops and volunteers with all their accompanying dogs and helicopters and news vans and Ohio University ROTC guys had, for now, vanished with them. Four days after the disappearance and still hours before daybreak, it was only Castillo and Jeff here. Even the woman's abandoned SUV had long since been towed away.

"What you looking for?" Jeff asked in the dark.

"Don't really know."

Jeff watched Castillo as the man stood alone in the vacant picnic area. The guy hardly moved, and almost vanished in the night's shadows himself, staring at different parts of the park. *Maybe he's totally nuts*, Jeff thought. *Why should he be any different?* Guy never slept. Like ever. He stayed up until three in the morning and was up again before sunbreak. It was totally weird. And the few times he had actually slept. *WTF?*

It'd happened twice now. The first time, Jeff thought he'd imagined it. But now . . . just the night before, Castillo'd woken up totally screaming. The most god-awful sound Jeff had ever heard, and his first thought had been to bolt out the motel room door, but he'd been too terrified to move. Afraid Castillo would jump up and shoot him, or snap his neck. So he'd lain as still as possible, pretending to be already dead. All the while, he'd been able to feel the guy staring at him in the dark.

Eventually Castillo had settled back into bed, his face to the wall away from Jeff, but the Army assassin had literally been trembling. This UFC-built badass with the guns, tats, scars all over, and amazing staredown. *Trembling in fear*. In the darkness, Jeff had been able to hear the guy's breathing going a hundred miles a minute, and it had gone like that for a good hour. Funny thing was, you'd think someone would never have been able to sleep again after hearing something like that. But Jeff'd ended up sleeping soundly for the first time since he'd left home; since his old life. Because it was the very first time he'd thought of Castillo as "normal." As human.

Not like me, Jeff thought now.

He drifted away from the empty swings and Castillo with deliberately slow steps, hopefully away from his own thoughts.

"Keep close," Castillo cautioned. "We're outta here in a minute."

Jeff nodded, stopped to shove the swing bridge that connected the two halves of the huge wooden castle swing set. Watched it sway back and forth in the darkness. Cozy midsummer wind snaked through the thick grass, surrounding him. He heard night bugs chittering. And frogs maybe. Or an owl.

Or the ghosts of a mother and her two children screaming.

Castillo said the witnesses who'd seen teens had been swept aside and that, instead, the woman's husband had been brought in for questioning.

Castillo also said a boy had been found murdered in Vincent, Ohio. That this guy was sixteen (*like me*), played varsity volleyball, and caddied at Pinehill Golf Club. His name was Howell. Rick Howell. Students from his school were crying and stuff on TV, saying what a supernice kid he was. No one understood why someone would beat a person like that to death.

But none of them had seen his father's notes. Like he had.

They didn't know Richard Howell was the clone of some guy named Richard Ramirez, the Night Stalker, a guy who'd murdered and raped, like, a dozen families or something. Would his classmates still be crying and carrying on if they'd known *that*? If they knew the truth?

H Powell.

The Starry Night. Van Gogh's most famous painting. Jeff's dad had taken him to see it at a van Gogh exhibition at the Museum of Modern Art in New York.

VINCENT van Gogh. Vincent, Ohio. *Really?*

Yes, Jeff answered himself. *Really.*

Another clue just for me. As if he was the one who was supposed to stop any of this single-handedly. *Or, maybe,* Jeff thought, *is it to help free the others?* Were he and his dad supposed to be together even now, unleashing teenaged serial killers onto the world?

Then why'd he leave me? And why won't he see me?

Jeff looked back, found Castillo preoccupied with the empty gravel parking lot. "A minute" was clearly going to become five or ten, though he knew Castillo wanted to get in and out as soon as possible. No telling when all the others might return.

With Castillo clearly lost to his own thoughts, Jeff wandered farther away, bearing toward a small skate park down the pathway. Eager to truly free his own mind. Of everything.

No such luck.

Whether Imagination, Fear, Exhaustion, or Insanity—maybe all of the above—he didn't know. He knew only that the New Truth had been lurking in the darkness waiting for him. Waiting to show him things.

By the time he got back to Castillo, he was surprisingly calm again.

Castillo gave him some shit for wandering off, but not much—probably saw something in Jeff's face that said leave it alone—and then they were back on the road again.

"Was it them?" asked Jeff.

"Don't really know."

"Yeah, you do." Jeff closed his eyes and tried to sleep. Not that there was much difference. His nightmares had all entered the real world anyway.

ROAD TRIP

The car held five comfortably.

Al did most of the driving, said it was relaxing. This, coming from a guy who'd tried jamming a couple needles into his gouche to see what it felt like. (Like his original had. It was ALL in his new book.) Ted always rode shotgun: Liked to hog the radio, could never settle on a song for too long, and followed their journey on the map with each town they passed. "Butlerville," he'd announce with some secret satisfaction only he understood. "Vernon is next." Henry sat in the back with Jeff and John. They kept the nurse tied in the trunk.

The car's AC was cranked and the windows down unless they were hot-boxing. (They'd gotten a bunch of pot from that Emily girl.) The new Avenged Sevenfold CD was in the player. The floorboards were covered with candy wrappers, crumpled Taco Bell bags, a couple of empty beer cans. (All bought with money they'd taken from her mom.) Henry smiled in memory. Emily had thought she'd be joining them after serving up her sister and mom like that. (And she had, for a whole day almost.) Because this girl thought she was the shit, someone important now. Like them. (And the stupid hole was wrong on every count.) He'd kept asking Ted all day if he could kill her. Eventually, Ted had let him help.

Indiana rushed by. No particular destination anymore. There was this one kid about an hour away and another near St. Louis who they were supposed to free. And it wasn't nothing to stop, he figured. More stuff to see. More fun to have. But everyone else wanted to get west now. California. Everyone in a fucking hurry. See the Pacific. Buy more pot. Maybe find one of those porn stars to party with.

Or even, Henry thought, looking down at his new book, try and visit some old stomping grounds in Texas. The home of the *original* Henry. The same places *he'd* once lived and killed.

Maybe Ted and the others were right. Maybe they'd done enough. Counting the ones Jacobson had helped with, they'd already sent half a dozen clones scattering into the four winds. Though Henry figured most hadn't gotten very far. A couple of the kids looked weak as shit, just didn't have it. Not that he saw. Hell, they'd killed that one kid themselves: Ricky Howell, the "Night Stalker" clone. *Total fucking pussy.* Some seemed down, though. Like John, the guy they'd picked up in Maryland with Jacobson. Pulled together the goofy clown suit like his predecessor had made so infamous. *Funny.* Version 2.0 had only killed four. *So far . . .* Yeah, he was happy they'd taken John along. Kind of nice knowing there were others out there. *Like us.* He thought about the Albert kid, one of the first they'd visited. Jacobson talked to the boy while they'd raped and murdered his mom in the next room. He and Ted did. *Fucked up.* It wasn't the kid's real mom, though. She'd been a phony. Just like *all* their moms. A fucking EMPLOYEE. Got a fucking paycheck to play mommy. Basically, Jacobson said she'd been paid to hurt the kid. *Bitch totally deserved it. They all did, really.* His own mom came to mind. Eventually, he'd head back east. . . . So, yeah, most of the other guys, the ones on the gay-ass list Jacobson had given to them—to Ted, actually, if he was being honest—had been freed. Mission accomplished. Mostly. A couple more left, if they felt like it. But fuck it. The other guys, even Ted, had had enough of that same old routine, driving up to houses and fucking with people. Deciding if some kid was worth killing or keeping. Basically tired of doing Jacobson's chores. *Seriously, fuck him. If he wants the shit done, he can do it himself.* That seemed to be the consensus.

Henry closed his eyes. Tried to rest. *Now, San Francisco . . .* THAT Jacobson chore they were all still into. July fourth. God Fuck America. Just pop that can's tab and watch the fun when the whole crowd went crazy. Started ripping each other apart and shit. *Totally gonna fuck some bitches up then.* He wondered if they could wait that long. If *he* could wait that long . . . but, there again, that was Jacobson's shit. Jacobson would totally get credit for those piles of dead people. *Not me.*

"They named a highway after me." He looked around again.

"Who did?" snapped Ted from the front seat.

"Cops did." Henry held up his new book. "Some highway in Texas. He dumped, like, a hundred bodies there. Pretty cool, yeah?"

Ted eyed the book, shook his head. "Stop reading that shit."

"Jealous?"

"*Encyclopedia of Serial Killers*? You're fucking retarded. Nothing but a bunch of ancient history. That guy, the one they named the highway for, that guy is probably dead and buried fifty years ago. HE killed a hundred people. You didn't. They ain't named shit for you."

"Whatever."

"You guys gotta stop obsessing over old files and those queer true crime books. Getting chubbies for shit you didn't even do. And this guy . . ." Ted pointed. "You and that clown outfit."

"I thought you liked it," John said. He seemed genuinely hurt by Ted's criticism.

"Dude, I love it. It's funny as shit and scares the fuck out of the moms, but it ain't you. I'm just sayin' it gets in the way of you figuring out you're not *that* John Wayne Gacy. You are *the* John Wayne Gacy. Get it?"

"No."

"Man . . . ," Al laughed, looking over nervously, "I . . . I never know what the fuck you're talking about."

John looked around. "The little kids like the suit. I like it. I thought you—"

"Then fuckin' wear it," Ted spat. "I really don't give a shit anymore. Assholes."

Henry retreated to his book. Opened up to a page and stared dreamily at the little black lines on the paper. Maybe it was time to finally cut loose. To ditch the others once and for all and finally go his own way. Forget California. Forget July fourth. Probably wouldn't even go down. They were bound to get caught eventually, traveling together. How long could the cops ignore a guy in a bloody clown suit buying gorditas and Mexican pizzas at the drive-through? Maybe he'd fucked up. Maybe they should have kept the Emily girl around a bit longer. And killed Ted instead, maybe. Emily, at least, had been up for anything.

So had Stacey. Nurse Stacey had always liked him best. Maybe the two of them could take off together. Get another car maybe. Go to Texas together. Fuck like mad. Bet she could fix his arm, too. Basically, there was something growing on it. Looked like a bunch of tiny little blisters grouped together. Most of the time, it just looked like dirt. But when he picked at it, it oozed like a popped zit. The stuff inside brown and kinda thick. Not like a zit at all. Nasty. It had started a couple days ago as a cluster of dark bumps on his lower left wrist but was spreading up his forearm a little bit.

Maybe he'd call Jacobson real fast. Ted and John both had his new number. And Jacobson always knew what stuff was, and what meds to take. He kinda wanted to talk to Jacobson anyway. About the shit that they'd been doing. But the other guys, Ted mostly, said to forget about Jacobson. They didn't need him.

Henry ran his fingers over the dark growth.

He wondered how David and Dennis were doing. They'd gone east. New York. Jersey. Boston. Promised Jacobson to pick up a couple of other guys there. *Maybe I should have gone with them instead*, he thought. "Maybe they'll name *this* highway for me," he said.

No one had heard.

"Name this highway for me," he said louder. "Route 50."

Ted laughed. "What the fuck for?"

"We could stop for a little bit, you know. Maybe have some more fun."

"Don't wanna stop. What kinda fun?"

"Best kind," Henry replied. "Fucking people up."

"Maybe, maybe. OK. Now you're talking, YOLO man. That's the

shit I wanna hear. Stop living in the past, pussies. This is *our* time now. Our life. Someone wake Jeff up."

"What about that house?" Al said.

"Which?"

All their voices had become one voice.

"There. With the swing set."

They could see the small farmhouse clearly from Route 50, though it would take a couple back roads to reach.

"You and the fucking swing sets," Ted said, and grinned. "Five miles to Barnhill. What's the vote, mentlegen?"

John squeezed his clown nose and made a HONK HONK sound with his blood-crusted mouth.

"Yeah." Henry's eyes and thoughts focused on the distant house. "That'll do nicely."

"Okay," Ted agreed. "Let's have some more fun."

NIGHTMARES SHARED

The rest of Ohio and eastern Indiana passed in a blur of fields, one-church towns, and Dairy Queens. Castillo drove like the devil was chasing them, but it was the other way around. It was newly morning. An hour or so down this same highway, there'd been a holdup a few days before. Couple of teens, a boy and a girl, tortured and killed behind the store. And on the wire this morning: the two missing Ohio women was now an apartment complex with three or four murdered. One of them purportedly chopped up. Another woman. Emily-something, Collins, still missing, *and* the main suspect. And *two* hours down the road, if Jeff was right, there was a teenaged clone of a famous serial killer living in Hitchcock, Indiana. It was, Castillo mused, quite the stretch of highway. Offering answers or only more questions.

Kristin called as they passed through somewhere called Loogootee, her number flashing on the cell's screen like a living thing. Castillo eyed Jeff in the seat next to him. The kid seemed preoccupied, lost to the monotony. "Hey," Castillo answered. "You find something new?"

"Nope," Kristin replied. "It's . . . It's been a couple days. I wanted to see how you were doing."

"Everything's fine."

"Wasn't asking about 'Everything.' I was asking about you."

"Are we on the clock now? This going in my little folder?"

"I'm asking as a friend."

"Well, that's very kind of you."

"And it's an enormous folder, by the way. The biggest Staples had."

"Naturally."

"Asshole."

"Yes."

"How much longer, Castillo?"

"Don't know."

"What can I do?"

"Probably done too much already."

"Probably. What else?"

"I don't know. Maybe check in every few days and ask how I'm doing."

She laughed, but it was a sad sound, full of regret and rumination.

He needed to change gears quick, to talk about something, anything, without the thoughts of what might have been. "Tell me," he said, his reflections shifting back to the day's latest discoveries. "Would a girl run with these guys? By choice, I mean? I've got two, maybe three women at least who may be involved in this. Not sure if they're victims or . . ."

"Superfreaks? Sure. Why?"

"I don't know. Some info this morning I got. Been wondering some if these women are victims or maybe even accomplices somehow. Would help if I knew even that much."

"It's hard to tell. The dirty truth is most women have *some* level of hybristophilia. It's a common psychological condition of arousal or attraction to individuals who commit crimes. Sometimes it's called 'Bonnie and Clyde Syndrome' for Bonnie Parker. Again, it comes in a thousand flavors and degrees, from SKGs, which is our abbreviation for serial killer groupies, to full-blown accomplices."

"Groupies?"

"It's a fact. As many lonely women sign up for Writeaprisoner.com as Match.com. These men are both the little boy you want to mommy and the bad boy you want to . . . well, you know. And, as a bonus, you know exactly where your man is on a Friday night. Locked safely behind bars. You've heard of Ted Bundy?"

Castillo could not help himself and snorted back his laugh. "Yes" was all he said.

"Bundy confessed to killing, what, thirty women, and he received *hundreds* of letters each and every month from girls across the country. Visited by dozens of them. Married one within a year. Henry Lee Lucas, another one of these guys, had only one eye and killed two hundred people. He also had hundreds of female admirers and also got married in prison. Gacy was overweight and gay, and even he got fan mail from girls every day and married a woman while in prison. The Night Stalker, Richard Ramirez . . ."

Richard Ramirez. Rick Howell. The boy murdered in Vincent, Ohio, two days ago. Apparently played varsity volleyball and caddied and . . . "I know that name also," Castillo replied.

"He raped and murdered twenty women, and there were lines of suitors outside the courthouse every day to see him. *Lines*. During the trial, one woman sent him a cupcake on Valentine's Day with the message 'I love you.' Want the punch line?"

"Do you have to ask?"

"That woman was on the jury."

"Jesus," Castillo breathed. He imagined the two girls still hanging with those motel assholes back in Pennsylvania. "That's fucked up."

"Maybe not. They've done several studies on orangutans and gorillas, and the most violent males in the group always get the most ass. It's a biological fact."

"You implying we're no better than monkeys?"

"I didn't run the tests, so no. But everybody knows girls always secretly like the bad boys best."

"And serial killers are as bad as it gets."

"I guess."

"Hybristophilia . . . incredible."

"Still a quick study, I see."

"Have to be. Or people die."

"Yeah." A long pause again. "Anything else?"

"Not that I can think of now."

"You know my number. Take care of yourself also, Castillo."

"Later." He hung up and laid the phone on the dashboard.

"Who was that?" Jeff asked.

"Don't worry about it." Castillo glanced at him. "What's that you're working on?"

Jeff tucked the list away. "Don't worry about it."

Castillo shook his head. "Fair enough."

After a moment, Jeff spoke again. "A list of states I've seen so far. License plates. The last car was Indiana, but it looked weird, so . . ."

"So, how many you got?"

Jeff pretended not to hear, and Castillo drove in absolute silence for another couple miles.

"Thirty-two," Jeff said. "Who is she?"

"She who?"

"Girl on the phone."

"A friend who knows a thing or two about how the mind works."

"What'd she tell you?"

Castillo said, "Thirty-two? Not bad for these back roads."

"I started in Jersey. What'd she say?"

She said once you were the worst of them all. And that the evil inside you was almost off the charts.

Castillo raised his brows, staring at the road ahead. "She said the world's a curious place."

"Oh." Jeff nodded, then asked, "What was your nightmare about?"

Castillo's hands reflexively tightened on the wheel. "What the fuck are you talking about?"

"You screamed the other night. Back in the motel when we were sleeping."

Ah, shit. "Did I?" He half remembered doing so, but . . . "I don't . . . nothing." Half remembering was enough. He grimaced. *You REALLY want to know, kid?*

He could tell that Jeff wanted to say something more. "What? What is it?"

"I have them too sometimes," the boy said.

"What? Nightmares? Good for you. You, me, and everyone else."

"Yeah, OK. Mine are kinda different, I think . . ."

Something cold twisted in Castillo's abdomen. Something primal. *No, no, no.* "OK. I don't really want to—"

"Mine happen in the daylight sometimes. Or, like, well, maybe stuff right before I fall asleep."

Despite himself, Castillo looked over. "What kinda stuff? You tell me 'I see dead people,' I'm gonna kick your ass right out of the fucking car."

"Nothing. I don't know. Nothing." Jeff's voice trailed off, his last thoughts held private after consideration. Fine by Castillo. The last thing he wanted to know about was the images rolling around in this creepy kid's head.

I dreamed about YOU, Jeff. Is that what you want to hear?

The cold knot in Castillo's gut tightened, still stronger than the guilt that came on its heels.

"How'd you get that?" Jeff asked.

Castillo glanced over again. The boy was pointing at the scar that ran the length of Castillo's arm. "Fishing," he replied. "Dude, take a nap or something."

"You want me to drive awhile?"

Castillo watched the road, half smiled. "No, thank you."

"So . . . ," Jeff asked again. "How'd you get it?"

"War." Castillo fixed his sleeve to hide the scar better.

"How?"

"Someone cut me."

"What about the others?"

He meant the other scars. They'd roomed together long enough now. Jeff had certainly seen them. "Yeah. Those too."

"Did you get the guy who did it to you?"

Castillo adjusted the rearview mirror a fraction.

"Did you?"

"No. Yeah. I don't know. But I think so, yes. I got rescued. Don't remember much."

"What's it like?"

Being tortured? Being meat? "What?" Castillo prompted.

"War?"

"War's hell."

"That's just a cliché."

"Well, it's a good one."

"What's it really like?"

"You going to war?" Castillo asked.

"No."

"Then what you askin' for?"

Jeff retreated to his window.

"Loud," Castillo answered. "It's mostly loud."

"Did you . . . did you kill anyone?"

"Original fuckin' question."

"Did you?"

"Shut up."

Jeff shifted in his seat, looked out the window at the car they'd passed. "What do you suppose they're doing with Ed right now?"

"Who? The Albaum kid? No clue. Told you before: He's not my job anymore." Castillo reached for the radio. Behind a chain-link fence, several children waved at them as they passed. "He's DSTI's job now."

"Perfect," Jeff said, waved back at the kids. "Then I'm sure he's doing great."

Castillo didn't reply, turned up the radio.

They drove another twenty miles without speaking.

Castillo imagined the nightmares the kid might have been having. Could only guess at what was in the boy's mind and hope he was guessing wrong. He tried fast to think of other things.

His own nightmares had changed. In the past, they were always about the boy, Shaya, or The Cave. Being back in the cave. But now this new one—two, maybe three times. In the past week. And it didn't help that the cause was always sitting a foot away. That the cause slept across the room from him each and every night.

He thought again of simply pulling over on the side of the highway and cutting the kid loose. Or making the call and turning Jeff Jacobson over to DSTI. Surely that would end the dreams. Would end the issue of having to lie to Stanforth every time they spoke. Of having to lie to Kristin.

But he couldn't. Not today. Not yet. Jeff actually had some good info, some good ideas. They were less than twenty miles away from a home that could have a clone in it, who was likely a target. If this lead panned out, he had no doubt the Jacobson kid could figure out some more of his fucked-up father's doodles. Figure out where more of these kids were.

More important, Jeff Jacobson was his good-as-gold insurance policy. If anyone ever got too squirrelly, from Stanforth to Erdman, if he ever felt a screw job coming, he had the boy. Leverage. An actual clone of Jeffrey Dahmer, paid for, in part, by the United States military. WikiLeaks or Rachel Maddow would sure have some fun with that. The mission had already gone too dirty for things not to get worst-case soon. *How soon?* Would he have enough time to dig back out?

He glanced over at the boy. Jacobson stared straight ahead, eyes half closed to the midday sun. His hand hung partway out the window, making tiny waves in the wind outside.

In the new dream, Jeffrey stood over Castillo's bed, his face continually morphing between the kid riding shotgun and the other man Castillo knew only from the file photos. The first Jeffrey Dahmer. The man who'd murdered, raped, and partially eaten at least seventeen men. The killer who'd infamously admitted, "I bite." That face blending with the boy's. Both faces were always slick with dark, dripping blood.

In the new dream, Castillo could never move. Could not look away as the inhumanly oversized teeth eventually widened, stretched even longer, and then sank deep into his flesh. He could only scream and pray it was solely a dream again. That he would wake. That the monster sleeping in the same motel room each night, hardly ten feet away, had not finally revealed its true self.

I bite.

"Got Alabama?" Castillo asked and nodded to the car they were passing.

"Thirty-three!" the monster beamed.

LIKE LIONS

Jeff waited in the car while Castillo went to check on the clone.

The Sizemore family lived on 7422 Oldegate Lane, but Castillo had parked the car a couple blocks away.

Hitchcock, Indiana, looked like anywhere else to Jeff. The same houses and fences and trees and dogs and families as any other town. All alike, except maybe for one. According to his fake father's notes, maybe one family in Hitchcock had a son who'd been cooked up in a lab. Maybe one family in Hitchcock was raising the clone of Gary Ridgway, the "Green Valley Killer," who'd murdered almost a hundred women in the Northeast during the '80s and '90s. Maybe one family'd been paid to molest the kid. Or to encourage him to drink. Maybe one family'd been paid to leave him alone. Or maybe one family had not clue one where this kid had really come from. Or maybe the bird pic in his father's lunatic notes had nothing to do with Alfred Hitchcock at all. Probably Jacobson hadn't wanted his freak son to ever help solve ANYTHING.

It'd been almost a whole week. Jeff could hardly wrap his head around it. It was clear there wasn't another person on earth who wondered where he'd gotten to. Not a single person. *His* name wasn't in the papers. No one was searching for *him*. His own dad didn't even care where he was. *What kind of life is this?* And to Castillo he was another dirty piece of the grand damn experiment. Another clone freak. Something to hunt and capture. Something to turn over to DSTI when it was time. No different than any of the other kids from the facility. *No different at all.* In the name of science. For the betterment of man. Etcetera. Etcetera. To understand what caused aggression, violence, evil. Isolate it. Cure it. Control it. Then to one day unleash it again.

The Cain Gene.

Is it really just a matter of the chromosomes and enzymes floating around our blood?

If so, Jeff wasn't stupid. He'd read enough Warhammer books and watched enough Syfy Channel and Jason Bourne movies to get the big picture. *"Imagine Greater."* Ha! Well, he could easily imagine biological weapons that would infect the enemy with a murderous rage. Or provisional injections to boost aggression and strength in battle-fatigued troops. No wonder the Department of Defense was running the show.

And where, exactly, does Castillo come in? That was still a mystery to Jeff. The guy clearly worked for DSTI and the government. But he also kept a clone of Jeffrey Dahmer hidden in his motel room. At first, he'd figured Castillo'd brought him along only to fill in some of the info gaps. But he had most of that now and was still dragging Jeff along. Sure, there were a couple more notes to figure out, but there was something else. As far as Jeff knew, Castillo hadn't told anyone about him yet. *Why?*

Castillo appeared around the corner, walked casually toward the car.

Jeff sat up as Castillo got in and started the car to pull away. "Sorry," Jeff said.

"For what?" Castillo frowned. "You just found another clone."

"What if someone comes?" Jeff asked in the darkness. "A Realtor or someone?"

"They won't." Castillo carried in a recently purchased foldout chair and a bag of groceries. There'd been two empty houses to choose from. One was directly across the street from the Sizemore house. The other was down the street on an adjacent cul-de-sac. FOR SALE! REDUCED

PRICE! Castillo set the food down. "I love this housing market," he said, setting the chair by the window. "Sometimes we'd have to commandeer a house for a base." He peered out the window onto the neighborhood below. "I was half prepared to do that here, too," he added.

He'd waited until two in the morning and broken into the home on the cul-de-sac. Empty, furniture removed, the last owners long since moved on. And, as Castillo surmised, its top-right bedroom window looked out perfectly over Oldegate Lane.

"Here," he said, turning and reaching into the food bag, and tossing Jeff a thick paperback.

"What's this?"

"You said you were a reader."

Jeff turned the novel over. Something by some guy named Follett.

"Sorry," Castillo said, positioning his chair. "Unless you wanted romance, that's all they had. Closest thing to a fantasy book I saw."

Jeff studied the back cover. "Thanks," he said.

Castillo watched him, looked like he wanted to say something, then turned to look out the window. "So, here we are," he said.

Jeff walked over behind the chair. "What now?" he asked.

"Now? Ever seen a lion hunting a zebra on the Discovery Channel?"

"Sure," Jeff said.

"Now we're lions," Castillo said and settled back in his chair.

Being a lion proved boring.

It had been two days of *nothing to do*. They never, ever left the house. Just sat and watched another house. Castillo never talked. Jeff slept on the floor in the upstairs room behind Castillo and his chair. They ate peanut butter sandwiches and cold hot dogs together in silence. Jeff tried reading the book Castillo'd bought him. It was actually pretty good, because it had stuff about the Hundred Years War and witches and the plague. But it was also, like, a thousand pages, and it made him sleepy. He spent time mostly wandering through the empty house. Tried imagining what the family who'd lived here was like. What furniture had been in each of the now-empty rooms? Were they a normal family with a mom and dad and kids? Or one like his? He explored each room, running his fingers across bare walls where once there'd been hanging pictures and knickknacks, their phantom outlines bound in muted stains. What had the pictures shown? he wondered. His own room back in Jersey had been turned into a space as empty and ghostlike. He took watch a couple hours each day so Castillo could get some sleep. Staring out a window at a house where nothing ever really happened was easy. Once they'd seen the mom drive out to do some food shopping. Big thrill, right? Once he'd seen the boy, little Gary Sizemore, play basketball in the driveway for a bit. Another freak his father had made.

Castillo said that according to the U.S. Department of Health and Human Services, 45 percent of adoptions in the United States occurred through private arrangements. That was about seventy thousand babies a year trading hands that no one really knew anything about.

Kids like me. How easily it might have been *him* Castillo was now watching. Adopted out to some unsuspecting family. Maybe even a family that was paid to abuse him. Jeffrey *Sizemore*. And how easily the Gary kid could have ended up as Gary Jacobson. All these little clone babies. It was nothing more than a dozen cosmic coin flips.

Jeff watched Castillo awhile, frozen half asleep at his post by the window. Guy was never really asleep. "Wanna know how Dolly got her name?" Jeff asked him across the darkened room.

Castillo shook his head.

"Do you even know who Dolly is?"

"Nope."

"Liar."

"Yup." Castillo sighed. Half smiled. "OK, how'd Dolly get her name?"

"The scientists made her from a cell that'd been taken from another sheep's mammary. *Mammary*'s a fancy word for 'breasts,' and there was this country singer named Dolly Parton who was basically famous for having really big breasts. So the scientists called the sheep Dolly."

"So," Castillo said as he turned, "the most significant experiment of the last hundred years, the scientific advancement which brought man closer to God than any other before or since . . . was a tit joke."

"Yeah," Jeff said. His back was against an empty wall, his legs out straight. "They're never gonna come, you know."

"Never's a long time," said Castillo. "It'll probably be less than that. Patience."

"Waste of time."

"Not if we're right. If *you're* right. All I know is there's a thirteen-year-old kid named Sizemore a hundred yards away. Kid who doesn't look a damn thing like his parents. These guys went to Delaware, and Ohio, and Indiana. They've got the exact same list we do."

"My dad's list? Yeah. You know anything about Mendel?" Jeff asked.

"Didn't he have really big tits?"

Jeff laughed. "Nooooo."

"Sure he did. The pea guy, right?"

"After peas, he worked on some plant called hawkweed."

"You and your dad ever talk about the Phillies?"

"Not even once. So, this famous biologist in Germany read Mendel's paper on peas and wrote to him, said he's gotta give this hawkweed stuff a try. The guy was, like, the only real biologist who ever wrote to Mendel. Said he'd experimented with hawkweed before and even sent Mendel some seeds to help get him started."

"I've heard about the peas."

"'Cause hawkweed didn't work. Has a very weird, um, 'reproductive pattern.' Random like. Even makes clones of itself sometimes, instead of true offspring, to keep things interesting. Mendel's notes and ideas on heredity suddenly made no sense. He wrote a paper and admitted to the whole world he couldn't repeat his pea experiments with the new plant. He admitted he could be wrong about everything."

"Rough."

"My dad said this German guy set Mendel up. Guy wanted him to fail. Wanted him to understand you can't predict shit."

Castillo shrugged, leaned back in the single chair he'd set up at the window. "They'll come." He turned to Jeff and winked. "Maybe."

Jeff smiled, tapped his head against the wall. "I knew it."

"Give me a break, kid."

Jeff made a cracking noise with his mouth.

"Hey," Castillo said. "You done good, man. Getting us this far. This close, I mean. Really."

"Hawkweed," Jeff said.

Castillo turned back to the window. "Maybe."

•   •   •

Castillo rested in his chair with his eyes closed, his own book opened and resting on his chest. He couldn't sleep. Two, four hours he'd been trying. But nothing, as he'd struggled before. Years ago. He'd been fighting insomnia all week. Maybe since DSTI. Each night, another hour less than the night before. Hell, he couldn't remember the last time he really had slept. Time had gotten funny. Always did when he was on a mission.

He'd tried counting slowly to relax, like they'd first told him when he'd returned to the States. But he'd gotten up to a hundred four different times with no dice. Then, he'd continued to the deep breathing exercises and meditations he'd learned from Kristin. Imagining his feet in the ground, rooted in the soil, growing out, drawing on the healing power of the earth, releasing his "negative energies." What kind of soil? the pacifying voice on the meditation CD had asked. And he'd always thought: *Sand*.

And, now, he thought of her.

So he tried reading again instead, but the words his eyes settled upon were all dark words, the passages filled with more doubts than solace:

```
The gods bestowed courage on me, and power
to break through ranks, sowing evils for mine
enemies. Such a one I was in war. But farming
was not agreeable to me, nor house-keeping, which
nurtures noble children. Rather, battle-equipped
ships were always loved by me, and wars, and well-
polished javelins, and arrows, mournful things,
which are objects of shuddering to others. But to
me these things were dear, these things heaven
placed in my mind; for different men are delighted
with different employments.
```

He was left staring at the flat white ceiling, searching a mental file of a career, a whole life, devoted to an idea. And for that same life, he couldn't articulate what that idea was anymore. Fifteen years. *"Nor did my noble mind ever set death before mine eyes; but having leaped on far the foremost with my spear, I slew whoever of hostile men gave way to me. . . ."*

Am I any different? Any different than Jacobson? Than Henry?

"*But to me these mournful things were dear . . .*"

He breathed deeper, his whole body and spirit pleading for sleep. Sleep. To sleep. "*What dreams may come must give us pause . . .*" There was no "may" about it. What dream *would* come? The Cave? The Boy? Or the latest one, the one with Jeff? (*I bite.*) Each nightmare no more, no less terrible than the last. *Which one would tonight's restful death bring?*

As if to answer, he heard Jeff step into the doorway behind.

"Yeah?" he leaned back to see him.

"Castillo?"

"Yeah, what?"

"Sorry," came his soft voice from the hall's darkness.

"No prob. What's wrong?"

"Nothing. I . . ." Jeff poked his head into the room. "Got tired of sleeping." Slowly, carefully. "How much longer are we staying here?"

"Don't know."

Jeff nodded, considering. He'd leaned back against the door frame, still half in the hall.

"Why don't you go read your book or something?" Castillo said.

"Already read it twice."

Castillo scratched his head to awaken. "Well, read it again, I guess."

"Ox seemed pretty cool."

"Yeah," Castillo agreed, curious as to where this was leading. "Can be."

"Why's he called Ox?"

"Beats the hell out of me. Why don't you—"

"Where'd you meet?"

Castillo leaned forward. "Afghanistan. Ten years ago."

Jeff thought about that. "What's the ghost thing he said?"

"'Ghost thing'?"

Jeff stepped farther into the room. "Um, *talking* to ghosts."

Castillo searched the ceiling for an answer. "Something someone taught some of us."

"Kristin?"

"How do you—"

"Ox asked about her."

"Oh. Yeah. Her."

"Is she the girl on the phone?"

"No," he lied. There was no reason to involve her any more than she had to be. "She's, she was a doctor. Psychiatrist. Worked mostly with soldiers. Most of the guys . . . You can come back home with a lot of bad memories. It's her job to help get rid of them."

"Were you one of those guys?"

"I was. Am."

"What do you mean?"

"Guys come home angry a lot. Always looking for a fight that never comes. Sucks. Guess I don't drink nearly enough, so it got to me pretty good. You come home with regrets, people you let down. Talking to them is the best thing, but sometimes . . . Well, sometimes you can't talk to them. One way or another, a lot of 'em aren't around anymore. So, she had this exercise where we'd try to face these regrets, these 'ghosts.' Instead of letting them haunt you, you kinda meet 'em head-on. Talk it through. I don't know."

"Does it work?"

"Some."

"You did it? You . . . you talked to ghosts?"

"In a way, I guess."

"Did they go away after?"

"The ones I talked to."

"Who's Shaya?"

Castillo jolted. *How in God's name . . .*

"You, um, kinda talk sometimes when you sleep," Jeff explained. "Who is she?"

"*He* was someone I knew in Afghanistan."

"Did something—"

"Not something I talk about." Castillo studied this boy.

Castillo knew that half of the other clones had been systematically abused, molested, neglected. Injected with varying levels of serotonin, dopamine. Tweaked and modified. It seemed that Jeff had not. His test group had been slated to be raised in a loving environment. An environment tolerant of his passive nature, of his possibly emerging homosexuality. The end result was a kid who was polite, curious, and sharp. Yet he'd still been crafted from the DNA of one of the worst serial killers in history. Castillo knew such men were often gifted socially. They could mimic and master, for a short time, social norms. They could use them to their advantage. *Is that what Jeff is doing?* Was he merely waiting? *Pretending?* Was it only a matter of time? *Where did the fabrication end and the true boy begin?*

Jeff stared right back. "War's stupid."

"War's simply the unfolding of miscalculations."

"What's that mean?"

"Something I read once in college. Basically means war's stupid. Comes around when people reach bad conclusions."

"Is it pretty terrible over there?"

"Sometimes." Castillo's mind tried to replace his instant remembrance of Shaya (*what they'd done to him, what he'd done . . .*) with other thoughts. The "good" ones. "I'd be lying if I told you it wasn't also fun sometimes, too."

"Like what?"

"I don't know. Some of the guys, I guess. Funny shit they do, say. The landscape, sometimes. Some of the locals you meet. I don't know . . ."

"What's your favorite memory?"

"Memory? Hell . . . couldn't even guess. Don't have one."

"Then you can make one up."

Castillo smiled in the dark room. "Fine. Early. October '01. Hell, the dust of 9/11 was still settling over New York. We hit 'em outside of Mazar-e Sharif. A thousand Taliban, back when they were still fucking dumb enough to amass like that. They had a couple ZSU-23 antiaircraft cannons, pair of T-55 tanks, and good fields of fire. Good defensive position, but not dug in too deep yet. We'd partnered up with a local warlord in the Northern Alliance who'd brought along a thousand guys of his own. Only way in was across an open field. 'Bout eight hundred yards. And we wanted all of us over at once, so we came in on horses."

"You making this up?"

"Does it matter?"

"Nope. Horses?"

"Ayup. Like real live cowboys. Or Napoleon or some shit. Six hundred guys on horses. To buy us some time, our side was hitting the

Taliban positions with 14.5mm machine guns and M-30s. Artillery. Even had a couple of old T-55 tanks. Bad guys came back with Soviet mortars and those damn ZSU-23s."

"Loud," Jeff said.

Castillo nodded, smiled again. "Yeah. And bad. The 23s, there's nothing left if one hits you. We went in six waves of a hundred men each. Crashed against the Taliban position. Hundreds of Afghans yelling 'Charge' in Dari. *Allahu Akbar.* 'God is great.' You know? Christ, I was twenty." He chuckled, turned to look out the window into the night. "Like I said, I'd be lying if I said it wasn't *any* fun."

"So, you liked it? Over there, I mean."

"I liked being good at something."

"Killing people."

"That's not all we did . . ."

"But you did."

"Yup." At this point, there was no reason to fight the discussion. "But it was never something I *wanted* to do." He realized it was a lie as he said the words. *There had been times . . .*

The boy must have seen something in Castillo's look to make him drop it. "You still think Ted and the rest of the guys are coming here?" he asked.

"Yes."

"What happens when you catch them?"

"Then . . . Then it's over."

"You gonna turn me over to them?"

"DSTI? Don't know. But this *will* end soon."

"I could run away. You'd still let me, yeah?"

"Then what? You're fifteen years old."

"Sixteen. And I'd manage."

"Yeah." Castillo shook his head, imagined the road Jeff was choosing. "People seem to. Here . . ." He handed Jeff his book.

"What's this?" The boy stepped closer, reached out a hand.

"Chapter called 'A Gathering of Shades.' It's about how to talk to ghosts."

Jeff riffled through the pages inside. "Thanks."

Castillo did not reply and turned slowly back to the window.

•   •   •

Jeff ran away the next night.

Castillo'd sent him out the back door to buy some more food and water when it got dark. It was a bullshit errand, but Castillo must have recognized Jeff was rapidly losing his mind in that house. Cabin fever. *Cain* fever. And Jeff was more than happy to seize the escape. He *also* thought he was rapidly losing his mind, but he wasn't so sure that being stuck in the house was the problem. The nearest convenience store was two miles away. By the time Jeff reached it, he'd decided to just keep walking. He had the forty dollars Castillo had given him. He figured that was enough to do something. Get a bus, or walk to the next town and figure out what to do then.

It had probably been an hour. He didn't know. Cars kept passing in the night. Black things filled with black shapes he couldn't see. A hundred people going God-knew-where. Just pairs of headlights racing past. It was colder than he'd first thought.

He would get back east and find his father. Because that man had more explaining to do. A hell of a lot about *when* and *who* and *where*. But mostly a whole lot more about *why*.

He didn't need talking ghosts for that. He needed his goddamn dad.

It was another mile before he realized he hadn't a single clue about how to find him.

All those journal pages and weird cartoons and "murder maps" and computer printouts and Castillo's little phone calls—they were all about finding the other kids. Not kids—clones. None of it was about his dad. The guy who'd basically told him to fuck off and die. Discarded him like a piece of trash blowing beside the street.

He stopped to shove tears away from his eyes.

"Where the hell were you?" Castillo asked.

Jeff did not respond.

"You get the water?"

"Fuck off," Jeff said.

WORK TO BE DONE

JUNE 09, THURSDAY—WILDWOOD, NJ

avid stared toward the ocean from the balcony, any view of it blocked by the umpteen enormous houses between. He couldn't even hear them, the waves. Instead, a couple of gulls cawed beside an open dumpster behind the pizza place.

He could also hear the others in the next room. Dennis and Andrei watching TV.

And, also, the girl they'd picked up on the boardwalk a couple hours ago. They were all in her apartment, which was half a dozen blocks from the beach. She was still crying.

"Yo!" Dennis called out above her. "Get in here."

Soon this will be over, David told himself. *Somehow, someway.*

He wanted out. Didn't care anymore if he was really the genetic clone of Son of Sam, some balding douche named Berkowitz. It didn't matter that his dad roughed him up some, called him stupid a little too much, or that he'd been prescribed access to porn and violent movies by a bunch of evil doctors working for the military. None of that mattered. He didn't want to hurt anyone. Not really. Or be around those who did.

He only wanted to go home. Boring old Pennsauken. Play some Xbox. Maybe even make some microwave popcorn and watch a funny Will Ferrell movie with his asshole dad. Maybe, even, look into that church thing.

David trudged back into the living room. The TV was on. Some countdown on VH1 about the fifty most "Outrageous Moments" in rock-and-roll history. The girl was hog-tied on her stomach over the wicker and glass table. Her clothing, which they'd cut, hung in dangling shreds. Andrei was naked, too.

"I'm gonna get some pizza," David said.

"Later." Dennis looked up from the girl, smiled. "Later."

"I'll be right back," David sustained. *Down the steps, down the street, forget the car, just keep walking.* Down the whole Atlantic if he had to. Call his dad to pick him up. *Would he?* "Kinda hungry, is all."

"What about you?" Dennis laughed and smacked the girl on her bare ass. "You hungry, bitch?"

Andrei grinned, his hand working between his own legs.

The apartment door opened.

Andrei jumped up. "Hey!"

"Who's that?" Dennis jerked up from the couch, lurching toward the hallway. David also turned with the noise.

The door had already shut again.

And something crept in the shadows within the hallway, then glided deeper into the apartment. A blur of darkness, no more.

Then Dennis gagged suddenly, blood spurting from his mouth. *No, his entire neck.* His hands clutched for his throat as the blood jetted out from between his fingers and sprayed the white walls and tiny paintings of lighthouses. The boy's head sloped back, half attached to the yawning neck beneath. His body toppling after it to the floor.

Something sleek and black slid away from him further into the room. A man—*obviously, what else could it be?* David asked himself—scurried low across the floor like, if David had to say, a gigantic insect, a four-legged wriggling thing.

Andrei suddenly lifted several inches off the floor, too quickly to see exactly how. His naked body jerked, a choked scream gurgling in the blood that sputtered from his mouth. David saw the wide tip of a blade exiting his stomach, then steadily lifting, carving, up to the soul-patched chin. Andrei's eyes, wide and glazed, tracked the knife's slow progress as his breath rasped and wheezed, then stopped. The body was tossed to the ground.

David looked toward where he'd left his backpack. Thought of getting his hands on the canister. Jacobson had told him to just open it early if it ever looked like they were going to get caught. Instead, he stood frozen as the dark man next killed the girl. Drove one of the blades into her back so hard that the glass table shattered and she fell through to the carpet beneath. The man wiggled the blade free from the floor.

Then came for him.

And, so, the decision to open the canister was never really his to make.

"Wait! What . . . ?" David started a half-formed question.

Two blades replied.

The boy spilled to the ground, suffocating slowly, the blood and air releasing together in cadenced surges from his severed throat. It sounded almost like the ocean.

His killer had already withdrawn to the front door. Stopped over the dead girl for an instant, considered her nude form, but continued ahead.

His other brothers were still out there somewhere. His fathers waiting.

And there was still much work to be done.

I KILL PEOPLE

JUNE 10, FRIDAY—HITCHCOCK, IN

Castillo shook him awake.

Jacobson! Jeff!

"What?" The boy rubbed his eyes awake, stirring from where he'd fallen asleep on the floor.

"Lion time." Castillo nodded out the window.

Jeff pushed himself up and stepped beside him.

"See the blue car? Pulled up five minutes ago. No one's gotten out yet."

"It's them!" His voice groggy.

"Relax. Relax. Haven't seen anyone yet."

So they waited another ten minutes. It felt like an hour.

"What're they doing?" Jeff asked.

Castillo watched.

Eventually, the car door opened. A man stepped out. A teenager.

"Jacobson?" Castillo murmured.

Jeff caught himself moving back from the window. He recognized the kid completely.

"That's Henry," he said.

Castillo nodded. "Go and get the car."

"What?"

"The car. Right now." Castillo handed him the keys. His voice hadn't changed at all. If anything, Castillo sounded even calmer than usual. "It's close to where we were the first day. Remember the spot? Good. Bring it to the top of the street. On Ashbridge. OK? Keep up top."

"Yeah. But . . . I—"

"Right now. Albaum's family was killed in minutes. I'm not letting that happen here. *We're* not. Go!"

Jeff was down the steps and out the back door in seconds. He sprinted around the side of the house toward where the car was now parked. He wondered what neighbors would think if they saw some kid bursting free from an empty house in the broad daylight, running on fire. The cops were probably already on their way. *Good!* In either case, no matter what happened next, he was never setting foot in that suckhole house again.

He was gasping for air when he reached the car. Felt like acid was pumping in his chest, and his hand shook when he tried the key at the door. It took several attempts.

Jeff got inside the car. Sat down. Got his hands on the wheel.

SHIT!

He'd never actually driven before. The temps and lessons meant for the summer had been swept aside by an ever-increasingly "distracted" father. By a man losing his mind . . .

"OK," he said to the empty car. "This is . . . this is nothing." He put the key in the ignition. *Thank God, it's an automatic!* The car started right up. He fumbled with the gearshift, found Drive. Foot on the gas. The car pulled forward.

"Yes! Yes . . ." He slapped the dashboard.

The car trolled down the street at about two miles an hour and eventually made the necessary turn to the corner of Ashbridge and Oldegate. As he inched up against someone's lawn, Jeff stomped on the brake and the car shuddered to a stop. He could see nothing of the scene down the street, the Sizemores' house and half the block lost beneath a low dip in the road. He thought about getting out of the car to see . . . wasn't sure if Castillo wanted him to stay with the car or not. His eyes glanced to the various mirrors: Rearview. Side. A hundred angles showing more of nothing.

He looked down to study the gearshift, finally found Park.

By the time he looked up, a car passed. A dark blue car. And Henry was driving.

Jeff froze. He'd met Henry a dozen times at DSTI. But in less than a month, Henry already looked different. Older. Darker. So much so that Jeff was half convinced it wasn't even him. Or hoped not, because if Henry turned and saw him . . .

The car passed. Kept going. It was totally Henry.

Jeff collapsed against the steering wheel.

The car door flew open.

"Move over." It was Castillo.

"What happened?"

"Move! Or get out!"

Jeff scrambled to his right. Castillo hopped in and tossed the car in reverse, then pulled a quick K-turn that would have made a stuntman applaud. "He just knocked at the door," Castillo explained. "Talked to the dad for a minute and then took off again."

"So what's that mean?"

"No clue. Surveillance, I guess. Running point, like we did. They're probably coming back later."

"Guess they're lions too," Jeff said.

"Whatever. Now we follow this asshole. See if we can find four more like him. Maybe your dad's with them."

"He's not."

"We don't know that for sure. Keep your head down a bit. I figure he'd recognize you as easily as you recognized him, huh?"

"Maybe. Those guys never paid much attention to me, to be quite honest."

"Well, they might now. Keep down."

"You see him?"

"He's two cars ahead. Not a problem. This twisted fuck isn't going anywhere." Castillo pulled out his cell. "It's me. Following Henry now. Affirmative. Hitchcock, Indiana. Yes, sir. OH plates.

Tango-Juliet-Delta-Zero-Four-Nine. Don't know that yet. Affirmative."
He put the phone away again.

"DSTI?" Jeff asked.

"Quiet. You done real good. Again. Just enjoy this part."

They had at least one of the original six. Adopted Name: Henry
Roberts. Aged seventeen. Birth Name: Henry/61. Parent Gene: Henry
Lee Lucas. He still looked like his DSTI photo, hadn't thought to
change his appearance in the slightest. He first stopped to buy some
Burger King, then headed out of town. Castillo followed every step of
the way, not even bothering to hang back after a while. Henry didn't
notice, didn't even seem to check his rearview mirror.

They drove like this, cat and mouse, for half an hour. Castillo didn't
make a single sound, and Jeff followed his lead.

Finally, Henry turned.

Pulled into something called the Paddy Creek Park. They'd never
been there, of course, but Castillo knew it well enough. It was like any
small community park, like the one back in Ohio—a crime scene waiting to happen.

Castillo drove past it and doubled back after a few minutes. Henry
had parked and already vanished. The rest of the parking lot was empty.
1500 hours on a Friday afternoon. How long before an evening crowd
appeared? Castillo parked far away from Henry's car. He got out of the
car. "Stay here," he said. The summer sun nuzzled atop the tall trees.
"If I'm not back in thirty minutes, you call this number. Tell 'em you're
with Castillo and that we're at Paddy Creek."

"This DSTI?"

"There's money in the glove box. You don't have to be here when
they arrive."

Jeff nodded, sliding down into the seat. "Castillo?"

"What?"

"Be careful," Jeff said.

Castillo considered the boy for a moment. The messy hair and glasses.
The uneven smile. He wondered what truly awaited the kid if he actually called that number. "Thirty minutes," he repeated. It would be,
he hoped, more than enough time. Still no other cars in sight. He

wondered how many more of the boys he'd just found. If any. There was no time to get backup, but it'd be difficult to take down half a dozen teenagers.

Castillo approached Henry's car. His eyes took in the playground, brickhouse restrooms, and the concrete buildings attached to a small amphitheater in the center of the park. His 9mm drawn, silencer threaded in place. The car was empty, but he found his target soon enough. Moving by the small amphitheater. Castillo thought of waiting until the kid headed back to the car. Too tough to get up to that stage unnoticed. But Henry had stepped out toward the center of the platform, half lost in summer shadows. Kneeling over something.

Some*one*. A form, a woman, reclined before him like some kind of Aztec sacrifice. She was not moving. Castillo aimed his gun, considered taking the shot then. Took one last look. No others around, teens or otherwise. Area secured.

"Henry," he called, keeping to the shadows of the closest tree.

The boy struggled to his feet. Fumbled awkwardly with his pants as a wide serrated blade shimmered in his one hand.

"Drop the knife," Castillo ordered and edged up the steps at the wing of the stage. "Drop it now, Henry." Another step closer.

"Who are you?"

The woman at his feet was nude. Set over a blue tarp. Her body undercoated in dirt, filth, old bruising and scratches. Even from twenty paces away, she smelled dead. Looked dead. *But what if she's not?*

"I'm a guy who can help get you home," Castillo said, looking back at the boy.

"Home? What the—" Henry laughed. "You got no idea, do you, you stupid fuck?"

"So tell me then."

Another step closer. Clearer shot. Leg, maybe. Shoulder.

"You know, I called that bitch two days ago. My 'mommy.' Told Mommy I'm coming back someday real soon. That I'm gonna cut her fucking head off. You from Massey? DSTI?"

"No."

"She beat me, ya know. When I was a kid. Made me dress up as a girl for her friends. Forced me to watch her fucking dudes. Then the men would . . . then they'd have a go at me. Nice, huh? Just like him."

"Like who?"

"Lucas. Henry Lee. Just like him, just like me."

"I don't know about any of that, dude. I just . . . look, how about you put down the knife. Then we can talk about all this."

"Suck me, faggot. Don't you get it? She was doing it on purpose. She wanted me to be like him. She did. Or *they* did. DSTI. Jacobson. *Someone* did."

Castillo could not argue. He'd seen the videotapes and read the reports. Traumatization in the formative years was textbook development for a serial killer, and it had been freely prescribed. Nothing in this kid's charts had said anything about it, however. Yet knowing DSTI, it wouldn't surprise. *Jesus Christ, what they did to these fucking kids . . .*

"Road trip's over, man," Castillo managed. "The other guys are already back home."

"Bullshit. Those guys? I left their bitch asses days ago. Told 'em I'd take care of this fucking Sizemore kid myself. Those guys are halfway to Cali by now."

"They're not. Police picked them up yesterday."

"Bullshit."

"No, it's true. Look, I'm putting the gun away, OK? Let's talk through this." Castillo did as he said and gradually returned the sidearm to its holster. He wasn't worried about this kid and his knife, knew he could disarm him easily if he got close. "OK? See? Now put that down, and we can end this thing before it gets any worse."

"Any worse?" The boy lifted his shirt so Castillo could see. Castillo had tensed, ready to draw his pistol again. But Henry hadn't revealed a gun. A giant purple-black mark covered half the boy's body. A bumpy bruise that ran from his nipple down onto his stomach. "This . . . this shit's all over me, man."

Castillo had no clue what he was looking at, but he played along. "We'll get you whatever medical—"

Henry laughed. It also sounded like a cry. "Whatever, dude. Fucking listen to yourself. You're so full of shit . . . you don't even know it. July fourth, you'll find out, pussy. You all will."

"Henry . . ." Castillo reached out his left hand. "Come on, man, don't let them win."

"Whatever."

"We could—"

"You wanna say hi to Nurse Stacey?" Henry looked down and toed the woman at his feet. "Me and her were gonna get married, I think."

"Henry, I can get you help." *Can I really?*

"But I'll probably cut her head totally off and then—"

"No. You won't."

"After, I'll cut you." Henry dropped to one knee, his eyes wild. Who knew what was running through his veins. What hellish venom brewed in some lab ran through his veins. He'd lifted the woman up to him with one arm. "You know who I am, asshole?"

"Henry Roberts," Castillo said. But his full attention wasn't on Henry Roberts anymore, it was back on the woman. Close enough, finally, to really see.

It *was* Stacey Kelso. One of the two nurses from DSTI.

Her face battered and swollen but recognizable from the ID photos. Abducted by six psychopaths a week ago. Officially, they'd reported to her friends and family that she was away taking an advanced training somewhere. *She looks dead.* Castillo tried not to think about how DSTI and Stanforth would ultimately explain her disappearance. And he certainly tried not to think about the reality of her last week. Still, he thought about both. And so shifted back to the here and now. The ol' black and white again. First: *99.9% dead. Can't tell absolutely. . . . It changes everything if a hostage situation.* He still needed to get closer to know for sure.

"Your name's Henry Roberts," he echoed, turning his attention back to the teen. "And some really bad men put you in a terrible mess." The words came out more easily, suddenly, more earnest. "You can beat this thing, man. Trust me. I know what it's like to—"

"You know nothing, you fuckin' liar. Don't you know what I am now? I'm Henry Lee Lucas!" It was a declaration and a question, too. He'd brought the knife to the woman's throat.

"No. You're just some kid who got fucked over by assholes who should have known better."

"I kill people. I like to rape dead girls."

"That ain't you, man." *Closer.* The boy'd shielded himself well with the woman's body. Head, shoulder exposed. *Maybe the shoulder* . . . "That was something else. Someone else. Now, please, put down the knife."

"Bet they name this highway for me. Route 50, right?"

"Sure, OK, man, I'll bet you twenty bucks. What do you think they'll—" *Still too far away. . . . Fuck!*

"Now let's see her head come off."

"Henry, don't . . ."

The boy tensed, knife perched to slice.

Two shots.

The boy flipped back, legs kicking out through the spray of blood, and landed awkwardly on the concrete stage.

"Motherfuck!" Castillo dropped to the woman first. She was, as suspected, dead. Had been for a day or even two, he figured. "Goddamn it," he cursed again. Crawled next to Henry's body. He'd gone for two in the shoulder. Drive the kid back. *Must have hit his neck somehow.* Nope, both shots in the shoulder. "What the fuck?!" *Why was he bleeding out so fast?*

Castillo grabbed the knife and cut the kid's shirt away. Bunched it up to help apply pressure to the two wounds. The kid wasn't lying. The black growth ran all the way down past his hip and onto his back some too. Castillo tried not to think about it as his other arm bent over the boy to start CPR. "Come on, kid . . ."

Two breaths. Elbow down twenty thrusts. But every time he pressed, the blood pushed through the bundled shirt against his fingers. It was as if he'd hit the kid's jugular. But he hadn't. *So why's this fucking kid bleeding out like this?* A pool of blood had already spread underneath them. It looked, felt, oily. Had a putrid smell. Castillo told himself the stink was from Kelso's body, but he didn't think so. *The kid's blood? What else could it be?*

He put his mouth to the boy's again. Blew air into his still body. "Come on, kid. You gotta want it. . . . Not like this. Not like this."

Two minutes. Five. Ten.

On the final press, blood came from the boy's mouth.

Castillo dropped back on his ass. Out of breath. Patted the boy on his chest.

"I'm sorry, Henry," he said.

He pulled out the cellphone. His fingers were dark with blood. "It's me," he said into the phone. "Yeah. Target down, sir. Need someone to Paddy Creek Park. Right, Henry's down. Kelso, too. Yes, sir. Affirmative."

He watched as Jeff approached slowly from the distance. Tried waving him away, but the boy still advanced. Castillo kept talking. "Yes, sir. The kid said something about California. The other guys. Could be nothing. Threatened his mom. Made some comment about July fourth. I don't know. Any news on the East Coast group or Dr. J? Yes, sir. Is something wrong? Yes, sir. I'll be here. Out." He put the phone away, didn't look behind him. "I thought I told you to stay in the car."

Jeff had stopped moving toward the stage. "Is that . . ."

"Yeah," Castillo said. "One of the nurses they took."

"Is she . . ."

"They both are. Why don't you get your ass back to the car."

"Why'd you shoot him?"

"He had a knife. I couldn't . . . I'd hoped she was still alive. Hit him in the damn shoulder. How was I supposed to know the fucking kid was . . . You know, fuck it."

Jeff stared at the two bodies again, both perfectly level with his view of the raised stage.

"Look, Jacobson, I ain't gonna apologize for this shit," Castillo said. "Fucker gave me no choice here. I just did what I was trained to do."

Jeffrey looked up from the two bodies to Castillo.

"So did he," the boy said.

BIRTH TO
THE 21ST CENTURY

JUNE 10, FRIDAY—RADNOR, PA

tanforth skated the note card across the table so that it settled directly in front of Dr. Erdman. There was dark, dried blood on it, and the doctor eyed it without touching. It read:

> *ShARDhARA*
> *ZODIaC BaBYSITTeR PhaNTOM*
> *Independence Day*
> *I also gave birth to the 21st century*

"This is the emergency?" Erdman asked.

"Love letter from Jacobson," Stanforth answered calmly. Behind him, another man stood in a textbook military at-ease pose. Solid and motionless, his hands crossed, no more than a few inches from the pistol at his hip. A similar-looking man had taken a position along the adjacent wall, behind Erdman. Though both were new to DSTI, Stanforth had introduced neither. "Found this morning laying atop a gutted corpse near Indianapolis," replied Stanforth. "Crime pics look a lot like the way your psychiatrist was butchered. Gallagher, was it? Handwriting's confirmed as Jacobson's."

"Who else has seen this?"

"No one to worry about," Stanforth said.

"I don't understand," Rolich said between them. "What does it mean?"

"Something we're all here to figure out," Stanforth said, looking at Erdman. "Anything you want to tell me, Doctor?"

Erdman read the note card again. "Well . . . I don't know. I can tell you that Zodiac was a notorious serial killer. Never caught. But he has nothing to do with any of our research as far as I know. I'm not sure about The Phantom or The Babysitter. I would assume they, too, are serial killers?"

"They are," Stanforth confirmed. "Also never caught. What else?"

Erdman eyed the soldier behind Stanforth. The man's eyes remained straight ahead, lifeless, as if he'd been the lone man in the room. The doctor picked up the card. "I suppose 'Independence Day' refers to their newfound freedom or, perhaps, July fourth. Some kind of threat from Jacobson. A prediction, a schedule. If the lunatic thinks he's Jack the Ripper . . ." Erdman frowned. "The Ripper once wrote to the police on a card much like this that he'd be remembered for 'giving birth to the twentieth century.'"

"It's plainly nonsense," Rolich said, reaching for the card. "Jacobson's fucking insane."

"Who is SharDhara?" Erdman asked carefully, handing the card over.

"*Where*," Stanforth corrected. "Afghanistan."

"Oh," Erdman said.

"Oh. Anything you need to tell me?"

Erdman studied the card some more. Too long. He could have memorized it backward by now. "I don't see how . . . SharDhara was used for testing, wasn't it?"

"Yes."

"I didn't know that."

"Few do."

"What kind of testing?" Rolich asked.

"IRAX11," Stanforth said.

The CEO's eyes widened. "That . . . that was terminated."

Stanforth stared hard at Erdman. "How would Jacobson know about SharDhara?"

"You tell me." Erdman shook his head. "Never heard of the place until now. I knew IRAX11'd been field-tested, but never when or where. I'd always believed Jacobson was the one who helped you guys pick the location, tabulate results, and so on."

"You believed erroneously. Dr. Chatterjee performed that duty for us."

"He's dead."

"Quite." Stanforth nodded. "I'll assume that he somehow told Jacobson before his demise."

"So what?" Rolich said. "So Jacobson knows where IRAX11 was tested. How much more damage could he possibly do? Go to the press?"

"How much more damage, Doctor?" Stanforth asked Erdman alone. His voice remained calm, but his eyes showed something else entirely. "I will not ask again."

"We're missing three canisters," Erdman said.

"Of IRAX11?" Rolich grabbed the desk for support. "Missing? You mean you didn't . . ."

"We discovered this three days ago." Erdman stared at something far past and away from the room. He looked like a man prepared to die. "In the confusion of the escape. The murders! The cleanup. We'd checked, but . . . These were test batches, canisters from deep storage. I can presume Jacobson took them. We believed . . . I don't know what. That there'd been a mistake or . . . We, I concede, should have apprised you more promptly." He looked straight at Stanforth.

The colonel reached for something below the table, and Rolich visibly flinched. From beneath the table, Stanforth brought out a short tubular canister. It looked like a can of tear gas or a beer can.

"Is that . . . ?" Rolich retreated back from the table as if Stanforth had placed a cobra there.

"Shall we open it and find out?" Stanforth put his fingers on the top. Erdman leaned toward it. "Where did you find that?" he asked.

"Three targets were eliminated in Jersey yesterday. Dennis, David, and another boy. One of Jacobson's secret adoptees, we assume. I've brought you all three bodies for testing. When we received the letter this morning, we made a closer examination of the cleanup, and there it was."

"IRAX11?" Rolich reclaimed his seat, looked between them, confused. "They had this? Out in the world?"

Stanforth nodded. "Most likely with instructions to open it on July fourth at some public event. Agreed?"

"San Francisco," Erdman murmured. "It's where The Zodiac killer operated. . . ."

"Yup," Stanforth agreed. "The Babysitter in Detroit. There was a Freeway Phantom in D.C. and a Phantom Killer in Texas. Could be either, but we assume it's D.C. Gotta be a dozen major public celebrations planned, and the symbolism alone would have been tantalizing. Three canisters, three cities."

"Astonishing. How many . . . ," the CEO stuttered, "I mean, how many people could he . . ."

"Ten thousand," Erdman said.

"Each canister," Stanforth added.

Rolich shook his head. "Astonishing," he said again. "I mean, guys, if we don't—"

Before the man could finish his thought, Stanforth shot him.

DSTI's chief executive flipped backward with the force of the discharge, his body and chair upended in an instant. Blood and brain had sprayed across the wall behind. The sound still reverberated throughout the room, and a single leg now extended from beneath the table, the pant leg wilted down to reveal a dark tartan sock; the leg's shoe apparently vanished alongside the gunshot.

"I told you: If you lied to me again, I'd kill both of you," Stanforth said as he laid his pistol atop the table. Erdman had stood during the shooting. The two henchmen with Stanforth hadn't even exchanged glances. "In this case, it seems, you'd not revealed the entire truth. A technicality that warranted, you'd agree, a reduced punishment. Next time, there'll be only you."

"How will you—" The geneticist stared in horror at the pant leg.

"Not your concern," replied Stanforth. "Hiking accident, maybe. Fell. Sit down, Doctor."

Erdman did as he was told. "There's no antidote," he said, one eye still on the extended leg. "July fourth is three weeks away."

"We stay the course. Keep fixing snags as they come along. Castillo's already found three clones, including one of the original six, and the second nurse. He has a strong lead on half a dozen more. In just forty-eight hours, our other solution has eliminated four more." Stanforth grabbed the canister, shook it slightly for emphasis. "We're missing two canisters now. Three weeks could be enough time to clean this up. From what the Ohio kid—Albaum, was it?—said, we suspect several are still traveling together. Heading west. Hitting houses along the way that have Jacobson's other private clones."

"And if not?" Erdman asked.

"Twenty thousand Americans tear themselves and their neighbors into small bloody pieces," Stanforth said. "And you'll be killed in the subsequent cover-up, which blames Al-Qaeda sleeper cells for contaminating the water supplies."

"Understood."

He most assuredly did. It was three days since Albaum, the Ed Gein clone, had been brought in. The first Castillo'd found. The boy'd arrived in the morning for a handful of various blood and DNA tests and a brief psychological exam. Diagnosis made. Prescription given. Done. Little Edward "Leatherface" Albaum was peaceful and drooling by the middle of that same afternoon. Utterly comatose. No more stories of killer clones or boys dressed as clowns from this kid. Stanforth had apparently taken care of the boy's dead family, with other hired "parents" even now also being disposed of. More "hiking accidents," no doubt. *The price of admission*, Erdman figured. *Progress always comes with an invoice*. With Jacobson, and now Rolich, out of the way, just maybe he could make peace with Stanforth. Prove he was on the same page, and always had been. "Understood," he said again, more to himself this time.

"You seem to be taking this all rather well, Doctor. Good. Always fancied you a practical man."

"Pragmatism and science have always gone hand in hand, Stanforth. The dreamers and bleeding hearts can stick to poetry and paint. You remember what Oppenheimer said when they first tested the atomic bomb."

"Sure . . . sure. He cited the, ah, *Bhagavad Gita*, right? 'I am become Death, the destroyer of worlds.'"

Erdman nodded. "Apocryphal. What we tell classrooms and the History Channel to make ourselves feel better. Want to know what he really said, according to half a dozen witnesses?"

Stanforth smiled. "What?"

"'It worked.'"

NEED TO KNOW

JUNE 10, FRIDAY—OLNEY, IL

They rested in an east Illinois motel. It was afternoon. Castillo lay on his back in his bed, fully dressed, staring up at the ceiling.

"What's wrong?" Jeff asked from across the room.

Castillo sat up, passed over his phone to the other bed. "They sent me this a couple minutes ago. What do you think?"

Jeff reached out to take the phone and looked at the image. "My father?"

"They think so. His handwriting." Castillo nodded. "They found it yesterday."

"Where?"

"Outside Indianapolis. This mean anything to you?"

His thumb flicked across the touch screen. "What the fuck?!" Jeff looked away from the phone. "Oh my God, Castillo . . ."

"Give me—" Castillo lunged up.

"I already saw it," Jeff said, handing the phone back. "You didn't think I know how to scroll back? Who is she?"

"Some woman. The card was next to her when they found her."

"I can see that. What's it mean?"

"They don't know." He watched the boy absorb the quantifiable evidence that his father was a murderer. "You OK?"

"Yeah."

It was a lie. Castillo figured it best to keep the conversation elsewhere. "The three names on the card there are serial killers from specific cities."

"Clones?"

"Can't be, apparently. Because no one knows who those three guys really were."

"You still believe in 'can't be'? I'm not sure there's such a thing."

"Maybe you're right." Castillo shook his head. "My bosses figure it's some kind of clue that something's going to happen in San Francisco and Detroit and Washington on July fourth. Henry did say they were headed west. Makes sense."

"SharDhara."

"That's what it says."

"But no one really knows what happened there."

"We know *something* happened there. A test of some kind. Some kinda biotoxin."

"That's going to happen here?"

"Who knows." Castillo thought a moment. "I know I don't like the way my boss sounded. He couldn't give a shit about Henry or these other two. Your leads on Salem. Sherwood Forest. Didn't care. It was about the guys heading west. 'Grave' was the word he used. Wouldn't tell me anything beyond that."

"You didn't tell him you know about SharDhara."

"Nope. When I asked *him* about it, he said it was outside my 'need to know' anyhow, but to keep an eye out for any references to it moving forward. Said the only thing I needed to know now was that it was a grave threat and to keep my eye out for a canister of some kind. So I didn't feel obligated to tell him anything about what Ox told us."

"Wow."

"Uh-huh."

"That pisses you off, doesn't it?"

"What's that?"

"That they wouldn't tell you what SharDhara is."

Castillo rubbed his head. "Maybe. But it shouldn't. I've spent fifteen years on a need-to-know basis. Goes with the job. And maybe they don't know much more than we do right now. Regardless, if . . . If your father's note or anything we've learned about SharDhara is any true indication, and these guys have a canister of some terrible biotoxin . . ."

"So are we still going west, then?"

"Like I said, he had no real interest in Salem or Sherwood Forest. Especially when I told him those two kids were either already freed or dead. He said they'd be taking care of it. Ordered me west to San Francisco. Those are the guys I was hired to bring in." Castillo lay back down and closed his eyes. "Anything on that card make sense to you?"

"What's the twenty-first-century thing?" Jeff asked.

"Nothing," Castillo replied.

"It's something."

"Something to do with Jack the Ripper."

"Oh."

Castillo yawned, a long groan that turned into a half-formed thought: "Gotta nail these little fucking monsters. . . ." He regretted the words even as they passed his lips. Looked at Jeff. "Hey, look . . ."

"Don't worry about it," Jeff said.

"Not the Sizemore kid," Castillo said. "Not *you*. The other six guys."

"Sure."

"You know what, fuck it. Here's the thing. Sorry if it 'offends' you somehow, but it is what it is. I've tracked down some real bad guys over the years. Men who've killed a lot of people. But I always knew what I was dealing with. I got it. The religious fanaticism. Or greed. Or power. Duty. Whatever it happened to be, I understood it. These guys were sadistic and terrible and damned, but there was a *reason* to be those things."

"But not these guys."

"No," Castillo admitted. "Not Henry. Or Ted. Or some little fuck dressed up like a clown. And I'm talking these kids *and* their original selves. They kill for fun. Period. They fucking kill because it's fun. And I just can't accept, I won't . . ." He could hardly breathe. The air in the room was suddenly warm and thick. "Physiological, biological . . . old or new. Nature, nurture. I don't give a shit anymore. They're . . . they've become only monsters to me. And, despite what your new pal Ox might think, I'm too old to believe in monsters."

"You've killed people," Jeff said. "Are *you* a monster?"

"War's different."

"You think *I'm* a monster."

"Didn't say that."

"That I'm just some clone. Evil incarnate."

"Jeff . . . I didn't—"

"My father told me they'd taken one of Dahmer's cells and re-trained it to become, like, an egg cell. Then they fertilized that egg with another one of Dahmer's cells. Never been done before, he said. I *am* one hundred percent him. I *am* Jeffrey Dahmer."

"In genes only. I guess that's how it works. Right? So what? So, you'll be tall and blond and probably need LASIK. And? Good for you. I wish I was tall and blond. So you're maybe genetically prone to being an alcoholic, so what? Go to AA meetings and keep away from alcohol. So you're genetically prone to, what, being gay? Good. You're not being raised in the seventies. Fall in love with whoever you want and live happily ever after."

"And the murder? The death? The corpses?"

Castillo looked away. "I never said . . . I'm not saying you're like Henry."

"Castillo."

"What?"

"I don't want to . . . to hurt people. I don't ever even *think* about hurting people. I don't care whose blood is running in my veins. That's why my father did this, you know. I understand that now. He wanted to explain the terrible thoughts in his own head. He wanted to prove it was all in his blood, that he didn't have a choice. So he took the most terrible person ever and raised him like a normal boy to see what would happen. To prove that the genes, the blood, that nature would win. But I never even think about . . . I'm not some disgusting monster."

"I know."

"Do you?" The words were a soft plea. "Do you really?"

Castillo looked at the boy. But he didn't reply.

"Well, don't feel too bad," Jeff said. He turned away. "To tell the truth, I'm not totally sure either."

They both lay in the silence for a long time.

Then Jeff said, "I want to find my dad."

"So do I."

"I mean now." Castillo could hear Jeff moving off the bed, and he opened his eyes to look over. "I want to find him now."

"Unless he's in San Francisco, can't do it. Not yet. You OK? You look kinda . . ."

"I'm fine. When?"

"After. You're shivering."

"I'm a little cold, is all. After what? July fourth? That's bullshit. We can start now."

Castillo stared hard at the boy. "'Bullshit'? Get your quilt. Jesus."

"I'm fine." Even as he said it, Jeff's face had scrunched in agony. Castillo could almost feel the shiver scrabble up his own spine.

"Sorry, kid," he said. "I've been ordered to San Francisco. Go yourself if you want."

"You'd let me?"

"Yup."

"But I need your help."

"Then we'll look *after* San Francisco."

"Can we start now?"

"Haven't we already? We've been fighting through two hundred pages of notes. What more do you want us to do?"

"We need books."

"What kind of books?"

"Books about Jack the Ripper. And I want you to use your FBI database thing to pull up any unsolved murders of women in the last five years. Women who've . . . who've been cut open. Like that teacher at DSTI. Like the woman in Indiana where they found the card."

Castillo looked at the boy, who'd freed the motel quilt and blanket from underneath and wrapped them around his shoulders so that only his small head pushed out.

His face the same as the monster from Castillo's dreams. *I bite.*

But, also, not at all.

Castillo sighed. "Tomorrow," he said.

FAMILIAR, ALMOST

A flash of light and noise. When the darkness returned, the thing in the doorway had already vanished back into the night with it.

Castillo fired two more times to make sure.

He'd rolled behind Jeff's bed as he'd shot, chasing away that last clutch of sleep, ignoring his confusion and shock of the door bursting open to put three bullets into his anonymous target. Whatever the hell it was. He'd worked Special Ops for ten years, on missions from Angola to Syria, and had never once fired at an unidentified target. Until now.

This guy had simply felt like something he was supposed to shoot. And familiar, almost.

The last two bullets had a moment ago chased after the retreating form as the door frame splintered out into the night. It'd moved so damn fast. Castillo steadied the gun over Jeff's still form beneath his arms. Tried to figure out if the kid was dead. *Hadn't Jeff screamed?*

Someone had screamed, a terrible sound. Castillo allowed that it might have been himself, and he focused even harder on waking completely. Had he simply shot the boy by mistake? *Or on purpose?*

The dreams. Such horrible dreams. Had he imagined the whole thing? Nope. Castillo reached out with his free hand and felt the kid's skinny leg. "Hey, kid." He shook him. "Jeff . . ."

"I'm good! I—"

"Quiet," Castillo snapped, and clambered over the foot of the bed toward the doorway. He kept low to the curtained window, clinging to the same darkness to which his enemy had recently retreated. "Get behind the bed."

He stole a glance out the door into the parking lot. Light from the La Quinta sign above cast a yellow sheen over the empty sidewalk and every car in the lot. The whole world looked jaundiced and diseased.

Castillo cursed. *When exactly did I become the prey?*

A fence rattled in the distance and Castillo gave chase.

"Stay put," he shouted back into the room.

His bare feet slapped loudly against the walkway as he sprinted toward the chain-link fence. Something ripped into his heel. He could see where the top of the fence still trembled, as if someone had climbed over a moment before. He quickly scanned the cracked doorway he passed, and then the ashen face behind a barely drawn curtain in the next room. No threat, only curious tourists alarmed by the clamor. Too afraid, too smart, to come out and do anything about it. The police would arrive soon, he knew.

He crossed the parking lot onto weed-covered dirt and finally reached the fence. Fingers of his free hand wrapped the links separating him from a deeply shadowed hill of weeds and an empty exit ramp. No blood on the fence or ground that he could spot. He thought about jumping it. Then his training kicked back in, and he shoved personal emotion aside.

"That's it," Castillo said, catching his breath for the first time since springing awake. "Cops and robbers ends now."

He'd shot the man. *I must have put at least two into the fucker.* He backed from the fence, tucking the pistol in the front waist of his jeans, keeping his fingers around the handle. Police would arrive in two, maybe five, minutes. He lowered his head, hurried past the other rooms.

"Hey," someone dared from one of the darkened doorways. "What the hell's—"

Castillo turned to the voice, and the man stalled midsentence. "Bunch of kids took off that way," Castillo said, waved toward the fence, moving past toward his room. "Firecrackers, looks like."

"Goddamn kids," the man's voice trailed after him.

You have no idea, Castillo mused. But had it been one of the "kids"? One of his targets? Couldn't have been, moved too fast. *Something worse?*

He darted back into his room, pulled the door shut behind him. It bounced back freely on its newly busted hinges. "Get your—"

"Good to go," Jeff said in the darkness. He'd already pulled his own bag together and was working on Castillo's. "Thought you'd want us moving," he added, looking over his glasses. His hair was tousled and pillow-shaped. He looked all of ten years old.

"Thought I told you to get behind the damn bed," Castillo said. Still, he couldn't help but smile. The kid was smart. Never complained. Eager to learn, to always do the "right" thing. Any parent would be thrilled to have a kid like this. *Does any of that other shit matter? That these same cells once ate dead flesh and fucked skulls?*

"I just thought—"

Castillo looked away. "Thanks, man. Good idea. You all right?"

Jeff nodded. "What *was* that?" he asked.

"Who," Castillo corrected, even as he noted that the boy had also felt the guy's *wrongness*. "I don't know." He crossed the room, pondering. Baffled. Something about their enemy, something still somewhat outside the periphery of his memory. "We'll talk about it later. I'm gonna have to deal with the local cops now. There's a Waffle House about half a mile that way. Go." He grabbed his wallet and fished out a twenty. "Buy breakfast. I'll get there as soon as I can. OK?"

"OK."

Castillo smiled again. No questions, no back talk. The kid did as he was asked so easily. He'd have been a good soldier in another life. "You sure you're not hurt or—"

"I'm good," Jeff said, lowered his head, and grabbed his book bag. "Um, how long will you be?"

"I'll get there as soon as I can."

"Sure." Jeff skirted the broken door and stepped into the sickly buttery light. "Thanks, Castillo."

Castillo half shut the door behind him and flipped on the light to check the room again. He saw where the door frame had taken a bullet. He finished tossing the rest of his own things into his bag. Some clothes. The Murder Map. Pictures of the family recently murdered in Delhi, Colorado.

He pulled out his cell and made the call.

"Castillo." It was 3:00 a.m., but Colonel Stanforth's voice was clear and alert.

"Yes, sir."

"Didn't expect to hear back from you so soon. What's the situation?"

"Don't know, sir. I think one of them might have tried to kill me tonight."

"But I'm talking to you, ain't I, kiddo?"

"You are, sir. I gave chase, but he escaped." Castillo pictured the dark shape sweeping into the room. Something glittering in its hands. Knives, he supposed. But something else was off . . . the guy'd moved like a ghost, floating across the darkness toward him. Again, familiar. No! It'd been toward the boy, Castillo now realized. Toward Jeff. "Real Hollywood, sir. Son of a bitch kicked in the door. Big blades twirling. Woke up in time. Pretty sure I dropped him, but—"

"Castillo," Stanforth stopped him. "Where are you?"

"Illinois. Town called Olney."

"Fine, fine. Locals on the way?"

"Affirmative. I took a couple shots at—"

"Clear out. We'll, ah, clean up with you off-site. And . . ."

"Yes, sir." Castillo stopped packing, really focused on the call for the first time. Something he'd noticed again in Stanforth's voice. "Sir? Come again?"

"You alone, Castillo?"

"Yes, sir," he said quickly, adding feigned surprise to his reply. *What did Stanforth mean? Jeff? Impossible.*

Unless . . . *Goddamn.* The tracking chips!

He'd completely forgotten about the tracking chips. Jacobson's hidden clones didn't seem to have them or the gang at DSTI would have already collected them all. But Jeff was something different—Jacobson's adopted son. He was official, just like the six who'd cut theirs out before going rogue. Would Jacobson have implanted a chip in his own son? Castillo'd never even considered it. But now the chip had led DSTI straight to them both.

Damn, damn it! Stupid, Castillo. You fucked up bad.

Stanforth asked again: "No one else was with you tonight?" Castillo heard the confusion in his commander's voice.

"No, sir," Castillo said.

"Olney," the colonel repeated. "You know what, Castillo, cancel that last. Hold until they arrive, is that clear?"

"*Who* arrives?"

And just like that: The Turn. The one Castillo'd always secretly expected but never dared imagine would actually happen.

"Buy some time with the locals. I'll get someone out as soon as I can to help clean up." Stanforth laughed—a terrible, forced sound. "Don't worry about it, kiddo," he said. "You're doing fine. We'll get this mess sorted out soon enough. Hang tight. We'll be right there."

"Thank you, sir," Castillo said and hung up. "Asshole."

It was over. All of it. He'd heard it in the voice, the instructions.

Stanforth had just decided to sell him out. If he waited for whoever showed up, anything could happen. He'd be in *THEIR* control. No better off than Jeff Jacobson or Edward Albaum or any of them. He'd trusted Stanforth with his life for twelve years and now couldn't dare give him another fifteen minutes.

He grabbed his bag and stepped out the door.

The world waiting outside somehow even more yellow. More diseased.

IV

Stochastic event n.

From the Greek *stokhos* for "an aim" or "guess"

(1) an event based on random behavior;

(2) scientific principle which asserts the occurrence of individual events cannot be predicted, although measuring the distribution of all observations usually follows a predictable pattern

Let us here devise his mournful destruction
And let him not escape us.
Do not think that, while he is alive,
these things planned will be accomplished.
For he is knowing, now.

THE ODYSSEY

LIABILITY

They broke into the Glenmoore Animal Hospital twenty miles away from the motel in Olney. Jeff watched in the shadows while Castillo hacked the alarm and opened the back door. There were just four dogs caged inside, barking as one and loud enough to wake half the state. Castillo told Jeff to find them treats while he looked around some. In five minutes, the dogs were quietly munching biscuit mounds and Castillo was testing something called a DR 3500 Digital Navigator Plus, the clinic's sole X-ray machine. In another ten minutes, Jeff was up on the table, looking skeptical. "The alternative involves cutting," Castillo said. "Trust me on that."

They x-rayed his feet first, which was where the other boys had had their chips injected. Nothing. They took another dozen close digital shots of different body parts. Hands. Legs. Neck. *Nothing.*

"What if I get cancer?" Jeff asked halfway through.

Castillo repositioned the machine's floating tube stand. "And if they find you, will that matter?" He took another X-ray. Jeff stayed quiet for the rest of the undertaking.

"You're clean," Castillo told him. He seemed disappointed, like Jeff had done something wrong. "Can't find a damn thing."

"How did it find me?"

"*He*," Castillo corrected again. "*They*. I don't know." Castillo deleted the images, had already tossed the clinic's two laptops and a box filled with various canine drugs to make it look like a routine break-in.

They now slumped across from each other on the office floor, Castillo with his back against a desk and his legs outstretched, Jeff cross-legged. Each had a dog resting at his side, piles of treats on the floor between them.

"What now?" the boy asked.

"What now? What now . . ." Castillo distractedly scratched at the dog nestled beside him.

"You gonna quit? The mission."

"If those have become my orders, sure. Don't know if they are yet."

"But you're not answering your phone. Is that, like, legal? Won't you get in trouble?"

"Already am. They know you're with me. I don't know how. But they do. I can probably talk myself out of that." He shrugged. *So damn tired.* "The real problem is that their objectives keep expanding. And never mind me. I think it may have gotten beyond what even Stanforth can do. That's the real danger. If he feels he's lost control of this thing, he'll fucking torch all of it. Including me."

"And me."

Castillo would not deny it. "Remember the Albaums?"

"Edward Albaum. Serpent Mound."

"Right. Their names came over the feed a couple hours ago. They were reported dead last night." Castillo eyed him from across the room. "House burned down. Fire started in the garage. Old paint cans. Community in grief. Etcetera, etcetera."

"Burned down? But the bad kids killed them before we even got there."

"*Seven* days ago."

"Did . . . did DSTI burn their house down?"

"Someone did," Castillo said. "I'll bet lots of adoptive parents vanish soon and that DSTI's missing some more employees at this year's Christmas party."

"God," Jeff said. "Can these people just do whatever they want?"

"Yes."

"What's that mean for us?"

"That your dad was right. You're a liability. A lot of people are now. I'm one now too, it seems. I get a feeling that if they catch either one of us . . ."

"What do we do?"

"Maybe we're not a 'we' anymore. Maybe it's time for you to just go your way, and I'll go mine. What do you think about that?"

Jeff looked away.

"I don't like it either," Castillo said.

"You don't?"

"Nah. I think if we went our own ways, you'd be dead in about forty-eight hours tops. I might last a couple weeks."

"Oh."

"I'll need to check in again eventually. I know enough to be dangerous to them. I have enough skills, maybe, to still be of value. I've been loyal for fifteen years. I just . . . You heard about what happened in SharDhara. All anyone should care about today is that these guys got ahold of some bad, bad stuff. Maybe, I don't know, maybe if I can find them, I can still clear this up."

"My dad gave it to them, didn't he? This 'stuff.'"

Castillo looked back at the boy, struggled for the next words. "I don't know. Don't care. If we don't find it, many people could die. Everyone assumes from the Ripper note they'll be in San Francisco on the fourth. And, or, D.C. and Detroit. That's three weeks. But I don't think we have that long to make my bosses happy."

"Couldn't you just find them on the Murder Map again?"

"Sure, sure. But mostly I'd be chasing dead bodies for the next three weeks. Likely off Route 50 now, and we were *always* one step behind them anyway. Maybe we get lucky again. Henry was the only one going for the Sizemore kid. The rest, he said, were probably already in California. It's a start, I guess. And a 'start' is fine when you have *months*.

There's just not enough time to do really anything. Just . . ." He closed his eyes, mumbled to himself in thought.

Jeff waited, and he thought Castillo had maybe fallen asleep.

But then his eyes sprung open again. "Fuck," he grunted. "Yeah . . . Still, I think our best way out now is through."

"What do you mean?"

"Means I need to stop bitching and finish the damn mission. Regardless of the time crunch, I gotta fuckin' 'fix' things."

"Find the other guys?"

"Yup. And stop whatever's supposed to happen July fourth."

"Find my dad."

"Yeah, that, too. And I think if we do all that, then . . ."

Jeff chuckled.

Castillo smiled back. "Right? Just catch all the bad guys. Save the world . . ."

"Then maybe they'll leave us alone?"

Castillo looked down and spoke at the dog. "Sounds reasonable, doesn't it?"

"So, then. . . . What do we do?"

"Beats the shit out of me."

"Oh."

"Need to sleep some first, I think. It's been . . ." Castillo rubbed at his eyes. They felt like bare slits. "Crash here an hour. Then we'll get moving again."

"West."

"Might as well. Let's try to get some sleep first, OK?"

"Oh." Jeff reached into his book bag. "Here." He handed back the worn copy of *The Odyssey*.

"You're done with it?"

"Sure. And you, um, like to read it sometimes before you sleep."

Castillo reached for the book, smiled wearily. "Try to tell myself it relaxes me."

"Does it?"

"Mostly. Obviously, not always." He tucked it aside. "Not even gonna try tonight."

"Did she give this to you?"

"Who's that?"

"Kristin. She gave you this book, didn't she?"

Castillo closed his eyes. "Yeah, she did."

"You guys used to date?"

"Get some sleep, Jacobson."

"Thought so. How come you—"

"She was already married."

"Oh."

"Oh."

Jeff slumped down on his side, reached out to pet a napping dog. "Good night, Castillo."

"Hey . . ." Castillo opened his eyes again.

"Yeah."

"Where would you go to meet girls?"

"I'm probably gay, remember?" Jeff made a silly face. "How would I know?"

Castillo smiled back. "Dude . . . seriously: Where? She . . . Kristin said some of the guys would be looking for girls. Specifically said Ted. Two days ago, they found the body of Emily Collins. Cops are saying she and some unidentified boyfriend butchered her whole family. Where would they go to pick up girls?"

Jeff thought about it. "Toss over your phone."

"Why?"

"'Cause I know a way to meet girls."

Castillo got up from the floor. "Facebook," he said.

Jeff mimed a slow clap.

YOURS TILL DEATH

JUNE 11, SATURDAY—RIVER GROVE, IL

[From the journals of Dr. Gregory Jacobson]

June 11—What a dance I am leading. The papers now carry the story. Perhaps this attention is what she has been missing? She is never satisfied. No details have been released yet, only that the authorities suspect a "serial killer." Ha ha ha. La police, ne t'a pas encore trouvé? [50W Parma drive, rebeca] I gave birth to the twentieth century. I've given birth to the twenty-first also the others called again today. Something troubling. Wanted to talk. It is because they are alone. So very alone. I know. Do I now destroy what I have created? Or will they destroy the creator? Either may still satisfy. What lies behind and before each of us is a tiny matter compared to what lies within. Iacta alea est. When I initiated the XP11 project, I feared this. Today, after all the tests and reports, splicings, mechano-synthesis and STR markers, I wholly embrace it. Reason, Observation, Experience—the Holy Trinity of Science.

This one was prettier than the others. When he cut her, he thought of the Buddhist monks who practice *Asubha Bhavana*, meditating in isolated graveyards, mounting fresh corpses bloated with putrescence. Contemplating the body's true foulness, seeing ourselves as we truly are. The spit and snot. Tears. Piss trickling down her legs. Putrid, soft, yellow-brown-colored shit. The bile of her vomit as she puked in fear. The sweat on her skin. Lymph slick. Inside, the synovial fluids greasing her joints, the mucus and phlegm lining the insides of her throat and stomach. And the blood. *Always the blood* . . . For a hundred dollars, she danced for him. "I'm Misty," said she. "Tumblety" was the name he gave. *What do I do? They say I'm a doctor now. Ha. Ha.* She touched herself for him in a dark motel room while he watched TV. Five hundred dollars more. Her real name was Gail, Abigail, and where once there was an alluring girl, a pretty smile, the teeth were now broken, jagged and bloody, gaping fetid sockets. He found two rotting wisdom teeth still lurking in the back of her mouth. Her hair, highlighted and long like an Olympian goddess, had, an hour before, lain across his waist. Now it was sticky with bloody stumps at the ends from where he'd torn it out. The tight, tanned flesh across her young stomach, once stripped, became dripping meat. Her mesentery, like a baby's blanket over her intestines, slips between his fingers. It reeks. She reeks. Long legs are nothing but bones. They are painted in blood and graying flesh is stuck to them. Breasts are no more than fatty tissue and two bags of saline. Where once there was an alluring girl . . . *Another illusion that baits such unspeakable things.* In one sutra he knows, the female bodhisattva becomes a rotted corpse to release her lover from his lust. In another, a woman gouges out her own eyes for the same purpose. *Sweet sweet Abigail.* He held her liver, uterus, and heart, fingers pushing through the membranes that held each in place, like reaching into a pumpkin to make a jack-o'-lantern. Her intestines spilled more vomit and fecal matter over his lap, then squirming in his hands before he lay them across the floor. *Samvega*, the monks call it. *Samvega*. The dreadful awakening that surely comes from such sudden awareness. He understands that it is all an illusion. He understands that science is one thing, wisdom another.

He writes again in his journal:

Is this why I have been summoned again? Fata viam invenient. Funny little games. I wonder each day how the others are doing. Jeffrey, most especially. To what have they been summoned? I wonder. Now that I've set them free in every possible way?

RABBITS

When Ted was nine years old, he'd hit a nest of rabbits with the lawn mower.

It had been an accident. Or, at least, he'd thought so at the time.

Later, he would learn the incident had been staged, prescribed for him as part of some test group to see if his MAOA levels would exceed those of another "Ted" somewhere else who *hadn't* killed rabbits. *Fucked up.* He still remembered the weird fhump-fhump-fhump sound, and then little black shadows running in every direction, scattering. He remembered screaming, and the blood misted over the grass. And his dad, who'd been watching, moving toward him. Not his real dad, he knew now. Some guy they'd hired with monthly cash payments. "A damn shame," the pretend dad had said. "But no use sniveling like some pussy girl. They shouldn't have been there." Ted had worked to stop crying. "Nothing to be done about it now," the pretend dad had continued. He'd handed the boy a shovel. "Here." Several of the baby rabbits had stopped no more than ten feet away. Even when Ted stepped right over them, they'd crouched perfectly still. As if he hadn't been able to see them, or, maybe, just that they'd been too afraid, too stupid, to keep running. "They're gonna die anyway," the pretend dad said. "You doing 'em a favor. Make it quick. Go on. I said, go on now, you little fag." Each time Ted lifted the shovel, they still hadn't moved.

He thought of those rabbits now while watching the other kids.

Seemed like the whole goddamn state had shown up. About every redneck in Orchard City between fourteen and seventeen, anyway. All he'd had to do was talk to some girls online and flash some of the money they'd stolen. *Party at Adria's! Free beer and drugs!* The rest had taken care of itself.

The lights were down low, and sixty-plus "bunnies" had already crowded into this rich ho's basement. She'd told Ted her parents were in Italy for two weeks, and he hoped they were having a good time. They were in for quite a surprise when they returned.

There was beer, as promised, and pot. A little coke. Even some molly they'd bought.

And also bleach and ammonia. Several big tubs of it for later.

What they really wanted, of course, was to open the canister Jacobson'd given them. See what that shit would *really* do. Guy claimed it'd be all sorts of badass awfulness. Why wait for July? They could have some real fireworks right here and now.

But Williford argued that Jacobson deserved their waiting—at least that much. They owed him still. And since Jeff Williford almost never talked, and fucking scared the shit out of all of them, they'd just agreed. And so then their thoughts all danced on to other poisons: Zyklon B, like the Nazis used when they were wasting all those Jews, but you couldn't buy that shit anymore. Not even on eBay or craigslist. So next choice was sarin. One drop could basically kill a dude, and on the Internet they even found how to make it, but it was way too hard to figure out. Isopropylamine and sodium fluoride and heating it and all . . . shit could kill you. *Forget it.* Googling some more, they found much easier ways to kill lots of people. Too easy.

"What about that one?" Albert nodded toward the crowd below. The music in the room was so deafening that Ted had to lean closer to hear him. "That one!" The three boys sat on the basement steps over-looking the rest of the party. "Tig ol' bitties, red tank top!"

"That one's Laura, I think," Ted replied. The room was hazy with smoke cut by a cheap strobe light. "Proof of God."

"So you like to say."

"Well, they are. What you want me to say?"

"Bet she's a virgin."

Ted laughed. He absolutely hated these guys. Albert and John mostly. Jeff Williford was terrifying but kinda cool. Ted said, "Yeah, OK. I guess."

"Wanna find out?"

"Not enough time," Ted shook his head. "Doors close in ten."

Ten minutes.

John had already returned into the crowd to take care of the back door. He was still in his clown makeup and costume. Ted had almost forgotten what the kid looked like without, and he supposed it didn't really matter anymore. John kept bumping into the locals and patting asses as he went, and everyone was laughing. Thought the outfit was a riot. *Bunnies.* If they knew the things he'd done this week. To his own family, to total strangers. Or knew he was a clone of some guy who'd butchered and raped thirty-plus dumb slobs. How funny would that be? If they understood who they'd been dancing with, throwing their arms around for Snapchat pics. Ted shrugged. They never would.

"What was that?" Jeffrey asked.

"What?" Ted leaned closer to hear.

"I don't know. Thought I . . . I don't know. Crunk, I guess."

"Yeah." But Ted had felt something also. Like the house's AC had kicked into balls-freeze cold for two seconds. He ignored the strange feeling. It was almost time to lock the doors.

There were all kinds of industrial materials to create toxic gas, they'd discovered. But ammonia and bleach had been the easiest to buy. Twenty gallons each, which they'd stored in three plastic trash cans they'd bought and hidden. One in the hallway closet, two just outside the basement door. All that was left was to mix it up a bit and let it go.

Chlorine gas.

They'd tried a batch earlier. The shit had burned green like a witch's cauldron, then burned their eyes and throats. And that had been standing outside. Down here, three batches of it would blind every eye and burn out fifty-six larynxes. Then, collapse and death. Beautiful. Not quite as personal as Ted usually liked, but it was something.

Something *different*.

He had to admit the rest was, well, getting kinda boring. Same shit over and over. Jacobson had finally called them back. Some of the other guys, John and Al, had been having bad dreams. Baby stuff. Shit, Ted had them too, but he wasn't crying like a pussy about it. But these dreams . . . Ted didn't know. Even he had to admit that the dreams were getting a little more fucked up than usual. *Someone, something, looking for him* . . .

The guys wanted to talk to their old pal Jacobson about this and some other stuff. Like when they used to all sit around in a big circle-jerk back at Massey and talk about their feelings and shit. So fucking gay. Jacobson was such an asshole. But he'd finally called back and was trying to put together some kind of meeting. Fine. There was history there. Something Ted might enjoy, maybe.

Albert had mumbled something beside him.

"Three minutes," Ted shouted back, ignoring Albert and whatever he'd felt a minute before. "Why don't you head down now to help John. We'll get the one up top."

"Cool." Albert stood.

"Who's this guy?" Jeffrey asked, pointing over the crowd to the back door.

"What the fuck?" Ted leaned forward on the steps to get a better look. "Dude's in a costume or something."

"John's got competition," Albert laughed. "Guess this town's got its freaks, too."

"Yeah," Ted said as he peered through the smoke. "I guess." His whole back tingled with ice again. He stood.

"What's wrong?"

"Nothing." Ted tried to shake off the feeling, but could not.

The new guy had shut and locked the back door.

"Who is that?"

"Looks like a black guy, an old black guy. Or—"

Someone screamed. The sound was half lost in the music, but Ted heard it perfectly. He knew all about screams now.

A girl fell in the back of the crowd. People pointed, laughing. Then another collapsed. A boy this time. He was tossed aside by the dark man, and Ted had seen something spray, and he didn't think it was beer.

Jeffrey stood up beside him. "Did he—"

"Yeah," Ted said. "I think he . . ."

"Dude!?"

"Yeah."

More screams. The dark man rushed into the room, making his way deeper into the crowd. Toward John.

"We should—"

Before Ted could articulate the thought, the man clasped John's costume from behind and spun him around.

"What's he . . . ?"

The hand slashed across John's painted face. Blood splashed out from the wide clown collar, sprayed the startled crowd still standing around the attack.

"We should—"

"What?" Ted asked, frozen, not taking his eyes off the thing. "We should *what*?" Another plunge drove a foot-long blade into John's juddering body, another. Another. The man tossed John to the ground and looked up at the steps.

The eyes found Ted's.

"What the fuck *is* that?" Albert shouted. "Ted? What the—"

"I don't know," Ted replied calmly. Too calmly. Warm piss had spread down the front of his legs. "Come on."

He, Jeffrey, and Albert turned and raced up the stairs. Behind them, the crowd squawked and gibbered as they scattered. (*Just like they'd been hit with a lawn mower,* Ted thought.) Their lame shrieks of terror and confusion totally drowned out the music as their shadowed forms barreled up the steps after them.

"What about the chlorine?" Jeffrey Williford asked.

"Fuck it," Ted shouted. They'd fallen in with several of the other kids. Each one running for their life. Exactly like he was.

Finally, he thought, covered in piss, bursting with the others out the front door and into the night. *Something different.*

He started laughing.

JUST AFTER DARK

JUNE 11, SATURDAY—ORCHARD CITY, CO

They'd been less than thirty minutes away from the house with all the dead kids.

Facebook and Twitter told them that.

Jeff hadn't been on either site in more than six months. He had only four new friend requests. Twelve new messages about nothing. He had only forty-two "friends." But David and Al were two of them.

Using Castillo's phone, they'd clicked onto Al's page and read the various threads and messages there. Clicked onto the pages of some of the girls Al was friends with. Took two hours. Jumping from site to site to site, scanning *their* posts. Everyone's privacy settings were for shit.

One girl, Laura Studer in Colorado, had posted random pics on Al's Facebook wall all damn day. Mostly links to videos of obscure bands and a pic of a Magic 8 Ball. Beneath it, she'd typed "i wanna . . ." Then, posts to other girls with various versions of "cu2nite, rofl," which quickly led to another site and a chain of tweets that included Cedaredge High baseball players talking about "crashing the party" and kicking some "Philly bitch's ass."

It didn't take long to piece together the kids' weekend plans.

"Where is Orchard City?" Jeff asked.

It'd been fifteen hours driving straight through. It wasn't yet 9:00 p.m.

Close. But still too late . . .

The girl's parents had not known what to make of Castillo. He told them he was with the DEA and that a lethal LSD drug was being sold at some teen party. *Where was Laura?* They didn't know exactly. Laura wouldn't answer her cell. *What about her friends?* Castillo asked and even gave the names. *Who might know where they went?* Nothing.

He tried two more of the girls' names, their houses. Nothing still. Only more parental confusion and more proof that they had no clue where their children really were for the evening.

And then, finally, the sirens. The flashing lights.

A lone police cruiser racing past in the distance.

Jeff and Castillo shared a look.

"Jesus Christ," Castillo said.

Then followed after the ghostly refrain of the retreating siren.

Castillo parked outside the flashing emergency vehicles. The gawkers of Orchard City were already gathering in full force. It looked like a thousand emergency vehicles were parked up and down the street, and the neighborhood twinkled and flashed like a pinball machine.

In reality, it was only four local police cars and an ambulance. For now . . .

Flashing a bogus badge twice had been enough to get Castillo into the house. The FBI was another hour away, the guys in Grand Junction another ten minutes, and the two hundred rubes of Orchard City, Colorado, still hadn't locked the scene down yet. None of them knew what the hell to do, what the hell was going on. None of them had seen something like this before. He had, and he moved and looked like he knew what he was doing. So they left him alone.

Colonel Stanforth, no doubt, was also already on the way.

Castillo had to move quickly.

He entered the basement, covering his nose and mouth with the top of his shirt. The whole house stank of ammonia. And blood. As he stepped carefully into the butchery below, he could see where both had splashed and soaked the carpet stairs.

There were five bodies here. He'd passed four more upstairs leading out to the front porch. None had been covered yet. They'd been cut. He recognized none of the death-contorted faces. And there wouldn't be time to look any closer. The place was crawling in confusion, but soon someone would show up who knew he didn't belong there.

But here, downstairs, he found the boy in the clown outfit.

Not one of the original six, but a clone nonetheless. John lay sprawled over a dead girl and had been stabbed half a dozen times. His throat was slit, and the blood had pooled out below several of the other nearby bodies. The cuts were deep and had clearly been done with great strength.

Castillo immediately knew who'd killed them, and he literally shuddered at the memory. Could still picture the dark man's retreating form. Castillo quickly inspected the dead boy.

He found two deep pockets in the side of the pants, from which he retrieved a handful of twenties and a cellphone. He left the money but tucked the phone into his own pocket. He patted the rest of the teen's body. There was nothing else but a half-eaten bag of Combos. Castillo looked around again. The head of one of the girls was twisted wrong, angled crookedly to one side. But most of the others looked as if they'd been stabbed, too.

"Who are you?" someone said behind.

"DEA," he lied again, standing.

More police had arrived. And paramedics. He retreated insouciantly from the house, weaving through them and back toward the car. A news helicopter from Grand Junction now swept overhead, no doubt already streaming promising images of carnage to Fox News and MSNBC. His eyes glanced over the crowd, again looking for a familiar face. Wondering what he'd do, what he *could* do, if he actually saw one.

He opened the cellphone he'd taken from John.

A cheap toss-away. No text messages. Any calls in or out already deleted.

Checked the boy's contacts.

There was only one.

Castillo eyed the number again. 215 area code, Philly.

The contact tag: *DR J*. The kid sure as fuck wasn't talking to Julius Erving.

"So, you've been calling Daddy," he mused.

Daddy . . .

Castillo withdrew his own phone.

"Would you . . ."

Scrolling through his own call history. Nothing.

He started for the car, but then stopped. Groaned.

Opened up Safari to sign directly onto the phone service's account. Records not so easily deletable. There Castillo skimmed the most recent calls made.

"Son of a bitch."

Castillo unlocked his car door and slipped inside, where Jeff clung to the shadows in the backseat. "Was it them?" Jeff asked. He sounded out of breath.

"Yeah. Here . . ." Castillo handed the boy his cellphone.

"What's this?"

Castillo started the car and pulled slowly away down the street. "Need you to make a call."

"OK, Castillo," Jeff said, inspecting the phone. "Who am I calling?"

Castillo checked his rearview mirror. They were not being followed, and the flashing lights had already become a wine-colored blur in the distance. It looked like someone had misted Orchard City in blood. He eyed the boy, suddenly uncomfortable with having Jeff that close behind him. *His teeth . . .*

In the mirror, he looked Jeff in the eyes.

"Same guy you've been calling all week," Castillo said. "Your goddamn father."

JEFF CALLS

Hey. Hey, Dad.
    It's me.
    Jeff. Jeff!
    No. Jeff Jacobson.
Yeah. I'm . . . I'm OK. I know you told me not—
Where are you? I need . . . I need to see you.
No. It's just . . . yes. I guess. Is that OK?
Winter Quarters. No. Utah? Yeah, I can look it up. Thanks. I . . .
Midnight. Yes.
Are you OK? You . . .
Dad?
When will you—
Yeah. OK . . . I—
Yes.
Yeah.
I love you too.

NOT WHO I EXPECTED

JUNE 12, SUNDAY—WINTER QUARTERS, UT

Winter Quarters, where they were to meet at midnight, was five hours away.

So Castillo and the boy slept while parked at a McDonald's outside Grand Junction and then, in the morning, Castillo found a Barnes & Noble and picked up the books Jeff had asked for earlier: books on Jack the Ripper.

Maybe find something to help better understand the man they were headed toward.

Jeff read quietly while they drove deep into Utah.

By noon, Castillo had posted up at Green River State Park, about thirty miles north of Winter Quarters, with another ten hours to wait. He tried sleeping again. Couldn't. Far too ready to get the day started for real. The boy kept reading, dozed off a little bit, too. Neither one much for talking.

He'd gotten over the initial surge of anger at Jeff for calling his dad. Knew he'd never really been mad at him anyway, the kid doing what anyone in his position—scared to shit—would have done: Call his own dad. No, Castillo was mad only at *himself*. For being so dumb as to not expect it, to look for it. Maybe even suggest it. How and when Jeff had managed to make the calls, he still didn't know. Supposed the kid had been handed the damn phone enough times over the week. Maybe when he was in the shower, or catching some Zs. *Had the blackouts returned?* Didn't matter. He had Jacobson now. Or would soon. And once you had Jacobson, you also had the other guys, too. Because if the clown boy and Jeff were talking to Jacobson, the others also probably were. Phone numbers traced easily.

But did he really have any business going in to deal with Jacobson directly? Or, later, Stanforth? He'd been totally played by a scared kid. *Fucking pathetic.* Maybe what all the others had said about him was true. Maybe he'd really lost it over in Iran.

Maybe . . .

There was one way to find out. So, he waited.

Hours later, the sun finally setting, the boy started mumbling about something.

"What is it?" Castillo asked, shaking himself, and his peripatetic reveries, returning fully to the here and now.

"In the book . . ."

"Found something?" Castillo looked over.

"Tumblety," Jeff said.

Tumblety, Castillo thought. *Tumblety is familiar.* His slow recall was further proof he'd lost a step or was too damn tired. *Tumblety.* Then he had it. "The dead guy, right? Secret room?" *The guy your freak father has a raging genetic chubby for.* Castillo grimaced. "How could I forget? He's in the book, I assume?"

"Big-time. So he's a prime Ripper suspect, right?"

"Seems so. What'd you find out?"

"After the Ripper murders, he escaped to America. The New York City police were always watching him and stuff. He settled in Rochester and got married twice. To Margaret Zilch and . . . ready?"

"We are," Castillo said, exhausted. Checked his watch: Five hours to go.

"Alice Jacobson."

"And there it is."

"There was a son. William."

"William Jacobson? Are we assuming then he kept his mother's name?"

"We're not assuming, it's in the book. Tumblety was a Jack the Ripper suspect *and* had also been arrested for being involved in the Lincoln assassination. Would you want the name Tumblety?"

"Not under any circumstance. So, you suspect William is your . . . what? Grandfather?"

"Great-grandfather. Maybe. But not mine. I'm not a Jacobson."

"So, your adopted father's grandfather?"

"Maybe. We could double-check."

"We could. But how will it help? This Tumblety guy, was he really—"

"Jack the Ripper? Probably not," Jeff said. He reached for the other book Castillo had picked up. "Most evidence now points to some guy named Walter Sickert. They've done DNA analysis and everything. It's pretty much case closed."

"Wouldn't your father know that?"

"You'd think. But maybe he didn't really want to know it."

"So if he still thinks he's a direct descendant, some kind of genetic rebirth of Jack the Ripper . . ."

"It's all totally in his sick head."

"Yeah."

"Yeah," Jeff echoed. "And if he's wrong about that . . ."

"Then he's wrong about a lot of things."

"Uh-huh."

Castillo nodded, his thoughts churning. He said, "My dad took off when I was nine."

"Yeah?"

"Yeah." Castillo looked ahead at nothing, the setting sun over the mountains maybe. "Hated the son of a bitch for close to twenty years. And the more I tried hating him, the more I became just like him. The way he moved, talked. Things he said. Fuck . . . I don't know. In a couple years, I'll probably *be* him."

And, so, will you be Jeffrey Dahmer when you grow up? I wonder if your daddy's so wrong after all. . . . His thoughts turned again, to paths too dark to traverse at the present. If ever.

Castillo started the car.

"OK," he said. "Let's go get Dad."

Past Colton and down Route 96 to Scofield, an isolated canyon where a coal-mine town thrived for two generations until the mine exploded. Every available casket in Utah was shipped to Winter Quarters the first week of May 1900, and there still weren't enough coffins. Two hundred men dead in a single day: burned, buried alive, poisoned by the coal dust's afterdamp. In ten years, the town was completely empty.

Jeff had looked it up on the Internet on the way to Utah. The web said the place was seriously haunted: In addition to the strange lights in the mines, tourists reported the desperate wails of the dying men and their mourning wives. All that stuff. But Jeff didn't care much about ghosts tonight. Tonight was about getting his dad. Getting ANSWERS.

He knew Castillo was still pissed about the phone calls. He'd only called a couple of times, but the fact remained that he'd called the number his dad had given him the night he'd left. It'd been pointless. The calls had all ended the same way. Confused. *Where are you?* No answer. *What should I do?* No answer. He wasn't sure his dad even knew who he was talking to. But that didn't matter either. Castillo would do what he said he would: Make things right. He'd find his father. Help him. Then they would all talk. Figure it all out. Make things better. Get back to the rest of their lives. The cursed dead could wail all they wanted. Tonight was about the damned souls still living.

In the dark, he saw someone walking the dirt road toward him.

Castillo was already coming back.

Castillo expected Jacobson would arrive ahead of them, that the madman was even now watching him. He'd made Jeff stay in the car again, a good mile back, then hiked over the fence and along the forsaken railroad grade. Jeff hadn't been happy about it, but the argument had ended quickly.

Midnight loomed. Below, caved-in cellars and broken foundations were all that remained. There was one two-story building still standing, two of its stone walls completely collapsed, the others desperately clinging to the rotted frame beneath. Castillo hiked along the top of the hill, watching every shadow below, keeping low, as unusually cool summer winds whistled up the canyon toward him. The old mine was beyond the canyon and ruins. He'd come in through the back.

Castillo leveled his gun and moved toward the mine. He thought again of calling for backup. Jacobson was insane. And he might not be alone. But Castillo had crawled into enough caves alone before. He could certainly handle this one more, capture Jacobson, and call it a day.

Mission over. Stanforth and the others could take it from there.

Success. He'd sort out everything, get his life straight again.

As for Jeff . . .

Castillo couldn't afford to think about him. Not now. Focus only on the direct mission: Capture Jacobson. He listened, then charily descended an overgrown footpath toward the boarded mine.

There, someone was clearly below, a shadowed figure half lost within the shaft's opening. Where and when he'd said he'd be. *As precise as ever.*

"Dr. Jacobson," Castillo said and cast his flashlight directly onto the shape.

A man shrank back from the light.

It was Jacobson.

The same man from the pictures Castillo'd studied for more than a week. But thinner. Clothes disheveled. *Maybe not so precise after all* . . . Disoriented. He looked unarmed.

Castillo dropped down after him and kept the light focused, finger ready on the trigger of his gun. Still, he wanted Jacobson taken alive.

For answers. For Jeff.

"You're not who I expected," Jacobson said.

"Understood," Castillo replied. "Put your hands out where I can see them."

Jeff's father shielded his eyes from the light. The tunnel extended another fifteen feet back, and then the mine behind was completely boarded over. "The boss man sent you," Jacobson said. "Yes?"

"Fucking hands out where I can see them. Hold 'em out!"

Jacobson did as ordered as Castillo scanned the rest of the mine's entrance. Except for the shifting doctor, it appeared completely empty. "Down now. On your knees. Get down. Understand?"

"Fine, fine." Jacobson lowered to the dirt floor, grunted with the effort. "How did you . . . Where are they? I don't understand."

"All the way down." Castillo moved closer, checking behind him, keeping the light on the doctor's face. "Relax. Everything is going to be fine."

"Of course. If you don't mind—"

"Down." Castillo closed the gap and drove the man's chest completely to the ground with his left hand and flashlight. "Easy now."

Jacobson's next words were garbled, his face buried in dirt. "Of course . . ." Both arms were already secured behind his back with custody strips. Castillo then patted the geneticist down, each movement reflexive and textbook. Still, touching the man proved palpably unsettling. Knowing the kinds of things he'd arranged, done, to kids.

To Jeff.

Castillo found the knife in a holster at Jacobson's hip. It was a seven-inch black carbon blade with a leather sheath, stained with use. Again, Castillo didn't care. It wasn't what he was looking for. He pulled the knife holster free and jammed it into the front of his own pants. "Where's the chemical?" he said, shaking Jacobson roughly.

Nothing.

"Did DSTI send . . . no . . ." Jacobson squinted against the light between them and studied Castillo. "I recognize your breed. One of Stanforth's boys? I'm not surprised, you know. What's your name, little soldier?"

Fuck this guy. "Where'd you park, Jacobson? Where's your car?"

"First, a brief riddle, a history riddle. Do you like history? Take five of the greatest scientific minds of their times. Galileo was hired by the leadership in Venice to design weapons. . . ."

"Come on." Castillo pulled the geneticist back to his feet. "The stuff you used at SharDhara?"

"Da Vinci was hired by the pope to design weapons," Jacobson replied, seemingly oblivious to the question. "Descartes was hired by the queen of Sweden to design weapons. Edison was hired by President Wilson to design weapons. Einstein—"

Castillo pulled Jacobson closer, brusquely. The man grunted. Castillo could feel his warm, foul breath on his face. "Your car?"

"Three of these scientists," Jacobson continued, grinning like something that'd emerged from its crypt, "did exactly as they were told and continued to make weapons. Two, however, decided their interests were not in 'military science' after all. Which two?"

Castillo shoved the man forward by his wrists. He didn't want any more riddles. Not from anyone. Certainly not from Jacobson. Best to clear out and talk with him elsewhere.

"Some more information first, perhaps. Galileo was jailed for life, declared a heretic, and the publication of any of his works was forbidden. Descartes was poisoned, buried in a graveyard for unbaptized infants, his writings added to the *Librorum Prohibitorum* by the pope." Jacobson stopped walking. Turned to stare Castillo straight in the eyes. "Now," he said. "Brave soldier; which two?"

"Drop the bullshit, Jacobson. You're no Galileo. You're just another asshole with a big knife. Another weirdo with a pile of chemicals. Another terrible father."

"Jeffrey? He . . . I believe he called me." Jacobson's gaunt face was surprised, wondering. "Yes, I know he did. My son." He spoke as if in a trance.

"Your *experiment*," Castillo corrected. "You only wanted him for your own perverse validations. To prove evil was in the blood. Got news for you, Doc. You were wrong. The only evil Jeff knows is what you fucking people did to him. But he's safe now," Castillo said, pushing Jacobson ahead. "Everyone's safe now." He realized that mentally, he'd included himself.

Jacobson laughed.

"Something funny?"

"'Safe.' Coming from you. From the kind of men you work for. It's, shall we say, ironic."

"Told you I'm not interested in your dogmatic bullshit, Doc. Not one bit."

"I see," Jacobson said. "But you are assuredly 'interested' in *them*. Yes?"

Castillo followed the man's eyes. And, up the hill and standing at the edges of the ruined city, were three figures who were not the ghosts of the Winter Quarters miners.

Three narrow shapes. Men. Boys.

"Who are they?" Castillo pulled the doctor closer as a shield. He'd put on his vest for the arrest but wanted the extra barrier in case.

"John, I think," Jacobson said. "John, Ted, and some of the others. When I got the call from Jeffrey, I . . . Well, I invited the others here tonight. I honestly thought we would be alone."

"How many? John's dead, by the way."

"Is he?" Jacobson's voice sounded even more distracted, distant.

"Murdered last night. Throat slashed, stabbed a dozen times. Some people will want to talk to you about that, I'm sure."

"Me? No, no, not me. They'll want to talk to me about other things, I suppose. But not about John. Slashed, you say?" Jacobson chuckled softly.

"More irony, Doctor?" Castillo found that he was moving toward the teens, not away.

"I wondered if they would . . ."

"Would what?"

"You'll find out soon enough."

"Stand still." They were fifty yards from the others. Castillo recognized every one of them. He'd studied their files enough to recognize each face.

Albert, Ted, and . . . Jeff.

No, Castillo cursed himself, then thought, *This is the OTHER Jeffrey*. One of the original six. A kid named Jeff Williford. Adopted to a whole other surrogate family. Three years older. Taller. More . . . *evil?*

Castillo stuffed his flashlight into his jeans pocket and retrieved his cell. His pistol remained trained on the three teens, who all stood perfectly still. Waiting.

"Castillo?" Stanforth's voice came over the phone, calm and forgiving.

"I've got Jacobson. Get whoever you can to Winter Quarters mine outside of Scofield. Now. There are at least three more targets here. Copy?"

"Copy. Air support out of Salt Lake in fifteen. Can you—"

"I'll manage. Jacobson doesn't have any sort of canister or vial on him. Still need to check his car."

"Fine work, soldier. Hey, kiddo, I wanted to—"

"Later," Castillo hung up.

"Your masters are pleased, yes?" Jacobson asked. "That's always important."

Castillo shook him quiet. "I have a gun!" he called out to the others. It was suddenly freezing cold. "Is that understood?" Castillo ignored the chill.

"'I've got a gun,'" one of the boys mimicked in a high, silly voice. "Eat my dick, asshole."

"One step closer, I shoot you."

"'One step closer . . .'" one of the other voices said, and the other two laughed.

Castillo pulled Jacobson still closer, tried to attach voices to the faces he'd come to know so well from file photos. It was always odd hearing their voices. . . .

"Jacobson?" the one named Al shouted. "Who's this loser? Jeffrey's new friend?"

Castillo scowled, wondered why they'd mentioned Jeff. Surely they meant the other Jeff.

Their Jeff. Williford.

"This is over," Castillo said. He was not sure if he was speaking to the kids, Jacobson, or himself. He thought of Henry, had promised him it was over, too. That he could help. And then . . . and then he'd killed him. *Will this play out the same way?*

The teens giggled.

"It's over," he said again, to Jacobson specifically. He wanted someone, anyone, to agree.

"For me," Jacobson said, "perhaps. But . . . over? No. This isn't over yet. Science without conscience is the soul's—"

"Save your babble for the fucking shrinks," Castillo snapped. Jacobson stilled, and Castillo looked over the dark horizon. It would be another twenty minutes, at least, before backup arrived. He needed to stall. "Quite a party you guys had last night," he shouted over at them. "The one back in Orchard City."

"Yeah, so? What do you care?"

"I don't, not really. Purely an observation. Nine dead, not including John, of course. You see it on the news?"

"Yeah, well. Wasn't us."

"We'd have killed sixty," said another voice. Jeff's voice. No, NOT Jeff. *Jeffrey*, rather. Jeffrey Williford. Yet he'd sounded enough like the boy Castillo knew . . . different, but enough.

Too much.

"The ammonia," Castillo offered, stalling. "Interesting idea . . ."

"What you know about it?"

"I also know about the family in Vernon. The women in Unity."

"Yeah. You're some kind of fucking genius, aren't ya?"

"I've been told." Castillo decided right then that he would, in fact, kill all three if one moved another inch. Only Jacobson was key. Only Jacobson knew every turn this Hell had. Only Jacobson had a son. And, in the end, no matter what happened here tonight, he understood these three were only more collateral anyway.

"You the guy who did John?" Al asked.

"No way," Jeffrey said. "It ain't him."

"You're a dead faggot," Al shouted.

Castillo checked the horizon again. These guys would probably run when the copters appeared. *Run*, he thought. *They'll get you easy.* Jacobson shifted in front of him, muttering. Sounded Latin maybe. Castillo pulled the doctor still and shouted back at the boys. "You guys kill anyone today?"

"Not yet," the last boy spoke, finally. Ted. His voice had been deeper and more serious than the others. He'd meant it. He'd also drawn a gun.

"Easy there, tough guy," Castillo warned. "Put the gun down or I will end you."

"Do it," the teen said, stepping forward. "You think I really give a fuck anymore?"

Castillo reset his own pistol, aimed at the boy's head. "No, I don't," he agreed. "I've read your files, asshole." The kid stopped, smiled broadly. For a second, Castillo thought the skin might actually split open against the ever-widening jaw. Almost as quickly, the smile vanished.

Ted turned, looking behind the other two into the ruined city. Castillo tensed, scanning the surrounding shadows. Jacobson had mumbled something again, then moaned.

"What's that, Doc?" Castillo crouched closer behind him.

"He's here," Jacobson said.

"Who—"

Then Castillo knew, too.

He twisted instinctively, reacted to the sudden movement from his right. One of the shadows had separated, leaped, away from the others. Castillo felt his entire body lift from the ground, weightless, reality suspended. He'd seen his attacker only a second, had felt the steel-fingered hand against his shoulder and rolled against the expected strike. Burning pain sank into his lower back, then he was slamming into the ground. Someone close was screaming. There were gunshots, not his own. Castillo knew he'd been cut, and deep. But he'd rolled with the blow, and the vest had taken the worst of it. He scrabbled to his knees, fought to pull himself back up.

Someone stood directly between him and Jacobson. The man was small and lean, almost completely lost against the night. The same from the motel room. But, *man*? *Not entirely* . . .

This guy held Jacobson by the throat, lifting him into the moonlight with one arm, studying him, while the geneticist's feet kicked inches from the ground. A blade in the figure's other hand was jammed in the doctor's middle, lifting also. Jacobson's screeches were pitched too high, like the wails of a ghostly widow.

Castillo put five bullets into the killer's back. The man stumbled forward with the impact but still did not drop Jacobson. Righting himself, he heaved his blade arm sideways. Blood sprayed across the distance between them and splashed hot across Castillo's face as Jacobson split open from the middle, his intestines bursting free with a wet slurp.

Jacobson's killer turned now toward the three boys. The clones.

This was an execution. Pure and simple. Stanforth, DSTI, had sent this man.

Castillo watched the boys sprinting back through the deserted town. *Do I just let it go?* he wondered. *Let this guy, whoever he is, kill again. Finish this.*

He felt the fresh wound burning in his back, straightaway thought of the basement full of dead kids he'd seen barely hours before.

Castillo fired another burst of shots. Each hit its target, and their reports echoed through the canyon. Probably scared a shitload of ghosts. The thing—Castillo could think of it as nothing else now—turned back to Castillo.

He emptied what little was left of the clip.

It spun backwards, black mist spraying from the side of the head, and whirled to the ground with a screech. Yet as quickly as he'd appeared, he sprang back up and was now sprinting away from Castillo deeper into the old camp. Crouched and loping.

Wounded. Dying.

Has to be, Castillo told himself. *I saw some of that damn head go POOF.*

He was suddenly fighting to keep conscious himself. *Who's the wounded one now?* He'd lost a lot of blood already. His body racked with pain, he chased after the shape as fast as he could, feeding another clip into his 9mm.

He looked for the others. The three teens were gone. Or well hidden. Jacobson's killer moved more slowly, scarcely fifty yards ahead. The man tottered, stumbled, crawled on his knees into one of the half-collapsed cellars.

Rounding the cellar's corner, Castillo had to admit that if he hadn't been looking, he never would have seen his quarry. The black-garbed figure was slumped against the far left corner of a shadow-filled cellar. He was twisted, misshapen, in his attempt to hide himself better. Like a giant spider or a bat that was only part human. And the long knife still glistened in the moonlight, like a single giant fang.

Castillo shot five rounds.

The man dropped from the corner, from the shadows, and onto the floor.

Castillo climbed down into the small cellar, using the collapsed rubble as stairs. He looked back, wondering if the copters would ever show up. *This guy has to be with Stanforth. How had he found them?*

He dared touch the body, to confirm what he already knew: The man was dead.

And it *was* a man. Mostly.

Castillo stared for a while. Tried to make sense of what he was looking at.

The guy wore a modified ballistics vest. Additional armor down its arms and around the throat and jaw. Just above, the left cheek and ear *had* been shot off. He was charcoal-skinned, black as the darkest African, but otherwise the facial features seemed more European. But no racial heritage could account for the too-narrow head. Like a sideshow freak. Or the too-wide mouth overcrowded with uneven, slanted teeth, or maybe the two gaping holes where a nose should have been . . . and not from any recent gunshot wound. An old injury, then, or . . . was this just the fucking guy's face?

Castillo kept staring.

Still so eerily familiar. A memory?

From his nightmares. *Is that it?*

Something about his nightmares. Something . . .

But any forthcoming remembrance vanished with the next flare of pain.

He winced. Cursed. Looked away. Climbed wanly out from the dark cellar, leery of the others: Ted, Al, and Jeffrey. They were probably still running, though. He couldn't blame them.

He touched his own side, wet and sticky with blood. Kept his hand against the wound and moved out of the canyon as fast as he could. It took forever. His breaths were long and slow by the time he reached the top.

Two helicopters glided swiftly into the canyon from the west. He'd not heard them over his own ragged breathing. Along the railway again, toward his car. He felt light-headed, knew he'd lost too much damn blood. Knew well how close he was to collapsing.

Castillo drew close to the car, tightening his hold on the pistol. "Jeff?"

The car's windows were busted out. Front and back. All four windows on both sides. *They've been having fun*, Castillo thought. *Teasing their prey.* Anger crawled through him again. Familiar. Not some damned PTSD phantom anger. Something that suddenly felt more real.

The shattered glass lay everywhere. There was blood on one of the back windows. His new books discarded in the backseat, Jeff's duffel bag in a heap in the front. The tire tracks of a second car were furrowed deep in the dark ground.

He checked the woods outlining both sides of the dirt road. "Jeff!"

They'd taken him. Jeff's "brothers."

Castillo rested against the front of the car, blew his breath against the chill. The ghosts of Winter Quarters mine whispered in the distance. Or maybe it was the helicopters.

Castillo didn't know which. Didn't care.

He just knew he had another boy to find.

THE DARK MEN

Zahir likes to watch men die, specifically treasuring the precise moment when the doomed reaches that unique awareness of having nothing more to give, helpless, and then, in that very personal and ultimate defeat, almost always a brief, final, futile, clench of life, a sudden gasp, optimistic, defiant, and the eyes almost always show it all because no man is ever as truly alive as during his very last breath and, by looking into their eyes, Zahir can truly see God and so runs his fingers along your face slick with sweat and blood, and you move your head into the touch. Well trained, Zahir thinks, and smiles. Where most would pull away from one who'd already brought so much pain, you've been taught to want the heft of reality against your cheek, something real to focus on. Zahir pats the cheek. Soon, he whispers again, promises, and moves again toward his bench of tools, the rusted kerosene lantern, fluid shadows along the cramped cave, the shadow twisted unnaturally under the low ceiling. Other men talking in the adjacent tunnels and holes, someone's laughter . . .

The first time Zahir sees a man die, he's maybe eight, and maybe in Cairo when some car bomb shatters half of some market and, as he cowers on the ground with the others, a dark shape maybe stumbles toward him from out of *the smoky wreckage and Zahir is still not sure if it was a man or a woman he sees that day, there was too much blood, and part of the head is missing as it lurches toward him as if every step might bring its final collapse, and the boy, the Zahir boy, has wiped the burn of the smoke from his eyes to watch it all. He sees half a face, the right side shards of bone and flesh and the skull behind almost completely lost. He sees the lone left eye glaring at him, yes, directly at him, with both amazement and resolve, the boy Zahir knows then that the bloody thing actually wants to kill him. That, even with half its face and brains splattered over the street behind, it has determined not to accept death alone. The man-woman lifts an arm at him, an accusing bloody stump that ends at the elbow, and then it collapses at your feet. Something wet and hot splashes on your face, Zahir's face, beside him then, the shattered jaw and what was left of its teeth gnawing on a lolling tongue, and blood gurgles from the half mouth, the limbs twitching against Zahir's legs. Still, the boy focuses on the eager and knowing eye watching him and the eyes shine like a star. The eye of God. He finds the same look again maybe six months later when he kills the old man with a brick. Then, maybe once more, when he strangled Ahmed's baby sister. And the others. When he joins the Fatah al-Islam Jihad, it soon becomes his sacred duty to hurt, to kill, and one of the group, a wealthy girl who goes to Alexandria University, a Ph.D. candidate in some-or-other bullshitty subject, she suggests his violent nature is surely caused by the trauma of that first car bomb, or perhaps the frequent beatings his father gave him. And Zahir does not think so, and, as he rapes and kills her, he tells her as much. He simply enjoys it, he tells her, it's not schtick, that was all. He'd enjoyed torturing the family in Herát, or the boy soldiers they'd kidnapped in Qal'at Dizah, or more recently, he'd enjoyed killing the people in Towraghondi. His team has captured the three Rangers outside of Towraghondi a week before and slipped them back across the border, no way the Americans come into Iran for them, says "John Penn" and "George Clooley" would never allow it, and chuckles. A good week after much pain, and much blood, he'd already seen God twice and he will enjoy this man's death too. Already hurt him, peeled his flesh, cut down to the bone. The American's so damn big he wants to see that muscle up close and, truth be told, he'd never been particularly interested in the politics, or in the spiritual matters of his effort, these secondary to his true passions, and in that regard, he is probably no different from this soldier that God has directly sent to him.*

Glance over to the two emptied chairs. Dark stains of torture pooled below each, memories of the broken bodies, only their heads remain each propped on the small wood table watching. Choosing his favorite scalpel, the two-inch carbon steel BD Bard-Parker lifted from the Red Cross tent, nice cutting control and strength, perfect to make some more shallow incisions along the chest and genitals. Start making garbled sounds, not words anymore. Havn't been for almost a day now. A pity, as Zahir wants to learn more about this man, but these are not normal men, these "Rangers" never once beg for mercy like the others, they curse and grow angry. He never even learns their real names, no identification on men like these. No man. Oud-eis. Don't do this. Not yet the true eye of God. Zahir steps closer and presses his thumb against your mouth to push back the upper lip. Writhe in the chair, the blood-speckled ropes holding tight. Scream as Zahir raises the blade, brings the scalpel once more to your gums. Then moves to the body again works quietly before the gunfire. The gunfire erupted in one of the tunnels. The sound echoes like thunder. Drops the wet scalpel onto the table beside the two heads and someone shouted somewhere, the sound of a man dying, and now Zahir reaches for his rifle. One of the others, Hasib you think, bursts into the cave, shouts something, and Zahir almost shoots him. Zahir grins at this thought. "What is it?" he asked. In reply, Hasib lifts into the air and, then, like a ghost, rises another full meter off the ground. Zahir stepping back in confusion and blood splashes across the cave's rock. Something shiny now out of Hasib's chest, then he is dropping to the floor. Something else moves in the shadows. A thin, dark shape that drifts like smoke directly toward Zahir who is firing his rifle. The strong hands at his throat and then something very cold sinking deep into his stomach. A large knife glinted in the dark cavern, stabbing. The man screams, Jacobson, opens at the middle, entrails spilling in a splash onto the cave floor. He feels the cold blade moving inside him and the shadow man stands before him and Zahir gazes into the pitch-black eyes that shimmer like oil, like a demonic jewel, but in their dark reflection he sees his own eyes, too, wide and shining, and recognizes the sensation of his body splitting apart as he screams, an almost joyful sound, and then, finally, in the reflection of the dark man's eyes, his own eyes shine like stars, the eyes of God, he thinks, and then, nothing. The body cast aside, knocking the table and the two heads rolling slowly obscenely almost comically tumbling over. Watching you. The heads of Second Lieutenant Wissinger and Specialist Koster. Become, because this is the dream, the faces of Shaya and Jeff. The dark thing turns next toward you in the chair. Struggling against the ropes. Turning away. Zahir's top half still squealing in a piercing sound that spreads and spreads until you wanted to explode from the pressure. The dark skeletal fingers digging under the chin now. Lifting your head. Blood trickling over one eye, you have no choice but to look straight into its face. The eyes . . .

Castillo lurched awake, a gasp caught halfway in his throat in the form of a lunatic's high-pitched scream, the terrible sound going into him, not out. The nightmare vanished again, but the pain lingered, as it sometimes did. He dreamily touched his mouth, and then moved down to his chest, where his fingers easily found the thick scar tissue. Both familiar and still alien. His hands moved to the more-recent bandaging and wounds. Here too the bleeding had stopped. His vest had taken the bulk of things, the cut since cleaned and sutured. The motel room bathroom was still covered with stained towels and the fresh stench of alcohol and blood.

It was the same man. . . .

Castillo sat up painfully once more at the small desk over a closed laptop and his notes. A gooseneck lamp cast the only light in the motel room, and it glowed hotly, like a rusted kerosene lantern. He leaned forward and put the heels of his palms against his eyes to rub away the sleep, the memory. His fingers wrapped around the sides of his head, a familiar pose. From afar, Castillo often thought, it must look as if he were literally holding himself together. *Maybe I am.* He felt the fusty chill of the room's AC move across his back and shoulders.

The man in the cave . . .

Castillo could hardly think anymore. He checked his watch. 0636. He couldn't quite remember when he'd dozed off. He remembered noting 0500 clearly and then reading more of Jacobson's damned notes. Time had become a damning factor. It had been less than four hours since he'd walked out of the Winter Quarters, but the pieces of his past were coming together, melding with the nightmares of his present.

Jacobson had been murdered by, and Castillo himself had shot and killed—as unbelievable as it seemed—the man from his own nightmares. The "Dark Man" he'd seen in the cave two years before.

Whether the same man or some sort of clone himself, Castillo didn't know. *And how had Stanforth . . . ?* and *What are these men?* and so on, but none of this mattered now, he told himself.

What mattered now was the boy.

He picked up Jacobson's opened notebook from the table and read. From the letters of Jack the Ripper: "*You an me know the truth dont we. ha ha I love my work an I shant stop until I get buckled and even then watch out for your old pal Jacky. Ps Sorry about the blood still messy from the last one.*"

"Your old pal Jacky."

Castillo turned the page and reread the words of Ted Bundy: "*We serial killers are your sons, we are your husbands, we are everywhere. And there will be more of your children dead tomorrow.*" Castillo ran the words through his head again. The boys truly had a whole country in which to hide. They had transportation, money. No ties anymore to real people beyond the files of the historic killers they'd been cloned from.

We are everywhere.

Castillo's mouth went tight. *How long does the boy truly have, left with them? And are there really any answers I can find in the notes of this mad-man? Any clues as to where Jacobson's creations might have gone? Or is this only more of the same lunacy? The same which drove the eminent geneticist to such horrors in the first place?*

He closed the notebook. Stared at the dark wall over the desk. He felt he should get up and drive somewhere to do something. But where? And what? He was too alone now, and as wanted by the Defense Department, he suspected, as the psycho killers he'd been tasked with bringing in. And even if he'd had the full support of Command, there simply wasn't time.

Castillo pushed back from the table and rose for the first time in hours. Limply, painfully, he moved toward the mirror in the dim light. Then, he looked up.

He saw the new bandaging taped around his side, and all around it, the pale scars that almost completely covered his stomach and chest.

The marks crisscrossed the defined muscles in continuous disfigure-ment and design, wrapped over his shoulders and arms. Many letters were Perso-Arabic, naturally. Others something else, symbols no one had ever determined. The man had cut snakes and trees into him. And eyes, staring eyes etched in flesh.

The Illustrated Man, Castillo thought for the hundredth time. He studied himself awhile. Curiously, almost, as he often had over the last two years. As if he was looking at someone else. He stared back into those other eyes. First, the ones that had been cut into him. Then, the pair in the mirror. His own. Behind him, the shadows of the room assumed their own shapes. Almost human.

Your old pal Jacky.

Castillo turned away from his reflection and reached for his phone. His call was answered on the first ring.

"I'm glad you called," Stanforth said. "We're in a new place here."

"Very true."

"And it's not a good one."

"Also true."

"You need to come in, Castillo, and you need to come in right now. This one's over. That's an order."

"Not yet."

"Shawn, if you continue—"

"Not yet."

"What do you want?"

Castillo flipped open his laptop. "I want you to release more of those things."

"I don't know what—"

"Sure you do," Castillo stopped him. "Super-soldier type, genetically fucked with artificial violence. Like the one that murdered Jacobson for you. Or all those kids in Orchard City. The same one you sent into Iran two years ago?"

"When I saved your damn ass?"

"Do this," Castillo said. "Or I go to the press with everything."

"Would you really?"

Castillo honestly didn't know. "Yes."

"But would they believe you?"

"Considering the current popular opinion of our bosses, I have a feeling they might. Release them."

"To what end?"

"What end do you think? So they can find the last few boys. Like the other one did. How'd he track them down before? Made somehow from the same stuff, I imagine. Some kind of psychic or chemical connection or . . . What the fuck does it matter? Just get it done."

"You killed him, Shawn. There are no others."

"Sure there are, *Brad*. You're the guys who love to make copies, right? Death's very own Kinko's."

Stanforth grunted a half laugh. "I don't know if we can do that now. You saw what happened in Orchard—"

"We can do it." Castillo moved back to his laptop. "Risk it. And I need to know exactly when they're found. I want to be there."

"Why? To end this yourself? Save the day? Everyone told me you'd lost your fucking mind over there. I should have listened more."

Castillo ignored him, tapped at his keyboard. "I'm sending you a private ICR to contact the moment you know something. Do that, and you won't have to worry about me ever again."

"It's my job to worry. And what about Jeffrey? Do I need to worry about him?"

"Who?"

"Jeffrey Jacobson. Jeff Dahmer. Whatever name he's going by. Jeff/82. His DNA's all over Jacobson's house. In your hotel room in Olney. It was only a matter of time before we realized where he'd gotten to. How long have you—"

"Kid helped me do my damn job," Castillo said. "He's not an issue. Never was. Besides, I'm pretty sure he's already dead." He almost hoped as much. "Just fucking get it done."

"I understand your request, but Castillo . . ."

"Yes."

"If we do this. If we do this your way . . . and if it goes bad, I can't help you when this is over. You'll be on your own. You understand?"

If it goes bad . . .

"One hundred percent," Castillo said and ended the call.

"*And there will be more of your children dead tomorrow.*" Bundy's quote echoed in his mind. *But how many?* Castillo wondered aloud, and his body trembled in the empty room. *How many?*

As he flipped off the light to let the darkness cover him completely, he could only think of one.

JEFFS

Jeffrey Dahmer sat in a chair before a rusted metal table, a small pile of bones spread before his hands.

Jeffrey Dahmer stood closely behind the chair, watching him.

The first, the one Jacobson had raised, had been stripped naked and looked as if he'd been crying. He had been. There were abrasions on his wrists and legs from the duct tape.

The other one, the one Ted knew from school, was a couple years older. Heavier, too. The young one's hair was brown. But there was no question about it: These two little dirty birdies came from the same dirty nest.

It really was something to see. And Ted could hardly take his eyes off it. Any of it.

When they'd first grabbed the kid in Scofield, it had been a pretty random act. But when they saw, when they really understood who this kid was . . . they thought it was AMAZING.

Another version of Jeff. 2.0 or 3.0 or 40.1. They hadn't a clue.

And the real kicker was this pussy had lived with Jacobson most of his life.

Al totally recognized him. Another lab rat who'd apparently been snuck into DSTI a couple times for counseling and testing over the years. One of the lab rats who'd gotten off way too easy. Didn't even have a tracking chip in him, when they looked—cutting him in the same places they'd been cut, and a few others, too. Not too much, though. Williford had other plans.

The bones were only animal bones. Small stuff, too. Mice and birds, mostly. A squirrel Jeff had found in Mt. Sterling. And a cat, that one family's cat. A fun little pile of tiny vertebrae, ribs, tibia, and skulls that Jeff had pulled together over the last few weeks. He usually kept 'em in an emptied box of Frosted Flakes, a box he'd recently had to reinforce with silver duct tape. Now they were dumped out onto the table again so the other kid, the other Jeff, could play with them.

Would play with them. Had to. Or be punished.

When Jeff'd been five, the crew at Massey made damn sure he'd find the bones behind the facility one morning, in the hope that he'd find them amusing and play with them. That's exactly what another Jeffrey Dahmer, the "real" one, had done when *he* was a kid. They must have been quite pleased with the results. But this other kid, this other Jeff, hadn't gotten any of that. He'd been in another test group. Until now.

"It's the sound," the older Jeff said. "When they rub together. Or when the pile collapses and they roll off each other. That click, click, click." He leaned in close behind the second Jeff as he spoke. "I don't think they ever understood that, the ones who were watching me all these years. *Click, click, click.* They'd call it something else, some psychobabble about a God complex, I suppose. Playing God. A power trip. But it was never that." He picked up some of the pile and let the tiny bones trickle back off his fingers onto the table.

Click, click, click.

Ted listened too, but he couldn't understand what the big deal was. To him, it sounded like dice rolling on a table. But he could see the look on his new pal's face. And he recognized THAT completely.

"Do you hear it?" Old Jeff asked New Jeff. "Do you?" He picked up and dropped another handful.

Click, click, click.

New Jeff didn't answer.

"Are you playin'?" Old Jeff's face sharpened like a knife blade. "Maybe you need another beer first." There was a half-emptied case of Budweiser on the table, and he angrily reached for a can. "Go for it, faggot." He pushed the kid's head back and poured.

Jacobson's kid spurted and choked as the beer ran over his throat and chin and piss-colored streaks traced down his bare chest. He thrashed against the weight of Old Jeff's hand, but throughout, Old Jeff held him in place.

Ted reached to scratch his arm again. It stung, and he reluctantly pushed back the shirtsleeve to get a better look. The blotch looked even worse than before. A rounded stain that today ran from the lower half of his bicep past the crook of his arm toward his wrist. *Growing.* It had bubbled up in the center with what looked like several giant whiteheads, but yellowy and the size of quarters. The skin was darker than brown now, almost black. A week before, it had been a small smudge. He'd thought it was a bruise.

But there were others now. A small one on his chest. And another growing up his calf, multiplying by the day, hour. He didn't know what it was, but thinking about it made him want to scratch it again. Made him want to cut it out.

Ted turned his attention back to the Jeffs.

"No?" the older Jeff was shouting. "Then we better give it some time, I guess." He tossed the empty can across the room. "You'll get used to it. Even start to like it, I bet."

The boy coughed, gagged as some of the beer spewed from his mouth.

"Pussy," Old Jeff laughed. "They had me drinking by ten. Wanted a genuine alcoholic. Like the original." He moved behind the boy again but kept his hand on his face. "Of course, you're really only a baby, aren't you? Still wet behind the ears with formaldehyde and whatnot. New and improved insta-clone." His fingers moved steadily over the chin, forced their way into the boy's mouth, where he slipped them in, long and wet, again and again. "I can tell from your look you have some idea what I'm talking about. Your daddy told me all about it. And since Daddy's all dead now, good-bye Daddy, I guess it's up to me to make sure you really get the whole picture. Ted, you think our boy here can handle this shit?"

"Whatever," Ted replied.

"Exactly." Old Jeff leaned closer. "Here's the thing, kid. You were made in a lab about nine years ago. Jacobson, your pretend daddy, and the other paragons of science at DSTI figured out how to alter gestation rates. How to accelerate the speed of clone production. . . . AH! Ted, I think our boy might already know all this."

Jacobson's kid tried speaking. Nothing came out.

"Save your strength, Jeff." He patted the boy's face. "You're gonna need it. So, while some of us have been here like real people from the beginning, you and another batch of clones have been alive for only ten or even three years. Daddy took one home, told it some lies, used an army of tutors and top-of-the-line learning modules to stuff your head with everything an average fifteen-year-old should know. And voilà! You got a kid. They could have as easily made you thirty. Which, technically, considering that your DNA was copied from a guy *in* his thirties, you already are."

"Just . . . ," the pathetic kid managed, "stop. . . ."

"Face it, you got any real memories from when you were a little kid? Anything? First Christmas, maybe? Learning to tie your little shoes?" Old Jeff said, his voice deep, like a god's. "Like I said, love. Clone in a box. Just add water."

"Please . . . I—"

"Relax, brotha. You're cool here. You're still one of us, right? Shouldn't care if you were made yesterday, love. Right here and right now, you and I are exactly the same. We are one."

"I'm . . ."

"You're what, Jeff?"

"I'm *nothing* like you."

Old Jeff grabbed the kid's face in both hands. "All evidence to the contrary." He smiled.

Jacobson's kid tried to wrench himself away.

Old Jeff held tightly. "Do you love me?" he asked. His voice had taken on a different emotion. And it was another that Ted was familiar with. Old Jeff's other hand moved down New Jeff's chest. "Because I love *you*," he said. It came out like a whisper as his hand slipped lower. "But you know what?" He pulled his hand away from New Jeff's mouth and leaned closer so their two faces were pressed together. It looked like one of them had mashed up against a mirror. "I fucking hate you, too."

Old Jeff's lips brushed across the boy's cheek, and Ted wondered if New Jeff was even listening anymore. If he was even there. He also wondered if it really mattered.

Ted smiled and stepped slowly from the room.

It was clear that Jeff needed some more time alone with himself.

THE EYE OF GOD

S tanforth, that Army Guy, was an asshole.

Even more so than the other stock Nazi Big Brother Dogs-of-War who sporadically appeared at the lab. This guy was another breed altogether.

Seven letters for Stanforth?

ASSHOLE. GESTAPO. CERTAIN. UNMOVED. MONSTER.

Ten letters for the current situation?

PRECARIOUS. INIQUITOUS. INEVITABLE. FUCKEDCITY.

An old word game DSTI's Dr. Robert Feinberg used to take his mind off the real task at hand. Not quite the same as his customary morning routine of the *New York Times* crossword puzzle, but it usually got the job done all the same. His hands were hardly shaking anymore. He looked across the lab to where Stanforth and some other Defense Department clown stood with Dr. Erdman. Watching him from the relative safety of the control room. Dr. Mohlenbrock was at the console next to his, reading out the latest vitals.

The specimen in the tank twisted again. Moved with new life. A single dark hand suddenly slammed against the side of the Plexiglas, and

Feinberg instinctively stepped back. Snot-colored bubbles rolled between the long, skeletal fingers as it dragged the hand across the inside surface. Feinberg would not look up. He knew that if he did, it would be looking straight at him. They always did that.

And he knew it would be smiling.

He refocused.

Nine letters for the things in the tanks?

PROCEDURE. EVOLUTION. DESTROYER. PAYCHECK.

They'd used these before in Afghanistan and Yemen. Lots of tests in Central America. Short shelf life on these fellas, they—

No, he realized suddenly. *"Paycheck" is only eight letters.* And then moved to the tank itself and typed in the last codes, unable to drown out the whirr and spurt of the remaining dark fluids. *I should be home playing my guitar,* he thought. *Rolling a nice big fatty and crankin' those new speakers.* Feinberg patted the release check, and the sealed hinges of the front panel hissed back at him like something alive. *I should be hunched over a binocular microscope, making better deodorant for P&G.* He could almost hear the other men talking behind him. Stanforth's and Dr. Erdman's words muffled, but about killing more children, no doubt.

By now, word among the staff was that DSTI had already eliminated the other waiting embryos, and that some of the developed specimens had been destroyed or chemically lobotomized. There'd been a million rumors after Jacobson had up and vanished. Some kind of accident in the "Cain" tests. Rumors, he told himself. Nothing more than that. He wondered again why he hadn't been sent home with the others. Most of DSTI was temporarily shut down, the employees shipped off to various university study or interim assignments in other development branches within the corporate mother ship. Instead, he remained part of the skeleton crew. For cleanup. He hadn't had a decent night's sleep in nine years. *Nine years.* His shrink felt that his anxiety attacks were induced by "stress" from work. *Stress? No shit.*

Legs wobbling like a newborn deer or someone who'd just cum for a third time, the figure stepped from the tank and grabbed the sides of the hatchway to steady itself.

The man—and it *was* categorically a man by all touchstones of the definition—was a by-product of biopharming. The use of recombinant

DNA technology to introduce genes into organisms, thus manipulating their genomic structure and function into a form not otherwise found in nature. Companies had been doing it with plants and livestock for almost thirty years to the tune of a hundred billion dollars a year. This organism—this *man*—here was merely another single step forward.

Feinberg thought again of a book he'd recently read all about the Nazis' work on V-1 and V-2 rockets at the Dora concentration camp. The mountain hideaway in Thuringia with its endless secret tunnels and twenty thousand slave laborers. The torture and hangings in the name of science. Fifteen thousand corpses to help "improve" mankind. *How many corpses will this one make?* Feinberg wondered.

Dr. Feinberg half closed his eyes to the thought and stepped aside to let the specimen pass by. But it didn't. It had stopped. And now stood beside him, watching him. Feinberg could hear the fluids dripping off its charcoal skin onto the floor. He could smell the synthetic stench of something between cheap fruity wine and formaldehyde.

A twelve-letter word for—

Then it opened the mouth. Fetid breath blew rank and hot over Feinberg's face. No words came to mind. He gagged, and a deep gargle burbled down the specimen's throat. He assumed it was laughing. Something gently touched his arm, tugging him closer, and he turned slightly.

A single eye caught his own, and he stood frozen before it again. His body trembled, yet he was too terrified to move a single step away. In that one glance, Feinberg would have sworn he'd seen everything behind the stare. In the novels he loved to read, the killers always had uncaring, vacant eyes. Shark eyes, glossy doll eyes. But in this gaze was something else. This eye was the collective refined chromosomes of men named Bundy, DeSalvo, Dahmer, Gacy, Ramirez, and a dozen others. This eye was the authentic "all-singing, all-dancing crap of the world" and empowered by that same truth. And this eye wasn't vacant at all. It was *totally* aware. It was all-knowing. This eye was the eye of God. And God clearly wanted Robert Feinberg dead.

The mouth opened, showing teeth, and moved toward Feinberg's throat.

"No," someone said behind them. It was Stanforth.

Jaws cracked, widening. Something sticky dripped down Feinberg's neck.

His mind racing, Feinberg thought, *Would there be a space age without the extraordinary work the Nazi scientists accomplished at Dora? Would . . .* He knew then he would die.

"No," Stanforth said again, beside him. "At least not today," he added and laughed, patting the technician on the back. "Move aside, Doctor," he suggested, and Feinberg quickly did as he was told. Colonel Stanforth stood directly in front of the dripping form. "We need you to find someone," he said, handing over a blanket. "Your brothers."

The specimen growled in understanding.

"Find them and then kill them," Stanforth explained.

"Castillo, too," Erdman added.

Stanforth turned and fixed the embryologist with an icy stare of endless contempt, then looked back. "Anyone," Stanforth agreed, "who gets in your way."

Grinned. Head tilted back in anticipated pleasures.

"First," Stanforth said, "some clothes and intel. There's a chopper leaving in thirty minutes. Better follow me."

Eight letters for fucked.

FEINBERG. Some guy named CASTILLO.

EVERYONE.

"Feinberg!"

He looked up to where Stanforth had his hand on the back of the swathed creature, leading it and Erdman from the room. "Yes, sir?"

"We'll need the other two, as well," Stanforth said.

GHOSTS

The room was dark and smelled like dirt and mold and spiders. Jeff lay curled on the concrete floor. Everything hurt. The cool and damp floor against his face the only feeling that wasn't burning, piercing.

They sat with him, the other boys from someone else's life.

The ghosts born in his head, lurking by a hairsbreadth outside his real world for years.

James and Matt and Ernest. (*Now the souls gathered . . .*)

Curtis, Tony, and both Stevens. (*From every side they came . . .*)

I'm sorry, he'd told them.

I'm sorry. I'm sorry.

They'd told him his apologies were unnecessary.

They called him brother. Whispered to him for hours.

His attempt to escape had been short-lived, failed.

I deserve to die.

Konerak, the youngest in the gathering, stroked Jeff's hair in the darkness.

Be brave, he said.

There was a hole drilled into the back of Konerak's head. Jeff could see it even in the dark. Long ago, someone had injected hydrochloric acid into the frontal lobes of his brain while he was still alive. Someone had wanted to make Konerak a "zombie."

Be brave, he said. Castillo is going to find you.

Jeff closed his eyes.

He heard the door open.

Konerak and the others were gone. Returned to the underworld . . .

(My heart longed, after this, to see the dead again.)

"Who you talking to?" a familiar voice asked.

It wasn't Castillo.

KRISTIN

JUNE 13, MONDAY—LAS VEGAS, NEVADA

Kristin was as beautiful as the day he'd first met her. She shined. Almost two years apart couldn't change that, Castillo thought. Not a hundred. Had it already been two years since he'd returned broken from Iran? Two years since she'd helped put him together again?

"Thanks for coming," he said, sitting in the opposite side of the booth while his eyes scanned the rest of the small café. "I know I . . . It means a lot."

"Cut the bullshit," she replied. "You knew I'd be here. You look terrible."

Castillo laughed, but his expression and body proved she was right. "Thanks, babe."

"I'm sorry." She found a genuine smile. She'd grown out her hair, darkened it. Her eyes, even with the smile, filled with both pity and anguish. "You know what I meant."

"This thing is almost over, I think."

"Thank God." She grabbed his hands together. He let her, and she squeezed them tightly in her own, the touch proving so very familiar.

"We can figure this thing out together. You and me. Whatever it is. Please."

"It's . . ."

"Can't you simply walk away?" she asked. "Just this once?"

"I don't think so. Thanks." He took the water the waitress set down, then waited for her to leave again. "It's . . . it's gone too far."

"'In this hole lives the Wicked King.'"

"What's that?"

"A quote."

"Lady Gaga or Gandhi?"

"Neither, smart-ass. It's Berkowitz. The Son of Sam."

"So close."

"He wrote it all over his apartment wall when he was killing people."

"Very Hallmark. Your point?"

"Sounds like you've climbed down into some dark places the past few weeks. Like before. The kind of pits that are sometimes tough to get out of alone."

"And you can only walk in Mordor so long before that evil dust gets in your boots. Is that it?"

"Something like that. I don't know where you're at anymore. No one does."

"Oh, let me guess. Our old pal Stanforth visited you."

"Fuck Stanforth, this isn't about him. They traced your phone calls, yes. They know you called me, and I've been ordered to give a full report to someone in the Pentagon. But this isn't about any of that. Or national security. Or about the goddamn job. Yours, or mine. It's gone beyond that now and you know it, too."

"Yes."

"Why so personal this time? And don't tell me it isn't."

Castillo took a long drink of water. Set the glass down again. "There's this kid . . ."

"Try again. There's always *some* 'kid.'" Kristin shook her head, took both his hands again. "Every village in the world, there's some kid. Some Shaya. There's something else."

"This isn't about him. And you don't know anything about that."

"Because you won't talk about it. I know he died. And I know you hold yourself accountable."

"'Did he smile his work to see? Did he who made the Lamb make thee?'"

"Perfect. Hide behind Blake."

"You started the quote bullshit. How 'bout Genesis?"

"Gabriel or Collins?"

"Funny," he said. "Bible. Mark of Cain."

He felt her hands relax. Release. "What about it?"

"Something in Jacobson's office. But the quote wasn't quite right. I looked it up in the Bible last night. Do you know why God marked him?"

"Who's Jacobson?" Her face tightened, deciding whether or not to follow him down whatever path he'd chosen. "Because Cain was a killer," she said.

"Yes. But why?"

"Jesus, Castillo, it's a made-up story. What's the—" She sighed with exasperation. "So others would forever know his sin. He was marked as a murderer."

"Nope," Castillo said, and smiled, and her reaction showed him it wasn't a pleasant expression. "I always thought that too, but I read it again," he said. "God marked Cain so that the others would never punish him. Never kill him. It was a warning to others to let Cain live. Said whosoever slayeth Cain, vengeance would be taken on him sevenfold. He wanted Cain to live."

"Right. To punish himself later. And?"

"No, not to punish. Never to punish. How could he? All of us," he said, wrapping his fingers around the water glass again. "We're all Cain. Always have been."

"We're all Abel too, Shawn."

"We were positioned in Towraghondi, a little village twenty clicks outside Shirabad. The Taliban set up shop there recently, and our assignment was to wait for an important commander to arrive and take him out. We'd taken position in one of the local homes, with a farmer named Sajadi. Shaya was his son, twelve years old. Cool kid. Funny, liked Metallica and PayDays. Could draw like he worked for Marvel. We'd spent two months waiting, waiting in their home, and then we completed the assignment. Couple days later, we got tip of a weapons stash one village over and moved in for a closer look. Ambush. Total ratfuck, but we got out. Got back to Towraghondi, I knew. I just . . . The whole fucking village was out, staring at us. Looking at me. They'd . . . the Taliban figured out where we'd been staying. The tip was bait. The farmer, Sajadi. Whole family dead. Tortured. His two daughters—"

"Shawn."

"Shaya'd been nailed to the wall. A brick wall with these metal spikes. They'd stripped him. Cut away his nose, his genitals. They'd taken—"

Kristin shrank away from the table. Away from him.

"Listen to me." He leaned forward to follow her, his words a hiss. "An American genetics company is cloning humans from the DNA of various serial killers."

Kristin eyed him more steadily, trying to work back to him. "Go on." Her voice still shook.

"The kids I'm chasing are clones built by the United States government. Kids who were systematically cultivated to become killers. You just quoted the Son of Sam. I'm chasing the younger version. Literally. His name is David. He's fifteen."

She looked away, collected herself.

Castillo leaned even closer to speak in a whisper. "When I was rescued in Iran, it was one of these same science projects that saved me. One of their 'distilled' killers. Something special. Stanforth, the Army, has been using these things for years. And this company's committed everything from murder to torturing children in order to make these weapons. And worse. In the name of science. In the name of national defense. In the name of cash."

"And?" Kristin suddenly looked back.

"And?" He sat back, smiling at her candor. Amazed he could smile at anything.

It was Kristin's turn to lean forward. Puzzled and challenging.

"And when has that ever bothered you before? You, of all people, understand that this"—she indicated the diner and everyone, everything, in it—"has a price. It's always been a double-edged sword, Shawn. When did you latch onto the puerile absolutes that the military is always dangerous, government is always corrupt, capitalism is always merciless?"

"Not always. Maybe not even usually. But sometimes. And *this* time."

He placed a flash drive onto the table.

"What's this?" she said.

"Everything I know. All of it. If I vanish, which is likely, you get this to Ox or CNN or whoever you can."

She laid her hand over the flash drive. "Just walk away."

"Can't."

"Shawn."

He looked up and she smiled at him, her blue eyes filled with such sadness. "This time," he said, "this kid, this boy. Jeffrey." His voice cracked a pitch at the end and he looked away in shame. He felt his hands squeezed again. "Not again. Not this time."

"God, I love you," she said.

"They made this kid," he continued. "They did, we did, I did. The clone of Jeffrey Dahmer."

"Jeff from the files?"

"Actually, that's *another* Jeff Dahmer clone. You'll get used to it. But, it doesn't matter which. They're both an actual by-product of everything I've devoted my life to protecting."

"You can't possibly think—"

"But I do. And if I'm willing to die for those ideals on some Pakistani hilltop, I'm sure as hell going to take full responsibility for them here, too." He glared at her, not seeing her eyes anymore but those of another: A boy. Lost, wounded, terrified. Abandoned. "I made this kid, Kristin. Like God made Cain. And I . . ."

"Hey."

"What?"

"I would have gone with you," she whispered.

"I know." His hands moved over hers. "But I hadn't really come home yet."

"And now?"

He shrugged, realizing even as he did, that he'd given a credible imitation of Jeff Jacobson's favorite response.

"Closer," he said.

"What do you want me to do?" she asked.

Wild Type n.

(1) The natural base genetic form of any living organism as distinguished from a mutant form (an organism with any genetic mutation).

     Note: Within the population of any organism, there is no such thing as a "wild type" as there are *always* mutations of some kind. The term is still useful for geneticists because it allows a simple definition of a theoretical standard or control organism.

Then Ulysses stripped himself of his rags,
and leaped upon the large threshold,
holding his bow and the quiver full of arrows:
and he poured out the swift arrows there before his feet;
and addressed his rivals: "Your final game is over,
but now I will see whether I can hit another mark . . ."

                                    THE ODYSSEY

THE WICKED KING

JUNE 14, TUESDAY—LA VERKIN, UTAH

Ted saw it coming: All that death.

Or, rather, he *felt* it. He'd experienced the exact same sensation in that house in Orchard City. Like there was something crawling inside of him, something alive with many legs, many legs with many teeny claws. Growing more and longer legs each day, each hour.

The "Dark Man."

The same dude who'd carved up that Johnny kid and a bunch of other kids too, without missing a step. It was the feeling that guy brought with him that struck Ted the most: Part dread and part relief. And part, well, *HOME.* The tickly sensation that everyone in the house was soon going to die had hung on him for a couple days, and he'd progressively gotten used to it. He'd even started to enjoy it. And it had gotten stronger as the night settled again on them all. Ted had to smile at that. *Even monsters are a little more afraid in the dark.*

They'd been in the house, another one of the rentals they'd broken into, for almost three days. *Too long,* he thought. *Probably best to go.* Kill the little faggot and get moving again. But Jeff wasn't done with the

Jacobson kid yet. Not by a long shot, from the sound of things. *Shit*. Ted shook his head. Those two had been going at it all day. And Al, fucking Al, was out of it. That guy was done, fried. A mumbling retard who didn't make sense anymore. Maybe he'd been feeling the Dark Man's approach. Maybe crazy Al also knew what was coming.

Ted thought, *He's upstairs with Al even now. I can about picture him cutting, cutting. Hacking around the spine and pulling out that muscle. Almost as if it was me doing the tasty knife work*. . . . He clung to the new feeling. It almost replaced the other that racked his whole body. The ever-growing sensation that he was stuffed, full. Like he needed to drop the world's greatest deuce but couldn't. Even his fucking fingers were swollen like little fat-kid sausages. And all that scratchy black shit on his skin.

He was in the basement again, watching the two Jeffs, when the door above pushed open and Al came down the steps. Only it wasn't really Al anymore.

This Al, the new one, was limp and floppy like a giant dick. All folded up on himself, sort of collapsed in the middle in a couple of unnatural places. And he didn't walk down the stairs as much as he seemed to float over them while leaving a dark trail of vivid red blood on the carpet beneath his feet.

Even Jeff had turned and stopped to watch. He was wearing some kind of blue wizard's hat with giant mouse ears on the sides. Other than that hat, he and the Jacobson kid were both totally naked again.

Al moved down the last few steps and into the light, and then Ted's recent minute-ago prophecies all came to pass. The Dark Man stood right behind the kid, holding Al up with one arm. The other arm carried a long blade. The man slid down the last few steps easily, like another shadow moving into the one-bulbed room. Ted could barely make out the skeletal body, the misshapen head.

As the two moved closer, Ted could see where one of the man's black arms was jammed up into Al's back. Behind the shoulder blades and up behind the kid's head. Ted half expected Al to start yapping, the man's fingers moving the dripping jaws from the inside like some kind of puppet. At the bottom step, Al's body—or, rather, the half-gutted *shell* of Al's body—pitched forward as if he'd been trying to fly.

More blood speckled the wall as Al arched and then crashed face-first onto the floor with a wet, heavy sound. His upper back lay open, hollowed, the peg from the top of his spinal column and some tendons lodged in the bloody cavity. Bulbous, pearl-colored lumps glistened in fields of black along the top of Al's shoulders and the lower back.

Al's killer stepped over the boy and moved toward Ted.

Ted was ready and lifted up his shirt. His own black lumps ran from his neck down to his groin. Several had sprouted long black hairs. "Look, man," he almost laughed. One on Ted's side had split open to reveal a pair of teeth and what looked like what might become a tongue. "Look at this shit. Yeah? You see that?" Closer still, Ted decided it was not something human. "Look, dude! I'm like you. You should see the shit I've done these past few—"

The blade slashed out.

Ted fell back, fire scorching across his chest and neck.

He collapsed to the floor, the dark thing looming over him. Bulging rat eyes stared down into Ted's, a mouth opening to release what Ted could only think of as a hiss. Breath hot with the stink of fresh decay.

The man-thing stepped away. Moved across the room toward the two Jeffs. Ted fumbled on the floor, brought his hands to the drenched gouge in his chest. So sticky and warm, the blood running freely over his fingers.

Jeff Williford had grabbed his knife from the table—the one he'd used on Jacobson's kid—and Ted watched dreamily as Williford moved toward the Dark Man.

Then that stupid wizard's hat and mouse ears were falling to the floor. Jeff Williford's head still inside. His naked body remained standing for one beautiful moment, gushing from its neck like a blood-filled fountain. Then it, too, fell to the floor beside the mouse ears.

The Dark Man advanced toward the other Jeff, the one in the chair.

Ted propped himself up to watch as best he could and wondered some if that damned Jacobson kid had seen it coming, too.

Jeffrey Jacobson felt the thing standing behind him.

Breath hot and wet against his scrunched, bare shoulder blades. The warmth off its body. Several jagged nails moving slowly under his chin.

And he could almost hear its thoughts. He'd imagined it upstairs for some time now. He'd pictured it chopping into the boy called Al, ripping away that muscle and weird fatty stuff inside. Almost as if he'd been doing it himself. A dark place he'd gone over the last two days while that boy . . .

While Jeff . . .

He was still tied to the chair, but he knew there was nowhere to go even if he wasn't. It seemed sort of silly now. All of it. He'd been wrong. If he'd been able to speak, he'd say it aloud. Tell everyone: There was no real Jeff Jacobson. Or Jeff Dahmer, for that matter either.

There was only Cain.

Warm water splashed over his back and soaked the top of his head.

The table beneath him turned red. Like a magic trick. Like a sorcerer's spell. And the red on the table was blood, he realized, and his instant silhouette—his own head and shoulders—appeared on the table outlined by the spatter.

All sound vanished. Then something like thunder pierced his ears.

This is DEATH, he thought.

He felt great weight fall against his body and then slide away again.

He heard more thunder.

Gunshots.

Something touched his face, lifted his head.

The light above burned his eyes, and he crept back into the darkness again. The burn from the ropes slackened suddenly.

Then nothing.

He felt himself being lifted from the chair.

Like flying.

He forced one eye open.

"Castillo," he said.

"I got you, pal."

NO MORE TALK OF SHAME

J eff woke. For all he knew, he was still in his own house in Haddonfield the night his father left. The night Castillo arrived. And all the rest, all of it, the worst of it, had been a nightmare. Imagined the whole thing. *For all he knew . . .*

Yet his entire body ached a thousand different ways. And a man stood at the end of his bed, fading in and out like another ghost. *Maybe that's all I am now, too.*

A small black man came into focus. The smile already so familiar . . .

"You're safe."

But Ox hadn't spoken.

The voice had been Castillo's, and Jeff tried turning to it.

"Take it easy," the voice said.

Jeff torpidly skimmed the rest of the room. Sparse. Bare walls, a cot, a rusted metal desk.

"You're safe," Castillo said again. "But, Jeff . . . Hey?"

"Yeah." His own voice sounded like high, cold wind far away. He followed Castillo's to train his sights on him. The man's face was exhausted, sorrowful. Jeff didn't need a mirror to see the damage Castillo was looking at. As much as Castillo was trying to hide it, Jeff could see it in his eyes. *I'm broken.* He fought to sit up. Couldn't. "Where are we?"

"My place," Ox spoke for the first time. "Everything's gonna be fine."

"Where's my dad?" Jeff asked Castillo.

Castillo shook his head. "I'm sorry, Jeff. I tried to . . ."

Jeff looked away. Fixated on the wall. "One of those things killed him," he said, and it wasn't a question.

"Yeah. How'd—"

"I just know."

"Jeff, I'm so sorry, man. But you've . . . ," Castillo said, refocusing his effort to make everything seem normal. "But I need you to only focus on *you* right now. On getting better. I got some more work to do before it's *over* over and then—"

"You're going to DSTI, aren't you? They'll just kill you, too."

"They're going to try to soon, anyway. This way, maybe my own timetable. My terms. Might help."

Jeff turned back. "I want to go, too," he said.

"Not possible. You should be in a hospital as it is. You should . . . You're going to need help for a long, long time. You've been through something terrible, I know. Believe me. And, as soon as we can, I'll get you all the help you need. But you're not going anywhere until we know for sure DSTI and Stanforth and all the rest are done with us. With you. Jeff, you need to understand—"

Castillo had only glanced, but enough. Jeff followed the look. Found his arm had been bandaged. "What's this?"

"We're gonna get you what you need."

"It's that stuff that Henry had, isn't it? That black stuff."

"Yeah," said Castillo. "A little bit. Yeah."

"I took some pills once a week." Jeff gently touched the bandage. "My dad said I had allergies."

"Guess it depends on how you define allergy," Ox said.

"The other kids . . ."

"At DSTI? Not your problem. You need to—"

Jeff shook his head. "Now *you* don't understand."

"Look, if there are any kids left . . ." Castillo looked over at Ox.

"We'll get as many as we can. I promise. Ox has a couple pals that are gonna help me. You're gonna stay here with him, where it's safe."

"But I can help!"

Castillo reached out to comfort, put a hand lightly on Jeff's shoulder. "You've already helped more than anyone. You're gonna stay put right here. We're waiting for one more guy to show up to help Ox here, and then I'm off to DSTI."

"Trust 'im, little man," Ox said. "He can handle it."

"Yeah?" Jeff lifted his hand. It was shaking. The nails worn to nubs. "Well, it'll be easier to handle it with this."

"What's that?" Castillo asked. He leaned back, curious. Half smiling, even.

This damn kid.

"Keys," Jeff said, and wiggled his fingers. "Five keys."

"Security system?" Ox said. "Oh, my."

Jeff nodded.

"No," Castillo said. "We can get around their security without that. Hell, I'm looking for a front-door invitation anyway."

"But I know DSTI. *And* Massey. Like where they keep all the drugs and stuff. And . . . and there's even this tunnel underneath the grounds that connects them. I've gotten into there a couple times. I bet—"

"I said no. Goddamn it, you're done. No more. Those fucking monsters ain't ever getting near you again."

"'*If you are curious, Father, watch and see the stuff that's in me.*'"

Castillo stared hard at the boy. "What did you say?"

"'*Watch and see the stuff that's in me. No more talk of shame.*' Telémakhos says it to his father right before that battle at the end."

"Yeah, he does." Castillo collapsed, head down on his chest, both hands out to hold the boy.

"I'm not gonna hide anymore," Jeff said. "Not from the monsters."

"No such thing, Jeff."

"You know that's not really true."

Castillo did. "I killed it," he said. *Killed two, actually.*

"But there's more." Jeff blinked.

Castillo knew that also. "Yeah," he admitted.

"And they're looking for me right now."

Castillo and Ox exchanged glances.

"I think they're real close," Jeff said.

Castillo sighed heavily, looked back at Jeff.

"Should we bug out?" Ox asked.

"To where?" said Castillo, still looking at the boy. "If they can find him here, they can find him anywhere. Can you think of a better place to do this than here?"

"Would I be 'here' if I did?"

Castillo smiled. "OK. Plan B, then."

Ox stood to leave. "I'll round up the guys."

"Soon," Castillo promised, patted Jeff's leg. "Give me one more day," he said.

The boy nodded.

Jeff shielded his eyes from the midday light. Trees surrounded them at every turn for what felt like a thousand miles. "Where are we?" he whispered. "Looks like the middle of nowhere."

"North of," Castillo replied, surveying the property with him, helping him with each step. "It's only another place. Come on."

Ox met them again at the foot of the ramp. Gave a brief tour of the encampment by pointing: Half a dozen different trailers and sheds spread haphazardly among the trees. Solar panels, generators. Paddocks for livestock, chicken coops, a small dog kennel. Barns for a couple horses. Down the road were another dozen lodges and trailers scattered throughout the three hundred acres, Ox explained. Several, he added, led to underground bunkers. "For the fallout," he said. "There'd be mass strikes in the west, you know." He smiled when he said it.

They walked slowly, matching their pace to Jeff's, who walked stiffly. Lifelessly.

They reached the camp's main provisions and armaments complex, a V-shaped structure of two long igloo-style halls joined at the bottom by a central kitchen facility. Inside the chow hall, three men waited. Two in summer camouflage appeared at the foot of the trailer's ramp. Twins, black-masked with ballistic vests and well-adorned AR-15s. The third of indeterminate age beneath a thick beard and long hair. "Sir," one of the men nodded to Castillo.

"How many people live out here?" Jeff whispered, sitting slowly.

"Classified," Ox whispered back, winking at Castillo.

The third man handed them each a tray of food.

Ox read Jeff's face. "Ain't never had T-rats before, huh?"

"Army food," Castillo explained. "Probably older than you are, knowing Ox. Never as terrible as they look, though. Regardless, you need to eat."

Jeff thanked the bearded man, worked at opening the packaging.

"OK, Mr. Classified," Castillo asked Ox. "This it? Six total, yes?"

"Including you and me. Last came in an hour ago. Best I could do. Already got him out on security to relearn the terrain with Rosfeld."

"Five more than I had a week ago. Thanks, man."

"They're coming tonight?" one of the men asked.

"Yeah," Jeff replied.

The entire room turned to him.

"I'm telling you . . ." Jeff's face braced, looked at Castillo only. His small shoulders shivered. "Tonight."

"Tonight," Castillo endorsed him. "Also could be in ten minutes. But these, ah, men, were specifically developed, trained, to work in the night."

"So," Ox drew a breath. "How'd you run it if you were them?"

"If they don't simply pitch a drone at us, I'd wait until early morning and put their super soldier, or *soldiers*, dead center. Run 'em straight up the gap or maybe MFF insertion." He made a dropping motion with his hand to indicate a high-altitude free fall. "Helicopters can't really get in here. Too wooded. Couple spots in close that they'll consider, maybe over by the paddocks, but we got those Russian SA-14s of yours for that."

"What kind of special forces guys we talking about?" one of the others asked.

"One or two men," Castillo said. *Keep calling them men. For their sake. And yours . . .*

"Who the hell are these guys?" the man returned.

"Don't know," Castillo said. *I really fucking don't.* "But I can tell you they travel light, fast. Fastest I've ever seen. They use special camouflage, face paint. Stick to the shadows and you'll lose 'em. Thermals won't work. But they'll come in close anyway. Like working with blades."

"Blades?" The other men exchanged looks.

"Uh-huh. And while they'll cut through you to get there, they'll only be after the boy."

The room looked at Jeff again.

"He'll be with me," Castillo said. "Just close on me if the fire lines break. You'll find the real bad guys there. And, bullets *will* work fine."

Ox cleared his throat. Smiled.

There ARE Bad Guys in this world, Ox. I know you know it, too. . . .

"So," Castillo pushed on. "These two, or one, or three . . . if I were them, I'd have another group. Regulars. Have 'em come in slow from the outside; secure the perimeter with maybe two dozen men. ATF, maybe. Local cops, I hope. They'll doubtless tell everyone we're some kinda whacko survivalist cult, or gun runners for the Taliban. Worst case, it'll be mercs or current Special Ops. If they go that route, our defensive position won't be enough. In any case, I'd set up snipers like this"—he pointed at the maps lying on the table—"here-here-here and so on, to take out anyone hoping to get out of the kill hoop. Steadily squeeze in. Let these special units do what they do best. That's what I'd do."

"Then, that's what they'll do," Ox said. "So what's *our* plan?"

"So we . . ." Castillo picked up his package of peaches and laid it on the map. "Stay tight. Here. Keep the bunker as the fallback. Work the interior lines up top. Take out the special units first. See if the others even have the orders to come in anyway. Regardless, reset your claymores to funnel them here and here. Couple of rounds to piss 'em off. If it's ATF or local boys, they'll be spoiling for a fight and take the bait. They like to pretend they're real soldiers. Some of our own sniper fire here, open up the snare some. Keep 'em honest. They'll have thermal imaging," he said, and turned to Ox.

"Just so happen to have a shipment full of those new German combat ponchos. Gortex, mylar insulation. We'll put everyone in masks. They might hit us with gas."

"Yeah," Castillo said, and looked at Jeff. "They might."

And maybe we'll hit them with what I now have. . . .

He was thinking of the small canister he'd retrieved from Ted's dead body. He had little doubt as to what was inside.

One of Ox's crew spoke up again. "Twenty or more against, what, seven? We won't hold out very long."

"If at all. We'll bend back pretty quick. Retreat. Create a gap here. The reserves come in after our retreat here and here. Draw 'em in."

"Like Cannae," the bearded man said.

"Yup."

"What's that?" Jeff asked.

"Like a pincer." Castillo made his thumb and finger into a U and squeezed them together. "Double envelopment. Sucker 'em down the middle, make it look like a retreat, and then hit from the flanks. Hannibal used it at the battle of Cannae, where he was outnumbered three to one against the Romans."

"It worked?"

"Big-time. Hopefully, they'll recognize it for what it is. That'll give us our chance to try a variation on Hannibal. Interlocking fire here, here. With four men, like this . . ." Castillo pointed.

"Yup, yup," one of the others agreed. "Ox didn't pick this property for its scenic charm."

"Yeah," Castillo agreed as he looked at him, then around the room. "Except for the special units, we will avoid enemy casualties where possible. Incapacitate, take prisoners, chase 'em off. But these aren't enemies. Most all of these guys won't even know why they're really up here. They're only following orders, doing their damn jobs. And they'll have been lied to. Understood?"

"Castillo's running the show," Ox reminded quickly.

All the men nodded in agreement.

"Our objective is to put up a good show," Castillo said. "Draw 'em in enough to make a mess of things."

"Why don't you guys double-check the claymores," Ox said, releasing them. "They might not wait until night. Get the roof stationed. Be out in a minute."

Castillo watched and waited as the three men filed out of the room. They'd spent the day sizing Castillo up. He'd done the same. They were a collection of "Misfit Toys," castoffs. The lunatic fringe of the

American Right. Or Left. He wasn't sure that even mattered anymore. Somewhere along the way (right or left, right or wrong), they'd all fallen off, or *stepped* off, society's great grid. *How many more months would he have spent waiting in a trailer in New Mexico before joining them somehow, someday, anyway?* He decided half of the men knew what they were doing. The other half were weekend warriors at best. Prepper militia types. How would they do when the bullets really started flying?

"You don't have to do this," he said.

"Sure I do," Ox replied.

"Why?"

Ox reset his glasses. "Let's just say I want my two sons living in a place and time worthy of them."

Castillo nodded. "And these other guys are just as sure about it?"

Ox replied, "'All experience hath shewn that mankind is more disposed to suffer, while evils are sufferable, than to right themselves by abolishing the forms to which they are accustomed.'"

"Uh-huh. I repeat, your guys sure about this?"

"Are *you* sure about the counterstrike after?"

"Nope," Castillo said as he picked up his peaches, tossing them onto Jeff's tray. "Not by half. But we'll cover after *after*."

"Copy," Ox said. "Then you sure about Now?"

Castillo shook his head. "Christ, I'm not even sure about Before anymore."

"Oh." Jeff looked up from his plate. "You'll actually get used to that."

UNFOLDING OF
MISCALCULATIONS

JUNE 15, WEDNESDAY—NEAR ROUTE 47, SD

Castillo watched the boy fuss with his gas mask, weaving his tiny head this way and that to counter the weight of the side respirator, the same type used by British SAS a decade ago. Castillo figured Ox had paid three hundred apiece for them. The combat ponchos they all wore weren't too bad either, would probably work for a quick TI scan.

Of course, thermal imaging was the least of their worries. The things looking for Jeff wouldn't be tracking by shape or heat or noise. They were after blood. *How* exactly, Castillo had no clue. But there was no doubt that it was how they'd found Jeff and the other boys. Maybe even how they'd found Castillo all those years before.

What the hell am I doing? Castillo stopped his assessment. Or, rather, amplified it.

I'm going to war with the United States.

By tomorrow, he and the others would probably be statistics, relegated to a Wiki page. Another Ruby Ridge or Waco. They'd talk about the crazies holed up in South Dakota for guns, drugs, religion, whatever. Who knew? The real story would never be his to tell. Only the victors told stories. And Stanforth and the others would surely come up with something for the news to talk about for a couple of days. It was easy enough to make everyone vanish. Him, Jeff, Ox, and the rest. Maybe even Kristin too, now, if they didn't pull this off. Like the kid had warned when they'd first met.

In any case, the truth would never be believed anyway. Cloned serial killers? Even more absurd than the notion of the Air Force shooting down Flight 93 or Goldman Sachs orchestrating a seven-*trillion*-dollar heist off the American people. So much easier to believe that brave Americans fought terrorists over an empty field or that a Peter-Paul bailout had been necessary to avoid the next Great Depression. So much easier. *As lex parsimoniae.* Occam's razor. It made the whole damn world go round. Men like Stanforth counted on the principle to pull off the unthinkable at will. A third of the country couldn't name the vice president. Less than half could find Afghanistan on a map. Most people were plain fucking ignorant.

In a shallow bunker on American soil, Castillo realized that he was no different. For the last two years, he'd stayed focused on the small picture. *His* own. The one that was always clearest, made the most sense. Work. Sleep. Fuck. Eat. Watch sports. Repeat. All the while, tell yourself you're one of the good guys. Not like those *other* stupid assholes. Not like those others . . .

"They're here."

Jeff's muted voice broke through his dark reflections, and Castillo turned to the boy.

"Castillo . . . ?"

He patted Jeff's shoulder, then tapped the transmitter on his chest. "Blue 8, message. Over." The boy shivered beside him. Castillo tried again: "Blue Team 8?"

"Send. Over."

"Anything?"

"Nothing yet," a voice from two miles away answered. A "team" of one man. There was no reason to disclose their true numbers.

"They're here," Jeff said again.

Castillo looked down the ditch-line toward Ox, who shrugged. Castillo shouldered his rifle, a modified G3, and surveyed the obverse field through the power scope. Nothing. "Gold Team 4?" He tried the scout hidden on the central bunker's roof.

"Negative."

"Roger. Out." Castillo eyed the scope again, and in the ethereal smolder of night vision and thermal imaging, the ghost world returned. It was a territory Castillo had long walked in. These otherworldly shapes and hues, smoldering and lucent like another reality hidden within our own. How many hours, weeks, years he had traveled here, he could not say exactly, but it was enough that it was as familiar and comforting as the real world. Maybe, he allowed, more so. How many men had he watched from this same spectral perspective? Following their every movement, sometimes for hours. Sometimes pulling the trigger, sometimes not. The thousands of ghosts he'd seen: Men, women, and children drifting over a dim landscape of green and black shadow.

> The souls of the perished dead assembled forth from Erebus. Betrothed girls and youths, and much-enduring old men, and tender virgins, having a newly-grieved mind, and many wounded warriors, possessing gore-smeared arms. In great numbers, they all wandered together about the blood-filled trench on all sides with horrific screams and clamour.

Homer's words came to mind, but no ghosts moved among his vision. Only the barren extraterrestrial terrain. Forsaken. Dead. *They're here. . . .* Jeff's words again echoing.

"Gold Team?" Castillo checked in once more.

"Hold up," the voice crackled back. "Something . . ."

"D2," Ox's voice now. "Message all signs. Movement left of the pickup."

Castillo knew the old pickup was to his right, but out of his line of fire. His discipline and trust remained solid. He kept an eye only on his area. Still nothing. Jeff tensed beside him.

"What the fuck . . ." Ox's electric voice rustled in his ear. "Gold?"

"Affirmative," the man above them, Wilke, confirmed. "What . . . What's he doing?"

"C2, engage?" Ox asked.

"Your call," Castillo replied.

"G4?" Ox's voice calling the sharpshooter above. "Alex? You got him?"

"Ah, affirmative . . . roger. In three, two . . ."

Two shots from the Barrett M107 sniper rifle exploded like a small cannon. Ox's automatic fire sputtered in the blast's echo.

Castillo bumped Jeff softly with his elbow in reassurance.

"Loud," Jeff said.

Castillo nodded, edged closer. Rifle up. Still nothing.

Blue reported in. "B8. Message over. Movement in the south and west," the muted voice said from four miles out in the dark somewhere in his thermal-guarded ghillie suit. "Five, six. Ten men. Spreading out. Setting the perimeter."

Ten. Castillo shook his head. That's all Blue could see. Might be another dozen covering the back side or to the east. Still, fifty men . . . it would be the least of their worries. "G4?"

No response. Jeff's gas mask stared up at him, and Castillo turned down toward Ox. The elfin man was huddled against the forward trench barrage, his back turned to Castillo, the AK74 aimed downfield. "Gold Team?" he tried again. "Ox?" No point using the handles. These people already knew who Ox was, where he lived, what he knew. . . .

"Send." Ox's voice emerging in his ear.

"Target?"

"Negative. I don't know . . . maybe. Had him dead in my sights. But now . . . I'm not so . . . and I'm not going out there to find out. I . . . What the fuck, man?"

"Copy that. G4?" Maybe Wilke, overhead with the sniper rifle, had a better look at what they'd done. If anything. "Gold Four. Come in." Castillo fought the urge to turn and eye the roof above.

Jeff mumbled something beside him. Castillo wasn't sure it had been words at all, and he turned. The boy stood frozen, hands and arms out before his own mask. Studying his suit. Tiny splashes, stars, of blood glistened on his suit. Twinkled almost. A dozen tiny red stars. Castillo stared in confusion as another appeared. And one more.

Then he understood.

The next drops hit him now. Spitting down on them both like dark, reluctant rain from above. He finally looked up. Jeff, too.

The moist stain started at the top of the concrete building, trailed unevenly in several distinct rivulets down the side of the wall. An arm dangled off the rooftop. The sharpshooter, Wilke. Braced by the elbow, the wrist and fingers sagging and lifeless above them. The blood dribbled slowly, steadily from the dangling hand. They watched as his arm slid backward, something unhurriedly dragging his body back from the edge.

"This is Castillo," he snapped. He grabbed the boy by the chest with his hand. "Red 1, go."

The voice came back. "Go?"

"Now!" Castillo roared, pulling Jeff toward him.

The whole night exploded, shook the hilltop. The boom, a long series of succinct succeeding detonations, heralded an unnatural and fleeting dawn in the western woods.

Castillo had lifted Jeff with his left arm and was already carrying him down the line toward the bunker's entrance. Random rifle fire returned from the forest indicated that the lure had been taken. Smoke rolled like mist out of the forest after them.

Ox and another man waited, providing cover, outside the barred entrance. They unleashed a hail of ammunition as another series of explosions shattered the western woodland. "Guess they didn't get the hint the first time," Ox said beneath his mask, unlatching the entryway. "Come on."

"Wilke's down," Castillo told him.

"Copy." Ox stepped inside, rifle aimed above toward where Wilke's body had been.

"C2 to all: Hands Out. Hands Out." Castillo gave the signal to retreat back toward the shelter in an attempt to keep bringing them closer, then he led Jeff, Ox, and another man down the long, dim hall. Thin muted green fluorescent lights lined the descending floor, blurring into one long line as they filed back together. Jeff shuffled behind him, knowing that every second counted. Ox and the other man, McLaughlin, fell into step to their rear. More gunfire trailed in ever-softening echoes behind them. Reinforcements, just two men, moved into new positions against the advancing ATF teams.

At the end of the tunnel, the passageway split into a T-shape, and Castillo guided Jeff to the left, pushing him into the waiting darkness. As quickly, he turned back, crouched to one knee. Ox had struck a similar position opposite them along the top of the T as McLaughlin wrestled with his harness. Castillo thought about taking his place, then glanced back down the long hallway.

Through the night vision goggles, nothing. Thermal heat scope, nothing. *If we're hard to see with stuff Ox found on eBay, what does this killer have at its disposal?* The egg that had given birth to Jeff had started as a single cell from a dead hair follicle. In a world that could do something like that, how difficult to genetically alter a man into something cold-blooded? Castillo'd been spraying his uniforms for more than a decade with chemicals to reduce his own infrared signature. How difficult to change the genetic makeup of skin?

Castillo pressed his eye tight to the scope, still picking up nothing in the hallway. *Will it wait for the others? Did it not take the bait?*

"Castillo?" The mask-stifled voice from behind.

"Hold on . . ." He gestured Jeff quiet, his other hand still on the trigger. He poured his whole self into the scope, trying to spirit a form that simply wasn't there. Still . . . nothing.

"Castillo . . ." Jeff's voice again.

Castillo looked down and discovered the boy had slumped against the wall. He was half curled into a ball, one knee up, hands up and crossed and bent awkwardly in front of his mask. Protectively.

"Take it easy, kid, we got you," he said, his voice sounding strange to his own ears, quiet. Comforting. "He'll come, but it's not here yet. We just have to wait—"

"It's *here*," cried Jeff. He was shaking uncontrollably, his fingers trembling over the hard shell encasing his face.

Castillo swung around, checked again, squinting hard into the scope—nothing at all, not the faintest blip of life. "There's nothing there, buddy," he began, only to break off his words at Jeff's near-incoherent moan, the sound thick. Primal. Not a sound any kid should make. Not a sound any human should make, but one he'd made himself once in a cave in Iran.

"You picking up *anything*?" he asked the others.

"Negative," both men across from him replied as one.

Damn it.

Jeff's fingers had peeled away from his mask and curled into a quivering fist. A slender finger jabbed into the darkness, shaking and crippled with fright. "It . . . it's," he moaned, his voice a mere whisper of sound, as if it was being ground out of him by sheer will. He couldn't unlock his hand, continuing to stab into the pitch black.

"Jeff, what?"

The boy said, "It's standing right there."

Castillo glanced down at his useless scope, then back to the kid, a one-human GPS for all that was sick in the world. "Fuck it," he growled. "McLaughlin! Go."

The man on the other side of the T jerked around to him, his surprise palpable even though Castillo couldn't see his eyes. "Go?"

"All of it!" Castillo barked and McLaughlin moved before the command had even finished, the flamethrower belching forth into the dark down the hallway.

But the thick blazing fire trail had already stopped and erupted in a hundred directions.

McLaughlin jerked the stream of flame upward. Blinding light, flames, and heat blasted back at them all.

"Fuck!" Castillo fell back, pushing the boy with him. Curses and shouting across the hallway. The flamethrower had stopped. The hallway glowed warmly, the burning gel still spurted in a line on the floor. And something else.

Something *was* standing right in front of them. Not three feet away. Something screaming. And on fire.

A man.

And a shape and presence Castillo recognized immediately now.

Castillo wrapped his hand into Jeff's collar, below the mask. Pulled him closer, and then behind.

WER MIT UNGEHEUERN KÄMPFT

Jeff stared down the hallway. The firestorm that'd lit up the blackness had dwindled to a single point: A man in flames. A man who was somehow part him. Screaming in agony, flailing against the floor and wall. Its mind now Jeff's mind, its thoughts Jeff's thoughts, culminating in rage and agony and fire. *Get out of my head!* the boy screamed in his own mind.

Two thunderous shots came from beside him. Someone—Castillo, he thought—putting the burning man out of its misery. Or, just maybe, it was to put Jeff out of his, as the alien thoughts vanished in an instant.

"We need to get back up top," Ox said, as if there wasn't a dead body still smoking in front of them. "The others will need cover."

As one, they went back up the tunnel, not speaking. Even through the mask, Jeff could smell its burning flesh, couldn't avoid looking at it, the man, as they stepped around—and it *was* a man, not a thing anymore. A man with open, staring eyes and a gaping, terrified mouth. A man that could have been him. Made from the same stuff. Made by his father.

"Keep moving," Castillo said, the words surprisingly loud in the sudden hush. His feet started forward again, and they moved up the hallway, the smoke finally clearing enough for the little green lights to come up again, guiding their path until the natural light from outside came clearer. "Wait here, keep down here against the wall."

Jeff blinked hard, lifting his arm to rub his sleeve over the mask, clearing away the greasy soot and grime of the flamethrower residue. "I'm good," he said. His throat closed up at that thought, and he stepped forward, even as a burst of gunfire sounded around the opening of the bunker.

"Nice job back there." Castillo gripped his shoulder. "You hear me?"

"Yeah."

"Give us one minute to collect the others, then we're out the back as planned. OK?"

Jeff nodded, swallowed. And then Castillo and the others were stepping outside. Through the opening, he watched Ox gesture. Another man's shaggy outline materialized in the trench line, silhouetted in the shelter's half-cracked opening. Rosfeld maybe, Jeff thought.

No sooner had Rosfeld appeared than a hissing whistle and several thunks surrounded them with sound. Smoke detonated from a dozen different places, enveloping the trench rolling down the hallway and cutting off Jeff's sight. He couldn't see three feet in front of him.

"Castillo!"

"Don't move, Jeff," Castillo's voice came back from outside, reassuringly close. "It's only smoke. I got you."

"Grenades!" someone—Jeff couldn't tell who—shouted.

"Down!" Castillo barked, yanking Jeff out through the doorway and throwing him bodily into a low trench as a tremendous boom filled the whole world. Jeff felt his body smack the bottom of the pit almost with relief, the tactile contact the only thing that kept him pinned to the earth. Ears ringing, gasping for breath in the stifling mask.

He fell away from Castillo, hugging the bottom of the pit and praying the wet, cold earth would stop spinning beneath him. Around him there were curses, orders, and the sound of more gunfire, but his pulse was pounding so loud in his ears that everything seemed an echo of the initial boom. He scrambled farther along the trench, seeking cover, safety, until he trusted his eyes enough to not see three of everything and lifted his head. Smoke everywhere, bodies rushing around like ghosts in an ash storm. Jeff looked left for Castillo—and he was gone.

Jeff spun back around. Castillo had been right with him, but he was nowhere. The trench was empty, and he was blind beyond maybe a few feet. "Castillo!" he yelled, but in the rain of gunfire his voice was completely lost.

Then the smoke cleared enough and he squinted into it. Castillo was crouched ahead, not ten feet away, waving at him—his face obscured by his gas mask and his body tight and coiled, as if he was ready to spring. "Castillo . . . ," Jeff shouted and pushed forward, relief washing through him for the first time in what seemed like hours.

As Jeff rushed forward, Castillo looked up and smiled at him.

Except you can't smile through a gas mask.

Jeff's feet skidded to a stop.

It wasn't Castillo.

And the face wasn't really a face at all anymore.

Just an open gaping maw, dripping, leering at him with terrible glee.

He'd seen that same non-face a hundred times before. The same face had reigned over his nightmares and stared out of dark shadows for as long as he could remember. It wasn't really a face anymore because it was *every* face. It was *his* face. His and Ted's and Henry's. And Al's and David's too. All of them. Even the one painted like a clown. Each and every copy of the same damned thing.

It was one of the things that he'd felt moving down the steps, crawling down the hallway toward him. Only he hadn't known this one was here, and he'd run right fucking toward it like some sort of idiot baby running to his daddy. Jeff turned. Fled.

Where was Castillo? He had to find Castillo! But Castillo could have been anywhere—he was probably fighting for his life, and if Jeff came up on him too fast, he'd be distracted. Maybe even killed. Jeff wheeled around, his eyes skipping off buildings, bunkers, men. Flashing bursts of gunfire. "No no no no no!" Jeff cried, though no one was listening anymore. The smoke had cleared enough that he could see the line of trees ahead, not thirty feet away. He didn't need to, couldn't really, get to Castillo. He'd fucked up the one thing Castillo'd told him to do. But it didn't matter, it didn't matter, Castillo would find him no matter where he went. He just needed to get away and hide. He'd be fine if he made it into the woods. He could hide there, he could be safe. *The woods!*

His lungs burned as he reached the deep black trees, stumbling over roots and fallen branches, his breathing coming so fast and hard that it steamed up the inside of his mask until it was dripping with condensation and his vision was entirely blurred again. Like nightmare running. With a grunt, he ripped off his gas mask, tossed it as he picked up pace, the sudden rush of oxygen all he needed to keep going.

He broke free so quickly from the trees that he stumbled, eyes quickly scanning the three buildings in this clearing and barns beyond. Which one to choose? He picked the smallest, farthest away, before the barns. Jeff rushed ahead and slipped inside the unlocked door, resisting the urge to barricade it shut. Nothing would scream out *Hello I am sitting inside this building* faster than some lame-ass chair stuck up against the doorknob.

The small storehouse held enough food to last well through an Armageddon or two. Jeff's eyes widened as he raced past row upon row of canned foods, foil-packaged MREs, and enormous drums of water. The drums were almost as large as he, and he skirted sideways halfway down one of the rows, stealing behind the first level of containers. The space wasn't large, but he could crouch here and wait. Wait for Castillo.

Hide. Survive.

The door opened at the front of the building.

Jeff felt the breath die in his throat. The footsteps that came into the room were a man's footsteps, but they weren't Castillo's.

Slow. Measured.

And coming his way.

Jeff tried to make his breathing more quiet. *Wouldn't Castillo call out? I got you, pal. I got you, pal. I got . . .*

The steps came close enough, he knew. Past the strongboxes of canned food and the MREs. Past the stockpiled oats and bags of flour and rice. Jeff could almost feel it viscerally as it passed the first row of water. Knew it was there as it had been before.

And coming closer.

Thoughts flooded through him, incoherent, but weirdly, terribly recognizable. Rage again, and death. Extreme focused purpose.

Hunting, always hunting. For something that seemed never to be found. It was Him again. It. The thing. Another copy.

I'm dead. The thought so clear and simple.

It was going to get him. Castillo wouldn't come. Castillo *shouldn't* come. It was just Him now, the dark shape who he would become, who he was destined to be. *I deserve this.* The thought came swift and hard, and he felt himself gasp. It felt it, too.

Jeff held his breath again, even though he was dead. Even though he was responsible for all of the people who had died already—how many were there, by now? He couldn't count. Didn't want to know. He'd been invented in a lab exactly like this thing had been.

It stepped into his aisle.

All those people who'd already been killed. All of those people who were still going to die. *All of this is my fault. They used me, the blood inside me, to make those toxins, these things, all of it . . .*

It walked down the aisle toward him. Almost as if it could smell him in his hiding place. Almost as if it knew the truth that Jeff was only now ready to see.

I'm the monster here. I *deserve* to die.

Without taking another breath, Jeff crawled free from his hiding place and stood in front of himself. The monster he would become. The monster he already, and always, was.

Jeff looked up at it.

And the monster looked right back.

HUMAN AFTER ALL . . .

Castillo froze in the storeroom as Jeff took position in front of the dark man. The way they were standing, they almost looked like father and son.

Except this father carried two long knives.

Jeff's gas mask hung from Castillo's belt like a talisman, the only way he'd known which way the kid had gone when the smoke had finally cleared enough for him to see the dark man barreling off into the woods. Castillo had known who he'd been after, but by the time he'd hit the tree line it had been a maze of possibilities. And then there had been the mask. And then there was here.

He took another step closer, but Jeff and the other man's stares seemed locked in an unholy embrace. Or reflection. And, they were too close. From this angle, Castillo couldn't get a clear shot. This one had the ballistic armor on again anyway.

Slowly, silently, Castillo laid his rifle aside and freed his own knife from his belt. The blade in his hand, he tried to think of something Odysseus might say, were *he* here instead . . . nothing. Not one damn thing came to mind.

He sprang forward. Felt it turn away even as he flung himself forward, his arm reaching out in a slashing arc that was meant for a jugular and ended up grazing a thickly clad arm. The fucking body armor again, U.S.A. approved and equipped.

Jeff fell back, out of the way, as the man came up screeching like some wild animal, rushing at Castillo. Knives in both of its hands.

Castillo grasped for his pistol, but it had closed the distance between them before Castillo had even gotten his hand around the grip. They slammed together, fire plunging into Castillo's back and belly. He knew what it was, knew he'd been cut open again. Gutted. He faintly heard the dismaying sound of his pistol skittering away across the floor.

Driven against an aisle of water barrels, liquid splashed out freely over the concrete and made the surface slick as ice. He shunted the insistent weight and blazing pain away. Rolled from it reflexively to his right, his own knife still clenched tight in his fist.

They both charged again. *Too close, too fast!* One swipe and it was on him again, pinning him to the ground. Leering as a black hand came down and encircled Castillo's throat. Clawed fingers digging into Castillo's skin. Ripping. Squeezing. The other hand brought up the blade. Lifted its arm high.

Castillo's eyes and face bulged from the lack of oxygen as he fought the hands, desperate to pry him off. Still, he could see it swing down at him; could see the sudden sharp, sideways lurch of the dark head.

Something striking that head. Blood splashing Castillo's face.

The hand let go of his throat and the man crumpled sideways, howling.

Jeff.

Swinging his arm again. Holding something thick and metal.

Another crashing blow upon its head and the man collapsed to the ground.

Still alive, Castillo knew, but stunned. Human after all, in the end. Of course. *Dear God, what fucking else could it have been?*

He hazily watched as Jeff, staggering, dropped the weapon he'd just used and, instead, retrieved the pistol from the floor.

"Jeff . . ."

The boy leveled the 9mm at the dark man's head.

"No." Castillo was up.

"I can do it!" Jeff shouted at him, his voice unnaturally loud in the dim, dusty storage room, loud and full of pain and self-loathing and fear. Castillo knew the sound. He'd made it himself many times before. Too many times. "I want to . . ."

And then pulling the pistol away gently from Jeff's hands. "No, you don't," Castillo said, and he looked hard into Jeff's eyes. "And you never will."

He watched as Jeff considered that, even as the man began to stir at their feet.

This same man, or more likely a brother, had probably saved his ass back in Iran. They'd been on the same team. Castillo aimed.

"You will never do this," Castillo said.

Then he fired three times.

"Enough," he murmured, securing the gun against his waist. He didn't know if he was talking to it, himself, the whole rotten world. He collapsed to one knee.

Jeff grabbed his shoulder. "Castillo . . ."

"What the hell you use, anyways?"

"I think it's a can of wheat berries."

Castillo shook his head. Holstered the pistol. "What the fuck is a wheat berry?"

"No clue," Jeff said. "But Ox has a shitload."

Castillo reached for the communicator at his hip. "Ox," he said.

"My friend, we got us one troubling shitstorm out here," Ox crackled back. His words were light, but the tone filled with genuine alarm. "Bad guys closing in fast. Two minutes, tops."

"Copy."

"How close are—"

"Negative."

"Castillo, we could—"

"Negative." Castillo closed his eyes. "Last Call."

"Castillo . . ."

According to the original plan, *all* of them would be escaping together under the impending commotion. But Castillo and Jeff were clearly cut off from that path. Best to at least get the other guys out. A start.

"Take it as an order if you'll still take one," Castillo said. "In the next life, pal. Over and out."

He hobbled across the storehouse and retrieved the automatic rifle he'd placed there. Jeff watched him. Somehow, the kid seemed older still, his light blue eyes quieter. Darker even. More aware. Too aware. They looked like eyes that'd seen a thousand years. *How could they not?* "Come here," Castillo said.

"What now?" the thousand-year-old boy asked. "Are we going back to—"

Castillo grabbed Jeff by the chest as, a quarter mile away, Ox's fortress went up in an explosion that seemed to take off the entire top of the mountain. The night outside lit like noon and the floor shook beneath their feet, cartons spilling from the shelving around them. Jeff was still screaming and their eyes joined again, Jeff's alight in shock and wonder at the enormous explosion that marked the total destruction of "Last Call." The amazed and horrified eyes of a child once more. *Thank God*, Castillo thought.

"There goes our way out," he said dryly, letting Jeff go. "Now we just gotta get off this damn hill ourselves. Somehow meet back up with these guys at the rendezvous spot."

"If they make it."

"It's not them I'm so worried about, man."

"Oh . . . So what do *we* do?"

"I don't know yet." Castillo'd pulled his own suit off, working at the warm, wet shirt beneath. *Really had quite enough of getting stabbed by these fuckers. . . .*

"Can you . . ." Jeff shuddered at all the blood, looked away. "I mean . . . what is that stuff?"

"Medical glue. Think Super Glue for skin."

"Will it work?"

"Nope. But, fuck, it's . . . it's better than nothing." He did what he could. There was no glue for what'd been *inside*. He had a couple hours, tops. It was the full boundary of his life now. "Maybe enough to get off this mountain," he lied and wondered who he was lying to most. He'd done as much as he could. In five, maybe ten more minutes, the ATF ass-clowns would figure out what had happened and move in. "Come on." He made it as far as the door, but each step proved harder to take than the last. He tried to figure out a way for Jeff to sneak by or fight through twenty ATF agents. He . . . His thoughts were already growing darker at the edges.

He turned to the boy.

Jeff was looking off to the west, beyond the storage sheds. "Castillo . . ."

"What?" he said and followed his gaze to the barn. His brow lifted when he saw what Jeff had in mind.

"The horses," Jeff said.

"Horses."

Jeff nodded.

Castillo's next step was easier. Not much. But enough. "That'd be cool," he said.

Jeff glanced back at him. "Yeah," he said. "It would."

WELCOME HOME

JUNE 16, THURSDAY—RADNOR, PA

A Sunday morning. Early. They'd stopped at Dunkin' Donuts on the way to DSTI and the Massey Institute. The car smelled like coffee and fresh aftershave. The whole complex had been empty, and he'd wandered the rec room while his dad took care of some work in his office. He'd played Xbox on the big TV, tried playing himself in foosball. Otherwise, it was still and quiet for miles in every direction, like the whole world was still asleep, or had disappeared, except for the two of them.

What's this? he'd asked.

Security system, his father replied.

How's it work?

His father had smiled, checked his watch. I'll show you, he'd said.

This memory was one of the few real ones.

Jeff held his hand to the touch pad. A back gate opened.

Held his hand to another touch pad. A door opened.

DSTI opened.

Castillo and Jeff stood in the doorway.

Ox and two of the men from the night before waited just behind them. Their prearranged escape strategy, rappelling down the sheer back side of the hill amidst the confusion of the demolition, had gone as planned.

The horse, too. Castillo had gotten them both down the hill, Jeff holding tight to his back as they'd snuck past the helicopter and escaped along the river.

The rendezvous location had been at a farm near Rosbys Rock, West Virginia. Jeff had never seen so many guns in his whole life.

"You're with Ox now," Castillo said. "First thing is find those drugs you need. There's bound to be a supply in there somewhere. Then keep using those fingers, get into the places you think they might still be keeping some of the kids. You've got ten minutes to find as many as you can. Ten minutes."

"All of them," Jeff said.

Castillo nodded in agreement.

There was no "good" or "bad" anymore. They were just boys.

"Wait." Jeff grabbed hold of Castillo's arm. "Where are *you* going?"

"I'm using the front door. They're already waiting for me anyway."

"No! They'll . . . I don't want you—"

Castillo put his hand on Jeff's shoulder. Stopped whatever words Jeff would have gotten out next. "It's gonna be OK, pal. Everything's good now." He slid his hand to Jeff's neck and pulled him closer for a hug.

"Castillo?"

"Focus on the job." The embrace was quick. Castillo pulled back, releasing him. "Take care of this. Then take care of the others."

"What others?"

"From your father's list. A friend of mine has all the files. Everything. You'll get it all again soon. There are still some other names, other families. Other boys who are going to be hunted ongoing as liabilities. Already out there, maybe."

"And we'll find them together."

Castillo smiled. "Hope so. Look, Jeff, I'm not sure what happens next and don't really even understand everything that's gone down. But I know one thing, and I don't need these scientist assholes or any of their damned tests to prove it either. There *are* good guys and bad guys. This I know. And I also know what you are."

"Castillo. Don't—"

"Go," Castillo said and then left before Jeff could say anything else.

Castillo lowered his head.

He'd only expected Stanforth and Erdman and some security. Instead, he counted nine in the room. Stanforth, of course; Doctors Erdman and Mohlenbrock and three other DSTI staff he didn't know. One of them was an older woman. Then there was Kapellas and Neff, two guys from Delta he'd met once before. Private security now.

And then one of the freaks: Dark Man. Shadow. Son of Cain. Man? Thing? Nightmare?

Did it even matter anymore?

How many more of them? Castillo wondered. *How difficult to make thousands?*

"Welcome home, soldier," Colonel Stanforth said. "Mission accomplished."

Jeff held his hand to another touch pad. Another door opened. Five boys were sleeping on cots inside this room. IVs dripping into their arms. Ox and another moved to collect them.

Another hallway, another room.

Three boys propped up in chairs. Metal held their arms and heads in place. Tubes fed them. Wires connected computers to their heads. Each skull opened at the top so that a dozen-plus wires connected directly to their exposed brains.

"It's OK," Jeff told them. "You're safe now."

The whole room grew comically still when Castillo entered. He noticed the look Stanforth gave the two mercenaries to lower their rifles, and took in each face slowly.

"We really gonna do this here?" Castillo asked.

Stanforth smiled. "No secrets here, Captain. We're all on the same team, remember? Always were. Only want to fix things up again. Are we good?"

"After you tried to kill me last night? Yeah, we're good."

"When you didn't wait for us at the house in Utah, as you'd promised, we didn't know what you were planning to do. One of my men had been executed. And something dangerous we'd expected to find was missing with you. My superiors got nervous. Should have contacted me right away, kiddo."

"Nervous about this?" Castillo withdrew the third and final vial of IRAX11. The one he'd lifted off Ted's corpse.

"Didn't say *I* was nervous. Curious, maybe. But then I'm curious about a lot of things, Castillo."

"As am I."

"No doubt. I told you the first day you would be. And that there was no going back."

"You did, you did. So you know they're all dead, then? Ted. Al. Jeff. All of them killed by your . . ." He looked at the dark man in the room. "In that regard, we're good."

"All of them?" Stanforth got up from his chair.

"Those I was contracted to find." Castillo watched one of Stanforth's henchmen fan out steadily to his right. "And the other Dahmer clone, Jacobson's boy. Killed last night."

"Was he?" Stanforth nodded, but Castillo could tell the colonel didn't believe him. "Did our other man also do that job, too?"

"He did." Castillo looked directly at Erdman. "Of course, looked like the kid was gonna die from some kind of cancer soon anyway. He'd gone bad. Like Henry had. All of them, really. Rotting like old fruit."

"It is not yet an exact science," Erdman interjected. "Certain test groups have—"

"That's fine, Castillo." The colonel held up a hand for Erdman to be quiet. "The biggest concern was always the biotoxin." He stepped toward it, then froze when he saw Castillo's warning stare. "We found the second in the trunk of Jacobson's car at Winter Quarters. Just as you suspected."

"The biotoxin used at SharDhara," said Castillo.

Every scientist in the room turned to Stanforth, who just smiled. "The same," he confirmed. "You saved our ass, Castillo. No doubt about it. Knew you would. So, now let's all figure out how to get out of this."

"OK. How?"

"That's almost entirely up to you. I can reassure you that there are some men at the Pentagon who are quite taken with you currently. We can probably still work this whole thing out."

"If I can just ignore all the dead kids. The state-sanctioned abuse, molestation. The murder of employees. The development and testing of illicit chemical weapons."

"Yeah," Stanforth said. "Something like that."

"Was it really worth it?" Castillo asked.

"All *this*," Stanforth agreed. "No fucking way. But Jacobson hit us all with a worst case, didn't he? Otherwise, the upshot always justified the risk."

"How's that?"

"Imagine the power to turn rioting mobs into sheep. Or super soldiers." He nodded to the dark-skinned killer. "Designed specifically to sniff out murderous terrorists and kill them."

"Imagine," Castillo added, "a bioweapon designed to infect an entire city with murderous rage."

"And all the cures the Cain project brought us? Is it fair to ignore those? I would think you, of all people, would appreciate the work these men have accomplished, specifically in the area of treating PTSD. This company has five *different* medications in clinical testing as we stand here. Several more tests are already scheduled to eliminate the affliction."

"Drugs can't solve that. And even if they could," Castillo glared, "it wouldn't justify the things we've done. These were children. *You* . . ." He turned to Erdman again. "You did this to children. *We* did."

"Only twenty percent of American combat infantry were willing to kill the enemy in World War Two," Stanforth said. "By Korea, it'd risen to fifty percent. Vietnam, ninety. Iraq?"

"One hundred percent," Castillo answered.

"Hooah." Stanforth nodded. One of his bodyguards nodded to Castillo. It was a look that said, *Come on, brother. You're still one of us.* It was also a look that said, *I'll kill you the second he gives the word.* "Because we trained them, trained *you*, to kill. Added a month to basic training specifically geared toward teaching our guys that gooks or haji or skin-nies are inhuman things to be stepped on."

"Yeah, you did. Had us train on moving human-shaped targets, as opposed to those little bull's-eyes our grandfathers trained with."

"And hard as hell to turn that off when you get home."

"Yes," Castillo breathed deeply. "It is."

Stanforth held out his hands as if a miracle had just happened. "Well, we've got something in the works that'll put that killer instinct in our men just long enough to win a war, and then take it right back out again. We won't *nurture* them into becoming killers over a few months. We'll let *nature* do it for us in minutes. And when the fighting's over, we just take that part of their nature right out again as if it had never been there at all."

Castillo shook his head.

"It works," Erdman said from across the room.

"Think of the suffering we could eradicate," Stanforth argued. "The drinking and drugs, spousal abuse, suicides, shootings. How many good men have come back unable to let go of that terrible rage?"

"Most," Castillo agreed.

"Then let's end this the right way. Let these guys do what they do best, and you and I can do what we do best."

Castillo closed his eyes, breathed in again.

A man may trust his brothers when a mighty contest should arise.

"Right. 'Freedom ain't free' and all that. So, tell me: How many kids and adoptive parents did you kill these last two weeks alone to help clean up the mess your new toys have caused?" Castillo eyed the crouched "Dark Man," dressed in black fatigues and mask, who shifted at Castillo's attention. He could feel the freak's hate, tangible and hot, from across the room.

"We've closed shop on the whole Cain project," said Stanforth. "Obviously, it was too risky, and we already had most of what was needed. Taking out these guys, and Jacobson's clone, was the last piece. This ends today." He added, "Once DNA testing confirms what you've told us about last night," he added.

"Well, fuck. Whole compound got torched, Boss."

"Yeah, we heard it was quite a show. Not a problem," Stanforth said, stepping closer. "I'm sure we'll be able to determine what happened there. Whether or not young Jeffrey Jacobson's DNA is found out there. And if we don't find him there, then—"

Castillo fired.

The first shot hit Kapellas in his vested chest, the next struck the Ranger's exposed shoulder as the man pitched backward off his feet in a shower of bone and blood that sprinkled over the computer monitors and microscopes behind.

Neff moved like a big guy; too slow.

Castillo shot him too.

Jeff waited with Ox in a van outside the gate.

There were twelve kids in the van with them. Most sprawled out like bodies in a crypt. Between them, a duffel bag stuffed with plastic bottles found in one of the rooms. Bottles filled with blue pills. Pills that looked exactly like Jeff's "allergy medication."

Ox and his man stood, automatic rifles aimed at DSTI as if they would shoot down the whole building if necessary.

"Five minutes," he told Jeff.

Jeff got him to wait ten.

Colonel Stanforth had not yet gotten his sidearm free.

"Don't," Castillo told him.

"You damn fool," Stanforth raged, pulling his hand away. "You god-damned fool."

Castillo eyed the dark man, the only other real threat in the room. Neff clutched his shattered leg, while Kapellas squirmed on the floor, blood seeping from his shoulder wound. The others, the scientists, were already crouched behind tables and chairs. The dark man, however, had not yet moved from its spot. And he seemed to be smiling with a childish curiosity, Castillo decided. Waiting to see how things might go. Castillo could literally feel this thought, its thoughts filled with un-imaginable bloodlust. Waiting to strike. *To kill*, though no decision as to whom to kill had been made quite yet.

"Toss the guns," Castillo told Stanforth and the two wounded soldiers. "All of them." He waved his gun at the pistol hidden and holstered on Neff's leg for emphasis.

"You gonna kill me, kiddo?" Stanforth asked.

"Probably." Castillo pointed his pistol at one of the scientists he didn't know by name. "You there. Collect all the guns."

Castillo knew the black-skinned science project wouldn't wait much longer to strike. He'd watched the man's eyes linger over this one doctor a second longer than the others.

"They were right about you." Stanforth handed his holstered pistol to the scientist. "Kristin was right about you. You've lost your mind."

"No," Castillo said. He moved deeper into the room, directed the scientist to collect the weapons of the two downed soldiers. "Bring it all over here." He'd never taken his eyes off Stanforth. "I'm quite sane, actually. That's the funny thing. So much money and so many deaths to isolate what? *This?* This urge to kill?" He grabbed hold of the scientist, pulled him close. "To kill. Is it deliberate or arbitrary? Anger or apathy? It's not under some damned microscope. What's your name, Doc?"

"B-b-b-b . . . ," the man stammered.

Castillo pulled him closer and read the name on his ID badge. "Feinberg. I'm gonna open this door, and you're gonna put all these nasty guns just outside. Got it? You do anything else, I shoot you in the head. Sure you got it?"

"Yeah."

"Good." Castillo pushed the door open with his right hand and watched as the scientist did what he was told. The guns safely outside, Castillo pulled the door shut again. "Feinberg, how long you worked for DSTI? Hmm? Long enough for that thing to know you, looks to me. See how he watches you?"

"I . . . I don't. Please. I didn't . . ."

Castillo wrenched the man around and brought the 9mm against his head.

He fired.

Feinberg's ear vanished in a crimson mist of blood and hair. The mutilated hole scorched black. Blood streamed down his neck as a large flap of skin fluttered against the side of his cheek. His screams filled the room.

Castillo shoved him forward toward the Dark Man.

It sprang onto Feinberg and the two collapsed to the floor as one, while long nails dug into the scientist's shoulders and neck and the DSTI doctor thrashed and wailed in agony. The black stunted head dipped into the spouting wound.

Started *feeding*. Tearing away the left side of Feinberg's face.

Alive still, the doctor roared, his words garbled and wet and lost beneath his own blood.

Castillo stepped over them both and fired. Emptied his gun into the back of the thing's head. The bullets pierced the dark head, vanished in mushrooming splotches. The scientist just beneath quivered in shock.

"Is it self-destruction?" Castillo asked, stepping away, moving to the door. "Yes. And see, a lot of time saved. No need to isolate anything at all. No need to breed and destroy children."

He shot the controls that'd open the door.

Fat Dr. Mohlenbrock was crying, clinging to the legs of the closest table.

Castillo pointed the pistol at Stanforth. "And," he asked, "is it maybe just a little fun?"

"What now, Castillo?" Stanforth asked.

"I don't know yet."

Castillo released the clip from his gun and thumbed out the last three bullets. Charged the chambered bullet free. Tossed the empty pistol across the room.

Listening to the others cowering, whimpering, dragging themselves across the floor behind him. He'd let Neff keep his knife.

The evil within. We can never cure or destroy it.

Because we are all Cain.

He moved for the canister on the table.

And we are all Abel.

"Don't," Erdman asked. "Please . . ."

Stanforth took a step back. "Shawn . . ."

Castillo held up the canister for the whole room to see.

"Let's find out what we're all really made of," he said.

And then he opened it.

CASTILLO ALONE

JUNE 16, THURSDAY—RADNOR, PA

The room filled with gas.

The toxic vapors coated the tall Plexiglas windows in greasy miasma.

Castillo could barely breathe. The synthetic stench of burning plastic filled his nose and throat.

His mind filling with a hundred thoughts. Such terrible thoughts.

Everything hazy.

Other bodies moved about the room.

Screaming. Thrashing.

And he could hear sounds. Such terrible sounds.

Someone moved toward him, and he pushed the body away. Could see it moving toward another figure.

He wanted to kill.

He wiped his burning eyes, breathed deeply. Focused.

I will endure it, having in my breast a heart that endures affliction.

He thought of the men lost.

Those who'd died beside him. Wissinger. Koster.

He wanted to kill.

He collapsed to the floor, choking.

I want to kill.

He pictured the boy, Shaya. Heard his musical laughter over the screams on the other side of the room.

He thought of his father.

Blood, someone's blood, splashed across his face.

He turned his head. Pressed it against the cool Plexiglas.

He wanted to kill.

For ere this I have suffered much and toiled much amid the waves and in war . . . Let this also be added unto that.

His whole body trembling with the blood of Cain.

More violent *wet* sounds from across the room.

He thought of Kristin.

And the boy.

Jeff.

He knew she would care for the boy as she'd promised. That she would "fix" Jeff as much as she could. He knew she would do that. That she was, even now, feeding the press information about dead employees, illegal experimentations.

And he knew they would be safe.

He could almost see the boy on the other side of the glass.

A heart that endures . . .

He closed his eyes again.

And then nothing.

ONGOING INVESTIGATION

DEATH TOLL RISES IN WORKPLACE RAMPAGE
BY JACOB HEUKER (JUNE 19)

Police officials have confirmed the removal of a tenth body from the burned wreckage of Dynamic Solutions Technology Institute (DSTI), a pharmaceutical research facility in suburban Radnor, Pennsylvania, fifteen miles north of Philadelphia.

On Friday, officials report, a former employee opened fire with multiple assault rifles and pistols and then set the two-story primary research building on fire using homemade explosives.

Yesterday, officials identified the gunman as Shawn Castillo, a recently retired captain in the United States Army who had been honorably discharged for medical reasons related to post-traumatic stress disorder a year before the incident.

Other casualties include Chief Executive Officer Thomas Rolich, 53, and the company's director of research, Gregory

Jacobson, 61. The bodies of geneticists Theodore Erdman, 46, Robert Feinberg, 33, and Martin Dechovitz, 37, and lab technician Catherine Callahan, 51, were identified earlier this week.

Three bodies, including the one recovered this morning, have not yet been identified by officials.

Castillo had been hired as a security guard at the institute six weeks prior to the shooting. Police officials are still unsure of the gunman's motive.

Castillo killed himself on-site following the incident and was one of the burned bodies recovered at the scene.

A spokeswoman for DSTI, Terry Maley, said today at a news conference outside the facility that the company would not comment on its security procedures, nor would she confirm whether there were any disciplinary or grievance issues involving Mr. Castillo.

Maley did say that officials "were aware of Mr. Castillo's mental history when he was hired but were not made aware of any violent tendencies or history."

Captain Kristin Romano, the Veteran Affairs specialist who'd treated Castillo at the Walter Reed Medical Center in D.C. for his PTSD a year prior to his medical discharge, stated the event was a "tragic reminder for this country to remain committed to advance the clinical care and social welfare of its veterans" and declined further comment.

Castillo was a decorated soldier who served in both Afghanistan and Iraq. No further information was made available concerning his military duties or record.

DSTI is a private biotechnology company with two hundred employees that specializes in the development of therapeutic, pharmaceutical, and cell-based therapies. The company had operated the Massey Institute as a hands-on charitable foundation that worked toward the mental health of teens and children.

Both the private boys' school and medical facility on the grounds were closed at the time of the attack, and no students were harmed.

The day of the attack, the company and its parent corporation, Goodwin Bio-Med, also faced national federal and media questioning following a critical *Philadelphia Inquirer* article detailing misappropriated government funds, the development and testing of prohibited biological contaminants, and the still-disputed circumstances surrounding the deaths of several DSTI employees.

Any correlation between the *Inquirer* reports and the shooting are unknown at this time. Radnor's police chief, Leonard Kerry, said at a news conference that the investigation was ongoing.

SOUTWEST OF EDEN

OCTOBER 8, SUNDAY—ALABAMA

Jeff tossed another stone into the dark waters of the small lake, and it skipped twice before vanishing into the blackness beneath. A small sunfish jumped briefly behind the splash as the setting October sun draped golden lace upon the opposite shore, framed in flushing treetops and spike-rush. His new book lay open facedown in the grass. The cold fall wind ruffled its pages at the corners and swept back his shaggy blond hair as he righted the Senators hat Ox had given him.

In the distance, he could still hear the laughter and shouts of some of the other guys tossing a football. Castillo had been right about this too: Ox's friends had enough room and supplies for all of them. For as long as they needed.

And also for any other boys Castillo and Jeff managed to collect along the way.

It was a good place. Not a single scientist for a hundred miles in any direction.

He was thinking of his father again.

For a week, the news channels had reported on the killing spree at a small research facility in Pennsylvania. About his father's death. And Castillo's. All of it lies, of course. And then another week passed—a month, three months—and everything, even the lies, just kind of went away. Almost as if none of it had ever happened. *Almost.*

He watched Castillo cross the field toward him.

He'd just driven Kristin back to the airport. She tried to visit every couple weeks. To talk with him and the other boys. She was good at that. Talking. It was nice.

Ox and his friends worked to make sure she and Castillo were never followed when she visited. Not that they were too worried about what would happen if they were. It was Kristin who'd worked with one of Castillo's old war buddies, some guy named Pete, and gotten special information to the papers. Enough of the truth to scare away DSTI and the government forever. Enough of a taste for what the full report would look like if anything ever happened to Castillo, or Kristin, or Ox, or any of them. *Or me.*

Castillo came up beside him.

How he'd survived the IRAX11, how he'd walked away from . . . from *that*, Jeff did not yet fully understand. But he suspected.

Since it was something in all of us.

Thank God, Jeff thought, looking up.

Castillo noticed the opened book and shook his head warmly.

Kristin had given Jeff his very own copy the first time they'd met. He thought of the last passage he'd underlined: *"I must not be found sitting in tears. It is not well forever to be grieving."*

He smiled up at Castillo, and Castillo sat beside him without a word.

Jeff turned back to the lake.

They would have time for talk later.

Epilogue: Any Boy

Jack moved slowly across his big green lawn.

The thick grass tickled his bare toes, and he let each step sink his foot in fully before moving to the next. In one hand he carried a small plastic cup that Mommy had filled with goldfish crackers. The cheesy pizza kind he liked the most. In the other hand was a grape juice bag. The driveway was hot under his feet, and he walked quicker to his destination. The shade of the big tree where his dinosaurs were waiting. The big T-rex that was his favorite, and the new stegosaurus his dad had brought home.

He sat down carefully on the natural mound under the great big tree and carefully set his cup of goldfish on the ground. Looked around for any ants.

Across the street, Alec was playing with his mommy. Alec got mad if you called him Alex. Maybe they would play later. He wondered again if it would be funny to kill Alec. To drown him in the pool. Or hit his head with something until he stopped moving.

Alec and his mommy both waved from across the street.

Jack did not understand why he thought these things.

Later, no one else understood, either.

There was no history of psychopathic behavior or violence in his family. There had been no physical or mental trauma. His serotonin levels and glucose metabolism were quite ordinary. He was not adopted. He was not a clone.

His blood and thoughts were entirely his own.

He was just a normal boy. He was every boy.

Any boy.

Jack waved back.

Acknowledgments

uthor Don DeLillo once described a book-in-progress as a hideously damaged infant that follows the writer around, dragging itself across the floor, noseless and flipper-armed, drooling; wanting love until fully formed by the writer. The writer, however, is not the only one made to endure this insistent childcare.

And raising two books (*Cain's Blood* and brother *Project Cain*) at the same time, all those extra hands/eyes/minds/hearts are much appreciated.

Special thanks to: Jason Sizemore and *Apex Magazine*, who first carried my Cain fetus; Foundry Literary & Media's Peter McGuigan and Stephen Barbara for suggesting twins and becoming steadfast godfathers, and Katie Hamblin and Matt Wise, the lads' favorite/coolest babysitters; the devoted fostering of Megan Reid and Stacy Creamer, and Kristin Ostby (who discovered this peculiar child in a blanket on her doorstep and still cared for it as her own). To family and friends who've supported the process throughout (one son finally asking, "Will you *please* stop talking about Jeffrey Dahmer?"), in particular Mary for encouraging, and accommodating, my own lengthy and selfish parenting of the Cains.

Turn the page for a peek at Geoffrey Girard's
young adult companion novel

PROJECT
CAIN

Available now from Simon & Schuster Books for Young Readers

I sat outside on the balcony of the motel's second floor, legs slipped beneath the lowest railing and dangling over the dozen rooms below. My fingers wrapped around faded cobalt-blue paint, arms stretched out fully in the warm summer dusk. The motel parking lot was still completely empty except for three other cars, and I think one of those might have even belonged to the manager.

Castillo was working in our room, just below. I had the sense he was getting kinda frustrated with the whole thing. He could talk about doing research for two years all he wanted, but it seemed like he was also ready to start kicking in some doors and finding some clones.

It probably didn't help that I'd been so pointless with my dad's notes.

I hadn't been able to give Castillo any worthwhile information or feedback.

How could I? I hadn't really even read that much of them, to tell the truth. Didn't want to. When Castillo came back into the room with some food and I handed the laptop back, he'd asked me what I thought and if anything had come to mind, etc., etc. I just made faces like I was thinking really hard and said stuff like "Yeah, some of it did" and "I'd have to think about it." I'm pretty sure he knew I was totally full of it. Worse, I had no idea what I was gonna say if he asked me again.

I didn't know anything about Jack the Ripper. And apparently I knew even less about my own father.

I spent the whole rest of the afternoon lying on the bed, mostly staring up at the ceiling. Wishing myself asleep, away from my rambling gloomy thoughts. The room was clammy and getting smaller by the minute. I could feel its walls closing in on me. And it was *cold*. I don't know how Castillo could stand it. My whole body was shaking at one point. I'd hoped Castillo might send me out for food again when it was dinnertime, but he'd bought stuff at lunch. Alas. Apparently bologna and bread, and water from the bathroom sink, was enough for lunch *and* dinner. So after my third bologna sandwich, I asked if I could get some fresh air.

Castillo eyed me suspiciously. It was a look I was getting used to.

I thought about saying something like "Hey, just think of it as another great opportunity for me to run away like you want me to" but didn't. Instead I went with "I've been in this room, like, all day."

I could tell he was trying to process this information, like he couldn't understand why this might be an issue for someone. I was living with a robot. He said sure and told me to stick close. (Maybe he didn't want me running off now, after all.)

Still, I got out of the room as quickly as I could. Castillo'd suggested I buy a soda or something from the main office, but I didn't feel like walking that way. I hadn't liked the way that manager guy had looked at me when I'd asked about the phone, and I didn't want to give him another chance of giving me any crap. So I just wandered along the walkways a couple times and slowly passed the other rooms. Most every one of them was totally empty. As I passed, I turned a couple doorknobs and peeked between some curtains into the rooms. They all proved locked, all dark and empty.

But I hadn't checked all the rooms on the second floor yet.

Halfway through, I'd decided to park it awhile. Just rest my elbows and head against the railing while kicking my feet off the ledge. Beyond the hotel I could see my Subway shop and streets and even the main highway heading east and west through Pennsylvania. I thought again of just picking one of those two directions (didn't matter which) and *going*, but the thought didn't last very long. Instead I watched *other* people heading these directions. Their tiny indistinct shapes inside the cars moving by at seventy miles an hour. I imagined what they were heading away from or toward. The options now seemed almost limitless to me.

I closed my eyes and really breathed fresh warm air into my lungs for the first time in what felt like years, but had only been a couple hours.

Felt the warmth of the concrete beneath my butt and legs, the strange chill that had latched on to me in the motel room slowly thawing away.

It was funny to think about the whole world just going on. I mean, when shitty things are going on in *your* life, everyone else just kinda carries on. Business as usual. All those people passing had no idea what was going on in the motel room below me. That some guy working for the government was trying to figure out where the teenage clones of serial killers had gotten to. That at a little-known technology lab in Radnor, Pennsylvania, walls were being cleaned of blood. That bodies there had been removed in the middle of the night.

A dozen people already murdered. Not that a dozen seemed all that much to me anymore.

Castillo's Murder Map showed that close to forty people were getting killed every single day. Not by cloned teenage serial killers, of course. But by *regular* killers. Your normal everyday kinda murderer types. And the amazing thing to me is that it doesn't really slow anybody down. All that murder, I mean.

Sure, if it was something local, you might see it on the news and think and even say, "Oh, that's terrible." But that wouldn't mean you aren't going to work the next day or going to a new movie that same weekend or whatever. It was just another "Oh, that's terrible."

Forty people murdered every day, and everyone just kinda shrugs it off.

I wondered how many bodies it would take to make people really notice.

• • •

I opened my eyes again. The declining sun had begun turning more red on the horizon, and a black pickup had just pulled into the motel lot under its crimson glow. I watched the truck coast across the empty parking lot. Looked like a guy and a girl, maybe college age. She glanced up at me for a second as they pulled in front of one of the rooms on the opposite side of the motel.

I wanted to get back before Castillo got annoyed and came to look for me. Or before I had to admit he had *no* intention of ever looking for me. Neither option was too appealing. So I pulled myself up, watching the girl lean on the back of the truck while the guy went into the office. I moved toward the stairwell to get a better look. She seemed pretty enough from afar. The guy, short-haired with random tattoos spotting up both arms, opened up one of the rooms and yelled something I couldn't hear at her.

I suppose I was being nosy, because instead of going down the steps like I'd planned to, I just continued walking slowly along the second floor to the other side. I'd moved away from the railing some so they wouldn't catch me spying. Below, they unloaded two cases of beer and a couple of backpacks. She asked where something was, and he cursed again, even called her a bitch. Up close she was still pretty, but now I wasn't sure if she was college age or not. Sometimes she looked no older than I was, but then again there was something in her voice that made her sound like she was, like, thirty. However old she was, she sounded tired to me. She sounded defeated. I figured it's what I would sound like soon. If I didn't already. Maybe the Subway guy had heard the exact same thing in my voice.

The two had vanished into the room. As the door closed, I heard the guy say something pretty crude about air-conditioning and her privates. She laughed, but even that had that same defeated sound I'd heard before.

I tapped the railing above their room and looked back toward the spot where I'd been sitting. I don't know what I expected to see. Maybe myself staring back, I guess. Some kind of *Alice in Wonderland* mirror thing. I only know I felt like I wasn't alone all of a sudden. I looked down to our room but the door was still shut. No Castillo. I shrugged off the feeling and started moving to the steps again. It was time to get back.

That's when I noticed.

One of the doors behind me was now open.

· · ·

Just the narrowest crack. Two rooms away.

I hadn't noticed the opening when I'd passed, but I'd been focused on spying then. Don't know if I'd even have detected it from that angle anyway. The only other cars in the lot were on the other side of the motel, our side. I suppose someone could have walked or taken a bus or . . .

I tried remembering whether or not I'd opened the door myself. My hands absently trying each door latch as I'd passed. I didn't think so. It didn't matter. I would just walk past the door and be on my way.

But I didn't.

As I got closer to the room, the door opening seemed wider and wider.

And I'd gotten slower and slower.

The gap showed only total darkness on the other side. The smallest hint of a dark green curtain that, I assumed, covered the inside window.

There were no sounds from inside. I knew it was just an empty room, the door left open by some part-time maid days before.

I eyed the darkness within.

Anyone could have been on the other side looking back at me. Anyone at all.

I did not, I'll admit, want to walk past the door and leave it open behind me. No way. So I moved my hand to the latch to pull the door closed, and instead found my hand *on* the door, applying pressure.

Pushing it more *open*.

"Hello?" My high voice vanished into the room like smoke up a chimney.

Nothing. My hand pressing more and more.

I saw blue carpet, the foot of an empty bed. Then the desk between.

It was just like the room Castillo and I were in, but everything was on the opposite walls. The room was empty. No one was here.

I put a foot into the room, my whole body now pressed against the door. My free hand searching for a light switch that I just couldn't seem to find. Everything awash in shadows and the dusk's red. Slowly peeked my head around the corner to see the rest of the empty room.

And then I saw her.

. . .

A woman.

Lying on the second bed, facing the ceiling.

She was wearing a long black dress. Her arms extended on either side like Christ, fingers hanging lifeless off the sides of the bed.

There was something wrong with her face.

It was too, too white.

She was wearing a mask of some kind, I decided. Its cheeks and lips painted dark, dark red. Redder than the sun. I could not see the eyes.

Until she turned.